an
impossible
choice

BOOKS BY ALISON RAGSDALE

ALISON RAGSDALE

an
impossible
choice

bookouture

Published by Bookouture in 2024

An imprint of Storyfire Ltd.
Carmelite House
50 Victoria Embankment
London EC4Y 0DZ

www.bookouture.com

ISBN: 978-1-83790-026-8
eBook ISBN: 978-1-83790-025-1

For darling Dad.

Nothing weighs on us so heavily as a secret.

Jean de La Fontaine

PROLOGUE

The peaceful, pre-dawn boat trip that Kenny MacLeod had planned for his wife Honour, to help her conquer her mistrust of the sea, had taken just over an hour to go horribly wrong.

The storm had closed in so quickly that their little fishing boat, the *Lila Rose*, was being tossed between raging waves, like a cork in a whirlpool.

It was a scene of pure horror; the very thing Honour had had nightmares about ever since marrying a fisherman. Her stomach was heaving with terror, her shoulder muscles threatening to rip apart, as she leaned over the siderail and gripped Kenny's icy fingers with all the strength she could muster.

A few seconds ago, carried by a massive foaming wave, he had been swept overboard halfway along the deck, behind the cabin. By some miracle, Honour had managed to grab one of his hands as he slid past her and now his legs were dangling below the guard rail. His life jacket, like a giant orange turtle shell, obscured the shape of him against the roiling water below. Panic was choking her, and her freezing fingers were quickly going numb, as she screamed, 'Kenny. Hang on.'

The boat tipped dangerously from side to side, making

Kenny's body swing like a heavy pendulum, the movement putting more strain on Honour's already exhausted grip.

Her heart thundered in her chest as the howl of the wind, and the cacophonous clack of metal lines smacking against each other, filled Honour's head. The sea thrashed beneath the hull, and each surge of the boat sucked her stomach back against her spine, as panic flooded her insides.

Another spray of frigid water coated her face, blinding her with a stinging mist. She shook the sodden hair from her face, tried to tighten her grip on Kenny's hand, and stared out at the heaving water, her fear as wild and out of control as the scene around her.

She heard Kenny, shouting into the wind, 'Honour, I'm slipping.' His wide-set hazel eyes were flooded with the same fear as her own. Looking into his, their entire life together flashed before her, and something deep inside Honour cracked. Kenny had never been afraid of anything. Ever. Least of all the sea, and seeing his customary, calm mask ripped away, Honour's own terror reached a new crescendo. But even as it twisted inside her, she knew she couldn't let him down. This time, it was her turn to be the strong one.

'I won't let go,' she shouted into the wind. 'I'll never let go.'

Kenny grasped her lower arm with his free hand, his fingers biting into her flesh. 'Honour,' he yelled again.

She felt the sharp tug of the rope that, when the weather turned, Kenny had used to tie her to the side railing of the boat a few feet behind the small cabin. The hard edge of the guard rail was cutting into her hips as she tried to adjust her footing, searching for the leverage that she would need to pull him back aboard, but her boot slipped on the waterlogged deck.

Just as she stumbled, the waves beneath them seemed to fall away, the prow of the *Lila Rose* dipping its nose into the churning water, and the stern lifting impossibly high behind them. Honour felt Kenny's fingers begin to slide from her grip as she clawed desperately at his cracked knuckles. 'Kenny,' she screamed, as his hand gradually and devastatingly left hers, his body splashing backward into the furious waters of her nemesis, the North Sea.

Honour watched, paralysed and powerless to stop time, shouting his name into the deafening wind, as his eyes locked on hers. She felt ripped in two as his mouth became horribly contorted by a silent scream, and his ashen face disappeared beneath the surface, taking her heart with it.

1

MARCH – THREE WEEKS EARLIER

Sunday was Honour's favourite day. It was the one time each week that they all ate breakfast as a family. Kenny's days off were precious, and a rare opportunity for him to take it easy, but rather than languish up in the cosy bedroom that he and Honour had shared for eleven years, he was always the first one up.

Today was no exception, and as Honour turned over, she saw that her husband's side of the bed was vacant, the pillow dented where his head had been. As she shifted closer to his side, she could feel the warmth his body had left behind and smell the buttery soap he used, a scent she loved, lingering on the sheets.

She pressed her palm onto Kenny's pillow, as, beyond the bed, the heavy curtains shielded the paned window that over-looked Crail harbour – the tight curve of the sea wall and the cluster of fishing boats tied up inside it.

The oldest Royal Burgh in the East Neuk, or corner, of Fife in Scotland, fishing had always been a major contributor to the local economy. In 1310, Robert the Bruce had granted Crail the right to hold a weekly market, and at its location on Marketgate stood a seventeenth-century Mercat Cross, crowned by the statue of a rearing unicorn.

Crail's charming, cobbled streets twisted down to the harbour, which was sheltered by the surrounding cliffs, and peppered with historic fishing cottages. Several of them had marriage lintels – long, smooth stones above the front door carved with the initials of the newly married couples who had lived there, and the date of their marriage.

Honour and Kenny's cottage, a sandstone, semi-detached home with a flight of wide steps leading up to the front door, was on Shoregate, set back slightly up the hill behind their neighbours' house. Honour had placed terracotta pots on each step and filled them with fragrant herbs, soft ferns, and heathers, giving the entrance a Mediterranean feel; the colours and smells of spring and summer a constant source of joy to her.

Above their front door, the lintel bore the initials CM and GD, dated 1711, and each time she passed under it, Honour would glance up and smile. Unable to find any historic records at the library to confirm the couples' identity, she had imagined them to be Charles MacPherson and Grace Duigid, married in their teens and excited about their new life in the cottage that overlooked the water where he undoubtedly earned their living, as her own husband did, more than three hundred years later.

Honour loved their little house, and the village she had called home since marrying Kenny. Every building was soaked in history, just as they were by the heavy rains that engulfed them in the winter. The people of Crail were kind, if a little cautious of outsiders at first, but underneath their quizzical glances, Honour had soon found them to be warm-hearted. A fishing community takes care of its own and as part of that community for three generations, Kenny and his family were family to the entire village.

Down in the harbour, tucked behind the high sea wall, Kenny's boat, the *Lila Rose*, named for his mother, sat among the lobster fleet. Its dark-blue paintwork was faded, stained from saltwater and weather exposure. The thin metal pole that rose from the stern speared slightly askew towards the sky. It was easily distinguished from the other boats by a small, navy-blue flag at the top of the pole, with the Clan MacLeod crest on it – a gift from Lila before she had passed away just months after Kenny and Honour's wedding. The wording of the Clan motto, *Hold Fast*, had faded, but the bull's head was still clearly visible when the wind caught the flag. It meant the world to Kenny, and every few months he'd bring it home to repair any tears and to wash it in the deep farmhouse sink in the kitchen.

Kenny's father, Allen, had survived Lila's passing by only eighteen months, lingering in the care home where Honour worked as an aid, his robust body fading away before their eyes. Soon after Allen had entered the home, Kenny's brother, Jack, had left Crail, and the family business, packing a rucksack and fleeing to Edinburgh. All their friends in the village had been dumbfounded at Jack's departure, which left Kenny to look after both the fishing business and their ailing father.

Watching Kenny suffer the slow and heartbreaking loss of his father, so soon after his mother passing, and before either of them could experience the joy of becoming grandparents, had been indescribably sad for Honour. She had considered it a privilege to be able to see her father-in-law every day at the care home and help to make him feel comfortable, loved, and valued, as he deserved.

When Allen had eventually passed away, Kenny had been devastated – his brother's continued absence deepening the wound of Kenny's loss. Seeing the hurt in her husband's eyes, and the depth of his sense of abandonment had brought up Honour's own conflict about Jack once more. It was like a painful hangnail that she couldn't leave alone, her lingering question loud in her head: *Did I do the right thing?*

2

A sliver of gold outlined the edge of the window as the street light glowed on the cobbled footpath below. At this time of year, the street lights came on around 5.30 a.m. and stayed on until sunrise, but as there was no clock in the room, Honour tried to guess what time it was.

Kenny refused to use an alarm clock, so as not to disturb her when he rose in the dark, slipping downstairs quietly to grab an apple before heading out to the *Lila Rose* and the early tide. From November to March, Kenny also volunteered on the Lifeboats – another risky endeavour that left Honour anxious, throwing herself into her job at the care home, her eyes drawn to her phone every hour or so as she'd wait for his text to say that he was home. When the message eventually came, she'd exhale, press her fingertips onto her eyelids, then text him back with something flippant like *Don't leave your sopping kit on the floor, you messy toad*.

When Kenny got up early at the weekend, Honour usually appreciated the extra time in bed before she dragged herself out from under the feathery quilt and then roused their children, Tara, ten, and Callum, eight, for breakfast. But today, rather than revel in that bonus time, Honour threw off the covers, craving more alone time with her husband. They'd been planning Tara's eleventh birthday party the night before, but Kenny had dozed off, and not having the heart to wake him, Honour had run her hand over his wiry hair and sighed. 'Sleep, my love.'

Now, the chill of the room made her shiver, and just as she was about to reach for her phone, Frodo, their giant Maine Coon cat, jumped onto the bed startling her. 'God, Frodo.' Honour huffed as she pulled the cat towards her. 'You scared the whatsit out of me.' She stroked Frodo's warm back as he stretched, then tapped her phone on the bedside table. It was just 6.35 a.m., so she had plenty of time to talk to Kenny about the party before the children woke up. 'Come on, you big lump. Let's go downstairs.' She set Frodo on the carpet and stood up, looking for her robe.

Her fingers trailing along the wall, Honour tiptoed past Tara's room, seeing the door slightly ajar. Her daughter's bedroom also faced the harbour. It was a bright, cosy space, with a single bed tucked against the left wall, and a tall, oak chest of drawers under the mantel of an unused fireplace on the right. The roof was steeply pitched at the front, giving the space a storybook feel, with a bubbled-glass window set into the thick stone wall.

Contrary to the soft floral wallpaper that Honour had wanted to put up when they had redecorated last year, typically, Tara had chosen a football design, with black-and-white footballs, strikers poised to score goals, and a net pattern behind it all. It was busy, and somehow made the room feel smaller, but Tara loved it and, therefore, it had grown on Honour.

Tara had been crazy about football ever since her dad had taken her to see Dundee United play when she was five. She had become obsessed with her father's idol, Peter McKay, the team's top scorer, and as soon as they'd got home from the match, she'd wanted to kick a ball around with Kenny in the back garden. She had taken to it instantly and had not looked back since.

Their garden consisted of a small square of grass with a narrow flower bed at the far end, filled with waxy rhododendrons. The whole area was enclosed by a thick, drystone wall at the back and on the left, and by the side of their neighbours' house on the right. With Bridie and Scott's permission, Honour had put a wooden trellis against that wall, and in the spring, a beautiful clematis bloomed, its dark-purple flowers visible from her kitchen window.

Now, as she peered into the dimly lit bedroom, she noticed Tara's hair, deeply waved and as red as Honour's own, strung across Tara's freckled face. Tempted to go in and gently sweep it away, Honour took a step forward, then thought better of it, knowing that if she woke Tara, she'd moan about being fussed over, so, backing up, Honour pulled the door almost closed.

Tara was a force of nature, her sharp wit matching her father's, and a touch of mischief perpetually glittering behind her sky-blue eyes. Honour adored her boisterous girl, and was proud of her drive, and determination to be the best player on the Fife under-thirteens football team that she'd joined the year before. The previous summer, Tara had been made their youngest ever striker, and her goal now was to play professionally. According to her coaches, Tara had the talent, so despite their concern over their daughter choosing such a physically and mentally demanding career, Kenny and Honour had agreed to support her dream, so long as she knuckled down at school and got good marks.

Despite being easily distracted, Tara had held her own in lessons so far, but Honour was vigilant about checking her homework and reports, ready to pounce if football started to detract from her academics.

Across the hall, Callum's door was tightly shut, as always. His room was bigger than Tara's and overlooked the back garden, which he said he preferred, as it was quieter. Their son was the polar opposite of his sister, academically gifted and studious, a classic bookworm. He had a shock of dark-blond hair, and dark-rimmed glasses which framed his wise, corn-flower-blue eyes.

Diagnosed at six, his Ménière's disease kept him from enjoying too many outdoor pursuits. The vertigo, nausea, vomiting, ringing in the ears, headaches, and loss of balance that the autoimmune condition caused left him easily exhausted. The maturity with which he handled his limitations constantly made Honour so proud, and angry that he had to deal with his condition every day, that she'd silently cry into her fist, behind closed doors. Listening to his sage logic about life, and reasoning about everyone just doing the best they could, she'd sometimes have to remind herself that he was the child.

Pressing her ear against the door, she listened for any movement inside the room. All she heard was the loud ticking of the giant clock that sat by Callum's bedside, the face dotted with various, luminous constellations, of which he knew every name, but that Honour could never remember. She'd make him laugh by saying, 'Is that arse-a-major or minor?' Pointing at the clock. 'Muuuum.' He'd chuckle, rolling his eyes knowingly.

When Callum was two, Kenny had built him a cabin bed. For all intents, it looked like a little fishing boat, with a captain's cabin at the head of the bed. It had a wooden deck that the mattress sat on, a porthole in the side, and a tiller attached at the bottom of the bed that hovered above the mattress.

As he'd grown up, rather than imagine himself at sea, Callum would spend ages lying on the bed reading about astronomy or looking through the telescope he'd been given by his grandfather when he turned seven. Honour suspected that Kenny was disappointed at his son's obvious lack of interest in the sea, never mind the family business, but, to his credit, he had never let Callum know. Just another reason why Honour loved her soft-hearted husband so intensely. His was such a pure love, and she knew without question that she and their children were everything to him.

Downstairs, Kenny was standing at the sink mixing pancake batter in a bowl. His hair was mussed up at the back, his faded grey T-shirt tight around his firm torso. His pyjama bottoms, loose around his narrow hips, were trailing on the flagstone floor and his bare feet caught her attention, his toes curling slightly as he concentrated on whisking the batter. Moving silently up behind him, she circled his waist and buried her face in the back of his neck. 'You'll catch your death being down here in your bareys.' She laughed as he jumped.

'Jesus, woman, are you trying to scare me to death?' He set the bowl down and turned inside her arms to face her. His eyes were bright as he fake-scowled at her.

'No. In fact I'm trying to keep you from dying of pneumonia.' Her eyebrows lifted. 'But, on second thoughts, I could do with a change. A newer model, perhaps?' She assessed him, her head tilted to the side, as his scowl deepened, and he blinked, comically quickly.

'Oh, really? I always thought you appreciated this classic model. No passing fads. Just timeless brilliantness.' He stepped back, breaking her hold on him, and swept his hands down his front. 'I'm the picture of sartorial elegance.' He couldn't hold back the grin that parted his wide mouth. 'Tell me you don't want to tear these off me, right here and now.' He tugged at the baggy pyjamas.

Honour laughed as she lunged for him, grabbing the sides of his pyjama trousers, and tugging them down until they reached his knees.

'You brazen hussy.' He lurched forward, awkwardly

covering himself with his hands, as a rush of love for him made Honour's heart flip-flop.

She stood in front of him and helped him pull them up again, letting her fingers linger on his waist. 'You started it.' She smiled at him, watching him tug his T-shirt down at the back as he shook his head at her.

'You're trouble.' He grinned, the deep dimple in his left cheek puckering the shadow of his unshaven skin.

'That's guaranteed.' She nodded, then moved over to the counter where the bowl sat. 'Pancakes, I assume?'

'It's Sunday.' He shrugged, then pulled her in to his side. 'If you get the bacon going, I'll go and get the kids up.' He kissed the top of her head, his breath warm, with a trace of coffee.

'Not yet.' She looked up at him, taking in the line of his jaw, the way his tawny eyebrows lifted as she shook her head. 'It's still early, and we need to decide what we're going to do about Tara's party. It's only two weeks away.'

'Ah, yes. Sorry I copped out on you last night. I think the Horlicks nightcap was to blame.' He smiled sheepishly.

'You're a real party animal.' She grinned, and bounced her shoulders. 'So, what's the plan?'

Having decided that it would be best to hold the party at the village hall, rather than trying to cram all Tara's school and football friends into their tiny home and garden, Honour and Kenny talked logistics, food, and games, as she set the table. The old pine table took up a good deal of room in the small kitchen, but the benches either side saved space, and it was where they spent the most time as a family.

Meals, food preparation, board games, homework, rainy-day snap marathons, colouring, or crafts, this was the place they came together. It was scarred by various ring marks, making a good portion of the surface appear to be covered in bubbles.

There were a few gouges from a dropped skillet, or the point of a sharp knife, and of course the ragged T and A that Tara had scratched into it with a teaspoon when she was five, then tried to blame Callum, who was only three and napping in his stroller in the other room.

This wooden table that Kenny's parents had given them when they'd moved out of their house on Marketgate, and into a retirement flat in Anstruther, had borne witness to many of their family stories, and as she wiped off crumbs, rubbed beeswax into it, or set cutlery at their places, Honour would let the memories come, each one a precious chapter in the book of their lives.

Now, with the table laid, the bacon staying warm in the oven, and the cast-iron griddle ready to go, Kenny rubbed his hands together. 'Right, shall I go up and release the krakens?' He pointed at the ceiling, then paused, just as Tara bellowed from the bathroom.

'Muuuuum. Callum finished the loo roll again.'

Honour closed her eyes, suppressing a laugh as Kenny shook his head. 'Will you do the honours?' She set the milk jug on the table as he nodded. 'And put some socks on, at least.' She widened her eyes at him.

'Aye, captain.' He tapped his forehead. 'Socks it is.' He turned towards the stairs, then he stopped and came back to her. He lifted her chin with his finger and kissed her, his mouth firm, and his lips parting slightly as his tongue sought hers. He leaned back. 'Love you, Red.' He'd called her that ever since their first date thirteen years earlier, because of her fiery mane that hung below her shoulder blades, and it always made her smile.

'Love you bigger,' she whispered, seeing his eyes taking in her features, one by one. 'Now, go before there's a mayday situation up there.' She gently shoved him away from her, watching him turn and run up the stairs, two at a time. As he disappeared around the narrow landing, heading for the bathroom, Honour felt a tugging in her core, and a rush of what felt like loss snatched at her chest. A sense of foreboding quickly took its place, and as she frowned, gathering her hair up into her hands and gripping it tightly behind her head, Honour took several deep breaths as she tried to banish the feeling that her world was about to spin out of orbit.

3

The following weekend, Tara's football game was running long, and Honour was freezing. She was standing on the sidelines in the misty rain, stamping her feet to restore the circulation. The community sports hub in Anstruther, just ten minutes away from Crail, was where most of the Saturday matches were played and Tara was out on the pitch, sprinting across the muddy grass – her fiery-red ponytail swinging out behind her. She deftly dribbled the ball, and then dodged two of the opposition, with ease, before heading for the goal. It was almost the end of the second half, and the score was two nil: the Fife under-thirteens team holding its lead.

Tara positioned herself and attempted to score, but the ball struck the crossbar and the little crowd of parents and supporters gathered around Honour groaned. Catching Tara's eye, Honour clapped above her head, as Tara lifted her hands out from her sides and shrugged, trotting back to the centre of the pitch. As Honour watched her daughter's normally fluid run, Tara suddenly stumbled, her left leg looking as if it might buckle.

Honour winced as Tara bent over and rubbed her shin, then

stood up and circled her ankle. The coach had seen it too, and walked over to Tara, leaning in as she said something to him. After a few moments, he nodded, patted Tara's shoulder, and turned away. Tara instantly sought Honour's eyes and, seeing her mother watching, gave a double thumbs up. Honour's shoulders relaxed with relief as she returned the gesture.

She checked her watch again. It was 3.35 p.m. and she wondered if Kenny would make it before the end of the game. When he and his fishing mate, Gregor, had got home at noon, Kenny had dropped Honour and Tara off at the pitch, then gone to St Andrews with Callum to get the car serviced. Kenny was going to come and pick them up, and as a treat, they'd planned to get fish and chips from Bailey's on the way home.

Bailey's was a local institution serving the best fish, chips and shellfish in the area. It was frequented by all the locals, year-round, and in the summer, the villagers would tut at the long queue of day trippers spilling out of the shop and snaking along Shoregate.

'We'll get fish suppers and watch a film tomorrow night – after Tara's game.' Kenny had grinned at them the previous evening, as Callum was about to go to bed, and Tara was curled up on the sofa, her nose in her iPad. 'Ice cream sundaes for afters.' The children had then both nodded enthusiastically as Honour, at the other end of the sofa, facing the fireplace, had pretended not to hear what was going on, her head buried in a book. 'Right, Mum?' Kenny had playfully nudged her leg, forcing her to respond.

'I suppose so.' She'd pulled a face. 'Chips and ice cream – so very healthy.'

Kenny had laughed. 'Once in a while it's OK.' He'd ruffled her hair, which he knew drove her mad, his eyes full of mischief.

'Get off, you eejit.' She'd laughed despite herself, smoothing her hair back down. 'Yes, it's fine.' Tara had been looking over at her, her left hand absently rubbing her knee. 'Is it bothering you, love?' Honour had frowned. 'Want some Deep Heat?'

'No. That stuff stinks. It's probably just growing pains.' Tara had shifted on the sofa, tucking both her legs under her.

'If you're sure? You could have an aspirin if it's really bad.' Honour had reached over and tucked a twist of hair behind Tara's ear.

'I'm sure.'

'She's such a hypo,' Callum had chimed from the top of the stairs.

'Oh, shut up, Call-umsy,' Tara had snapped back. 'Go to bed.'

'You shut up, Tara-dactyl.' Callum had made a hissing sound that had made Tara roll her eyes.

'He's such a pain in the bum.'

Honour had shushed them both, telling Callum to go to bed and Tara to be kinder to her brother. Kenny had watched it all from the old leather armchair next to the fire, his eyes glowing with amusement at the usual goings-on of his family.

Now, recalling Tara's sore leg the night before, Honour frowned, deciding it would be a good idea to have the doctor take a look, just to make sure she wasn't getting shin splints again, which had happened once before when she'd over-trained.

Just as Honour made a note in her phone to call the surgery on Monday, she caught sight of the old Audi turning into the car park and sighed in relief. Tara hated when her father missed her matches, and Kenny did too. At least he'd catch the last few minutes before they headed home.

The next morning at 3.15 a.m., the taste of salt on Honour's lips woke her as she sat bolt upright in the bed. Her face soaked with a mixture of sweat and tears, she turned to see Kenny, sound asleep next to her. The sight of the hill of his shoulder under the covers, and the shock of tawny hair on the pillow made her close her eyes and offer a silent thank you to the universe.

Her heart threatening to tear through her chest, Honour lay still for a few moments, then she moved in behind her husband, slid her arm around his chest and pressed her face into his back.

He shifted closer to her, moving his arm back and slinging it over her hip. 'You OK, Red?' he whispered hoarsely.

His nickname for her prompted the usual smile as she nodded against his back. 'Yes, just had my dream again.'

Kenny squeezed her thigh, then took his hand back. 'We're all present and correct.' He sighed. 'One of these days you'll need to stop worrying. Go back to sleep, love.'

Honour briefly tightened her grip and then released him, turning onto her back. Relief was calming her racing heart as she stared up at the ceiling, wondering what had prompted the recurring nightmare this time. She turned her head and looked at his outline again and exhaled. After all the years she'd been married to a fisherman, she'd never let go of the fear.

The daily bargains she made with the sea were a mantra she whispered as she watched the sun rise, then moved around inside their wharfside cottage, knowing that her husband was already out there – focused on the catch, skilled, seasoned, and yet, at the mercy of the North Sea – a notoriously moody mistress.

She ran a hand over her clammy forehead, then up into her hair, massaging her tingling scalp. Rather than lean into the relief that normally came on waking, a voice deep inside Honour – a sound she could not silence – whispered that she should not let her guard down. But as she heard his breathing slip back into the gentle rhythm of sleep, right now, Kenny was safe, and for today, at least, she could relax.

.   .   .

The rest of their Sunday was peaceful with a typical, family pancake breakfast and then they piled into the car and drove to St Andrews to see Honour's parents.

Marion and Kirk Dunn lived in the same Georgian house where Honour had been born, close to the castle ruins on College Street. After the usual hugged greetings, they sat in the sunny conservatory drinking coffee, while the children went out into the garden to play with Major, the Dunns' old black Lab.

'You'll be glad when the summer comes, Kenny.' Kirk nodded to himself, his white moustache quivering as he spoke. 'Warmer mornings for you, out on the boat.'

Kenny nodded, picking up a second Ginger Snap. 'Aye. It's always welcome.'

Marion smiled at her daughter. 'The kids are looking well?' She glanced out at the garden, where Tara was chasing the dog while Callum sat on the grass, pointing out where the old tennis ball was in the flower bed. 'Callum feeling OK these days?'

Honour smiled into her mother's sky-blue eyes, understanding only too well the constant nugget of fear that hovered inside them all, over Callum's health. 'Yes, Mum. He's doing fine.'

'Good, good.' Marion nodded. 'Anyone for more coffee?'

When they got home, the weather had warmed up enough to allow them to go for a walk on Crail's Fossil Beach. It was only five minutes from home, just past the harbour, but in the time it had taken them to get there, Callum had tripped over his own feet twice, and Tara had begun limping slightly. 'What a state you're both in.' Kenny laughed, helping Callum up. 'It's like an outing from the old folks' home.'

Honour laughed too, but underneath, it unsettled her to see her children, both struggling with the gentle walk.

They wandered the beach for half an hour looking for

fossils, one of Callum's favourite things to do, until the sky turned a dangerous purple, and the breeze picked up, bringing with it the sharp tang of seaweed. 'Right. Everybody home,' Honour announced, linking her arm through Kenny's as he squeezed her hand in his.

They'd played Monopoly at the table after dinner, Tara winning by a mile and Callum complaining that she had been cheating. 'She always lets herself out of jail and doesn't pay up when she loses,' he'd whined.

'Don't be such a bad loser,' Tara had teased.

Unsure exactly why, but wanting a little extra time alone with Kenny before he collapsed into bed, and fell instantly asleep, Honour had sent the children upstairs at the same time, causing complaints from Tara. 'But I always get to stay up later.'

'You have bags under your eyes and your leg is sore. It won't kill you to have an early night,' Honour had insisted, and Tara had grudgingly climbed the stairs, grunting her goodnights.

Now, with their customary evening Horlicks made, Honour patted the cushion next to her. 'It's a bit lonely over here.' She smiled, watching Kenny yawn widely, his arms stretching above his head and a strip of pale skin appearing below the waist of his sweatshirt.

'Righto.' He heaved himself out of the chair and crossed the room, flopping down next to her and slinging his arm around her shoulder. 'So, what's up, Red?' He leaned his temple against hers.

'Nothing much, really. I just wanted you to myself for a bit.' She pressed in closer to his side, catching a whiff of garlic on his breath. Lasagne was his favourite, and he always requested she use plenty of fresh garlic in the meat sauce.

'No complaints here.' He nuzzled her cheek.

She ran her hand down his thigh, suddenly needing to

touch him more – feel his presence more deeply. 'You know how much I love you, right?'

Kenny turned to look at her, his eyes warm. 'Aye, I do. About this much.' He pinched his forefinger and thumb, then separated them about an inch.

'That's it exactly.' She rolled her eyes. 'So, I suppose you want to go to bed, too?'

Kenny smiled bashfully. 'Pathetic, I know, but I'm done in.' He kissed her temple. 'Got an earlier start tomorrow, too.'

'Why?' She frowned.

'The creels were a bit light yesterday, so I'm going to drop a few a bit further out.' He leaned his head back against the cushion. 'Gregor's going to meet me at the boat at four rather than five.'

'God, Kenny.' She shifted to face him. 'That's you getting up at half three then?'

He grimaced. 'Sorry. It's worth a try, though. If the new spot is better, it'll pay off.'

Honour placed her palms on his cheeks and held his gaze. 'You need a break. You work so hard.'

He smiled, his cheeks puckering in her hands. 'You do, too. How many days are you going in this week?'

Honour thought about her schedule for the upcoming week, with three half-days at the care home. She'd found it hard to go to work after Allen had passed away, his absence a wound that had yet to heal. She had even considered leaving, but the staff were so kind, and the residents meant a lot to her, so she was glad she'd decided to stay on. 'Just three half-days. I hope Professor Smythe is doing better. His leg ulcers just won't heal.' She pictured the wizened face of one of the residents, a retired music professor with a lisp, who listened to Schubert all day long.

'I heard honey works.' Kenny shifted back from her, her hands falling into her lap.

'We've tried that.' She nodded. 'It's helping, but it's not cleared up completely.'

Kenny stood up and held his hand out to her. 'Coming up?'

Honour grasped his fingers. 'Not yet, but I won't be too far behind you.'

He pouted. 'OK. I'll see you up there.' He lifted her hand and kissed the back of it, then met her eyes. 'How about you come out with me next Saturday? The kids are sleeping over at your mum's on Friday night, and we could be out and back by noon.' His eyebrows lifted as she started to protest, then he continued. 'Honour, it's time you get shot of these nightmares. Make peace with her. Look old mother sea in the eye and tell her who's boss.'

Honour shook her head. 'There's no doubt in my mind who is boss, and it isn't me.'

'Come on, Red. We can make a morning of it. Take a picnic breakfast. Watch the sunrise. Maybe even catch a thing or two.' He grinned. 'Say yes.'

Honour laughed softly at his expression, the same one that Callum had recently learned worked when he wanted to persuade her into something she was unsure about. 'Kenny, you know how I feel about the water.' She sighed. 'Don't make me.'

He shrugged. 'It'll be romantic. You're always saying we need to do more stuff together, just us.' He paused. 'I promise you it'll be fun. Trust me.'

Feeling cornered, but with the promise of a sunrise break-fast, time alone with Kenny, and how happy it would make him if she agreed, Honour sighed. 'OK, fine. But it better be the date from heaven, or you'll never hear the end of it.'

'Yes!' He punched the air as Honour shushed him.

'You'll wake the kids.'

'You think they're asleep? Not likely.' He laughed. 'So, you and me. Saturday. No backing out, right?'

She shook her head. 'No backing out.' She smiled at him. 'Now go to bed.'

Watching him climb the stairs, once again Honour felt a strong tug of loss. She missed him when he left a room – even more so now than when she'd married him, twelve years ago – and she loved that that was the case.

When she'd met Kenny at a pub in St Andrews, she'd been twenty-six and he'd been thirty. He'd been a bit of a wild man, partying more than she'd liked, and spending much of his free time propping up bars around the Fife coast. His drinking had caused tension between them and, after they were married and living in the cottage, he and his brother Jack would often come home rolling drunk, even when they had to get up just a few hours later to fish.

It had come to a head one awful night, ten years ago, and Kenny had stopped drinking completely, much to Honour's relief. Their lives had taken on a calmer energy since, and with his partner-in-crime's departure from the village, Kenny had lost all remaining interest in frequenting the pub.

The brothers had not spoken since Jack had left, and when he didn't even show up for their father's funeral, despite Kenny leaving him multiple messages, Kenny had gripped Honour's hands at the crematorium, told her that Jack was no longer his brother and asked her to never to have any contact with him again.

Letting the uncomfortable memories come, Honour pictured Jack's face. The angular jaw, more prominent than Kenny's. The chocolate-brown hair and piercing green eyes, and the way he held himself – altogether more self-assured and aware of himself than his brother. She was sad for Kenny that things had turned out this way, but at the time she'd been sure it was for the best. Now, she wondered if that was still the case.

4

The week had flown by and Honour's promise to join Kenny had been weighing on her. She had attempted to find an excuse not to go, but he hadn't allowed her to get out of it. So, having dropped the children and Frodo at her parents' house for their sleepover, she had bought supplies for a picnic breakfast and decided what she'd wear, the spring mornings frigid out on the water.

Kenny had been excited on Friday night, talking about taking her to the new spot he'd found, further out to sea, and how beautiful the sunrise would be. She'd cleared their dinner dishes and circled the house turning off the lights, while Kenny showered, her stomach in knots.

Climbing the stairs, she had stopped halfway up and squared her shoulders. 'This is ridiculous, Honour. Get a grip.' She'd shaken her head at her irrational anxiety over doing what Kenny did almost every day of his life. She'd then continued up the stairs, glancing into the children's empty rooms before heading for bed.

Kenny had dived onto her, his hair wet from the shower, and as she'd shoved him off, laughing, her worry had seemed to

seep away. Kenny had a way of doing that. Of making everything she doubted she was capable of feel possible, even excit-
ing. She'd curled up next to him, imagining their special
morning together, and sleep had soon overtaken her.

Down at the harbour, the sky was inky black. The *Lila Rose* was
all but still, the water beneath it glass-like, mirroring the amber
street lights behind the sea wall, and the few illuminated
windows in the cottages lining Shoregate.

Honour shivered, pulling the collar of her wax jacket up
around her jaw, waiting on the dock while Kenny got the life
jackets out of the cabin. As she looked down at her feet,
cumbersome in the wellington boots he had insisted she wear,
she heard him laugh. He held a life jacket up and beckoned to
her. 'Gregor's will fit you.' He swung it towards her. 'Come on,
Red. Step aboard.'

'That grotty old thing? It reeks. I can smell it from here.' She
huffed, then laughter bubbled up inside her at his hangdog
expression. 'All right, give it to me.' She took it from him and
held it up to her nose, grimacing. 'God, Kenny.' She slid her
arms through the holes. 'You're lucky I love you so much.'

'You look great.' He held a hand out to her, helping her
board the boat. He had already stowed the bag of food she had
prepared, and as she walked along the port side, her hand gripping the icy-cold railing, she could smell the sea – ripe and
briny around them. 'Right. Ready for the off?'

She sat on the narrow bench that ran along a section of the
side of the boat beneath the railing. 'Yep. Let's get on with it or
we'll miss the sunrise.' She smiled at him, seeing his eyes
twinkling.

Kenny started the engine and backed the boat away from
the dock. While he turned and then steered it smoothly into the
mouth of the harbour, Honour could see other fishermen

making their way along the jetty towards their boats. Kenny raised a hand in greeting as Scott and his son Malcolm waved back – their boat tied up next to the *Lila Rose*. 'OK. Here we go, Mrs MacLeod.'

He smiled over his shoulder at her as she relaxed into the rhythm of the engine thrumming beneath the deck, and breathed in the tang of the water as they left the shore behind them and headed out into the last hour of darkness before the dawn. Honour looked back at the harbour, a flicker of anxiety making her blink as they eased further away from home.

An hour and a half later, Honour stood at the back of the boat by the big winch that pulled the lobster creels onto the deck. She was watching the sky. The water had been getting gradually rougher as the wind picked up. They'd had their breakfast on the back deck a few minutes before, then Kenny had checked the creels he'd left out the previous day and loaded them at the stern. Honour had enjoyed watching him work, the ease with which he moved around on the boat, and the way he talked quietly under his breath to the catch, complimenting a particularly large lobster for its impressive claws. She was glad she'd come out with him, despite the unsettling lurching of the boat in the rough water.

The sunrise had been murky, and he'd been disappointed at the lack of colour, but when she'd asked him why the sky looked opaque, he'd avoided her question. Now, as she looked back at him, inside the cabin at the front of the boat, checking the navigation instruments, something in the line of his back made the hairs stand up on her arms.

Rubbing her biceps through her jacket, she walked across the deck and paused at the cabin door. 'Is everything OK?' As she waited, a gust of wind slammed into her back, pushing her inside the cabin. 'God,' she sputtered, shoving her hair away from her eyes. 'Kenny?'

He looked over at her, the frown that he instantly tried to cover not lost on her. 'All's well, Red, but I think we'll head back in now.' He nodded at the stern. 'Looks like there's a wee bit of weather come in behind us, so we'll try to go around it.' He smiled, but his eyes clearly weren't cooperating.

'Are you worried?' She stepped in closer to him and looked at the dashboard of instruments, green lights flickering in a collection of circular screens behind the steering wheel, and next to them the rectangular face of what she knew was the radio.

'No. But we'd better get going. Taking the long way home will add some time to the journey, that's all.' He turned back to the wheel, frowning now as he began to turn the boat. 'Just stay close, OK, love?' he said distractedly, his eyes glued ahead.

Honour's heart quickened as she nodded, easing herself out of the cabin and gripping the side rail next to her. As they turned one hundred and eighty degrees, the sky in the direction of home was now ominous, dark-grey clouds layered upon each other, making patches of the sky look like night again.

The boat was now dancing over a steady series of waves that seemed to be growing in magnitude, their white tops reaching high up the sides, and a cold spray rising from the water that coated Honour's face.

She had heard of storms that rolled in from the west within minutes, taking sailors by surprise, but she refused to believe that today, the first time she'd been on the boat for years, Neptune could be so cruel as to send one their way. She'd agreed to meet the sea halfway, surely it wouldn't let her down.

Frowning, she sat on a section of bench that ran along the side of the boat, and gripped the rail just as a huge wave hit them from the port side. She let out a scream as icy water soaked her face and chest, its saltiness seeping into her mouth. Wiping her stinging eyes, she looked at Kenny, who was in the cabin on the radio, his back to her and his free hand on the wheel. Afraid to let go of the rail but wanting to hear what he was saying, she stood up, took a few steps forward and steadied herself against the outside of the cabin until she could get back inside.

Kenny clipped the radio back into the holder and turned to her, as another wave slammed into the left side of the boat. He jerked forward, his arms going around her as he stopped himself from falling. 'Right, we need to get ready. It's going to get a bit rough, Red, but we're OK. The *Lila Rose* has seen worse, and she won't let us down.' He held her face in between his palms. 'Trust me?'

Honour swallowed over a growing knot of terror, but nodded. 'Yes.'

'Good. Just do what I tell you and we'll be fine.' He passed her and, holding her hand tightly, led her back out to the deck.

Huge waves were now coming in steady succession, making walking difficult, and as they made their way towards the middle of the boat, rain began to pelt down as if heaven had cracked wide open and was leaking on them. Honour looked out at the sky ahead, which was now so dark it had turned almost aubergine, the blanket of cloud obscuring what little light they had seen earlier. Her heart was now thundering in her chest as she gripped Kenny's hand.

'Sit here and I'm going to secure you to the side.' He pointed at the narrow bench seat she'd been sitting on a few minutes earlier. 'Whatever happens, stay here, OK?' His eyes were piercing as she stared at him. 'Don't untie this, Honour. Do you understand?'

Her hands were shaking as she watched him take a short length of rope and tie it through the metal hook on her life jacket, then loop it through a large metal ring at the bottom of the rail. 'What about you? You need to be tied on too?' She watched him tighten the strap on his life jacket, then turn away from her. 'Kenny?' she shouted into the angry wind that was now buffeting her face, moulding her skin with its power.

'Stay there. I'm going to radio in again and then—'

The end of his sentence was whipped away by the wind as another giant wave crashed across the prow, taking the nose of the *Lila Rose* down into a basin of froth. Honour's stomach somersaulted, her body being forced away from the railing. 'Kenny?' she screamed now, his name ripping into her throat like a knife.

He emerged from the cabin, clinging to the narrow door frame as another massive wave hit the boat. This time, it seemed to come from above, drenching the entire deck on both sides of the cabin in foamy water. The force of it picked Kenny up like a twig, sweeping his feet from under him, and dragging him back-wards. He seemed to be suspended in the air for a few seconds until, to her horror, Honour saw his head smack into the metal frame in front of the winch. He folded over, his hand going to his temple, as another wave hit them on the port side, shoving him forward onto his knees.

'Kenny,' Honour screamed again, her numb fingers fumbling with the knotted rope that held her tight to the rail-ing. She needed to get to him more than she needed to breathe.

She watched the stern of the *Lila Rose* begin to lift out of the water, a surreal sight as the stack of creels that had been secured at the back of the boat broke free from their bonds. Honour's lungs were burning as she shouted his name again and again, powerless to stop him as he began to slip towards the port railing. As the boat then tipped further to the left, lifted by a surge of water that made such a roaring sound that Honour clamped her hands over her ears, the loose creels slammed into Kenny, knocking him onto his front. Horrified, and still screaming his name, she watched him slip across the deck as if it were ice, unable to grab onto anything to stop his progress towards the side.

Lurching forward, but anchored by the rope, Honour reached for him, catching only one of his hands as his body, lifted by the roiling water, rolled over the top of the rail.

Honour couldn't feel her fingers as she tried to grip his hand, her mind blank to everything around her, to all that she was feeling. Everything went quiet inside her head, except the certainty that she must not let go.

She could never let go.

5

Honour lay on the hospital bed, her head turned towards the window where the mid-morning sky was now clear – a final, cruel slap in the face. Her head ached dully and the skin on her cheeks stung as if she'd used sandpaper on them. She touched her chapped lips, her fingers shaking so badly she dropped her hand to her stomach, gripping the cotton blanket that covered her.

She'd been checked for concussion, treated for shock, and hypothermia, but otherwise she was physically fine. The irony of that, considering what had happened, was unbearable.

Chief MacPhail from the lifeboat station, or Geordie as he was known locally, had just left the room, and having what Honour already knew reconfirmed had left her paralysed, her heart shattered into a million pieces.

She'd come around in the lifeboat, and the first word she'd spoken was 'Kenny'. Geordie had held her hand tightly and told her that they hadn't found him, and then Honour had heard a wail, animal-like and disconnected from her body, and realised it was her own voice.

Now, just three hours later, turning to look at the door of

her hospital room, she pictured Geordie's bulky form, wearing the familiar dark-blue jacket with the distinctive Lifeboat Institution logo on the chest.

She'd been unable to speak, so had just listened, letting the tears track down her face unchecked as he'd described the way the lifeboat had responded to Kenny's distress call. How the *Lila Rose* had capsized, the hull splitting. Honour had turned her face away and stared out of the window, unable to look at him as he went on.

'We pulled you from the water. You were tied to a section of railing, Honour. It's the only reason you weren't washed away.' His voice had been laden with sadness, the weight of his sympathy like an anvil settling on Honour's chest.

At this, Honour had forced a swallow, the words she needed to say stuck in her throat. 'Geordie, is he definitely... Is he...?' She couldn't bear to say out loud what she knew to be true.

'I'm so very sorry, Honour.'

'Will you keep searching?'

'The coastguard will continue to search for a couple of days, but honestly...' His voice had failed him, and Honour had known that what Geordie couldn't say was that there was little hope of finding Kenny alive. 'He was a good man. A great sailor, a trusted crew member and friend.' He'd paused. 'If there's anything we can do. Anything at all.'

Honour had squeezed her eyes closed, the pain in her chest like a red-hot blade slicing through her heart – separating her from Kenny, with one brutal stroke. *Kenny. My love. My best friend.* This could not be happening. Perhaps if she bit her tongue, or pinched her forearm hard enough, she'd wake up, and leave this sickening scenario behind her – emerge into the warmth and safety of their bedroom, shaken by her recurring nightmare but seeing Kenny next to her, his shoulders quivering slightly as he snored.

Geordie's voice had faded, and Honour had heard a

sloshing in her ears, as if the sea was rushing in – filling them up as it had Kenny's... Could it be true that he was gone – finally, and victoriously stolen by his jealous mistress, the sea? She had forced herself to breathe in and out, knowing that this time there would be no waking up. This time, her nightmare had become her reality.

Geordie had offered to phone her parents, but as much as Honour craved their arms around her, the strength of her mother's heart, and her father's way of knowing just what to say when there were no words, she knew that she needed to be the one to tell them the news herself. No sooner had she thought about them than the children's faces had materialised and the thought of finding the words for Tara and Callum had been utterly unbearable.

Geordie had also offered to take her home, and then told her not to be alone for any longer than necessary. Honour had heard the word alone like a claxon, tearing at her eardrums. *Alone.* Her heart had felt suddenly flattened by a weight of such profundity that she'd curled up into a foetal ball, gathering the blanket into her chest. How could she contemplate moving on in this life alone, caring for her children and keeping them safe, without her anchor? How could she possibly do any of it, alone?

By 2 p.m., Honour had been released from the hospital and Geordie had dropped her back at the cottage. She had called her parents to tell them the awful news, and predictably her mother had been devastated. 'Oh, Honour. My love.' Marion had been crying. 'What can we do? Do you want the children to stay here? Shall we come to you? Do you want me to tell them?'

'No, Mum. I need to do it myself. Please don't say anything yet. I just want them home.'

Marion had said they'd pack up the children's things and bring them home by 4 p.m.

After hanging up, Honour had showered and put on a baggy tracksuit. She'd blindly tidied the kitchen, boiled the kettle twice, without making any tea, and was now sitting at the table, staring at the clock. The smell of the cleaning fluid was sharp and oddly comforting, as she tasted salt on her tongue – tears steadily trickling down her cheek and seeping between her lips.

As she'd cleaned, she had glanced at the calendar, numbly relieved that the spring term finished on 24 March, just a week away. With this unimaginable loss about to hit them, there was no way Tara and Callum would be going back before the holidays. More than ever before, Honour needed to keep them close, be there to hold them, comfort them, be their strength and share in their sadness. They in turn would be her strength, and she knew that Kenny would have told her the same.

Shoving the chair away from the table, she stood up. A shiver ran up her back, making her wrap her arms around herself, the chill of the room finally penetrating her tender skin. Passing it, she let her palms settle on the Aga, the gentle warmth of the cast iron easing away the pins and needles that had been present since she'd been in the lifeboat.

Feeling gradually seeped back into her fingers, so she tore off a sheet of kitchen paper, blew her nose and stuffed the paper into her pocket. Then, she walked to the sink, ran the tap and splashed a little water on her face, the sting of the cold against her hot cheeks, shocking.

Honour pulled her shoulders back, and tightened the drawstring belt around her middle, just as the doorbell rang.

She stood at the door, her insides twisting into a knot as she heard Callum's voice, light and filled with laughter. His peace was about to be shattered in a way that no child should have to bear, and knowing that she couldn't protect him or his sister from that made her own pain a thousand times sharper. Kenny was Callum's hero. Always patient and kind – especially when

Callum was having a bad patch with his Ménière's disease. Kenny never made him feel anything less than perfect, and as Honour's hand lingered on the doorknob, she wondered how she would ever be able to fill Kenny's shoes, in Callum's eyes.

Opening the door gingerly, Honour jumped back and yelped as Frodo dashed past her, his furry hind legs disappearing up the stairs as she clamped her hand over her mouth. 'God almighty,' she whispered into her palm, waiting for her heart to settle.

Callum was shoving past Tara, his backpack dangling behind him. 'I'm first.' He laughed as Tara grabbed his pack, trying to hold him back.

'No, you're not.' She held him for a few seconds, then let him go, rolling her eyes at Honour as he barrelled past her and dashed up the stairs. 'Hi, Mum.' Tara walked into the room. 'It's cold in here.' She frowned, then met her mother's eyes.

'Hi, love.' Honour managed to find a smile. 'Go and put your things away while I talk to Grandma and Grandpa, OK?'

Tara shrugged her backpack off and dumped it at the bottom of the stairs. 'In a minute. I want a glass of milk.' She walked into the kitchen, as Honour turned back to the open door.

Marion and Kirk stood on the top step. Marion's eyes were red-rimmed and her nose pink. Kirk was grey-faced and watery-eyed as he guided Marion inside, then carefully closed the door behind them.

Marion instantly pulled Honour into her arms, her skin cool against Honour's flushed cheek. 'My darling girl.'

'Oh, Mum.' Honour gasped. 'I don't know what I'm going to do.' Her voice cracked and fresh tears pressed in behind her eyes.

Her father came up behind her and circled them both with his arms. 'We're here, love. Just tell us what you need.'

Honour shook her head. 'I don't know. I don't know what I

need. I don't know anything anymore,' she whispered, easing herself from their arms and glancing towards the kitchen door. 'I've got to keep it together until I tell the kids.' She wiped her nose with her palm, then accepted the clean white hanky her father held out to her.

'Understood.' He cupped her chin in his palm. 'You can do this, Honour.'

As she imagined sitting the children down, meeting their questioning eyes and breaking their little hearts, Honour felt nauseated. 'I know it might sound odd, and I don't want to hurt you, but could you please go home?' She met her mother's startled gaze. 'I'm sorry. I don't mean to be cruel, or cold, but I honestly don't think I can do this if you're here. I'll fall apart.'

Kirk took Marion's hand in his and nodded at her, Marion taking only a second or two before she nodded back. Seeing the tacit communication between them, the same way she and Kenny could speak to each other with mere glances, was a knife to the heart.

'Thank you both. I love you so much, and I promise to phone you later.' Honour took their free hands in hers. 'I'll be OK. We all will.'

Marion looked dubious. 'Phone us. I can come back tonight with some dinner for you all. I want to help, Honour.' Her voice was raspy.

'I know, and this is helping me, Mum. Please come back tomorrow, maybe after lunch? I just need to focus on the children right now.'

Hugging her tightly, Marion kissed her cheek. 'I'm so, so sorry, my love.'

'I know.' Honour hugged her back, then wrapped her arms around her father's neck. 'I'll phone you tonight.'

He nodded, patted her cheek, and led her mother out the door and down the steps.

A movement behind her made Honour glance over her

shoulder. Tara was standing in the middle of the living room, frowning. 'Did Grandma and Grandpa leave?'

Honour willed her voice not to betray her. 'Yes. They were in a bit of a hurry.' She surveyed her daughter's face, taking in the bright eyes, the long, aquiline nose.

'Where's Dad?'

Honour took a moment, then said softly, 'Tara, can you come up to Callum's room, love? I need to talk to you both.'

Tara's hands dropped heavily to her sides. 'His room smells like cheese.' She grimaced. 'Can't he come into mine?'

'Let's just go upstairs and find him so we can have a chat.'

Tara looked puzzled. 'Why? Did we do something wrong?'

Honour's heart contracted. 'No, sweet girl.' She held her hand out to her daughter. 'Nothing like that.' She took Tara's fingers in hers, feeling the soft skin under hers. 'Something has happened, and I need to tell you together.'

Tara moved in closer, her eyes widening. 'Is it something bad?'

Honour took in the anxious shadow behind Tara's eyes. *How can I do this? How can I find the strength to destroy her world?*

6

Callum lay with his head in her lap as Honour gently stroked his hair. Tara sat next to them on Callum's bed, her head on Honour's shoulder and her hands lying limp on her thighs. They had cried together, held each other close, then, as quieter, more profound pain took hold, replacing the initial sparks of shock, they'd slipped back into silence.

Honour caught a whiff of seaweed as a wisp of wind floated in the partially open window, but she wanted to shut it out, to never smell or see the sea again. Seagulls called loudly from the roof, their voices a clanging and yet soothing harmony, and the only sound in the room.

Tara shifted, her hand going to Honour's arm. 'Mum?'

'Yes, love?' Honour gently slipped out from under Callum and moved him back onto his pillow. He had fallen asleep, so she pulled the duvet over his chest and kissed his forehead.

'What are we going to do?' Tara's voice was thick with tears, her face flushed and her eyes full of fear.

Honour's heart was so broken that she didn't think there was room for more damage, but seeing her daughter so distressed, it fractured a little more. 'Let's go down and make some tea,' she whispered, holding her hand out to Tara. 'It's going to be OK, Tara.' She willed herself to believe her own words.

Tara took her hand and followed her silently out of the room, along the hall and down the stairs.

Despite the late-afternoon sun filtering through the thin veil of clouds over the harbour, inside the cottage it still felt chilly, so Honour grabbed the blanket from the back of the sofa and wrapped it around Tara's shoulders. Honour guided her daughter to the sofa, then opened the curtains wider on the remains of the day – a day that Honour suddenly realised she had no idea how to navigate anymore – not without Kenny.

Glancing at the view, the cobbled lane that led from their front steps, past their neighbours' Bridie and Scott's door, and then down the gentle slope to Shoregate, where the village was getting on with its Saturday afternoon – with life – as if it hadn't all changed irrevocably, was hard to process. Imagining getting the children ready for school in a couple of days, dropping them off and heading to the care home, watching the phone waiting for Kenny's 'I'm home' text then smiling, as she changed a bandage, or carried a lunch tray to one of her old friends, made her breath hitch, so she closed her eyes and exhaled her pain into the room. None of that would happen now.

Sensing that Tara was watching her, she turned around and forced some power into her voice. 'Why don't we light the fire? It's a bit nippy today. We can have some tea and toast in here, and when Cal wakes, maybe we can go for a walk on the beach.' Honour hoped that any or all of her suggestions might sound appealing, but Tara just shook her head.

'I don't want to go out anywhere. It's going to be dark soon, anyway.' She dipped her chin to her chest and picked at the fringe of the blanket on her lap. 'Dad is always with us on the beach.' She sniffed, her fist going to her eye. 'It won't be the same.' She looked up at Honour, her eyes brimming with tears.

'Nothing will ever be the same again.' Tara's voice broke as she folded forward, her face going into her palms.

Honour sat next to her and pulled her in to her side, rubbing Tara's back as she sobbed into her hands. 'Oh, my darling girl.' Honour swallowed over a lump, tears streaming down her face. 'I know it won't be the same, but in time we will be OK.' She hiccupped. 'We'll find new ways to do things, you, me, and Cal. It won't be easy, Tara, but as long as we are together, we'll be all right.' She rocked her daughter, whose sobs were easing a little. 'I will never leave you, Tara. I promise you. I'll always be here.' She'd made a promise that she knew that her daughter needed to hear but, eventually, would be impossible to keep.

Having called her parents later that night, Honour had asked them to give her a little more time alone with the children, so, two days later, her mum had arrived around 11 a.m. Marion had brought a meal for them all and had been wonderfully strong, hugging Tara and Callum, and telling them that she and their grandpa would help with anything they needed. Callum had cried and clung to her, his arms clasped behind her back, and then Tara and he had both curled up next to her on the sofa.

Honour's father had said he'd join them the following day, as he couldn't get Major into the kennel, but Honour sensed that her mother had suggested that he wait, to let them get the children through the worst of the first days without their dad. Kirk was a gentle-natured man who adored his daughter, and his grandchildren, but as he got older, he found emotionally charged situations difficult to handle. Honour realised that Marion knew that she needed them to be strong for her and would wait to bring Kirk with her until Honour and the children were able to handle a weepy grandad.

Marion had eventually coaxed the children to eat some eggs

for lunch, and Honour was grateful beyond words as she'd kissed her mother's cheek, gone upstairs, and showered, exhausted and crying alone in the bathroom as the water thundered into the old bathtub.

Once she had pulled on some clean clothes, she had taken a few moments to close her bedroom door and call her closest friend, Lorna, Callum's best friend Dougie's mum. Lorna had been supportive, and kind, already having heard the news on the village grapevine. Crail was a small place and news travelled fast, bad news even quicker than good, it seemed. 'Honour, I just can't believe it, I'm so sorry.'

'I know. I'm numb, Lorna. It doesn't feel real.' Honour had spoken with Lorna for a few more minutes, but her head had been pounding from all the crying and she felt utterly bereft up in the room where Kenny would never lie next to her again.

Now, the children were back in their bedrooms, and Bridie and Scott had dropped in to bring a bag of provisions from the farmer's market, and a freshly baked gingerbread. Marion had answered the door and then asked the couple in.

Bridie, a renowned local artist, whose stunning scenes of the villages along the Fife coast were sold at a gallery on Marketgate, was carrying a canvas wrapped in white tissue paper. Her long silver braid swung behind her, and her steel-grey eyes filled with tears as she walked straight up to Honour and wrapped her free arm around her. The strength of the hug took Honour by surprise. 'Honour, love. I just don't know what to say.'

Honour hugged her back, catching the smell of the gingerbread on Bridie's floral shirt. Behind her, Scott was hovering in the doorway, twisting his flat hat between his ruddy hands. His grey hair was fluffy over each ear, and the baldness of his shiny, tanned crown stood out in stark contrast. His chocolatey eyes were hooded as he stared at the ground, while Marion talked to him in a hushed tone.

Sensing his discomfort hanging like a raincloud over him,

Honour smiled at the soft-spoken man who lived next door, whose boat was tethered next to the *Lila Rose* and whose son, Malcolm, his fishing mate, used to sometimes play football with Kenny and Tara, on the beach. 'Hi, Scott.'

He lifted his eyes, sucked in his bottom lip, and crossed the room to stand next to his wife. 'Honour, lass.' He cleared his throat. 'It's just no' right. Such a young man and with so much to live for.' His eyes filled and he swiped at them, turning his back on her and Bridie, who stood next to Honour, holding her hand.

'Get a grip, Scotty,' Bridie said, not unkindly. 'That's the last thing Honour needs.'

Honour squeezed Bridie's fingers. 'Thanks, Scott. You know how fond Kenny was of you.' She patted his shoulder as he turned back to face her.

'I should've talked him out a' going out so far. He mentioned it to me on Thursday, and I had a bad feeling.' He shook his head. 'I should've said something.'

Honour smiled sadly. 'No one could tell Kenny MacLeod anything he didn't want to hear, Scott. You and I both know that.' She swallowed hard. 'Stubborn as an ox.'

Bridie sighed, then held out the canvas to Honour. 'I don't know if it's the right time, but this is for you.'

Puzzled, Honour took the package from her. 'Thanks, Bridie.' She hesitated, looking for her mum, and realising that Marion had left the room. 'Shall I open it now?'

Bridie's shoulders bounced. 'Whenever you want, love.'

Taking a moment, Honour set the package on the sofa, sat down and gently tore off the tissue paper. Before she could say anything, Tara appeared at the bottom of the stairs, then walked across the living room. Her eyes were puffy, and her hair was a matted red mess.

Honour's attention was pulled back to the painting and as she looked at what Bridie had created, her vision blurred, obscuring the outlines of the image. It was a family portrait, the four of them sitting in the back garden, on a checked blanket, all smiling at the camera. Callum was leaning against Kenny's arm, her son's glasses typically close to the end of his nose, and Kenny and Honour's fingers were laced together on the blanket between them. On her other side, Tara's hand was draped over Honour's shoulder, completing the chain – the simplest series of touches, links, connecting them in a circle of family.

Honour was speechless, her eyes burning. She looked up at Bridie and shook her head. 'I don't know what to say.'

Bridie sat next to her and took her hand. 'I hope you don't mind, but I asked Malcolm to see if he could find a good photo on Facebook. He got it from Kenny's page, I think.' She smiled sadly. 'I don't normally do portraits, but Kenny asked me if I'd give it a go.' She paused. 'It was supposed to be a surprise for you, for your birthday.'

Honour focused on the painting, seeing the depth of joy and pride in Kenny's eyes. The adoration in Callum's and the ever-present sparkle of mischief in Tara's – all expertly captured. In her own, she saw only peace. A blissful lack of awareness of what was to come and, more than anything in the world, she wished that she was back there, in that moment. That they all were.

Finding her voice, she gripped Bridie's hand. 'It's absolutely perfect. Thank you, Bridie.'

'It's us.' Tara was leaning over Honour's shoulder, looking at the painting. She peered closer, then a tear dropped onto Honour's collarbone. Fighting tears herself, she propped the painting against the back of the sofa and opened her arms to Tara, as Bridie stood up and joined Scott over at the window.

'It'll always remind us of who we are. Our family,' Honour whispered against Tara's temple. She smelled of soap, and the peanut butter she'd eaten out of the jar a little earlier. 'Dad will always be here, looking out for us.' Honour swept the fringe away from Tara's eyes seeing the heavy lashes clumped together, like the bristles of a wet paintbrush.

Watching Tara say goodbye to Scott and Bridie, then slump up the stairs, still favouring her left leg, Honour heard her phone ringing from upstairs. She stood up stiffly. 'If you'll excuse me a sec, I just need to go and check who phoned, in case it was the coastguard, or...' She halted, seeing her mother's and neighbours' eyes widen at the reminder of why they were all here. 'Back in a bit.' Honour turned towards the stairs, unable to handle the sympathy that she saw welling up in them.

Her phone was face down on the dressing table under the window, next to her hairbrush and the little tray that Kenny tossed his watch, wedding ring and loose coins from his pocket into each night. Seeing it empty struck a fresh blow, the absence of his things another reminder of the gaping hole that seemed to be sucking in things from her life. If he'd been knocked down by a bus, she'd at least have had his belongings to keep, but that greedy crone, the sea, had even snatched away those small tokens of his life, and Honour hated her for it.

She slowly crossed the room and opened the curtains wider on the sunny March day. A handful of people were walking around the harbour, one man taking photos while a young couple sat on the seawall, staring at their phones. The boats were all out, not due back until after midday, and Honour couldn't help but stare at the spot where the *Lila Rose* would not come in today. The spot where there would be no creels to unload, no banter between Kenny and Gregor. No noise, or briny smells of the catch, or presence of her husband, or his boat, today – or ever again. Clamping her eyes shut, Honour pushed back the swell of tears. Until she was completely alone, her visitors gone, her children asleep, her mother quietly reading on the fold-down bed in Tara's room, Honour would not allow herself to cry again today.

Opening her eyes, she lifted the phone, turning it over in her hand. The missed call had come in eight minutes ago, from a number she did not recognise, but as the police and coastguard could call from various numbers, and she couldn't afford to miss any updates or news they might have, she hit call.

It rang a few times with no answer, and as she sighed, ready for it to go to voicemail, she heard a deep, husky voice that struck at her heart with such force that she gripped the dressing table. 'Hello, Honour, it's me.'

7

Honour's insides somersaulted as she tried to focus on the harbour below, her mind suddenly flooded with memories, images she wanted to banish. As her heart rate spiked, she calculated that it had been over ten years since she'd last spoken to this man. What was he calling for, and what the hell did Kenny's brother, Jack, want from her now?

'Honour, are you there?' His voice was familiar and yet like an unwelcome shadow materialising behind her. 'Honour?'

Every impulse rushing through her was pushing her to hang up – and the swoop of the anger she still felt towards Jack took her by surprise. The memory of the hurt and abandonment in Kenny's eyes when his brother had left was glaringly bright once again. The way she'd fought tears soon after, when she'd caught Kenny looking at old photos of him and Jack, as boys, that he'd shoved away when she came into the bedroom, and how she'd wished she could talk to her husband – tell him things that he didn't know. But most of all, right now, the promise she had made Kenny at the crematorium, never to speak to his brother again, came rushing back.

Each time Jack said her name, she told herself that, even

though Kenny was gone, she should not break that promise, but she straightened her back, stared at her bedraggled reflection in the little mirror standing on the dressing table and found her voice.

'Jack.' Saying his name left a sour taste in her mouth as she straightened her rumpled shirt and combed her fingers through her mop of hair, snagging painfully on the knots behind her neck.

'Hi.' His voice was soft now, tentative in response to her curt greeting.

'Hi.' She wished she could rewind time and ignore the call. 'What's up?' She grimaced, the casual question, *so* not her – and she knew that he knew that, too.

'I wanted to call. To say I'm sorry.'

Honour frowned. 'About what?' There were several things he could potentially be apologising for, so she was unsure what he was talking about.

There was a pause, then he said, 'About Kenny, of course.'

Honour's heart skipped – him knowing about Kenny feeling like an intrusion rather than a comfort. How did he know, anyway? In the days since the *Lila Rose* had capsized, and her husband had been lost to the sea, Honour had told no one outside the village, except for her parents. Crail was a close-knit community and it had been many years since any one of them had been lost. Typically, the villagers had closed ranks around Honour and the children, and no one she could think of would have taken it upon themselves to share her loss outside of the community.

When Jack had left the village, over a decade earlier, as far as Honour was aware, the entire community had cut him off, taking pains to show Kenny and Honour where their loyalties lay. So how the news had leaked out to Jack, in Edinburgh, was beyond her.

'How did you find out?' Her voice threatened to crack.

'Malcom.' Jack hesitated. 'He was a friend, Honour. He's the only one who's kept in touch.'

An image of Scott and Bridie's son flashed behind her eyes. Malcolm, an immature thirty-five-year-old, with peroxide white hair and a gappy smile, who often skateboarded around the harbour with the local teens, and sometimes fished with his father. Malcolm had been friends with both Kenny and Jack, often joining them at the pub, back in their drinking days. Honour had believed that Malcom's loyalties had been with Kenny, but as she let the thought settle, it seemed unfair to assume that Malcolm couldn't keep in touch with friends – regardless of his parents', or anyone else in the village's, opinions.

A rush of guilt made her face begin to burn. Jack was Kenny's brother after all; he did have a right to know, and perhaps, in death, there was room for forgiveness. She hated that he could affect her this way, after all the time that had passed. 'Oh, right.'

'Look. I just wanted to say I'm sorry. He was a good lad, and I'll miss him.' Jack paused as Honour felt the guilt give way to anger. His words felt utterly inadequate.

Honour bit back. 'He spent that last ten years missing *you*, Jack. So perhaps this will even the playing field.' She gulped, choosing her next words carefully. 'Whatever else happened, Jack, and irrespective of how it affected anyone else, you owed your brother, and your father, more than radio silence.'

'That was below the belt, Honour.' He sounded hurt. 'You and I both know that things weren't as simple as that.'

Unwilling to open this particular Pandora's box, she cut him off. 'Jack, listen to me. We all make mistakes. Have regrets and make crappy choices. But, as adults, we do our best to move on, repair things where we can, and learn to accept when they are irreparable.' She was trembling, her legs beginning to feel unsteady, so she sat on the floor and pressed her back against the wall. She knew that she couldn't give him whatever it was he wanted. 'It's too late, Jack. If things were going to be different...' Her voice caught in her throat as she fought to find the words she needed. 'I mean, what do you want me to say?'

'I don't want anything from you, Honour. I just wanted to let you know that I'm sorry. He was my brother, and I loved him.' There was pain in his voice and, for a moment, Honour wanted to acknowledge it, but fear of where that might lead held her back.

'OK, Jack.' It was all she could come up with.

'If you need anything. I mean, some help with the kids, or the house...' He halted. 'I could come and see them, maybe get to know them.'

The idea of him trying to inject himself into her children's lives suddenly made her truly angry. 'I don't need you, Jack, and neither do my children. Just stay away from me, and my family.' Tears were coursing down her cheeks.

She could feel his shock pulsing in the silence as she tipped her head back and stared at the ceiling. The arrogance of this man. The idea that he could swoop in, act the hero after everything he had done, made her want to scream. Then, a memory that had been long buried surfaced again. She saw Kenny, drunk as a skunk, being elbowed back into the cottage by Jack, and them both giggling like schoolchildren until they saw her expression. She felt again the hurt and the crippling disappointment of that night.

She fought to banish the memory, as sympathy for her brother-in-law snuck back in beneath her anger. Not all of it was his fault. She took a moment, then said quietly, 'Just move on with your life, Jack. And be happy, OK?'

'You too, Honour.' He sounded defeated. 'Give my love to the kids. I'm their family too.' Then, he was gone.

I'm their family too. Honour set the phone on the carpet and took a deep breath. Tara and Callum knew they had an

Uncle Jack who lived in Edinburgh, but Kenny and Honour had seldom spoken of him, and the children rarely asked, so Jack had remained a mythical figure that had no impact on their lives.

She pushed herself up from the floor as her thoughts went back to Kenny's expression when he'd told her that Jack was no longer part of their family. Now that Kenny was gone, could she keep her promise to him?

8

Four days later, Honour was rushing to get out to the shop while the children were occupied up in their rooms, when her phone began to ring – an unknown number – once more. As she tried to slip her jacket on, with the phone wedged awkwardly under her jaw, she scanned the living room for her bag.

'Is this Mrs MacLeod?' The female voice was unfamiliar.

'Yes. Speaking.' She frowned, spotting her bag on the floor next to the sofa. 'Who's this?'

'I'm calling from the MCA. My name is Helen Sanderson.'

Frowning, Honour crossed the room and picked up her bag. 'The MCA?'

'The Maritime Coastguard Agency. I am a team lead and have been coordinating the search and rescue mission for Mr Kenneth MacLeod.'

Hearing his name, so formal and impersonal, so out of context, was like a hard slap that drew Honour to a standstill. 'What?' The word 'coastguard' the only other word that she had retained from the statement she'd just heard, she turned and stared at the front door, the morning sky grey and overcast through the glass panel. 'Kenny is my husband.' Hope began to push its way up inside her as Honour walked to the window, the lane outside quiet, the cobblestones glistening from the light rain that had fallen in the night.

'I have some information to share with you, if this is a good time?'

Honour dropped her bag and leaned against the windowsill. 'Now is fine.' She straightened up, her body tense, steeled for the next blow – the news that they had found Kenny's body – that he would be coming home so that she could bury him – but what she heard next sucked the breath from her.

'We have received a report from a hospital in Stavanger. They have an unidentified male who was picked up by a local vessel in their care. The person is unconscious and has sustained head injuries. He has no identification on him, but his physical description is somewhat close to that of your husband.'

Honour felt as if she were falling, her insides tumbling around the empty space where her heart once lived. 'How long ago was he found?' she croaked, her head snapping to the stairs, where, up in their rooms, her children were struggling under the weight of their grief.

'He's been there just under a week, in Intensive Care. He can't be moved, but the hospital is trying to establish his identity.'

Honour's heart was rattling under her shirt, her fist clenched tightly on her thigh. 'OK.'

'I have their contact information, Mrs MacLeod. If you would like to talk with them directly, they have some questions.'

'What questions?' Honour frowned, wanting with every molecule of her being to believe that this could be real.

'I imagine they'd like to see if you can help them establish whether this is your husband, or not.' The woman sounded guarded, as if unsure whether Honour was hearing her correctly. 'Mrs MacLeod, I realise that this must come as a shock, but I felt you'd want to speak with them. Maybe even go to Stavanger to see if you can identify him. One way or another.'

Even as hope began to take root, it was overtaken by a sense of deep certainty that this man – whomever he was – was not her husband. She recalled Kenny's hand slipping from hers and saw once more him fall into the thrashing waves and disappearing. No. Her Kenny, her love, was gone.

'My husband drowned...' She hesitated. 'He was lost at sea over a week ago. If this man was found a few days ago, it can't be Kenny.' She pressed her eyes closed, the image of a faceless, broken human being, bandaged, and floating in a state of unconsciousness invading her mind. She pictured herself standing at the bedside full of hope, then seeing the wrong colour eyes, a strange face, a different body than the one she wanted to see, and she choked back a sob.

'I understand that it's highly unlikely, Mrs MacLeod.' Helen paused. 'But I'll leave the hospital information with you, and if you could please speak with them, it would be extremely helpful.'

Honour walked unsteadily into the kitchen, in search of a pen, the floor feeling spongy beneath her feet. Opening the middle drawer in the Welsh dresser, she fished around amongst the mess of string, elastic bands, books of stamps and a half-empty box of birthday candles, until she felt the cool surface of a pencil. Taking it out, she scanned the room for something to write on. Seeing the calendar hanging on the wall by the fridge, she passed the table, and cleared her throat. 'OK. I'm ready.'

Helen read the information out to Honour, who scribbled it on the edge of the calendar, seeing the words she was writing as hieroglyphics – a language that she had no understanding of. As she stood back and looked at what she'd written, the floorboards above her creaked, then she heard Callum's bedroom door open.

Startled, and wanting to get off the phone before he could come down, catch her in a lie as she told him it was Lorna on the phone, she lowered her voice to a whisper. 'I'll phone them as soon as I can.'

'Thank you. I'll follow up with you if we get any more information.' Helen's tone was back to the formality of the situation. 'I appreciate your willingness to do this, Mrs MacLeod.'

Honour nodded as she said goodbye and set the phone on the table just as Callum walked in. His face was pale as he shoved his sleeves up has forearms and, smiling at her, he opened the fridge.

'I'm hungry.' He leaned in, surveying the sparse selection of food inside. 'There's no yogurt.' He stepped back and shut the door, his mouth dipping.

Snapped back to reality, Honour smoothed his unruly hair down at the back. 'I was just going to pop to Green's. I'll add it to the list.'

He glanced at the fruit bowl on the table. 'Bananas, too.' His young eyes met hers, his seeming to slide beneath the surface of her practised smile, spying the turmoil inside her. 'What's wrong, Mum?'

Honour suddenly imagined herself talking to him and Tara, explaining about the poor soul who had been found in Norway, nearly four hundred nautical miles away, and days after their father had been lost. The scene was surreal, and while she wanted nothing more than to believe, to have hope, the facts of the situation blotted out blind optimism.

Seeing Callum still staring at her, she shook her head and lifted the canvas shopping bag from the hook by the back door. 'Nothing, love. I'm just trying to remember if there's anything else we need.' She stuffed three recyclable vegetable bags into the shopping bag and looked at Callum, face on. 'I'll be back in a tick, OK?'

He studied her face briefly, then to her relief, nodded. 'OK.'

She kissed his forehead and turned away from him before her face could betray her again. Hearing him climb the stairs, she snapped a photo of the information on the calendar, then shoved her phone into her pocket.

She would phone the hospital, try to find out as much as she could, and, to help them all find closure, she'd even go to Norway. If she could see the man in person, it would take a matter of seconds to know the truth. Her head told her that Kenny was gone, but her heart was holding on to a question that she couldn't shake off: *What if I'm wrong?*

The afternoon crept by, as Honour tried to focus on the mundane tasks that she usually took in her stride but that now felt monumental. She made a casserole for dinner, pushed the vacuum cleaner around the downstairs, and put some laundry into the machine, all the while distracted, struggling to process what she'd learned from the brief call she'd made to the hospital in Stavanger, on her way to Green's.

The hospital administrator had been a soft-spoken man, asking if Kenny had any distinguishing marks, any scars or tattoos that might help identify him. Honour had told him no, remembering the way she'd teased Kenny about being the only seaman she knew who didn't have at least one tattoo. He'd laughed, telling her that the only thing he'd ever consider having permanently marked on his body was an image of her face, and that no one would be able to capture her sufficiently. Honour had found it incredibly touching, and as she wasn't a fan of the inky tattoos that Allen and Jack had both sported on their forearms, she'd kissed him gratefully.

The administrator had asked her if she could describe Kenny, his build, his hair colour, and as she'd recited all that she could he had sighed. 'It's hard to say precisely, but this man's eyes look dark brown.'

A swoop of disappointment had made Honour suck in her bottom lip, the gold-flecked hazel irises of Kenny's eyes something she loved best about his face. 'My husband's eyes aren't dark.' She'd shaken her head sadly. 'It doesn't sound like him.'

After speaking with the man for a few more minutes, a feeling of conviction had grown inside Honour. She needed to see this man they'd found. There was only a tiny chance that it was Kenny, but she owed it to the children to pursue it, so she'd told the administrator that she would try to come to Norway within the next day or so.

'Ah, good. We hoped you would say so.' He had sounded grateful, but cautiously so. 'We know the chance is a small one, but until he wakes, we can't do more.'

'I understand.' She'd scanned the road by Bailey's, anxious not to be seen hovering in this odd way outside the shop. 'I'll phone tomorrow when I've made the arrangements.'

'Very good. Talk to you then.'

After a restless night – Honour spending much of it reading or sitting up in bed staring at the dark square of the curtains – she'd got up at 5.30 a.m. She'd snuck downstairs and made some tea, then spent some time looking at how she might travel to Norway, flying from Edinburgh looking like the only viable option since there were no ferries. Now, as she calculated the time in Norway, she lifted her phone and called the hospital again.

As she waited for them to answer, she estimated that she could go there and be back in a day, so all she'd have to do was figure out what to do with the children. She wasn't prepared to raise her parents' hopes by telling them what was going on. If she could tell anyone about what was happening, it would be Lorna, so deciding that she'd have to enlist her friend to cover for her, Honour heard the administrator she'd spoken to the previous day come on the line.

'Hello, again. This is Honour MacLeod. We spoke yesterday.' She waited for the enthusiastic acknowledgement that she'd received the day before. Instead, the man's voice was guarded.

'Ah, yes. Mrs MacLeod. Good morning.'

'I'm trying to figure out getting over there, but it's going to take me a day or so. I wondered if—'

Before she could go on, he cut her off. 'Mrs MacLeod, I'm afraid I have some bad news. The patient has left.'

Honour frowned, her heart sinking as she focused on the back door. 'Left?'

9

The administrator cleared his throat. 'Yes. He woke late last night. His vital signs were weak, but we talked to him, trying to explain what he had been through. We asked about his identity, who we could contact or whether he had a family, and while he appeared to understand us, he was unwilling to speak. We advised him that he needed to stay in the hospital until he was out of danger, but he signed a waiver and left early this morning – against medical advice.'

Honour let the information permeate, her initial inability to allow herself to believe that it was Kenny now feeling like a buoy that she should have clung tighter to. 'So, he's gone.'

'Yes, he is. We have no more information, I'm afraid.' He sounded defeated. 'I'm sorry to have raised your hopes.'

Honour nodded, tears that she'd been holding back now springing over her lower lids. 'It's not your fault. I knew, in my heart, it wasn't him. He would have contacted me as soon as he was able. I know in my soul that if he was alive, he would have let me know.' Her voice broke. 'I'm sorry,' she croaked.

'Please don't apologise. I wish it had been different.'

Honour wiped her cheeks on her pyjama sleeve and stood up. 'Me too. You have no idea how much.'

She walked out of the kitchen, trying to picture the man who had survived a situation that Kenny had not been given the grace to, and Honour swallowed a sob. Today, somewhere in Norway, a woman might be welcoming her husband home, a family might be reunited, but here, in this cottage, this fractured little family would never be complete again.

Ten days later, April bringing the spring rain that made the streets smell like clean linen, the small service they'd held for Kenny at the harbourside was behind them. They had been surrounded by their friends and neighbours in the village, and Honour and the children had each floated a red rose out onto the water, as her parents had gently held her up on either side.

A bagpiper had played 'Sleep, Dearie, Sleep' and the heart-rending tune had floated out over the water, the surroundings amplifying the mournful sound around the small group of villagers, as if they were all standing in an auditorium. Based on a Scottish lullaby, the song, about a soldier being urged to go to sleep after a long and difficult day at war, had felt painfully apt as Honour had held the children's hands and blinked away her tears.

It had been hard to hear Gregor talk about Kenny, his fishing mate and friend, and when he'd spoken, his salt-and-pepper head had been dipped towards his notes, the pock-marked cheeks pulsing as he markedly avoided Honour's eyes.

She had been surprised, and a little disappointed that Gregor was the one person who had not come to the cottage since the *Lila Rose* had been lost, but as she'd heard him speak about her husband, the depth of respect and fondness Gregor felt for Kenny had shone through. Honour suddenly under-stood that facing her, when it very well could have been him who'd been lost that day, was more than this shy, soft-spoken man could manage.

As she considered her own mounting guilt at surviving when Kenny hadn't, and what might have happened if he had chosen to tie himself to the railing, too, she'd smiled kindly at Gregor when he'd eventually looked up, and the relief on his face had been her reward.

Her mother and father had left four days later, her father hugging her tight, and gruffly whispering, 'You're going to be all right, my girl.' She'd wondered if he knew her at all, as being strong felt as beyond her as being happy again did.

Her mother had gathered the children in her arms, her eyes brimming. 'You're my wee angels, and I'm just half an hour away if you need me.' Her eyes had held Honour's as she'd nodded gratefully. Seeing them drive away had been a wrench, but Honour had also felt slightly relieved. She needed to find a way to do this on her own.

Now, she sat on the floor of her bedroom, staring at the open wardrobe; the reality that it was just the three of them now, her and the children, her altered family, sinking in. The concept that this was permanent was as unfathomable as it was painful, and, consequently, Honour was doing everything she could to stay busy, and keep the children occupied, too.

Filling the silence her parents had left with activity felt essential and, so far, they'd been for a walk on Fossil Beach, but quickly had to smile and thank the various villagers they passed for their condolences. Deciding that they needed to go further afield to avoid too many reminders of what they'd lost, the next day, Honour had driven them to Edinburgh, to the zoo. The following day, they'd been to the cinema in St Andrews, then come home and fired up Kenny's old barbecue, burning some perfectly good steaks to a blackened mess.

Each day, when they left the cottage, the gentle April sun felt glaringly harsh. The seagulls' calls that usually comforted were like clanging symbols above them, and the faces around them appeared like grotesque masks of normality to Honour's bruised soul. Despite all that, her new strategy seemed to be helping the children to avoid the weight of Kenny's absence, until this morning, as they'd got ready to go to Lomond Hills Park for a walk.

Honour and Tara had been waiting in the living room for Callum until Tara had grown impatient, eventually bellowing up the stairs, 'Come on, Call-umsy. You're such a flippin' slowcoach.'

Honour had frowned at Tara. 'Don't do that at the moment. He's not up to it.'

Tara had rolled her eyes as Honour had dashed up the stairs to check on her son. There had been an instant zap to her heart when she'd found him crying in the bathroom, trying to tie his shoelaces, with painfully stiff fingers that wouldn't do his bidding.

'I can't do it. My fingers hurt, and when I bend down, I feel dizzy.' His eyes had been awash with tears, his chin wobbling as he'd kicked the bathmat, angrily.

'Oh, Cal, I'm sorry, love.' She'd knelt and tied his laces for him.

'Can't we just stay here, today?' he'd pleaded. 'I'm tired of going places.'

Honour had been crushed. Angry with herself for not paying more attention to how he was feeling. Numbed by her own pain, she had missed the cues she would normally have picked up on. 'Of course we can.' She'd noticed that he'd wet his hair and tried to comb it back from his forehead, like Kenny used to when they went somewhere special, and seeing it had made her throat knot. 'What would you like to do, then?' She'd held his chilly fingers in hers, gently rubbing them to help increase the circulation.

'Watch TV. Have Dougie over and get fish and chips.' His

lips had been quivering with the effort of not crying, and his sweet attempt at bravery had all but destroyed her.

'Then that's what we'll do. I'll phone Lorna now and see if she and Dougie can come for tea.' She'd tried to sound upbeat, then she'd spoken softly. 'I'm sorry if I've been tiring you out, Cal.'

He'd eyed her, swiping at his nose with the back of his hand. 'It's OK.' He'd looked miserable. 'Tara bosses me around when we're out places, too. She acts like she's the mum sometimes.' He'd hiccupped, sending a bolt of maternal protection sparking through her.

'She doesn't mean to be bossy, Cal. She's just looking out for you.'

His mouth had dipped at the corners. 'I can look out for myself. I'm not a baby.' His voice had taken on a forced, gruff quality. 'I'm eight, for God's sake.'

Honour had scolded him for his language, and then tentative laughter had bubbled between them as she'd imitated his odd voice. He'd tossed his shoes aside, put his slippers on, and they'd gone downstairs to find Tara curled up on the sofa with the TV on.

'What're you watching?' Callum had flopped down next to her.

'Hearts versus Kilmarnock.' She'd nodded at the screen. 'Recorded from last week.'

Callum had sighed. 'Football is so boring.'

'You're so boring.' Tara had nudged him. 'Shut up. I'm watching.'

Callum had pouted, but rather than slope away as he might have before, he'd stayed next to his sister, making Honour's heavy heart feel a little lighter.

. . .

Outside the bedroom window, the sky was now heavy with clouds and big, fat raindrops spattered against the glass – a late-afternoon storm passing slowly across the harbour and heading out to sea, making Honour glad that they'd stayed at home. She pictured the gloss this type of rain left on the cobbled streets of the village, the way the plants in the pots and hanging baskets that lined the streets seemed to glow after an April shower.

The gulls were strangely quiet, leaving only the sound of the rain and the faint rumble of the TV downstairs, where Callum was watching *Star Trek* re-runs – waiting for his best friend to arrive, while Tara practised dribbling a football in the back garden.

In front of Honour, Kenny's clothes were hanging in the usual jumble in the wardrobe. Multiple pairs of jeans, and khaki trousers, often more than one pair to a hanger, filled much of his half of the big oak wardrobe. The two formal shirts he owned were crushed at one end, with a Dundee United scarf wrapped around both hangers. His shoes were tossed in chaotically, trainers and walking boots piled on top of flip-flops and canvas sneakers. Honour looked at the mess, then the three large plastic bags she'd brought upstairs with her, and her vision blurred.

Kenny was still here, present in every item of clothing, every brine-stained shoe, and the thought of moving things from where he'd last touched them was so overwhelming that she could barely breathe. She tried to imagine *ever* being ready for this step, then she folded at the waist and let the tears come.

Within moments, a shuffling behind her made her sit upright and swipe at her eyes before turning around. Tara stood in the doorway, a pinched expression on her face and her hands twisting in front of her.

'What is it, love? Are you finished practising?' Honour pushed herself up from the floor, kicked the plastic bags aside and crossed the room to her daughter.

'Do we have any aspirin?' Tara shifted her weight to her right leg, and lifted her left off the ground, like a wounded animal might. 'My leg's bad today.'

Honour closed her eyes briefly. She had not called the doctor yet. With everything that had happened over the past three weeks, it had completely fallen off her radar, and as Tara had not mentioned being in pain since the football match, Honour had let it slip.

'God, I'm so sorry, sweet girl. Yes, I'll get you some aspirin, and an ice pack, and I'll call Doctor Ford, right now. I think you might need some more PT, Tara. It really helped with your shin splints the last time.' She hugged her daughter to her, noticing that Tara's head now almost reached Honour's chin. At five feet seven, she had always been the tallest in her class at school, and now it seemed that Tara was heading down that same path – tall for her age.

Tara sighed, looking up at her mother. Tara's eyes were cupped by dark shadows and her usually bright complexion looked dull and waxy. 'I'm tired, Mum. I don't want to go to practice tomorrow.' She leaned into Honour's middle. This was unprecedented, but then so was this remarkably strong girl losing her father, and faced with another layer of unknown territory to navigate, Honour did her best to pivot.

'I think it's fine to miss it, Tara. Everyone will understand. I'll just phone and let the coach know.' She rubbed her daughter's back, alarmed by its boniness through the thick cotton of her hoodie. 'But first, I'll phone for an appointment, then you can take some aspirin, and once Dougie gets here, we'll go and get fish and chips. OK?' She stepped back from her daughter and caught a sad, half-smile twist Tara's mouth.

'OK.' Tara scanned her mother's face.

'What is it?' Honour tipped her head to the side.

'You're brave, Mum.'

Taken aback, Honour's eyebrows lifted. 'Brave, how?'

Tara stuffed her hands into the front pocket of her hoodie. 'Sleeping in here without Dad.' She gestured towards the bed. 'Are you scared at night?'

Honour frowned. 'Not at all.' She held her daughter's gaze, hoping for a clue as to where this was coming from. 'Why would I be scared, love?'

Tara shrugged. 'Because you have those bad dreams, but now he's not here to make you feel safe.' She stopped, one hand emerging from the pocket to go to her mouth, where her chin had begun to tremble.

Honour was rocked, having no idea that Tara knew about her recurring nightmares. 'How did you know about my dreams, sweetheart?' She held her hand out, and Tara grasped it.

'Dad told me. That time when you were staying with Grandma and Grandpa, after Grandma broke her knee, I had a really bad dream. He came in and read to me, and he told me that you had bad dreams, too.' She eyed her mother. 'What are yours about?'

Honour took a few moments to process what she'd just been told, picturing Kenny gently tucking Tara in, then lying across the end of her bed as he read to her. The image was so vivid, and so beautiful, that Honour swallowed hard. 'Oh, mine are about various things. Usually about getting lost or being late for something important. One time, I dreamt that I lost you and Cal in the supermarket.' She rubbed her thumb over the back of Tara's ivory hand. 'But then I woke up and realised the real nightmare was that you were both still here.' She pointed to the hallway, waiting for Tara to catch on.

Tara's eyes narrowed, then she laughed, a sound that had been missing from the house for three entire weeks, and hearing it now, for Honour, was like a life raft to a drowning man.

Tara's features blurring, Honour grabbed her daughter to her and rocked her in an exaggerated way. 'You are my baby, Tara MacLeod. No matter how tall and clever you get.' She smiled above Tara's head. 'Now, let's go and make that phone call. Then we all need to eat piles of chish and fips, or I'll be sending two stick insects back to school next week.'

The thought of them going back to school in just a few days, and her to work after bereavement leave, was hard to process. Now that her get-out-and-do-things tactic had crashed and burned, Honour realised that in the cottage they were safe, surrounded by Kenny's presence, in every room. Outside these walls, the world had a taken on a new shape that felt foreign, and frightening, without him in it.

Half an hour later, Honour called the doctor's surgery and got an appointment for Tara the following week. Doctor Ford's receptionist sounded busy and distracted but didn't forget to tell Honour how sorry she was, about Kenny. 'It's just tragic, Mrs MacLeod. We're all so very sorry.'

'Thank you, Carla. I appreciate it.' Honour pressed her eyes closed. Why was sympathy so hard to accept gracefully? 'So, Thursday at half-four. We'll see you then.' She turned off her phone and went to write it on the wall calendar that hung next to the fridge. As she lifted the pen on the string that was pinned to the board, she spotted Kenny's handwriting and it brought her to a standstill. It was a reminder for a dental appointment for him, in three weeks' time, and as she imagined herself phoning to cancel it, she went into the little pantry between the kitchen and the back garden and gave in to tears.

Tara had swallowed the aspirin, then gone back outside with the football, which she was now kicking against the side wall of the house, marking her location with a series of regular thumps that took Honour back in time, to all the Sunday afternoons when Kenny and Tara could be out there for hours, weather permitting, while Honour cooked dinner.

In the living room, while Honour read, Callum lay on the sofa in his navy-blue Space Camp tracksuit, waiting for Dougie to arrive. Dougie had been to Florida the summer before to attend Space Camp at Cape Canaveral and had brought back the tracksuit for Callum. He had worn it perpetually ever since, the logo beginning to fade from the jacket with all the washing.

When Dougie had come home, full of stories about all the fun in the dormitory, mission activities and team assignments, Callum had only done a passable job of hiding his envy. Kenny had seen it, and that night had whispered to Honour, up in their bedroom, 'Do you think we could save enough to send him next year?'

Honour had smiled, Kenny's need to give his children everything he possibly could, regardless of whether it was practical or not, making her love him even more. 'I don't know, Kenny. I'd love to, but we have so many other commitments, and the car is on its last legs.' She'd snuggled in closer to his side, her lips brushing his collarbone.

'So what?' He'd bent his head and kissed her. 'A car is a car. We can figure out another one somehow, but imagine Cal in America? Surrounded by all those other kiddos who love the same things as him. All the spacey experiences he'd have there that we can't give him here, in Crail.' He'd sighed as Honour had felt the ground giving way under her objections.

She'd wound her fingers through his and whispered, 'OK. Let's do some sums and see if we can manage it. But, Kenny MacLeod, don't you dare say a word to him until we know for sure it's possible. Do you hear me?' Sensing his excitement, she'd twisted to face him, and even in the dark, she'd spotted the tell-tale dimple in his left cheek. 'You're a nightmare.' She'd laughed softly as he'd rolled on top of her, extending his arms and legs like a starfish and pushing the air out of her lungs.

'Say yes or I'll sleep just like this, all night.' He'd sighed theatrically. 'Much comfier than the mattress.'

Honour had shoved at him, laughing under his weight. 'Get off, you arse. I can't breathe. OK, OK. We'll find a way.'

Kenny had kissed her cheeks, her forehead, her nose, her eyelids, as she'd wriggled beneath him. 'I love you, Honour MacLeod. You are the best mum in the world.'

'I love you bigger,' she'd whispered, as his kisses had focused on her mouth, and then gained in intensity.

Snapping her back to the moment, across the room, Callum sneezed, several times, his legs lifting off the sofa and his arms flying dramatically above his head each time – something comical he'd picked up from Kenny. Callum's book about the Apollo missions was lying open on the floor and his socked feet had been moving in time with the music playing in the background.

Honour was sitting in Kenny's chair, trying to read a book about Anne Boleyn that she'd been enjoying, before her world had imploded. The words to the song were distracting her, prodding at her heart with a bony finger, making it hard to hold back the tears. Callum had chosen the CD from the rack and as Adele crooned about one more chance, Honour had read the same paragraph three times. Giving up, she closed her book as Callum sneezed again.

'Bless you.' She stood up, pulled a tissue from the box on the shelf by the fire and handed it to him.

'Thanks.' He took it and flapped it under his nose, but rather than use the tissue, he then wiped his nose on his sleeve.

'You little monster,' Honour tutted. 'Raised by wolves, I swear.'

His eyes widened at her, and all she could think about was how happy Kenny would have been to tell him that they'd saved up enough to send him to Space Camp that coming summer. Kenny had sold the stamp collection his grandfather had given him and had patched the bilge pump on the *Lila Rose* rather than replace it to reach the amount they needed, and now, all Honour wanted to do was make her son smile again.

Tara had the football season to focus on, and with more away games this year, they'd be busy getting to all those matches. Honour pictured herself, standing on the sidelines by herself, watching Tara play, and the empty space beside her in the image felt so cavernous that she turned her back on Callum and closed her eyes briefly, trying to banish it.

'Mum?' He sounded concerned. 'Sorry. I'll use the tissue next time.' He was behind her now, the bubble-gum smell of shampoo giving away his closeness.

'It's not that, love.' She turned to face him, taking in the frown on his young brow. 'I'm just missing Dad so much today.' She drew him into her middle, raking the thick fringe away from his forehead. His glasses were densely smudged with fingerprints, all but obscuring his hazel eyes – a carbon copy of his father's – but she knew her son's eyes well enough to know that he was worried, and she regretted not editing her thoughts. 'Listen, I have something to tell you. Dad wanted to be the one to tell you but, well...' She gave a closed-lip smile. 'I'll have to do.'

10

Callum's frown deepened. 'What is it?' He let her lead him back to the sofa, where they sat next to each other.

'It's good. Nothing to worry about.' She smiled as encouragingly as she could. Why wasn't Kenny here to do this? To assure her that this was the perfect time to tell their son about fulfilling a dream, and to share in the joy that brought about. How would she ever get used to witnessing moments like this, alone?

Callum was staring at Honour, looking dubious. 'So, it's something good?'

'Yes. Stop worrying and listen.' She laughed softly. 'We've been saving up to send you to Space Camp this summer.'

Before she could continue, Callum's eyebrows shot up and his face was flooded with a light that she had not seen in far too long.

'Well, we managed it, Cal. We have enough for you to go.' She paused, readying herself for the hurdle that would come, along with this experience. 'Dad was going to go with you and stay a few days with my old friend Amy, who lives out there, while you're at camp.'

No sooner did she mention Kenny than the light went out of Callum's eyes.

'Oh.' His chin dropped. 'So, I probably can't go now.'

She shook her head, trying to hold onto the moment of joy for them both. 'Well, I wanted to ask if you still wanted to, and, if you do, I thought I'd ask Grandpa Kirk if he'd take you. I just can't be away in August, because of all Tara's tournaments, and training.' She watched his eyes widen, then narrow, as if he was playing out the scenario she'd described, in his mind. 'You can be one hundred per cent honest about what you want, Cal. There is no wrong answer here.'

He nodded, his mouth pinching as he fought some internal battle that she wasn't party to. After a few moments, he met her eyes. 'Wouldn't it be bad for me to go, and be having fun and stuff, when Dad is dead?'

Honour felt the air leave her in a rush. This was typically thoughtful of Callum, but also somewhat brutal. The honesty of her children could often unseat her, and as she let her heart settle, she shook her head. 'It wouldn't be bad, because it's what Dad wanted – more than anything.' She took his hand in hers. 'So, what do you think?'

Callum took his glasses off, rubbed the bridge of his nose and slid them back on. 'Then, I want to go.' He smiled, a genuine smile that transformed his face from concerned young adult to excited child, and this picture of joy was one that Honour wanted to commit to memory, forever.

'All right, then. I'll start by asking Grandpa Kirk, and if he's able to take you, I'll look at booking camp, and getting your flights, et cetera.'

Callum suddenly looked concerned, his brow knitting above his glasses.

'What is it, love?'

He took a moment, then said, 'What if I'm not well on the plane? Or at the camp? What if my legs get bad and I can't do the activity stuff?' He sucked in his bottom lip, the new mask of tension on his face tugging directly at Honour's heart. His Ménière's disease often reared its head when he was faced with a new challenge, something that took him out of his safety zone, but Honour wanted this for him – more than she'd known.

'Callum, you will be fine. And if, worst-case scenario, you really aren't feeling good, Grandpa Kirk will only be half an hour away, and you can FaceTime with me, any time you're worried.' She squeezed his bony knee. 'It's only four days, Cal, and imagine how much fun it's going to be. You'll get to see an actual space shuttle.' She smiled at him, willing him to focus on the positive, but understanding with her whole heart why he was nervous.

She had witnessed him during a bad flare, and Ménière's was no joke. It could leave him nauseated, listless, dizzy and in significant pain. 'We'll check with Doctor Ford before you go, and make sure you have your hydrocortisone with you, and you'll wear your Medic Alert bracelet.' She glanced at his narrow wrist, currently bare. 'I think it's upstairs in the bathroom cabinet.' She frowned, trying to remember when she'd last seen it. Callum rarely wore the bracelet, as he was seldom out anywhere without either her or Kenny, but if this trip was to happen, Honour would need to inform everyone concerned about Callum's condition, and him wearing the bracelet would be essential.

He was staring at her, his eyes flitting from her face to the window. 'And Grandpa will be near?' He blinked, his free hand going to his glasses again.

'Yes. Less than half an hour away.' She released his hand and did what Kenny would have done. 'Callum, you can do this. I have no doubt that you can. We'll go over each step together and do our very best to make sure you're ready. And you'll be full of stories about it when you get home. You and Dougie can natter until you both turn blue in the face.' She pulled a comical face and waited.

'OK.' He nodded purposefully. 'Can we phone Grandpa now?' The excitement was back.

Honour laughed. 'Once Dougie's gone, after tea, we'll phone together.' Just as she stood up, the doorbell rang. 'There he is, now.' She crossed the room and headed for the front door, steeling herself for another first time, seeing a good friend, and the sympathy that would engulf her, once again. Something that still felt like a gut punch every time.

Lorna had gladly agreed to stay for a glass of wine and join them for some dinner. She was a tiny, flaxen-haired, mossy-eyed nurse from St Andrews, whom Honour had first met at a party when she'd moved to the village as a newly-wed. Lorna had later married an American serviceman she'd met at the air force base in Prestwick. Eight years on, she was divorced, and she and Dougie lived in a pretty, high-ceilinged flat, above a gift shop overlooking the water in Anstruther.

They'd moved home from Prestwick to be near Lorna's parents when her ex had returned to Florida, and each summer, Dougie would spend two weeks with his dad – hence the Space Camp experience.

Honour was fond of Lorna, and while the boys played together, they'd often exchange stories about their experiences working in the healthcare industry. Lorna now worked part-time nursing on the paediatric ward at Victoria Hospital in Kirkcaldy, and Honour envied her feisty friend her selected independence – something that Honour had not sought but had had thrust upon her.

Tara had eaten her dinner at lightning speed and asked if she could watch football on the laptop in her room. Honour had agreed and kissed Tara's flushed cheek as she'd waved at Lorna and disappeared up the stairs, two at a time.

The boys were next to each other on the sofa watching the *Apollo 13* movie for the umpteenth time, Dougie's white-blond head highlighting how much darker Callum's hair had grown over the past year – the sandy-red tone of his father's replacing the strawberry-blonde of Cal's babyhood.

Lorna sat opposite Honour at the kitchen table as she topped up their wine glasses. 'Oh, I never even asked if you're driving.' Honour halted as Lorna patted the air.

'Nope. Taxi. I had a feeling.' She nodded at the bottle. 'Well, more that I was hoping.' She shrugged, a smile twisting her ruby mouth.

Honour smiled. 'Incorrigible, as usual.' She poured Lorna a hefty refill, added a splash to her own glass, then slid onto the bench, opposite her friend. Behind Lorna, the kitchen was in disarray. Dirty dishes sat in the sink. In the corner, near the back door, the flip-top bin lid was sitting proud of the rim, the greasy paper from their fish and chips messily crammed in. The tea towels that normally hung in crisp, military order on the handle of the Aga were crumpled, one dangling down almost to the floor, and various cereal boxes were open, sitting on the counter next to the stainless-steel kettle that was spattered with oil. Shutting out the unaccustomed mess, Honour focused on her friend as she touched her wine glass to Honour's.

'To you, my friend. I know this question is probably like nails on a blackboard, but how are you? I mean, really.' Lorna took a sip. 'I know it probably feels like shit at the moment.'

Honour swirled the wine in her glass, for the first time taking stock of the myriad sensations that were occupying her, mind, body and soul. 'Fractured. Numb. Disbelieving. Scared. Sad. Angry.' She met Lorna's eyes. 'Mostly scared.'

'I can only imagine.' Lorna's eyes glittered as she shook her head sadly. Then, she lifted her chin, her expression clearing.

'Not that my situation is anything like yours, but in my case, when I saw Dale's big, stupid back walking away from the house, I was just angry. Angry, fed up, angry again, then bloody relieved.' She stared at her glass, then met Honour's gaze. It took a few seconds for Honour to clue in, then the two friends laughed together.

There wasn't a whiff of pity in Lorna's words and Honour was unspeakably grateful.

Tears pricked her eyes as she took a mouthful of wine, letting the earthy tang sit on her tongue until it burned. 'You are a breath of fresh air, Lorna.'

Lorna shrugged. 'At least I'm good for something.'

Honour pushed her glass away and leaned her chair back against the wall. 'It's like I'm floating. Trying to feel the floor, but my feet go through it.' She paused. 'The kids are all that's keeping me going.' She gestured towards the living room, where the sound of an explosion on the TV floated into the kitchen.

Lorna nodded. 'Dougie was my saving grace, too. He had this way of knowing what to say, when I felt totally useless.'

Honour let Lorna's comment permeate, its truth a spark of light inside her murky head. 'God, that's it exactly. They don't edit anything and while it hurts sometimes, it's a reminder that I'm still alive.'

'Totally.' Lorna took another sip. 'So, when are you back to work?'

Honour sighed. 'Monday.' She would have to put on her scrubs, choosing which pattern to wear to amuse the residents of the care home. She had become known for her fun choices, everything from Smurfs to pink unicorns, bumblebees to golden starfish, and her personal favourite, a pair that were covered with hundreds of mini-Saltires – Scotland's national flag. The residents would take bets on what she'd be wearing, and the winner got a KitKat or a Milky Way that she'd stuff in her bag before leaving the house. 'I'm not ready.' She shook her head.

'I don't think you'll ever be, honestly. The first day will be hellish, then, hopefully, it'll get better.' Lorna set her glass down. 'How are the kids feeling about going back to school?'

Honour shrugged, guilt at not thinking to ask them warming her cheeks, and the sense that there was so much she was not coping with making her slump back in the chair. 'Dunno. I haven't asked them yet. That's the narcissist I am.' She sighed. 'I suppose I won't win the mother-of-the-year award, this year.'

Lorna frowned. 'In all the years I've known you, you've never been the self-pitying kind.' Her eyes were bright, her chin set in a firm line. 'That's not who you are, Honour.'

Honour caught the slight edge in her friend's voice and rather than take it as a shot of strength, Honour was filled with a rush of rage. Before she could stop herself, she snapped, 'Well, perhaps it's who I am now that my husband is gone.' Her throat drew into a tight knot, and she instantly regretted her tone.

Lorna's eyebrows jumped and she blinked several times. 'Wow. Well, I asked for that.' She nodded to herself. 'I'll defi- nitely need to ask for a refund for that *How-To-Help-A-Friend- Whose-Husband-Just-Died-Get-On-With-Her-Life* book.' She held Honour's gaze until Honour exhaled, a bubble of laughter breaking free as she leaned forward and let her head rest on her forearms.

'I'm sorry, Lorna. I'm just a bloody mess.' She felt her newly washed hair spilling over the skin of her arms, the sensation like a flood of cool water on her tender skin.

Lorna's hand was on hers. 'Forget it. I pushed too far. I always do.'

Honour shook her head against her arms, then sat up. 'No. I need to get a grip. I mean. I don't want pity, and then when you give it to me straight, I jump on you. Sorry.'

'It's quite all right,' Lorna said, rubbing her shoulder.

'Thank you. And speaking of truths, look at this place.' She swept her hand in an arc. 'It's a tip.'

Lorna spun around, taking in the mess behind her. 'I have no idea what you're talking about.' She shrugged, her narrow back to Honour. 'This is what mine looks like *after* I've cleaned.'

Honour snorted. 'OK. I can't take it anymore.' She slid out from behind the table, twisted her hair into a ponytail and secured it with a pencil that had been lying next to her wine glass. 'Talk to me while I clean this up?' She tipped her head to the side. 'There's more wine in the fridge, and some leftover caramel shortbread my mum made.'

Lorna grinned. 'Sold. I'm such a cheap date.' She stood up, circling her head and stretching her arms across her front, as if she was about to start a boxing match.

'Just talk to me. I'll clean everything.' Honour lifted the dishcloth and started moving the dirty pots out of the sink.

'Bugger that,' Lorna huffed, rolling up her sleeves. 'Where do we start?'

With Lorna and Dougie gone, the kitchen looking more like it usually did, and the children bathed and tucked up in bed, Honour lay on top of the covers in her and Kenny's room. The nights were the hardest, when the house was quiet, the children asleep, Shoregate gradually emptying of people, and the harbour activity fading away, until dawn.

As she closed her eyes to block out the ugly wound of Kenny's undisturbed side of the bed, she suddenly remembered that she hadn't phoned her father about going to Florida. Surprised that Callum hadn't asked about it as soon as Dougie left, she rolled over and lifted her phone from the bedside table, and as she was about to scroll through her contacts, she noticed one of the last incoming calls, from an Edinburgh number. Her thumb hesitated over the Delete button, then, without analysing why, she created a new contact, adding simply JM as the name. Seeing Jack's presence re-acknowledged, after more than a decade, by such a simple gesture, was disturbing and yet, even as she questioned herself, a whisper from deep inside told her that it was the right thing to do.

Honour pressed her parents' number and waited, her father's voice what she needed to hear for more reasons than to ask him a huge favour. Her heart ticked under her nightshirt, as Honour pictured his face, the pale moustache, the red hair, the gentle blue eyes behind frameless glasses, the way he rubbed his palm across the bridge of his nose when he was considering something important, but, mostly, the way he looked at her mother with the same, steady affection, after nearly forty years of marriage.

'Hello, my girl. It's late for you,' Kirk said, making Honour snap her head back and check the time, seeing that it was 10.26 p.m.

'Oh, sorry, Dad. I should've looked at the time.' She grimaced. 'I can phone tomorrow.'

'Not at all. I was just watching telly. Mum's already gone up, though, if you wanted to talk to her.'

Honour shook her head. 'Actually, I wanted to ask you something.' She sat up and leaned against the headboard, catching a waft of vinegar from their dinner, lingering in her hair.

'OK, well, fire away.'

Honour took her time to lead up to the question, explaining how much Kenny wanted to do this for Callum, and before she even asked if Kirk would go, he cut in, 'Why don't I take him?'

'Oh, Dad. That's exactly what I was going to ask you.' Tears pressed in at the back of her eyes. 'It's a lot to ask, and of course I'd pay for your ticket.' She pulled a tissue from the box by the bed. 'Amy says you can stay with them, and she'll drive you to Cape Canaveral to drop Cal off and pick him up. She's only five minutes from a lovely golf course, too.' She scanned the partially open window, the clear night sky sparkling with a dusting of stars that made her think of her son, and his love of all things astronomical.

'Well, that makes it an easy decision, then.' He laughed softly. 'And I won't hear of you paying for my ticket. This will be a priceless opportunity for me to have some time alone with Callum. A boys' trip if you will.'

'No, Dad. It's too much. And we saved enough to do it.' She frowned, the thought of Kenny's excitement over this a painful dart to her heart.

'Listen to me, Honour. You're going to need to be careful with expenses now. Mum and I want to help where we can, so let me do this.'

She felt the warmth of the love in his voice, the notes of concern that he was trying to disguise, and her heart felt as if it might burst. 'Thank you, Dad. You and Mum are the absolute best.'

'We're the best *you* get, anyway.' He chuckled. 'Now, you need to get to sleep.'

Honour nodded, slid down the bed and covered herself with the duvet. 'I'm in, and pretty tired, so hopefully I'll sleep.'

'I'll say goodnight, then.' Kirk sighed. 'We love you, Honour, and we're so proud of you.'

Honour closed her eyes against the tears that were pressing in again. 'Love you, too.' As she set the phone down and switched off the light, she felt she didn't deserve their pride.

If they knew the truth, how would they feel?

11

Honour woke with a start as the duvet was slowly lifted off her shoulder, letting a waft of cool air creep down her back. Thinking, for a second, that it was Kenny, when reality struck like an arrow, she kept her eyes tightly closed while Tara slipped into the bed behind her.

It had been a long time since Tara had crept in for a morning cuddle, and feeling her warmth, the faint scent of coconut lingering in Tara's hair, Honour was reminded how much she'd missed this. 'Hello, love.' She shifted towards Kenny's side, to give Tara more room.

'Morning,' Tara whispered, curling around Honour's back. 'It's cold in here.' She burrowed her chin into Honour's shoulder.

'Just snuggle in. You'll warm up in a sec.' Honour reached behind her and tucked the duvet tighter around Tara's slender hips. 'What time is it?' Honour wasn't ready to wake up yet, willing herself to melt into the mattress and linger in that gentle place, between being awake and asleep, that cradled her – keeping her safe from the new day.

'About seven.' Tara slung her arm around Honour's side. 'I've been awake for ages.'

Puzzled as to why her daughter, who was certainly not a morning person, would have been awake so early, and on a Sunday, Honour frowned.

'Try to sleep a little more.' She yawned, suddenly sensing that Tara needed more comfort than a simple snuggle could provide. 'Are you all right, love?' She moved away enough to turn around, catching sight of Tara's bright blue eyes for just a second, before they clamped shut.

'Yes. Just my knee was hurting, and I couldn't get comfy in my bed.'

Honour took in her daughter's features, noticing that the angles of her young face had become more pronounced over the past few weeks, the bone structure reflective of Honour's own – the prominent jaw and the long slender nose. This face was, to Honour, utter perfection, but underneath the serene exterior, she knew that Tara was suffering, in more ways than one.

Taking away her children's pain had always been paramount, and overcome with the need to soothe Tara's discomfort, Honour scooped a long hank of hair away from Tara's shoulder and began gently rubbing her back. As soon as Honour started to sing, 'You Are My Sunshine', the song she'd sung to her daughter since the first day she'd brought her home from the hospital, Honour could feel Tara begin to relax and slip back towards sleep.

Within moments, Callum's heavy footsteps along the hall alerted Honour to his arrival. He hesitated in the open doorway, so she smiled and beckoned to him, putting a finger against her lips. Callum nodded, tiptoeing around the bed, and getting in on Kenny's side. Callum was wearing his Buzz Lightyear pyjamas, which were far too small for him now but that he refused to part with, and Honour rolled onto her back and pulled him into her side. 'Hi, Cal,' she whispered against the top of his head, the usual spike of unruly hair tickling her under her chin.

'Why's she in here?' Callum asked, his feet wrapping around Honour's shin.

Catching the slight edge to Callum's question, she said, 'Same as you, love.'

Over the last year or so, he had come into their bed less often, but of the two children, he was still more likely to wander in, now and then. He'd sometimes stay in bed with Honour while Kenny made the Sunday pancakes. Occasionally, Callum would fall back to sleep, but more often they'd talk about the coming week, school events, doctor's appointments, anything that he was worried about or needed help with. Honour loved those precious moments with her son, and this was the first time since Kenny had been gone that Callum had come into their room. She flicked her eyes from one child to the other, filled with such a rush of love for these two amazing humans, that she and Kenny had created together, that her throat twisted into a tight knot.

A few minutes later, Tara stretched her arms above her head, and yawned. 'What's for breakfast?'

Callum groaned, nestling his head against Honour's shoulder.

'What do you fancy?' Honour smiled at her daughter, glad that she was hungry, having been somewhat disinterested in food since the accident.

'Can you make French toast?' Tara eyed her mother, her mouth dipping at the corners as if she doubted Honour's ability to dip a piece of bread in an egg and fry it.

'Why on earth would you want that?' Honour laughed softly, it being the first time Tara had ever asked for this.

'I keep seeing it on the telly. French toast with cinnamon and icing sugar, or syrup.' She shrugged. 'It sounds good.'

Honour pulled Tara closer, squeezing both her children

tightly into her sides, their proximity the only comfort that felt acceptable, recently. 'We don't have syrup, but we have everything else.' She looked down at Callum. 'Do you want that, too?'

Callum's eyes were hooded, his chin beginning to tremble, each tiny ripple driving a spike into Honour's heart. 'No. It's Sunday. We have pancakes.' His voice gave way and he turned into Honour's cheek, his face warm and damp.

'Oh, Cal, love.' Honour felt as if the bed had jolted beneath them, the very foundation of the cottage shifting with Callum's pain. 'Of course it is.' She patted his back. 'I'll make both today. How's that?'

He nodded against her, his breaths coming in little hitches. 'OK.'

Honour looked up at the ceiling, the overhead lightshade hovering above the bed like a big glass eye – staring at them – intruding on this private moment. 'Right. Let's get up, and how about this? How about we have a pyjama day? We've got all the shopping done. We've got everything you both need for going back to school tomorrow, and it's going to be rainy, so we can cosy in the house, eat junk food, watch telly, play games, and do whatever we like.'

'Junk food? You never let us eat that.' Tara huffed. 'Do we even have any?'

Honour gently shed a child from each shoulder, threw off the duvet and eased herself upright. 'Today is a new day and we can choose to do whatever we want with it. We have ice cream, and biscuits, and some crisps and popcorn, I think. I can even make us cheesy nachos for tea.' She gathered her hair into a twist at the back of her neck. 'Anything goes, for one day only.' She stood up and held a hand out to each child. 'Come on. Let's be lazy buggers, all day.'

Callum chuckled softly, wiping at his shiny cheek. 'You're crazy, Mum.' He grabbed her hand and let her pull him from the bed.

Honour helped Tara up, and then slid her slippers on. 'Right. Last one downstairs has to clean Frodo's litter tray.' She pulled a face.

'No way.' Tara shrieked. 'It's so gross.' She bolted for the door and just as Honour laughed, about to follow her, Tara stopped in her tracks, bending over, and grabbing her left knee. 'Oh, God,' she hissed, as her face drained of colour.

Honour was next to her in seconds and slid her arm under Tara's. 'Sweetheart. Let's get you an ice pack, and after you eat something, you can have some aspirin.' Honour felt the squeeze of concern under her ribcage. 'We're seeing Doctor Ford on Thursday, and we'll get this figured out, once and for all.'

Tara nodded, her face gradually regaining some colour. 'I'm sick of it.' She held Honour's gaze, something behind Tara's eyes worrying Honour.

'We'll get you some ultrasound treatments, like last time.' Honour waited until Tara righted herself and seemed to have regained her balance, before releasing her arm. 'As soon as we can,' she said, hoping that it wouldn't take too long to arrange.

Honour was washing up the breakfast dishes while Callum sat at the kitchen table, his glasses slipping down his nose as he read an astronomy magazine. Both the pancakes and the French toast had turned out well, and the house now smelled of cinnamon, reminding Honour of Christmases past. As she mentally flicked through the hundreds of precious memories they'd made in this house, her vision blurred. She couldn't picture a Christmas without Kenny. The way he wore a Santa hat for two days straight, played the Nat King Cole carols CD constantly and dutifully ate the two mince pies that Callum still left out when he went to bed on Christmas Eve, even though Honour knew that he no longer believed.

Their wonky tree that Kenny would drag out of the attic

each year would sit at the fireside and all the ornaments that the children had made, out of paper plates they'd coloured in, would dangle among the delicate glass snowflakes, and the glittery stars that Kenny loved.

When she thought about all the things he loved, the fun and laughter he brought to their family, and the acts of love and kindness he performed for them daily that would be missing from their lives from now on, she became so overwhelmed that she felt paralysed. As she shook the hair out of her eyes and tried to focus on the soapy basin in front of her, Honour could swear that beneath the thundering of the rain on the pantile roof, she could hear Kenny's voice.

Frowning, she turned off the hot water tap and tried to concentrate on the rain, but there it was again. Kenny speaking, then his laugh, the guttural sound that was contagious.

Her hands still covered in soap, she began to run towards the door.

12

Honour rushed into the living room, seeing that Tara was sitting on the sofa, her leg propped up on the trunk and a bag of frozen peas clamped around her knee. Her fiery mane was in a messy ponytail, with long coils of red having worked loose and framing her striking face. She was staring at Honour's phone and didn't notice her mother come in.

Honour walked quickly to the front door, panting slightly, her heart beating fast. Looking through the small window, she was crushed to see no one there. About to ask Tara if she'd heard anything, and beginning to think she was losing her mind, Honour heard it again – Kenny's voice. Where was it coming from?

Walking to the sofa, Honour saw what Tara was watching. A video Honour had recorded over a year ago of Kenny making breakfast one morning. He'd been standing at the Aga, barefoot as always, his tartan pyjamas trailing on the flagstone floor. Seeing him, Honour's hand went to her mouth – his broad back and mess of tawny hair seeming to scream their absence at her. That she couldn't touch him, feel the warmth of his breath on her skin, was nothing short of torture.

Honour stood, frozen to the spot, as Tara sniffed, held the phone closer to her face and tapped the screen to play the video again.

Kenny laughed. 'Right, who's for another pando' or three? I've got piles left and you know your mum hates to waste these bad boys.' He laughed again, his obvious joy floating out of the phone and wrapping itself around Honour's fractured heart. 'Cal, mate. You've only had three. Don't tell me you can't poke one more back?'

Next, Honour heard Callum's voice. 'I'm full, Dad,' he whined.

Kenny then turned towards the table and caught sight of Honour, filming him from the doorway. 'Ah, there you are, Red. I've saved some for you.' He waved the spatula at the frying pan.

Then, Honour heard herself say, 'Kenny, they're the size of my head. No wonder Cal only had three.' She laughed, walked closer to the stove, aiming the camera at the pan, where one giant pancake sizzled.

Kenny leaned in and kissed her cheek, making the camera wobble. 'Sit down and prepare yourself. This batch are my best yet.'

Honour watched as the image of his face froze in a cheeky smile, then the video ended.

The silence in the room was deafening, the rain having suddenly stopped, too. Honour was afraid to move, or speak, to shatter the fragile sensation that she'd just spent a moment or two with her husband, and as she waited for Tara to turn around and notice her, she willed the iron clamp around her heart to ease its grip.

Wiping her eyes, feeling the delicate skin beneath them raw and sore, Honour took a shallow breath. There were going to be many more of these moments, snapshots of the past, painful reminders of how their family had once been. Her darling man wasn't coming back, and her wrecked heart screamed that it simply wasn't fair that the world would go on, without Kenny MacLeod in it.

The next morning, Honour dropped the children at school, grateful that she was a tiny bit late, therefore missing most of the other mothers, who'd have wanted to condole with her. It was a sunny April day, the smell of toast in the air and the sky strewn with a band of lambswool clouds. The row of ancient oak trees along the front of the school were full of starlings, their speckled bodies catching the light as they flitted between the branches.

Callum seemed calm, slinging his bulging backpack over his shoulder, accepting Honour's peck on his cheek as he waved at Dougie across the playground, then made his way to the main door.

Tara was less at ease, lingering inside the car longer than usual and rummaging through her bag for an inordinate amount of time, her back to Honour, who was holding the door open for her. Tara's best friend, Jenna, a sweet-faced girl who also played on the under-thirteens football team, and whom Tara had known since primary school, was waiting at the gate, smiling nervously at Honour. Jenna was shifting her feet, her pastel-blue eyes flicking between Tara and the front door of the school where the sound of the last bell for assembly filtered out into the playground.

Despite Honour suggesting a couple of times over the previous two weeks that Jenna come over to the house, perhaps join them for dinner or to watch a film, Tara had dully shaken her head each time. 'No. I'm too tired,' she'd sighed, or muttered, 'She talks too much, sometimes.'

Honour had been taken aback. 'Are you sure? Dougie is coming over, so you could take Jenna up to your room, or I could make you both some sandwiches to have out in the garden.'

Tara had simply shaken her head again. 'No thanks. Not today.'

Honour had let it go, struggling to understand, and to provide each of her children what they needed to deal with their pain, but seeing Callum apparently coping better than Tara had been unexpected, and unnerving.

Tara had always been the more gregarious one, enjoying her large circle of friends from both school and football. She had the tendency to collect strays, children who were floating between groups, and bring them together. Honour remembered with a tug of sadness her discussions with Kenny about the size of Tara's birthday party, which had never taken place. This switching of behaviours between her children was as puzzling as it was sad to see, but Honour knew that she had to respect their individual coping mechanisms, regardless of the path they took.

Seeing Jenna's obvious discomfort as she waited for Tara, her fingers twisting a long section of her hair into a rope, Honour waved at her. 'Hi Jenna, love. Looking forward to getting back to school?'

Jenna pulled a face. 'Not really.' She grinned, then her eyes darted back to Tara, who had finally emerged from the back seat. 'Hi, Tara.' Jenna took a tentative step forward, as Tara approached the gate.

'Hi, Jen.' Tara's voice was pitched low, and rough, as if she'd been crying, and as Honour took in her daughter's face, she noticed the shiny tip to Tara's nose, the heightened colour in her cheeks and the slightly dipped chin – all tell-tale signs of tears having been shed.

Honour's heart contracted, her instinct to wrap Tara in her arms and tell her that she needn't go to school if she wasn't ready. But before she could get out of the car, and give Tara one last hug, her daughter turned and waved.

'See you later, Mum.'

Honour hesitated, unsure whether she should leave Tara without making sure she really was OK, but seeing her daughter turn and walk away, her ponytail tipped companionably towards her friend's raven-black mane, Honour decided it was OK to go. 'See you later.' She waved at Tara's back. 'Have a good day.'

Tilda, the manager at the care home, was predictably kind, hugging Honour and asking how she was coping. Tilda's grey-streaked hair was in a tidy bun, the frizzy coils around her hairline sprayed into submission, and she smelled of the lavender oil she put on her pillow at night, to help her sleep. Her dove-grey eyes glittered as she scanned Honour's face. 'You've been through so much, Honour. Are you sure you want to come back already?'

Honour nodded. 'God, yes. The kids are back at school, and if I wasn't here, I'd just be cleaning again, or staring at the walls – or, more likely, climbing them.' She laughed softly. 'I need to stay busy, Tilda, and besides, who else will put up with old Stanley and his bunions, or talk Schubert with the Professor?'

Tilda smiled warmly. 'You're a star, and they all love you so much.' She squeezed Honour's hand. 'Just shout if you need a break, or anything.'

Honour felt a trickle of the worry that had kept her from falling asleep after tucking the children in the previous night resurfacing. 'Actually, I wanted to ask you about picking up some extra shifts.' Money worries were not exactly new to Honour, a fisherman's salary not being that of a king, but never had they been as prevalent as they were now.

Tilda's eyebrows jumped. 'Oh, right. We can talk about that, for sure.' She studied Honour's face, her expression giving away her concern. 'We always have night slots available, but you can't really do that, now...' She caught herself, her implication clear, and painful. Honour no longer had Kenny at home to be with the children.

'Right. I can't do nights, but maybe a couple of extra afternoons? Or a weekend here and there. I could ask my mum to help with the kids.' Honour shrugged, unsure how practical this would be, or how it would go over with Callum and Tara.

Walking along the overly warm corridor, heading for the locker room, Honour was blindsided by a sudden wave of anger. Focusing on the row of metal lockers where she'd hang her jacket, change her shoes and check herself in the sliver of mirror behind the door, to her shock, Jack's face had materialised in her mind's eye.

If he hadn't left Kenny to cope with everything – their sick father, the struggling business – perhaps Kenny wouldn't have taken the risk he did by going so much further out – beyond his usual fishing territory? Perhaps he'd still be here? Perhaps she wouldn't have had to lie awake at night wondering how long she could afford to stay in the cottage, cover the small mortgage they'd taken out, afford Tara's football kit and match expenses, or continue to scrimp to be able to send Callum to Florida with a little spending money.

If Jack had been a better man, a better son, brother, and brother-in-law…

Honour stopped herself, the customary tug of guilt that always followed thoughts of Jack, his departure from the village, and all their lives, making her swallow hard.

In Professor Smythe's room, Schubert's Eighth, or Unfinished, Symphony was playing on the bulbous CD player on the oak dressing table. As he gave her his sincere condolences on her loss, the blissful music floated around them, soothing her fragile heart.

Honour always looked forward to her time with this

thoughtful and knowledgeable gentleman, and over the two years that he had been in the home, she had learned much about classical music from him, which both pleased and surprised her. Music had been a comfort to Honour at various trying times in her life. A language that needed no translation, she marvelled at its ability to bridge the gap between loneliness and fulfilment, or pain and joy, and today was no different.

Kneeling on the spotless vinyl floor as she gently tended to the old man's ulcerated leg, Honour let the undulating melody filter through her skin, the familiar notes softening the tension in her shoulders, and settling the turmoil at her centre that now seemed ever present. The invisible knot of anxiety inside her unravelled itself as she worked deftly, wrapping a new dressing around the withered shin, until she felt a hand on her shoulder.

'Honour?' Professor Smythe's voice was soft, loaded with concern.

She looked up at the kind man's face and saw his pale eyes, filled with affection. Realising that her face was soaked with tears, she stood up and, embarrassed, pulled two tissues from the box at his bedside. 'Sorry. It's the damn Schubert.' She tried to smile. 'Gets me every time.'

The Professor's eyes held hers. His face was a network of wrinkles, his bald head littered with large dark spots, and freckles, and a patch of feathery white hair puffed out over each ear. 'He has a tendency to do that.' He smiled, revealing his surprisingly white and regular teeth. 'We can't take him to task, though, as he's not here to defend himself.' He tipped his head to the side. 'We could put something happier on, if you prefer?'

Honour smiled at him. 'No, this is perfect.'

'I always thought so.' He nodded to himself.

Seeing a profound sadness occupy the rheumy eyes, Honour took his hand, noticing the fingernails, long and ragged at the ends. 'How about we tidy these up a bit?' She patted his hand. 'Tilda will be after me if she sees these talons.'

The old man tutted, but a smile tugged at his mouth. 'Aye, well, you'd better sort me out fast, before I start howling at the moon.'

As she walked to the little bathroom adjoining his room, she missed her father-in-law with such force that she leaned against the door frame for a second. Despite all the time that had passed since Allen had left them, Honour still felt his loss keenly, and as she let that thought sink in, the realisation that she might never get over losing Kenny was overwhelming.

The cottage was chilly when they got back from school and, despite it being April, Honour decided to light the fire. Before the kindling had even begun to crackle, Callum was stretched out on the sofa, his feet crossed on the arm and a digestive biscuit in his hand.

Honour took in the scene, and tutted. 'Don't have too many, Cal. I'm making shepherd's pie tonight.' She placed a log on top of the now glowing sticks in the grate. This would be the first time she'd made Kenny's favourite meal, and even saying it out loud felt like a tiny step towards healing.

'I won't.' Callum stuffed the remainder of the biscuit into his mouth. 'Tara took two upstairs, though.' He jabbed a thumb towards the kitchen.

Surprised, but pleased, Honour's eyebrows jumped. 'Well, she can't have any more either.' Honour stepped back to assess her fire-making skills and caught sight of the painting Bridie had done of them, propped up against the wall by the front window. Seeing their faces, the smiles, the close grouping of their bodies and their connectedness, Honour suddenly wanted the painting up on the wall, front and centre, where she could soak it in every time she walked through the room.

She put the fireguard in place, wiped her hands on her jeans and walked to the slanted door of the cupboard under the stairs, where Kenny kept his toolbox. As she turned on the overhead light, she squinted into the dark, triangular space. Seeing the box of Christmas decorations and the wreath she hung on the front door each December, Honour sighed. Behind them was a pair of Kenny's boots. They were water-stained and warped, and the ghostly shape of his calves, and the high arches of his feet seemed moulded into the worn leather, as if he were standing in them at this very second. Swallowing hard, she blinked away the press of tears and shoved the box of decorations aside, spying the giant, blue metal box of tools behind it.

Pulling it towards her, she hunkered down and eased the lid open, careful not to push it back all the way. The hinges had given up the ghost years ago, and unless you held onto it, the lid would slide right off the back of the box.

She lifted the inset shelf out and set it on the ground, looking for the small, handheld drill, then Honour spotted a small tin with the faded picture of a bagpiper on the lid. It was approximately the size of a can of tuna, or maybe a little larger, but not something she recalled seeing before. Curious, but anxious to protect whatever was inside, she flicked a glance at Callum, who had turned on the TV and was staring at the screen, his fingers absently twisting a lock of hair at his temple.

Satisfied that he was unaware of what she was doing, Honour picked up the tin and, using her thumbnail, pried the lid off. Her heart began to tick faster as she focused on the contents, and it took her a moment to register what she was seeing.

Rather than the collection of strange, oversized coins she thought was before her, instead, she realised that it was Kenny's AA sobriety medallions – tokens of the pledge he'd taken over a decade ago, and one that he'd kept religiously until the day he'd left them.

Honour's breath hitched as a sea of memories crowded in: Kenny at the bar in the pub, slurring his words as he smacked his glass against his brother's. Kenny's face, florid, his eyes unfocused as he bounced off the wall in the hall on the way to the bedroom. Him bursting through the front door, almost twelve years ago, closely followed by Jack, the two of them laughing loudly as she shushed them. The next image followed quickly, crashing into her mind and her heart, and no longer able to face what was there, she slammed the box shut.

13

On Thursday, Honour and Tara sat in Doctor Ford's office, in Anstruther. Fiona Ford had recently taken the practice over from her father, James, the doctor whom Honour had been seeing for years, who had seen her through both babies' births, Callum's diagnosis, and several other health landmarks. His daughter, Fiona, was as approachable and attentive as her father had been, and Honour found herself relaxing as she described what had been happening with Tara, as she sat on the examination table.

'She had physio for shin splints the last time. The ultrasound treatments really helped, so perhaps we can do that again?' She watched the doctor as she tapped Tara's knee with a rubber-topped hammer.

'Possibly.' She tapped again. Seeing Tara's leg twitching in response. 'Is this painful, Tara?' The doctor lifted Tara's leg and manipulated the kneecap.

Tara flinched. 'Yes. A bit.'

Doctor Ford nodded. 'Can you describe what the pain is like, when it happens?'

'It's like hot, then tingly. I want to bend my knee, but when I do, it hurts more.'

'Is it mainly behind your knee, or here, under the kneecap?'

Tara considered for a moment. 'Both, but more inside.' She squeezed her knee. 'When it's really bad, it goes up and down, too.' She pointed at her shin.

'Thanks, you can get down now, Tara. That was very helpful.' She smiled at Tara and helped her off the examination table. Then, she returned to her desk, swivelled her chair to face them. 'I'd like to send Tara to St Andrews hospital for an X-ray, and I'll also do some blood tests. Just to eliminate anything else going on.'

Honour's chest tightened. 'What else?'

'The blood tests will show if there's excessive inflammation, or any kind of infection.' Doctor Ford's eyes were almost too big for her face and a shade of blue Honour had never seen before, somewhere between turquoise and green. Her long, wavy blonde hair was caught up in a half-ponytail, giving her a youthful look – younger than her early thirties certainly. The classic, Celtic complexion spoke not only of genetics but of long hours spent inside, a creaminess to Fiona's cheeks that made Honour feel tanned and weather-beaten.

Honour shifted her hips, her eyes slipping to Tara, who was staring out of the window, drumming her fingernails on the metal frame of the chair. The tang of hand sanitiser was lingering in the air, and mixed with the scent of lavender seeping in the open window, the bright room felt crisp and clean. 'What can we do in the meantime?'

'Ice is a good idea, and paracetamol or aspirin is fine, in moderation.' The doctor nodded. 'I'll see if I can get the tests expedited.' She winked at Tara. 'You won't want to miss too many practices, I'm sure.'

Tara smiled weakly. 'That's OK. I'll catch up.'

Honour reached over and rubbed Tara's back. 'Should she maybe not play football for the moment?'

The doctor sat back and studied Tara. 'I think if you feel good, play. If the pain is too bad, then sit it out. How does that sound?'

'Fine.' Tara nodded. 'Thanks.'

Fiona stood up and spoke quietly. 'You're doing everything right, Mrs MacLeod. Tara is a wonderful, active young girl. We'll get to the bottom of this.' She held her hand out to Honour. 'I'll phone you when we have the appointment.'

Honour shook the delicate hand. 'Thanks, Doctor Ford.' She paused. 'It feels funny saying that but not to your dad. If you know what I mean.' Honour laughed softly.

'Oh, believe me, I know.' Fiona laughed. 'I get that every day. And I feel the same way. In this building, Doctor Ford was always my dad, so it's taken some getting used to.'

'Thanks, then. We'll talk soon.'

Honour and Tara stopped at the shops on the way home to get something for dinner, and to pick up a prescription for Callum, who'd be at Dougie's house for another hour until Lorna brought him home. After they'd left the pharmacy, they headed for Green's Market – Honour's favourite place to shop in Crail.

The shop had been family owned for generations and stocked local, excellent-quality fresh fruit and vegetables, a wide range of Scottish cheeses, wine and even some local gin. It housed a cornucopia of goodies and Honour inevitably left with more than she went in for.

The emerald-green canopies above the tall basket displays of produce fluttered in the breeze as they stopped in front of the shop. Honour scanned the baskets, taking in the vibrant clementines arranged next to tidy rows of striking green apples.

As Honour lifted a clementine and inhaled the citrus tang of the skin, Tara spotted a large tub of stunning sunflowers, their black, seeded centres thick and glossy. 'These are so pretty.' She bent down and made to sniff the giant flowers. 'Can we get some, Mum?'

Honour replaced the clementine and stood behind her daughter, instantly calculating how much the flowers were, and whether she could justify them, until she noticed Tara's expression – so engaged. Without another thought, Honour said, 'Why not? They are lovely. We could do with a bit more sunshine in the house.' Honour pointed at the big wooden tub. 'You pick the ones you want.'

Tara looked over at her, then, smiling, pulled a bunch of sunflowers out of the bin. 'These ones are good.' She handed them to Honour.

She pushed the door open and walked into the shop, instantly catching the scent of freshly ground coffee as she waved at Craig Dunn, the young man behind the counter whose parents owned Green's.

Tara headed over to one of the tightly packed shelves, as Honour approached the counter. 'Hi, Craig.'

He grinned, his tanned face smooth and enviably innocent of worry. 'Hello, Honour. Hi Tara.' He waved at Tara, who was carrying two tins across the shop.

Honour set the sunflowers on the counter and suddenly their vibrant colour, a shot of pure sunshine inside the dimly lit shop, felt like a sign. There was light to be had, even on the darkest of days, and today they had found it in some beautiful blossoms. If she focused on that, rather than everything they'd lost, perhaps Honour could guide her little family through their grief, and eventually they'd be able to think about the future, and healing, instead of wishing for the past.

With the concept of healing still feeling so very far out of her own reach, as she handed her credit card to Craig, Kenny's face flashed behind her eyes. Some wounds she could work to heal, but there were some that could never be made right. Not anymore.

Three days later, Honour's parents had arrived mid-morning. After a picnic on Fossil Beach, a walk around Marketgate, then a stop to get some ice cream from Green's, Marion and Kirk now sat next to each other in the living room. Their feet were crossed identically on the old trunk, and mugs of coffee were balanced on their mismatched thighs, that were touching – as always. Honour smiled, as she often had over the years, at their tendency to mirror each other's body language.

Her father was tall and reed-like, his limbs long and loose as if they were hard to control at times, while her mother was petite, toned from all the gardening she did and the weekly yoga class she took at her local community centre. Physically, they were as different as they could be and yet they were two halves of the same whole. As Honour looked at them from the door to the kitchen, so at ease in each other's company, she blinked her vision clear.

She and Kenny hadn't had long enough. Time to grow to look like one another, to speak simultaneously and still hear the other's point, to argue about Tara's partner, or Callum's choice of university. Their time had been stolen from them, and as Honour's heart ached for her lost love, and all the moments they wouldn't share, so her anger towards Jack twisted inside her, like a bitter vine. She knew that Kenny leaving her had been a terrible accident, but she needed someone to blame.

Kenny had suffered after Jack had left, supporting their father alone throughout his illness, and trying to keep the business going, with only Gregor to help him. Honour had seen the toll it had taken on her husband, essentially losing his brother, and then his father, too. His confusion as to why Jack had gone was the hardest thing for Honour to witness, her desire to take away Kenny's pain so overwhelming that, at times, despite her promise to him, she'd considered phoning Jack and asking him to come home. But with that notion came so much anxiety, and fear of the consequences, that she never had.

Snapping her back to the moment, her mother spotted her in the doorway. 'Where are the kids?' Marion leaned in closer to Kirk's shoulder.

'Tara's getting changed and I'm not sure what Cal is up to.' Honour frowned. It was after 4 p.m. and she knew that her parents liked to get home before dark, due to Kirk's developing cataracts. They were old school, her father doing most of the driving, and as she smiled at them both, she recalled road trips to Edinburgh, and the west coast, when she was a child. Her father would resist stopping the car for anything other than toilet emergencies, often making the journeys less pleasant than they could have been. That had been one of the many things she'd loved about Kenny, that no matter where they were going, how late they were or how pressing their mission, he had happily made as many stops as she and the children had wanted – nothing more important than them all being happy.

Letting the memory warm her, Honour walked up the stairs to see what the children were up to, and to tell them to come down and spend a few more minutes with their grandparents before they left for home. As she approached Tara's half-open door, she heard Callum speaking, a loud whisper the best way to describe it. The manner of his tone implying secrecy, Honour instantly halted her progress along the hall. She stood still, waiting for Callum to continue, then leaned her shoulder against the wall, her fingers going to her mouth, where she began to nervously nibble the cuticle around her thumb.

'But why is it a secret?' Callum asked.

'Because I don't want to make her worry,' Tara hissed back.

'Listen, Cal. I need you to promise, OK? If you tell, I swear I'll never tell you anything again.'

Honour's heart flip-flopped as she heard Callum sigh, one of his deep, melodramatic ones that were often accompanied by eye-rolling. 'OK. But—'

Tara's tone was emphatic. 'I'll tell her soon, but not today.'

14

Honour's insides churned as she tried to imagine what Tara was keeping from her. That her daughter would be protecting her from any more worry was heartbreakingly sweet, and yet not something Honour wanted – that burden too heavy for her girl to carry.

Just as she was about to turn around and tiptoe back down the stairs, Callum said, 'Your leg's going to get better, Tara. And even if you don't want to play football anymore, we can still race and do roly-polys on the beach, and ride bikes and stuff.' He sounded so young and caring, but Honour was so alarmed by what he'd said that she clamped her hand over her mouth.

Could it be true that Tara didn't want to play anymore? Football had been her passion for so long that Honour couldn't imagine her daughter willingly leaving that behind, but as Honour worked through her shock, and then the myriad of questions that started to spiral through her mind, she had a revelation. Football *had* been Tara's love, but more than that, it had been a special connection that she had with her father. Perhaps now that he was gone, Tara found it too painful to play, knowing that her dad wouldn't be there to watch her, practise with her or encourage her, ever again.

The clarity of what she'd just realised was sickeningly sad, and yet she could relate to it. Kenny would have been heart-broken to think that Tara would give up, but Honour would never make an issue of it or make Tara feel bad about any decision she made, if it was well considered. Getting over Kenny's death was as unique a journey for both of their children as it was for Honour, and as she walked silently down the stairs, she resolved that until Tara mentioned it to her, Honour would keep this new, upsetting information to herself.

Marion was drying up their cups when Honour came back into the kitchen and, seeing her mother's narrow back as she worked at the sink, Honour was overcome with the need to hold her close. She was so grateful for her parents and the calm, balanced way they had lived, and brought her up, that a little more of that calm, and inherent sense of safety, was what she needed right now.

Moving in behind her, Honour slid her arms around Marion's waist and pressed her chin into her shoulder. 'I love you, Mum,' she whispered. 'You and Dad are so fantastic with the kids.'

Marion dried her hands and turned inside Honour's arm. Marion's fair hair, peppered with silver streaks, was fluffy around her face, ruffled by the breeze at the beach, and her sky-blue eyes were full of sadness as she took Honour in. 'We love you all so much, sweetheart. I just wish we could do more.'

'I know we're all over the place at the moment, emotionally, but having you here seems to level us out again.' Honour paused. 'You have no idea how much it helps just knowing that you're coming, and we can feel normal for a little while, at least.'

Marion frowned. 'You're doing a wonderful job with them – supporting them through an unimaginable thing, with no map to

follow.' Marion hesitated. 'I just worry that you're not taking care
of yourself enough.' She swept Honour's fringe aside and cupped
her chin. 'Perhaps you need to talk to someone other than us, or
Lorna. A grief counsellor maybe?' She tilted her head to the left,
something she did when she was considering an important issue.

'I don't need a counsellor, Mum. I'm OK.' Momentarily
frustrated at the suggestion that she wasn't coping as well as she
might, Honour stepped back, seeing the frown that pulled at
Marion's forehead. 'Well, I *will* be.'

Marion draped the damp tea towel over the handle of the
Aga and then unrolled the sleeves of her checked shirt, rebut-
toning them at the wrists. 'Just remember that asking for help is
not a sign of weakness. It's a strong thing to do.' She eyed
Honour. 'Your dad and I can only offer so much help, and grief
can be a tricky beast. It's pervasive and all-consuming and takes
careful handling.'

'Excellent metaphor, Mum. Sounds like I'm in a bullfight
rather than my life.' Honour sighed.

'You know what I'm saying, Honour.' Marion pursed her
lips. 'Just try to pay attention to what you need, too. OK?'

Feeling bad for her tone, Honour closed the gap between
them and pulled her mother back into her arms. 'I will, Mum. I
promise.'

Behind them, Kirk had walked into the kitchen, his dry
cough startling them both. 'Hey. What's with the sneaky hugs?
Shove over.' He walked towards them, a gentle smile on his
face.

'Get in here.' Honour opened one arm and invited him in.
Then, as Kirk slung his arms around both her and her mother,
Tara and Callum also came into the room, to Honour's surprise,
holding hands.

'What's going on?' Tara asked, taking in the circle of adults
in front of the stove.

Callum was blinking furiously, Honour suspected to keep back tears.

'Come here, you two.' Kirk smelled comfortingly of coffee, and Imperial Leather soap, as he lifted his arm from Honour's shoulder and beckoned to the children. 'Family hugs before Grandma and I go home.'

Callum and Tara released their hands and walked into the circle, Callum's head slipping under Marion's arm and Tara leaning into Honour's middle. Then Kirk closed the circle by wrapping his arm behind Honour's back. 'There we are. Everyone's in.'

As his well-intentioned words floated around them, Tara wriggled inside the circle, her voice low and fragile. 'Not everyone, Grandpa.'

Honour lifted her chin and met her mother's eyes, Marion's flooded with concern. Wanting to assure her that all was well, Honour shook her head almost imperceptibly, and pulled Tara a little closer to her front. 'He is here, love. He always will be.'

Callum sniffed, and afraid that if one of them started to cry, they might all be unable to hold it together, Honour broke the circle and stepped back.

'Right, say goodbye to Grandma and Grandpa. Then we need to get you ready for school tomorrow.' She smiled at Callum, who was pouting. 'What's wrong, Cal?' She tucked the T-shirt label back in at his neck and raked her fingers through his messy hair.

'I miss Dad.' He sniffed.

'I know, love. So do I.' Honour held his hand. 'You're so brave.' She squeezed his fingers, then glanced over at Tara, who was leaning against her grandpa's arm. 'You two make me so proud.' She gulped the last word, then, seeing her mother's eyes fill, Honour shook the hair from her eyes. 'Right. See you soon.' She hugged her parents in turn, then they all trooped through the living room, where Honour opened the front door. 'Love you both.'

Marion kissed her cheek, hugged the children, walked out the door and started down the steps.

Kirk hugged the children, then Honour, gently easing her out onto the top step. Sensing that he had a message to impart, Honour turned to Tara and Callum. 'I'll be in in a minute. Can you both please go and check your bags for tomorrow, and make sure you've got everything you need?'

Tara sighed. 'I've checked mine already, and Cal has gym, but his stuff is already in his backpack.'

Honour took a moment to take in what Tara had said. Obviously, knowing that it was something her mother did every Sunday evening, Tara had taken it upon herself to check that Callum was ready for Monday morning. This, coupled with them holding hands a few moments earlier, made up a picture of such touching emotional maturity in her now eleven-year-old girl that Honour had to swallow hard. How had she and Kenny, with all their flaws and insecurities, made such incredible human beings? 'Thank you, Tara. That was really sweet of you.'

Tara shrugged. 'S'OK.' She looked slightly embarrassed as she turned and headed for the stairs.

Callum waved at his grandpa, his smudged glasses reflecting the early-evening light as it filtered in the front door, rendering his eyes invisible to Honour. But even without seeing them, she knew he was battling another wave of sadness.

She turned back to her father, realising that he was scanning her face, his red hair – his legacy to both her and Tara – lifting from the back of his head as a salty breeze rolled in from the harbour.

'What is it, Dad?' She found a smile.

'Is there anything else going on?' He frowned slightly. 'I mean, is there anything you need help with?'

Honour shook her head, puzzled as to what he meant and,

for a moment, nervous that she was transparent to him – her innermost fears laid bare. 'Like what?'

Kirk cleared his throat, then looked down the lane towards Marion, who was standing near the harbour wall. 'Do you need any money?' He patted his thigh as if looking for his wallet.

'No, Dad. We're fine.' Touched, and somewhat relieved, she looped her arm through his and walked him down the steps. 'The insurance money for the *Lila Rose* will come through soon, and I've picked up some extra shifts at work. We're all good – but thank you.' She tried to sound upbeat, as her heart swelled with love for her father.

It is said that women look to marry men with qualities that exist in their father, and in Honour's case, she knew that to be true. Kenny had the same kind heart and trusting, generous nature as Kirk, and since Kenny had been gone, every time she remembered that, Honour wondered if she had truly deserved either of them.

The following week, Honour was at work when her phone buzzed in her pocket. Before losing Kenny, she might have ignored it until her next break, but not having the luxury of another parent on call in case there was a problem with one of the children, she scanned the cosy room, looking for an excuse to step out. Seeing her opportunity, she picked up the empty teacup and plate from beside Professor Smythe's armchair. 'I'll just take these to the kitchen, and I'll be back with a top-up.' She smiled at him and waggled the cup. 'Unless you've had enough.'

'Right you are.' He flapped a hand. 'And I've never said no to a top-up.'

Honour walked into the hallway and quickly pulled the phone from her pocket just as the call went to voicemail. Seeing the number of Doctor Ford's office, her heart faltered for a second. As she waited for the caller to leave a message, she ran through the imaginary conversation she'd likely have with Carla about Tara's blood test results – that they showed nothing concerning, and that they had an appointment date for the X-ray.

Honour waited for the message symbol to appear on the phone, then she walked briskly to the kitchen and deposited the dishes in the large metal sink. Taking a clean mug from the shelf, she poured a fresh cup of tea for the Professor, adding just the splash of milk he liked, then she walked back into the corridor.

As she approached his door, she listened to the voicemail, and hearing the doctor's words, her hand began to shake violently, tea sloshing over the side of the mug.

15

'Hi, Mrs MacLeod. This is Carla from Doctor Ford's office. Doctor wanted me to let you know that Tara's blood tests came back, and her ALP level is elevated, which is a little concerning. We have requested a priority X-ray appointment and the first available is next week, on April twenty-eighth, over at Victoria Hospital in Kirkcaldy. If you could please phone me back, I'll give you all the details, and then we'll make a follow-up appointment with the doctor to discuss the results. Talk to you soon, then. Bye for now.'

Carla's voice seemed to fizz inside Honour's head as she took a moment and listened to the message again, her breaths coming in shallow gasps. What exactly did *a little concerning* mean?

It was two hours before Honour could call Carla back and ask the questions that had formed since listening to the voicemail: What exactly was ALP? What did the doctor think was causing the elevated numbers? How worried should she be? Could they get in for the X-ray any sooner?

Carla had been kind but evasive, telling her that ALP stood for alkaline phosphatase, but all she would say further to that was that the doctor would explain everything when they came in for the next appointment.

Now, as Honour listened to the instructions for where to go at Victoria Hospital, and what time to arrive, she battled a wave of nausea that reminded her of the way she used to feel every morning, carrying both Tara, and Callum. She tasted bile at the back of her tongue as she stared out of the break-room window – the same view she'd taken in each day that her father-in-law had been here, under her care.

The pantile rooftops of Crail, the sandstone of the houses and the cobbled lanes created a warm, earth-toned palette of colour that covered the gentle hill from Marketgate to the harbour. Beyond the harbour, the mid-morning sky was clear, with a few strands of gauzy cloud breaking up the expanse of blue, and tucked behind the harbour wall bobbed the collection of fishing boats, safely back home from the day's work. There was a gap where the *Lila Rose* would have been, next to Scott's boat, and seeing that was like squinting into the sun, the image burning painfully onto the back of the eye.

Honour closed her eyes, recalling the briny smell of the damp nets, and creels, the chilling spray on her face that the breeze often lifted from the surface of the water, until Carla coughed in her ear. 'Did you get that, Mrs MacLeod?'

Startled, Honour answered a little too emphatically. 'Yes. The twenty-eighth of April. Arrive at ten o'clock. Go to the radiology department in the north wing to register.' She turned and leaned her hips against the windowsill, hoping she hadn't missed anything else she'd been told. She couldn't wait to get home and look up elevated ALP, even though she knew that researching medical conditions online usually led to misinformation – generally considered by the medical profession to be a form of self-generated fear-mongering – as Lorna had told her once.

Carla continued. 'Right. And as soon as we get the results, we'll phone you so we can get you and Tara in for a follow-up. It usually takes about a week to get the report, so don't worry if you don't hear from us.'

Honour closed her eyes again, her chin dipping. *Don't worry* was possibly the most fatuous advice ever given when it came to being a parent.

She looked back out at the sea, her old nemesis, and she bargained with it once more. *Please keep Tara safe... Haven't you taken enough from me to at least grant me that?*

Having found out through her research that elevated ALP often indicated liver problems, or certain bone conditions, Honour coasted through the next few days on autopilot – driving, working, doing school runs, laundry, cooking, and shopping – all the while feeling numb. She was afraid to let herself think about what she'd learned, or the appointment the following week, and yet she couldn't keep her mind clear of it.

At home, the TV was constantly on, not something she usually allowed, but she couldn't stand the silence, as it let frightening thoughts of what might be wrong with her daughter seep in.

When she'd called her mother to tell her what was happening, Marion had been as comforting as she could, but after everything that had happened in the past month, her usual ability to calm Honour had lost some of its power. 'Doctors are so overcautious these days. Any little thing they run off for X-rays, or CT scans,' she'd huffed. 'Tara is just a healthy pre-teen, whose bones are growing faster than her muscles and tendons can keep up with. It happened to you, Honour, and it's a sign of good health and nutrition. Not a cause for concern.' She'd paused, as Honour willed this to be true. 'But I suppose it's always good to eliminate any concerns, and in the meantime try to remember how strong and fit Tara is, rather than focus on the negative.'

Honour had slid down the wall in the kitchen, her phone digging into her cheekbone. The lingering scent of their curry dinner had tingled the inside of her nose and the cool of the flagstone floor had quickly filtered through her jeans as she'd steadied her voice. 'I'm sure you're right, Mum.'

'If you think you'll be late home from Kirkcaldy on Thursday, I'll come and pick Callum up from school. He and I can do some baking, or we can read some of his astronomy books.'

Honour had thanked her mother, ended the call, pulled her knees up to her chest and hugged them. Feeling drained, she'd let her forehead drop to her forearms and listened to the murmur of the TV floating in from the living room, a programme about dinosaurs and the Mesozoic era. Callum had said something to Tara, who was curled up on Kenny's chair across the room, but Honour couldn't pick up what it was. Then Tara had replied, the two of them laughing softly, making the knot under Honour's breastbone ease a little.

Losing Kenny seemed to have brought Tara and Callum closer, or at least made them more tolerant of each other. They'd rarely have sat and peacefully watched the same programme a few weeks ago, and this tiny positive that had surfaced from the ocean of sadness they were all floating in had been an unexpected blessing.

The following afternoon, Honour dropped Tara off at Jenna's house after school for a few hours, and Callum was at Dougie's for a sleepover – the first time he'd wanted to stay there overnight for over six weeks. Lorna had invited Honour in for a drink, but too distracted by everything she was juggling in her mind, Honour had gently refused, saying she had work to do at home.

Now, she sat in the kitchen looking at her bank statement, the familiar weight on her chest, when she thought about finances, pressing in a little more. So far, they were doing OK with just her salary, and knowing that the money they'd tucked away in a savings account was there felt like a security blanket, until the insurance company paid out. But being unsure exactly how long that would take, Honour questioned whether she should have said anything to Callum about Space Camp. No sooner had she had the thought than she recalled the sheer joy on his face when she'd told him he could still go, so, no matter what else happened, or how she would make it work, she resolved not to take that away from him.

She slid the statement into the folder and put it back in the drawer of the Welsh dresser that stood opposite the Aga, then eyed her blue-and-white willow-pattern dinner plates that were propped up along the three shelves. The dinner service had been a wedding present from her parents and as she let her eye settle on the one plate that had a chip out of it, thanks to Kenny's clumsy washing-up skills, the need to touch him, feel his presence, was overwhelming.

She lifted the damaged plate from the shelf and ran her finger around the rim until she felt the rough section, the slightly grey, powdery inch or so where the glaze had chipped off. Stroking the gritty surface brought back images of Kenny, his mortification at what he'd done, and afterwards, whenever they used the plates, for family dinners when her parents came over, he would make a point of ensuring that he got the 'duff one', as he called it.

Smiling sadly, Honour sighed. 'Oh, Kenny. I miss you so

much.' Her voice caught and she glanced at the door, hopeful that the children had not heard her. Seeing no movement, she held the plate up and pressed it to her lips. 'Tara's going to be all right, isn't she? She has to be,' Honour whispered, the fear that she'd been keeping at bay suddenly bigger than her.

16

Lorna held Callum's backpack out to Honour. 'Don't be angry, but I saw the request for Tara's X-ray.' She kept her voice low, as the boys were standing close by, in the sunny bay window of Lorna's kitchen, overlooking Anstruther's Shoregate.

Taken aback, Honour glanced at the boys, their mismatched heads inclined towards each other as they peered at an electronic tablet. 'How did you see it?' She took the backpack, noting how heavy it was, then realised that in all the turmoil of late, she had forgotten that Lorna worked at Victoria Hospital.

'I spotted it when I was checking on an X-ray for one of my patients. I don't want to intrude, but I saw that it was an urgent request.' Lorna's moss-green eyes were fixed on Honour's. 'Is there anything you need? I've been there a while now and if you want me to try to get you in to see someone specific, or...' She shrugged, a bloom of pink appearing across her cheekbones.

'No, bless you.' Honour smiled at her friend, the need to sound in control suddenly paramount. 'It's just Doc Ford being cautious. We're pretty sure it's shin splints again, but it's best to be certain.' She shrugged, hearing herself say the words her heart wanted to believe.

'Well, let me know if you need me to shake a tree or two. They're good at Victoria, but sometimes a friendly shove from within can help move things along.' She scanned Honour's face. 'Are you OK, though?' She sounded concerned. 'Are you sleeping?'

'Lorna, I'm fine. Stop worrying.' Honour widened her eyes. 'I already have a mother, you know.'

Lorna snorted. 'Right. Message received.' She lifted a Tupperware filled with a few Rice Krispie treats. 'Don't forget the doggy bag, or Cal will be hitchhiking back here tomorrow for the rest. I swear he ate five of them last night.'

Honour smiled, took the container, and shoved it into Cal's backpack. 'Thank you. If at some point I do need any help, though, I'll definitely ask you.'

'Absolutely.' Lorna nodded. 'I'm on shift on Thursday, so I'll come and find you both. Just to say hello. You know – a friendly face.' She gave an exaggerated, sightly grotesque smile.

'God, that's enough to scare anyone off.' Honour laughed softly. 'You're a star, Lorna. I'm so grateful for...' Her voice failed her as Lorna moved in and hugged her.

'No mushy stuff, now.' Lorna's voice was raspy. 'All will be well.'

Honour leaned in to Lorna's embrace, missing the sensation of being held, then righted herself. 'I always forget what a short-arse you are until I hug you.' She made a face at Lorna, who mocked offence, then grinned.

'Five-feet-two of sheer perfection.' Lorna swept a hand down her side. 'What can I say.'

The friends smiled at each other again, their understanding of what the other needed unspoken, and invaluable.

'Right, Callum. Let's go.' Honour beckoned to him and as he walked towards her, she caught a glimpse of Kenny in the turn of Callum's head, and the way he held his shoulders, which made her heart skip.

Seeming to see something in her eyes, Callum frowned. 'What's wrong, Mum?'

Honour took a second, then shook her head. 'Absolutely nothing. Everything's fine, love.'

Four days later, Tara's appointment was over, and Honour and she had made it home well before Callum got out of school. Rather than go straight home after picking him up, they got ice cream from the Gallery Tearoom at the harbour, then walked out to the old sundial, on Castle Promenade. The walk was short and within a few minutes they were standing behind the wrought-iron railing that ran in front of the remains of the castle.

The sundial dated from the seventeenth century and had reportedly served sailors, fishermen and townspeople for more than two hundred years. It had originally been down in the harbour, but in 1883 it had been removed for repairs, then relocated up to the Promenade in 1890. It was considered somewhat of a talisman for the local fishermen and Kenny would often take them up there to walk along the castle wall, then look out over the Firth of Forth. He'd touch the stone pedestal of the dial and then kiss his fist. The first time she'd seen him do this, when she'd been pregnant with Tara, Honour had asked him why he did and he'd simply said, 'It's just something Dad always does.'

With that in mind, she now stood at the sundial, with Tara and Callum on either side of her. The afternoon sun was watery, labouring behind an ominous blanket of cloud, and a flock of seagulls was squawking in the distance, their calls muffled by the heaviness in the atmosphere. Honour breathed in the tang of seaweed wafting up the hill and blinked away the painful memories that were once again crowding in.

'Can we go home now?' Callum looked up at her, quizzically. 'Why are we here?'

Tara licked at the trickle of ice cream that was running down the outside of her cone. 'Because we always came here with Dad.' She sounded irritated. 'Just be patient.'

Honour could sense the tiny wound that Tara's tone had opened up in Callum, so she beckoned to them both, drawing them in beside her. 'Let's take a moment to think about your dad and remember how much he liked this spot. OK?' She smiled down at Callum, who was nibbling at the honey-coloured cone.

'OK.' He nodded, transferring his ice cream to the opposite hand, and wiping the other, now sticky fist down his trousers.

Tara rolled her eyes as Honour let the breeze sweep the hair from her forehead, twists of white froth topping the bands of waves rolling in towards the shore below. Before she could say anything more, Callum eased forward, touched the pedestal, and then kissed his clenched fist.

Tara looked shocked, as if he had beaten her to the post, as she immediately followed suit. 'Love you, Dad.' Tara spoke into the quickening wind. 'Miss you every day.'

Touched that they had remembered Kenny's ritual, Honour let her fingers linger on the stone pedestal, kissed her fist, then blew another kiss into the wind. 'We love you, Kenny.' She watched a single gull riding an updraught near the horizon, and she felt a loosening at her core, a sensation of falling that made her grab the pedestal. He'd never see this again, stand here and perform this ritual, and acknowledging that was letting go of yet another piece of him.

On the Tuesday after Tara's X-ray, Honour was in the back garden cutting some lavender for the pottery jug on the kitchen table, when her phone buzzed in her pocket. Dropping her clippers into her gardening bag, she saw the doctor's number on the screen. Fending off a picture show of dark outcomes, she took a moment to calm her heart, then answered.

'Hello, Mrs MacLeod. It's Carla. Doctor Ford would like to speak to you if you have a moment?'

Honour's stomach folded over.

17

The next few moments crept by and yet at the same time seemed to whirl past Honour as she tried to grasp what the doctor was saying. Fiona Ford spoke clearly and deliberately as Honour slowly backed up to the house and leaned against the wall, feeling the curve of the stones meet the back of her hips. She pressed into the stones, willing them to ground her, as she closed her eyes and tried to concentrate on what she was hearing.

'There's a spot on the X-ray, which is concerning, so we'll get a CT scan next, to eliminate a few things.'

Honour found her voice, her stomach fluttering alarmingly. 'What things, exactly? Is there something wrong with her bones? I read online...' She stopped herself.

'I can't make a diagnosis without more extensive testing,' Doctor Ford said. 'The CT will fill in the gaps of information.'

Honour looked over at the wall that joined their house to Bridie and Scott's, suddenly compelled to launch herself at it, kick and claw at the stones until they yielded the answer to her burning question: what had her family done to deserve all this?

As she listened to the doctor explaining that the request for an urgent CT had gone over to the hospital, Honour's mind was pulled to a shadowy memory that she had not faced for years, and she was suddenly convinced that *she* was to blame. Her actions, her choices in the past, and the consequent karmic forces had brought this bad luck upon them, and now, rather than Honour paying her dues to the ferryman, it looked like he might be coming for her daughter.

The next ten days went by in a blur and, feeling as if she might implode until she knew what was going on with Tara, Honour had asked her mother to come over for a couple of days for moral support. Marion had gladly agreed, turning up with her little suitcase and a giant cloth bag of knitting.

Bridie had been coming in regularly with fresh-baked bread, comics for the kids or a casserole. She'd stay for half an hour, sometimes sipping a glass of sherry with Marion, then she'd hug Honour and leave them to their evening.

This evening, Bridie was sitting on the sofa with Callum next to her, while Marion was upstairs helping Tara dry her hair. Honour had poured them both a little wine and Bridie was nursing the glass in her lap as Callum flipped through his favourite book on black holes.

Honour crossed her legs under her and flicked her long braid over her shoulder. With May well underway, she was surprised that she still felt so chilled most evenings, and as she stared into the empty grate, she pictured the roaring fires Kenny loved. He'd bank the logs up at night and rekindle the fire before he left in the mornings, so that Honour would come downstairs to a cosy room.

All the little things he did for her and the children, on a daily basis, were signs of his love – a love that Honour knew she would never find again. Feeling the press of tears at the back of her throat, she swallowed them down with a sip of wine just as

Frodo appeared, his long tail twitching as he crossed the room, then curled up next to Honour, as if he too was looking for the comfort of the fire. She stroked his back, the thick coat smooth beneath her fingers as the cat stretched out languorously, then re-coiled himself into a tight ball next to her thigh.

Bridie was staring at her, her brow deeply furrowed, and her eyes narrowed. 'Honour, is there anything more that Scott and I can do, to make things easier for you all?' She paused. 'However small.'

Honour smiled at her neighbour. 'No, but thank you. We're just taking it a day at a time.'

Bridie seemed unconvinced, her eyes holding Honour's until Honour felt uncomfortable, and looked away. It was enough that her parents and Lorna knew what was going on, and the thought of sharing it any further was unsettling.

'I know you've all been through hell, but don't hesitate to tell me if there's anything...' Bridie stopped, seeming to sense Honour's discomfort. 'Sorry. I never know when to shut up. You know I'm here, and I'll leave it at that.'

Honour nodded. 'I do. And it means the world.'

Callum shifted, tugged his T-shirt down at the back and adjusted his glasses. 'Bridie? Have you seen this?' He pointed at the page he was looking at. 'Did you know that a black hole isn't a hole? It's actually lots of matter packed into a really small space.' He looked up at her, his eyes bright. 'It says here that it's like a star, but say ten times bigger than the Sun, squashed into a sphere about the diameter of New York City.' He shook his head in amazement, and Honour followed suit, as always, touched and deeply proud at his innate intelligence and his constant thirst for knowledge.

'I did not know that.' Bridie smiled widely. 'You're a walking encyclopaedia, young Callum.' She put her hand on his shoulder.

Honour finished her wine and set the glass on the brick

hearth just as Marion and Tara came into the room. Tara's hair was floating around her shoulders, the deep waves like a flaming shawl.

'Want to watch a film on the iPad, Cal?' Tara leaned on the back of the sofa and, catching Honour's eye, rolled her eyes theatrically – as if this was the last thing in the world she wanted to do. But after recent events, Honour knew better.

Callum looked up, surprise and pleasure flooding his face. 'OK. But nothing mushy.'

Tara pulled a face at him. 'I don't watch mushy stuff.' She leaned over and batted his shoulder. 'And no more *Star Trek* or *Star Wars* or star anything.' She dodged the slap he aimed at her arm and laughed. 'Come on. Let's go.' She pointed at the ceiling.

The children said goodbye to Bridie and climbed the stairs, then Marion spotted Honour's glass on the hearth. 'Did I miss the wee tipple?'

Savouring the warm glow that her children's new closeness left inside her, Honour pushed herself up from the floor. 'The bar is still open.' She smiled at her mother, seeing the network of lines around Marion's mouth and the creases at the edges of her eyes a little deeper than just a few weeks ago. Worried that she was leaning too heavily on her, Honour wrapped her arms around her. 'Sit yourself down, Mum, and I'll get you some. Bridie? A top-up?' She smiled at her neighbour.

'Not for me. I'm off home before Scott sends out the lifeboat.' Bridie chuckled, then instantly paled. 'God, that was thoughtless.' She met Honour's gaze.

Honour shook her head. 'Bridie, it's fine. The best thing you can do for us it to be yourself and speak freely. We all need that normality, not to have people walking on eggshells around us.' She nodded decisively. 'And tell that sweet man of yours to stop avoiding us, too.'

Bridie looked relieved. 'Will do.' She opened the door. 'Shout if you need anything. Bye, Marion.'

Once again seeing the question behind Bridie's eyes, Honour crossed the room and closed the door behind her, then turned to her mother. 'She doesn't know, does she?'

Marion pulled her chin in and frowned. 'I don't think so, love.'

Honour sighed. 'Right. I suppose I just feel see-through. Like every emotion, thought or concern is plastered across my face – like a ticker tape that people can read. We just need to get this CT done and then I'll be able to breathe.' She pressed her palm on her chest. 'Was it like this for you? I mean, whenever I was ill?'

Marion gave a soft huff. 'You mean like when you broke your collarbone falling off your bike? Or when you had the worst case of measles Doc Ford had ever seen, and I sat up with you for three nights in a row until I fell asleep at the kitchen sink?' She smiled at her daughter. 'Yes, love. It was exactly the same.'

Honour nodded, memories of her mother singing to her, dabbing her feverish face with a damp cloth, bathing her in bed when Honour was too weak to get up, flooding back. 'How did you keep functioning?'

Marion held her arms out and Honour walked into her embrace. 'One day at a time. Just like you're doing.'

Honour caught the lily-of-the-valley scent that her mother favoured, feeling the strength of Marion's wiry arms around her, holding her up – keeping her broken pieces together.

'You are not alone, Honour. And Tara will be fine,' Marion said. 'Just believe.'

Honour tried to control the slight tremor in her legs as she wished for the strength to do just that, but faith felt beyond her grasp. She was already damaged, bruised and afraid, and without Kenny here to share the worry, she felt as if she might drown.

18

As June rolled in, and over three months since their lives had changed forever, Honour stared out of the living-room window at the gentle, cobbled slope leading down to the harbour below. The sky was grey, and fat raindrops splattered against the window, distorting her view.

She could hear the wind buffeting the gutters and the trickle of the rainwater running down the gulley at the edge of the lane, and even though the windows were tightly closed against the summer storm, she could smell the smokiness of the moss that grew in the joints of the paving stones on her front steps.

Her world was already on shaky ground and the phone call she was now taking had the potential to shatter its foundation completely. The CT scan had taken place within days of the request for the appointment, and now, Honour was listening to Fiona Ford, every word like needles pricking Honour's skin. She tasted bile rising at the back of her throat as she forced a swallow, grateful that the children were at school for another two hours.

'I have some difficult news, Mrs MacLeod.' Doctor Ford

paused, as Honour's insides flipped over. 'The CT shows a tumour in Tara's knee, at the top of the tibia. It appears small, but the indications are that it could be malignant.'

The air seemed to be sucked from the room as Honour dipped her chin to her chest. Her pulse thrummed in her ears and a sudden wave of nausea made her sway. Taking a moment to steady herself, she whispered, 'Malignant, as in cancer?' The word tasted cumbersome, bitter, and associating it with her sunny, active girl was horrific.

'It's a possibility, but we won't know until we do further tests.'

Honour leaned her forehead on the window, feeling the cool of the glass against her skin. Her mind was racing, filled with everything she did not know, and her imagination filling in the frightening gaps. 'How bad is this?' The question seemed ridiculous, as any degree of cancer was the worst-case scenario, but faced with this nightmare, Honour felt horribly ignorant of what it might mean for her daughter.

'The tumour looks to be contained in the knee joint, so the next step is to do a biopsy. Once we get those results, we'll know exactly what we're dealing with.'

Honour pictured a frighteningly long needle piercing Tara's delicate skin, spearing into the bones of her leg, and she shuddered.

'The biopsy will be done by an orthopaedic oncologist at Victoria Hospital. Tara will be slightly sedated, and they'll use local anaesthesia, so it should be relatively straightforward, and not too painful.' She paused. 'You can be with her, and the results will take about a week.'

The thought of waiting for an entire week, bearing the agony of not knowing, and handling her own fear while keeping Tara positive, was overwhelming. 'How soon can it be done?'

'I'm pulling every string I can to get her in soon. I'll let you know once we have an appointment date. And, in the meantime, let me know if Tara's pain increases, or if she starts to have a temperature. I can also arrange for some stronger pain medication if she needs it.'

Honour turned her back on the window, her skin feeling suddenly tender under her cotton sweater. As she listened to the doctor's voice, one question loomed larger than all the others, and as soon as there was a moment of silence, she said, 'What do I tell her? I mean, should I tell her everything now, that it might be cancerous, or wait until we know for sure?' The outline of the sofa, Kenny's armchair, the doorway to the kitchen all began to blur as Honour willed herself to hold back the tears until she had ended the call.

'My advice would be to wait. But Tara is very bright, and mature for her age, so I'm sure she will have questions. If I were you, though, I'd hold off on talking about the potential for malignancy, just now.'

Once again, it was shocking to hear those toxic words associated with her daughter, and Honour flinched.

'There is no perfect way to handle these situations, Mrs MacLeod. You know your daughter better than anyone, so trust your instincts.'

Honour nodded, her throat now tightly constricted. Lorna's offer to help replayed itself in her mind and, right now, she needed the doctor to stop talking so she could hang up and call her friend. 'OK,' Honour croaked. 'So, I'll wait to hear from you, then.'

Honour ended the call, every muscle and tendon in her body feeling taut and stretched to snapping point. Losing Kenny had all but ended her, and the children had been her anchors – her reason for getting up every day. But if the unimaginable happened and she lost her darling Tara, there would be no coming back from that.

.   .   .

Lorna sounded out of breath, her voice being distorted by a strong wind. 'Hang on, Honour. I'm running. Give me a minute to find somewhere quiet.'

'OK.' Honour's face was streaked with tears, her insides quaking as she paced across the living room. Each second seemed elongated, the third hand on the clock on the mantel dragging itself between the two and the three, as she waited for Lorna to speak again. Honour counted the tiny, erratic jumps of the gilded hand until Lorna eventually came back on the line.

'OK. I'm in the bus shelter. What's going on?'

Honour struggled to control her voice as she brought Lorna up to speed, all the while Honour pacing back and forth, hearing herself talk about things she never, in a million years, imagined would pass her lips.

When she stopped speaking, Lorna was silent for a few moments, then her voice was strong, and clear. 'So, Doctor Ford has requested the biopsy already?'

'Yes.' Honour sucked in her bottom lip and bit down, instantly tasting the cloying tang of blood.

'OK. So, I'll go in tomorrow and find the surgeon. I'll say Tara is family and see if we can get her in immediately.'

Honour nodded to herself. 'Thank you. That's exactly what I was hoping.'

'They're a lovely group up in orthopaedics, so I'm sure they'll do whatever they can.'

Honour nodded again, her legs beginning to give way. Rather than sit on the sofa, she crossed the room and lowered herself into Kenny's chair, feeling the soft leather yielding beneath her hips. She ran her free hand over the arm, searching for the worn area at the front where his hand would rest as he watched TV.

She laid her fingers over the stain where he'd spilled coffee years ago and tried to channel her husband, connect to his energy – his strength. He would have told her that Tara was going to be fine. That there was no way their strong, clever, athletic girl would succumb to cancer, and Honour would have believed him.

But Kenny wasn't here and as she listened to Lorna, the positive way she was talking about early detection, surgical success rates, new forms of chemotherapy and Tara's odds, Honour let herself slip into a memory.

She was standing at the side of a soggy football pitch watching Tara racing across the midfield. Her football boots were sending a spray of muddy droplets into the air behind her with every stride she took, and the backs of her socks were spattered with dark stains. Her fire-red ponytail was swinging wildly, her face was flushed, and she was biting the tip of her tongue, as she always did when she was concentrating on her footwork. Across the field, the coach was gesticulating, his face pink as he watched his protégé dodge a defender and, seeming to freeze, suspended in the air, with her dominant left foot shoot the ball past the goalie's outstretched hands and straight into the top right corner of the net. Honour closed her eyes and tried to summon the sound of the referee's whistle, the clapping from the crowd around her, and the whoop of joy that had risen from the entire team, until Lorna's voice broke through again.

'Honour. Are you there?'

'Yes, sorry.' She cleared her throat. 'Anything you can do to help would be wonderful. I'm kind of frozen. I should know what to do, and I don't. I need to fix this, but I can't.' The sob that was gathering in her chest burned – demanding to be released.

'Do you want me to come over? I can grab the kids from school and bring them home. In fact, what if Dougie and I stay the night, as it's Saturday tomorrow? The boys can have a sleepover, and we can watch a girlie film with Tara. I'll bring wine, and once they're in bed, we can drink ourselves into oblivion like bloody pirates.'

Despite herself, Honour laughed. 'Oh, God, Lorna. I am so scared.' Her voice splintered, and an animalistic groan escaped her. Unable to control the force of her fear, Honour buried her face in her thighs. The sobs rendered her speechless and, panting in between each racking wail, the pressure built inside her skull until it felt as if it might explode. All the while, Lorna spoke to her – soothing words that faded to white noise, but her presence was essential – a tenuous lifeline that Honour needed more than oxygen in this moment.

As Honour's rapid heartbeats began to even out and she sat upright, the idea of being alone with the children that evening was terrifying. Having her friend there, not only as a distraction from the negative spiral that waited for Honour behind every thought, but as someone who knew everything that was happening, felt like the only way Honour would be able to get through it. 'Yes. Could you come over, and stay the night?'

'Definitely. Dougie will be over the moon. I'll chuck some stuff in a bag for us both, grab the kids and be at your place around half past three. We can get a takeaway, so don't worry about cooking.'

Honour was shivering. The storm had passed, leaving a frothy mist in its wake, and she stood up and made her way to the front door, suddenly desperate for fresh air. She opened it and filled her lungs. 'I'll clean up my face and pull something out of the freezer for dinner. My two won't eat takeaway anything, other than fish and chips.' She swept the hair away from her forehead. 'They'll turn into a plate of chips if they have any more.'

'Honour. I know you're scared, but they are really good in oncology at the Victoria. Tara will get the best treatment, you can be sure, and I will be there, every step of the way. If you'll let me.'

'Thank you.' Honour gulped, Lorna's kindness threatening to strip away the last vestiges of Honour's control. 'Just don't be so nice all the time because I'm not sure I can handle it.' Tears blurred her vision again, so she blinked them away.

'Fine. You're a shitty mum, a terrible cook, and a crappy friend. See you soon.' With that, Lorna was gone, leaving Honour staring at the trail of watermarks on her window and wondering how she was going to break the news to Tara, and to her parents. The prospect was as daunting as anything Honour had ever faced as one question dominated her thoughts.

Do I have the strength to do this, without Kenny by my side?

19

While she waited for Lorna to arrive with the children, Honour dragged the air mattress out from the cupboard under the stairs and took it up to Callum's room. As she began to use the old foot pump to fill it, her thigh quickly began to burn.

The last time they'd used it, just a few days before Kenny had drowned, she'd suggested to him that they get a new, more modern one with an electronic pump, but he'd called her a wimp. 'Oh, come on, Red. Get some exercise in.' He'd poked her hip, his hazel eyes full of mischief.

She'd retaliated, swatting at him as he dodged her palm. 'Cheeky sod. I get more exercise in one day than most people around here get in a week.' She'd picked up a pillow and thrown it at him.

He'd grabbed her, pulled her into his arms and blown a raspberry on her neck.

'Oh my God, I married a child.' She'd shoved him off, laughing. 'Go and do something productive please.'

He'd laughed loudly, his head tipping back and the dimple in his left cheek deepening. 'You're a feisty one, Red. That's

why I married you. You take no prisoners.' His face had softened then, as he'd looked at her. 'You're the very best part of my
life, Honour. You and those two vagabonds downstairs.' He'd
gestured over his shoulder.

Honour had been taken aback at the sudden switch to seri-
ousness, and now, as she recalled that feeling, she wondered if
Kenny had somehow known that his days were numbered – that
the sea would win out eventually. Had he sensed that he
needed to tell her how much she and the children meant to him
in case he didn't get many more chances?

She switched to the other foot and carried on pumping, a
sadness so profound that it had a salty taste to it floating up from
her centre, into her mouth.

The doorbell rang, jolting her back to the present so
Honour secured the plug in the mattress to retain the little air
she'd managed to put in it. She spun around, checked herself in
the porthole-shaped mirror above Callum's bed and straightened her crumpled linen shirt. She still looked flushed from
crying, and her hair was wild, long twists trailing over each
shoulder. Grabbing a tissue from her sleeve, she wiped under
her eyes to remove the smudges of mascara, then, satisfied that
the children would likely not even notice her slightly dishev-
elled appearance, she headed for the stairs.

Two hours later, Lorna was sitting across the room, with her
bare feet crossed on the trunk. Her damp, rainbow-coloured
sneakers were at the front door next to her overnight bag, and
her and Dougie's jackets were draped over the radiator under
the window. They'd got soaked by another bout of rain as they'd
run up the lane to the cottage from where Lorna had parked,
near the harbour.

Once inside, Dougie and Callum had predictably disappeared immediately to Callum's room and Tara had hung about the kitchen as Honour and Lorna talked and prepared the dinner. Honour had found a steak pie in the freezer that she'd made a few weeks ago and with a pot of mashed potatoes, and some carrots and peas, their meal had come together easily.

They'd all sat around the table and Honour was thankful that opting to have company had been the right decision. Callum and Dougie were animated, making Tara laugh and roll her eyes in equal measure, and with the three children so at ease, Honour had been safe in her silence, shooting grateful glances at Lorna, who'd smiled back.

Once the boys had gone up to bed, Honour and Lorna had watched a funny film, letting Tara sit between them on the sofa, a giant bowl of popcorn in her lap that they had all dipped into. Tara had been yawning since the halfway point and Honour had tried not to stare at her, looking for Tara to grab her knee, or complain about the pain. She had made it to the end of the film and, without being asked, stood up, hugged both her mother and Lorna goodnight and headed upstairs.

Now, Honour nursed her wine glass, her back against the front of Kenny's chair and her feet crossed under her. Her heart was ticking under her breastbone as she glanced at the clock, waiting a few more minutes for Tara to be in bed before she went upstairs to talk to her.

Lorna drained her glass and set it on the floor, her eyes catching Honour's. 'So, are you comfortable with what you're going to tell her?'

Honour nodded. 'As I'll ever be.'

'I think you're right to downplay it for now. She's bright as button, but she's not likely to make the leap from another test to cancer.' Lorna chewed her bottom lip. 'Plus, there's every possibility that it's benign, Honour. You can't discount that.'

Honour swallowed hard, the word benign sounding like a

parachute that she desperately needed as she faced a free fall, from a great height, into uncharted territory. 'I'm keeping that top of mind,' she lied, seeing Lorna's chin dip. 'I'm trying to, anyway.'

'Go and get it over with. I'll fill us up.' Lorna stood up, lifted her glass and walked towards the kitchen. At the door, she turned around. 'You're going to be fine, Honour. You're a great mum and you'll see her through this. Whatever happens.'

Honour sighed and heaved herself up from the floor. 'God, I hope so.'

Tara's bedside light was on and her back was to the door, but her iPad was lying open in front of her. Spotting Tara's school uniform in the customary heap on the floor by the radiator, Honour smiled to herself, then crossed the room. As she approached the bed, she saw Jenna's face on the screen, just as the one creaky floorboard in the room gave Honour's presence away.

Tara turned over and smiled at her mother. 'I knew you'd come up.' She turned back to her friend. 'Got to go, Jen. See you tomorrow.'

Jenna grinned, moving her face comically close to the camera. 'Night, Tar. Night, Mrs MacLeod.' She waved at the camera.

'Goodnight, Jenna love.' Honour waved as Tara closed the cover on the iPad and tossed it to the end of the bed. She then shifted back a little, to make room for Honour. Tara's hair was in a loose ponytail and the sleeves of her football-covered pyjamas had ridden up, her wrists and forearms looking spindly and vulnerable. Honour carefully lay next to her daughter, then propped her head up on her hand and smiled. 'Is Jenna coming over tomorrow then?' Honour was pleased, as Tara had still been keeping herself to herself outside of school. Not playing football matches at the weekends, she wasn't seeing her team-mates and Honour had had two concerned phone calls from the coaches asking when Tara would be back. Knowing what she now knew, Honour suspected the tumour could mean that Tara's absence might be indefinite, and that was heartbreaking.

Tara nodded. 'Yeah. She said her mum could drop her off after practice, and I said she could stay for lunch. Is that OK?'

Honour smiled. 'Of course. Jenna is always welcome, sweet-heart. Shall I do a roast with all the trimmings?'

Tara tipped her head to the side and sighed. 'Yes, that'd be good. We can't have Dad's Yorkshires, though.' Her eyes dimmed a little as Honour pictured the spectacular Yorkshire puddings that Kenny would make, golden clouds with the perfect-sized dip in the middle to catch the gravy Honour would make from the rich juices in the pan.

'True.' She gave a sad smile. 'I can make some if you like. They might not be as good as Dad's, but I can give it a go.'

Tara shook her head. 'No. That's OK.'

Sensing that this was something else that must remain sacrosanct – a precious memorial to Kenny – she nodded, readying herself for what she had to tell her daughter. 'Tara, I wanted to have a chat with you, if you're not too tired.'

Tara looked mildly surprised but shook her head. 'I'm OK.'

'Good. Well, I spoke to Doctor Ford today and she has seen your X-rays.' Honour willed herself to keep her voice steady, not give Tara any hint of the inner turmoil that was making Honour light-headed.

'Uh-huh.' Tara yawned, her arm stretching above her head.

'She told me that there is a small growth in your knee, at the top of the tibia. That's the bone that runs up the inside of your shin.' Honour pointed at Tara's leg. 'It's what causing your pain, so Doc wants to do another test to see what the growth is made of so she can decide how to treat it.' Honour watched her daughter's face, the sky-blue eyes trusting, taking in every word as gospel.

'What kind of test?'

Honour shifted her elbow back. 'It's called a biopsy. They'll give you some medicine to make you sleepy, then they'll make your knee numb, then put a needle into the growth to get a little sample that they'll send to a lab. I'll be with you all the time and you'll be in and out in about half an hour. It'll take a week or so until Doc Ford gets the results.' Honour found a smile. 'It's nothing to worry about, Tara, and hopefully we'll be able to get some answers.'

Tara frowned, her fingers going to her mouth. 'I won't feel it, will I?'

Honour shook her head. 'No, love. Your leg will be numb, so you won't.'

Tara looked dubious.

'If we can get you out of pain, that's the main thing. Won't it be good to get back onto the pitch and play again, and not be hurting?' Honour felt herself wandering into the realm of untruths, but her need to soothe Tara's fears was bigger than her resolve to be honest.

Tara's eyes slid to the left and she sighed, her chin beginning to tremble. Each tiny quiver tugged painfully at Honour's heart.

'What is it, love?'

Tara slowly sat up, shoving her ponytail behind her before she leaned back against the headboard. 'If I don't play football anymore, will you be cross, or disappointed?'

Honour's chest tightened as a spark of shock at hearing Tara confirm what Honour had overheard a few weeks earlier overtook her. 'Tara, I could never be disappointed in you. You know that Dad and I supported you with the football because you loved it so much. If you decide you'd rather not play, or maybe do something else instead, that's fine, and totally up to you, sweetheart.' Honour sat up and drew Tara into her side, catching a waft of toothpaste. 'You can always talk to me and must never be afraid to tell me what you're feeling, about anything.' She rocked her daughter, feeling Tara lean in to her ribs.

'OK.' Tara sniffed, her nose turning rosy, as always happened when she was emotional. 'Do you think Dad would be upset?' Tara lifted Honour's hand and wove her fingers through her mother's.

'I think Dad would have understood. He only ever wanted you to have fun with it and be happy. He was so proud of you, Tara, but not just because of the football. You know that, right?'

Tara nodded, her fingers tightening around Honour's. 'What if they find something bad in my knee?'

Honour fought the shudder that crept up her back at the candid question. She had suspected that Tara would have questions, but her going straight to a dark place was Honour's worst fear. 'Whatever they find, we'll be in a better place than now, where we don't know why you're in so much pain. If we know what's going on, we can make a plan to get you better.' She paused, unsure whether she'd said enough, or whether Tara would challenge her further. 'It's natural to be a bit scared, but Lorna says the doctors at the Victoria are the best. They'll do a really good job of taking care of you.' Honour forced a swallow. 'Do you have any more questions, love? You can ask me anything.'

Tara took a few moments to look up at her mother, then she shook her head. 'No. But don't tell Cal. He'll only get all weird and wobbly about it, and it'll make him more of a pain.' She eyed Honour, then a smile tugged at Tara's mouth. 'He's such a drama queen.'

Honour felt a lifting inside – a surge of love and pride so powerful it rendered her speechless. Rather than reply, she simply nodded, cupped Tara's chin and kissed the top of her head. How was it possible that she, Honour, had had a hand in making this magnificent creature, a child that, on the outside, looked to be in perfect health.

But, despite appearances, deep inside the cells that made up her daughter's bones, was it possible that something had gone horribly wrong?

20

————

Ten days later, Honour's hand was shaking as she stared at the word *osteosarcoma* on her phone. When the call from the hospital had come in while she was at work, her boss, Tilda, had seen her crying in the break room and, without pressing her on what was wrong, had told her to go home.

Honour's eyes were burning and her head pounding as, next to her, her mother was holding her free hand, Marion's words soothing, but her voice fractured.

'At least you know what's happening, Honour. Early detection goes a long way, and these days, the treatments are much more effective. And she'll get the best care. We're here for her, and you.' Marion released Honour's hand and wrapped her arm around Honour's shoulder. 'Do you want me there when you tell her?'

Honour leaned in to her mother, letting the phone drop to her thigh. 'No,' she whispered. 'It's better if I do it by myself.'

Marion nodded, glancing at Kirk, who was hovering by the window, his face a mask of concern. 'So, what's the course of treatment?' Marion asked.

'The doctor said they'd probably want to do chemotherapy

first, to see if they can shrink the tumour, then surgery to remove it.' She swallowed. 'Then, depending on how big it is and how much it's affected the knee, she might need a knee replacement.' Honour winced, picturing her precious child on an operating table, the intrusive procedures she'd have to undergo and the uncertain outcome.

'When you get back from the school, I can take the wee man out for a wander on the beach. Get him an ice cream or something,' Kirk offered. 'Whatever is most helpful.'

Honour couldn't muster a smile, but she nodded at her father, grateful that, once again, no sooner had she phoned to tell them the news than they'd turned up on her doorstep an hour later.

Honour had known that her daughter had cancer for less than a day, and in that time Honour's world had imploded again, for the second time in three months. Every resource that she had been drawing on to get the children through losing their father had run dry, and now she only had a few hours until she'd have to pick them up from school. She had no notion of how she was going to keep it together enough to ask them about their day, focus on driving, listen to them talk about homework, or hear them ask her what they were going to do this weekend, all the while hiding her terror.

Typically, needing something to do, Kirk circled the room and collected their empty mugs, taking them into the kitchen. She watched him go, then Honour looked down at her legs, her scrubs today covered in ladybirds. The bright design seemed to burn her eyes. The happy colours, the normality of the tiny insects, and the ridiculousness of being covered in them, when she knew what she knew, felt unbearable. 'I have to change.' She stood up, gathering her hair behind her neck. 'Can you come up, Mum?'

Marion was already standing. 'Yes.' She followed Honour to the stairs and walked up behind her, Honour sensing that her mother's hands were hovering behind her shoulders as if Marion was afraid that Honour might topple over under the weight of what she carried.

Honour lifted one leaden leg, then the other, until she could not support herself anymore and her knees gave way. She knelt on the step ahead of her, her stomach contracting as she let the tears come. Marion sat on the step beside Honour and stroked her back as Honour shook, every fibre of her being quivering with fear and dread at what was ahead of them.

'Just let it out, my love,' Marion whispered. 'I'm here, and so is Dad.'

An hour later, Honour had showered, washed her hair, tidied up her face and put on a clean shirt and jeans. As she took in her reflection in the bathroom mirror, her eyes were puffy and her nose was still pink, but otherwise there was little evidence of the meltdown she'd had. She brushed her hair, feeling the bristles of the brush sharp against her neck, then closed her eyes, the rhythmic strokes calming her jangling nerves.

Her father had walked round to Green's and picked up some provisions, and now, downstairs, her parents were talking in hushed voices.

Honour checked the time, her throat catching as she saw that she had only a few minutes until she needed to leave for school. She made one final check in the mirror, then took a deep breath, shook the hair from her eyes and spoke quietly to herself. 'This isn't about you. This is about Tara, and what she needs. So, get it together. Be the parent your daughter needs. Be strong, like Kenny would have been.' She nodded to herself. 'Your tears are over, for now.' She blinked her vision clear, angry that her eyes were betraying her determination to be strong. 'You can do this, for Tara.'

Downstairs, her parents were in the kitchen, her father at

the table flipping distractedly through a *House and Garden* magazine, while her mother dried up the few dishes that had been on the draining board. Honour stood in the doorway and took them both in, their gentle, steady energy, their practised calm that she knew was for her benefit, and she was overcome with love for them both. Feeling as if she could draw on their strength, she said, 'I'm going to be OK. Don't worry. I can do this. Whatever happens, we will get through it, and I know that I can come to you if I need help.'

In sync as always, they turned to look at her, both sets of eyes glistening reflections of their own inner turmoil. 'Always, Honour. Whatever we can do, we will.' Her father held his hand out to her, so she moved over to the table and stood next to him.

'Thanks for understanding that I'd rather tell them alone.' She watched her mother's brow knit, then Honour glanced at her father, who was nodding. 'We need to talk as a family, and I've decided to include Callum in the conversation. I think it's important that we share this with him from the start.' She paused. 'He's too clever to keep it from for long, and I don't want him to feel excluded, or that we hid something this big when he finds out later.'

She watched her mother round the table and sit next to her father, Marion's face grey and her mouth pinched. As Kirk took Marion's hand in his, Honour continued.

'They are so much closer since Kenny...' She swallowed the words that were still hard to say out loud. 'They've formed a new bond, and I think it'll help Tara to know that we are all in this together. Taking it on as a team.'

Marion blinked several times, then nodded. 'We support you one hundred per cent.' She tipped her head to the side in question. 'Are you sure you want us to go, though?'

Kirk released Marion's hand and stood up. 'I think Honour is right. She knows we're here if she needs us, but she knows those children and what they need better than anyone.' He gave a half-smile, as Marion slowly stood up. 'We've always knows how strong you are, Honour. That was never a question.' He drew Marion into his side, the mismatch in their heights, as ever, endearing. 'Kenny knew it, too, and he'd be so proud of how you've coped, these past few months.'

Honour felt her new-found resolve waver. 'Do you think so?'

'Absolutely.' Her father nodded. 'He always said that you were the one with the backbone of steel.'

Honour felt a bolt of surprise run through her, her belief that Kenny was the rock was something that had existed for most of their relationship. That he had thought this about her was surprising, and yet it was precisely what she needed to hear. Her father had given her the very thing that would help her get through the next phase of what the universe was throwing at her. If Kenny believed she could do this, she would not let him down. Not again.

As soon as she'd found the right moment, Honour went up to Tara's bedroom to break the news.

Tara was initially, and understandably, shocked, pushing Honour away when she tried to hold her, but after a few moments, started asking questions about the chemotherapy.

'What's a port? Will I have to stay in hospital? Will I miss school?'

Honour battled to keep her voice steady, and explained as calmly as she could everything she understood would be happening, until Tara eventually leaned into her mother and cried in Honour's arms.

As Honour pushed her own worries aside and found words of comfort from a source deep inside that she had never tapped before, Tara stopped crying, angrily swiped her hair from her damp cheeks and pulled her shoulders back. 'Why did I get cancer?' She stared at Honour, her eyes on fire and her mouth pinching. 'It's not fair, because I didn't do anything wrong.'

Honour fought her tears again, taking Tara's anger as fuel for her response. 'It's not fair at all, and you definitely don't deserve it, my love. But you are so strong, and fit, and healthy otherwise that you will win this fight.' Honour made a fist and punched her own thigh, the spark of pain sending a bolt of power straight into her aching heart.

Tara took in her mother's expression, a depth of understanding in her eyes that robbed Honour of her voice for a few moments. Eventually, Tara walked to her chest of drawers, wrapped a band around her hair and tossed her ponytail over her shoulder, all the while sniffing loudly.

Honour handed her a tissue. 'Do you have any more questions, sweetheart?'

Tara shook her head. 'Not now.'

Aware that there was only so much Tara was willing to absorb at once, Honour said quietly, 'How about we go downstairs and tell Callum what's happening?' To her surprise, Tara immediately nodded.

'Yes, OK.' Lifting her iPad from the bottom of her bed, as Honour's heart twisted painfully in her chest, Tara followed her mother down the stairs.

Honour sat at the kitchen table and read to the children from her phone. Her need to get this absolutely right was making her teeth clench, her jaw aching with the intensity of the bite. Taking a moment, she continued where she'd left off: '"Osteosarcoma is a tumour made up of cancer cells that occurs in and/or around bone. It is the most common type of bone cancer in children and adolescents, and usually occurs when their bones are growing rapidly. The most common tumour locations are the lower end of the thigh bone or femur, around the knee and the upper end of the tibia." That's the shinbone, Cal, and where Tara's tumour is.' The words sounded toxic, their message now hovering above them like an ominous cloud that Honour felt she was absorbing with every laboured breath.

She looked at Callum, who was leaning against Tara's shoulder, his glasses tight to the bridge of his nose and his mouth slightly open.

Afraid that if she stopped now, she might never be able to get through this, Honour read on. "'It can also occur at the upper end of the arm or humerus, all of which are the fastest-growing ends of the long bones.'"

She took a moment to check their faces again. Tara's expression gave little away, her eyes flicking back and forth between Callum's profile and the half-open window overlooking the garden.

The faint sound of voices floated up from the harbour and Callum kept looking over at his sister, as if a breeze might sneak in the window and whisk her away, the angst in his eyes breaking Honour in two.

'Do you understand, my loves?' She forced power into her voice as they both nodded, silently. 'OK. It also says that when most osteosarcomas are diagnosed, they are localised, meaning the cancer cells have not spread to other parts of the body.'

As she read ahead, Honour knew that she couldn't absorb, let alone share, what she was seeing there – the text referring to the situation where the tumour might have metastasised.

Desperate to find something positive to close with, she switched off her phone and stood up. 'So, we're going to get Tara's special port fitted in a few days so the chemotherapy can start. It's a device that will allow the medicine to go straight into her bloodstream. After a few weeks, once the tumour has shrunk, the surgeon will remove it and that could be the end of it.' Willing with all her being for that to be the case, she dusted her palms against each other as if banishing some crumbs, and eyed Tara, who was chewing her bottom lip. Her eyes were clear, no sign of tears, and her right arm was draped around the back of Callum's chair.

'Will my hair fall out?' She lifted the end of her long pony-tail and studied it as if she needed to record the colour, texture, the way the ends twisted into curls of their own volition – feel the weight of it in her hand.

Honour hesitated for a moment, then shook her head. 'Not necessarily. Not everyone's does.'

Tara nodded, her mouth dipping at the edges. 'I bet mine does.'

Honour walked around the table and hunkered down next to Tara's chair. 'Worst case, if you do, your hair grows like a weed, so it'll come back so quickly, you won't believe it.' She scooped Tara's free hand up, feeling the slender fingers warm to the touch.

Callum looked over at his mother, his eyes now full. 'Is Tara going to die?'

Honour felt the question like a thump to her chest, taking a moment to collect herself and stand up again. 'No. She abso-lutely is not.' She forced power into her voice. 'One – because I forbid it, and two because she's far too loud and annoying to die and leave us in peace.'

Callum looked shocked, then a hint of a smile tugged at his eyes. 'She is very annoying.' He bumped his shoulder against his sister's. 'And she smells a bit manky, too.'

Tara shoved him off, gently cuffed the back of his head and stood up. 'If I do die, you can't have my room, Callumpty-dumpty. If you take it, I'll be a ghost by then, so I'll come back and haunt you. I'll hide under the bed, come out once you put the light out and bite your bum.' Tara made a gruesome face, and a pinching motion with her thumbs and forefingers.

'I don't believe in ghosts,' Callum pouted. 'Dad told me they're not real.'

'Well, we'll just see. Won't we?' Tara poked his shoulder as Callum stuck his tongue out.

'If you're a ghost, at least you'll be quiet, for once.'

Honour was staggered, this being the last kind of response she had expected. That her children were able to process this frightening news and yet still find humour in the unimaginable made her so proud that she could hardly breathe. It also made her certain that her amazing daughter would defy the odds, and that her fragile but intensely intelligent son would survive this next challenge, too. There was no other possible outcome that was conceivable. Was there?

21

Lorna's voice was low, on the phone, suggesting that Dougie was somewhere nearby. 'When does her chemo start?'

Honour rolled onto her side and pulled Kenny's pillow under her chin. 'She gets her port in on Tuesday, then the first round will start at the weekend.' Honour calculated the dates, realising that the school term ended in two weeks, on the twenty-eighth of June. It was a good thing, as one of Tara's worries had been whether she would miss school because of the chemotherapy, and if her friends would find out what was going on. Her questions about this had alerted Honour to Tara's fear of being pitied, or treated differently, and while it made Honour sad, she could entirely relate.

'I've requested a temporary transfer from paediatrics to oncology, Honour. I want to be around as much as I can while you're both going through this.' Lorna paused. 'It's going to get rough for her, but once it's over, and the tumour is gone, it'll all be worth it.'

'I can't believe you've done that, Lorna. Thank you.' Honour stared at the crack in the curtains, the street lamp's glow seeping in from the lane. She'd left the window open a little, taking in the smell of the sea and hearing the gentle waves lapping against the hulls of the boats – the clink of rope against metal – sounds that blocked out the frightening whispers inside her head. 'The surgeon said it'll be an eight-week course. That's going to take her beyond the start of the autumn term, in August.' Honour grimaced. 'She'll be weak, and probably still sick, and if she does lose her hair, she's going to hate that.'

Lorna took a few moments to reply, then spoke cautiously. 'Honour, all being well, she'll be heading for surgery as soon as her strength returns from the chemo. She'll likely not be going back to school for quite some time.'

Honour sat up and leaned against the headboard, once again feeling so ill-equipped and naïve – unprepared for what was to come. 'God, Lorna. I didn't think that through. How the hell am I going to tell her that it could be months. Her whole summer is going to be shit, and even then, we have no idea if any of this is going to work.' Her voice gave way, and she dropped her chin to her chest.

As she pictured delivering yet another blow to Tara, Honour felt the bitter sadness inside her turn to anger. How the hell had they ended up here? *Damn you, Kenny, for leaving me to deal with this, alone.* Just as quickly, her anger turned to something more painful. Guilt surged through her. She was still here, and her darling man was gone, and if anyone was to blame for that, it was her.

If only I could have kept a hold of his hand.

An hour after Honour had turned off her light, she was startled to hear footsteps in the hall. Lifting her head from the pillow, she checked the time, seeing it was 1.55 a.m. The floorboards creaked again and then the door opened slowly, inch by inch, until she could just make out Callum's tousled head peering around it.

Sitting up, she beckoned to him. 'What's wrong, love?'

Callum climbed onto the bed, but rather than curl up next to her, he sat at the bottom of it, as, puzzled, Honour switched on the bedside light.

'Cal?'

He crossed his legs, his bare feet tucked under his hips and his arms folded purposefully. 'I want to know the truth.' He frowned, as if examining something that made no sense.

Honour pulled the duvet higher up across her chest and focused on his hazel eyes. 'About what?'

'About what's going to happen to Tara.' He paused. 'I'm not scared unless I don't know things. If I know things, I can work out what to do.' He held her gaze. 'Do you know what I mean, Mum?'

Understanding him implicitly, Honour nodded.

'So, when people get cancer, they have chemotherapy, and operations, and then other medicine and stuff, like you said, but then they usually die.' He blinked several times. 'I've seen it on the telly.'

His earnest expression threatened to undo her. Honour was overwhelmed by the sage and frightening logic coming from her eight-year-old. 'Not always, Cal. Lots of people survive and have good lives after cancer.' She hoped she sounded convincing because she believed this, too.

'Hmm.' His frown deepened. 'When will Tara get chemo-therapy?'

Honour shifted her hips, unsure where he was going next. 'She'll start next weekend.'

He eyed her. 'How many days?'

'What do you mean?' Honour frowned.

'How many days will she get the stuff into her blood, at the hospital?'

Feeling cornered, Honour cleared her throat. 'She'll have it three times a week for the first two weeks, then have a week off.

Then again, three times a week for two weeks, then another week off, et cetera.' Relaying what the surgeon had told her on the phone made it solidify a little more as the image of Tara in a hospital chair, lines and IVs going into her port and Honour being next to her every single moment, became blindingly real.

'So, all the summer holidays?' He tipped his head to the side as Honour wondered if he'd overheard her talking to Lorna earlier.

'Pretty much, yes.' Honour nodded, working to keep her face unreadable.

He dipped his chin, then lifted it again as Honour waited for whatever was coming. 'I think I won't go to Space Camp, 'cos if she's ill and stuff, then you'll need me. Dad's not here anymore, so I'll help you.' He nodded once, as if the decision was his, and was final. 'I can go next year, maybe with Dougie.' His eyes were boring into hers and, without his murky glasses shrouding them, the rich, hazel irises were so much like his father's that Honour's throat narrowed.

Shocked by his statement, she leaned forward, her elbows on her knees. She had forgotten completely about Space Camp and now felt like a rotten mother, having her little boy bring it up, especially in such a poignant way. If she were honest, having him gone for a few days would mean that she didn't have to worry about making sure he was OK while managing all Tara's needs, but seeing his face, she knew her son well enough to know that he'd be hard to persuade.

'Cal, that's very kind of you, and so thoughtful, but I don't want you to miss out, and neither will Tara. It's just a few days and you'll enjoy it so much.' She smiled at him, watching as he began to shake his head.

'No. I'll stay here. Maybe I can have Dougie for a two-night sleepover, and we can build a space capsule in my room.' His eyebrows lifted as he scanned her face. 'Or maybe three nights?' His mouth twitched as if he was enjoying the negotiation.

Honour couldn't help herself, letting out a strangled laugh. 'You are so like your dad, Callum MacLeod. Always wiggling things around until you get your own way.' She held her hand out to him and was relieved when he crawled up the bed and slid in beside her. 'But I want you to know that I love you all the way to arsa major and back for what you've just said. You are the kindest boy and sweetest brother in the world.' She hugged him close, then raked her fingers through his matted hair, noticing how long it had got. 'And you need a haircut, young man.'

He huffed, then chuckled. 'We will make Tara better, then she can be a pain in our arsa major for a long time.'

Honour's laughter was mixed with tears as she held her son close, wishing with all her might that his words were a portent of what was to come.

The following weekend, her port in place, Tara had begun chemotherapy at the hospital. Her treatments took three hours, and as Honour sat with her daughter, watched films on the iPad, played cards or read to her, Honour had also planned for the coming weeks. The more she'd tried to manipulate her schedule to allow her to be with Tara, work, take care of Callum, and the house, her sense of isolation had grown.

Lorna had been a godsend, taking Callum to her flat at the weekends, then, during the week, making sure to come by to check on Tara whenever she was having treatments. She would bring magazines and ice lollies, was upbeat without being patronising, and as she would leave the room, Honour would step out into the corridor and hug her tightly, words simply inadequate to express her gratitude.

Honour's parents had offered to move in and help her with the children once the summer holidays began, but something deep inside Honour still wanted to handle this by herself.

Protecting her little family was all she could think about, and despite Lorna telling her that she'd need their support, Honour had gently told her parents thank you, but no.

She was happy for them to come over for visits as often as they liked, take Callum out while she took Tara to the Victoria or when they got home and Tara was dealing with the bouts of nausea the chemo induced, but when the sun went down on the harbour, Honour treasured the moments of quiet when the cottage finally fell silent, the children in their beds. She would slip on an old sweatshirt of Kenny's and talk quietly to him, think about the next day, and tell him everything she intended to do to get them all through it.

Callum had taken to sitting on Tara's bed when they got home from the hospital. Tara would be tired and pale after her chemo treatments but would lie and listen to Callum chat about his latest copy of *Junior Star Gazer*, or they'd sit side by side with a blanket over their knees and watch programmes on the iPad. Their growing bond gave Honour something to smile about during the hardest days, and as those days folded into weeks, and they all began to find a new rhythm, albeit odd and sometimes jarring, Honour felt her strength returning.

Tara was handling the treatments relatively well and, once the bouts of nausea had passed, would ask for toast with a sliced banana on it – a sign that she was through the worst, until the next treatment. Honour had begun giving her protein shakes and nutritional supplements as the weight was falling off Tara at an alarming rate. She would drink half the shake, then leave the rest, but even that was reassuring to Honour.

In an attempt to do anything she could to make Tara feel better, Honour had also taken to keeping fresh sunflowers in the jug on the kitchen table, and a single bloom in a green glass bottle on Tara's bedside table, and each time they got home from the hospital, Tara would gently touch the golden petals and smile.

As the summer holidays slipped by, and Honour juggled the immense strain on her resources, both physical and emotional, the end of the first round of treatments was just days away. Tara had been seeing Jenna every few days, and today – and this being the end of a treatment-free week – Tara was brighter. They were upstairs in her room and as Honour ironed in the living room, she could hear them giggling – a sound that lifted Honour's spirit more than anything else could.

That morning, she'd been helping Tara wash her hair over the bath, and as a few long lengths of molten red had come away in Honour's hands, she had stuffed them into her jeans pocket rather than let Tara see them. Remembering that they were still in her pocket, Honour walked into the kitchen and pulled them out, the strands now feeling dry and lifeless as she spread them across her palm. Her heart tearing, she pushed the hair into the bin and covered it with a piece of kitchen paper.

Honour walked back into the living room just as the doorbell rang. Checking the clock and noting that it was too early for Lorna to be bringing Callum home from his playdate, Honour frowned. She squinted through the glass panel of the door, trying to make out who was standing on her step, wishing the world would leave them alone to enjoy these few moments of peace. She contemplated stepping back and pretending to be out, but then she saw the long silvery braid and the light tanned face. It had been a few days since she'd seen Bridie and, suddenly, Honour was glad that her neighbour was here.

'Hi, Bridie.' Honour managed a smile. 'How's things?' Surprised to see Scott standing there too, Honour smiled. 'Hi, Scott.'

Bridie's face was strained, her mouth pinched into a thin line. 'Hello, love.' She hesitated as Honour stepped back.

'Come in.' Honour moved further back into the room, surprised to see them still waiting on the step. Suddenly alarmed, Honour stepped forward again. 'What's wrong, Bridie?'

They took a moment, then both walked into the room as Honour gently closed the door behind them. Bridie was carrying a tray of something covered with a tea towel. 'I made you some millionaire's shortbread. I know the wee ones like it.' She held the tray out awkwardly, then, as Honour watched, Bridie's eyes filled.

'Oh, Bridie. What's happened?' Honour took the tray from her and gestured towards the kitchen. 'Come through.'

Bridie blinked furiously, but she and Scott followed Honour, then each dragged a chair out and sat at the table, facing the window. As Bridie shifted the chair in closer, the feet screeching against the flagstone floor, Honour flinched. Kenny always made such a noise when he moved the chairs that Honour would scold him. Hearing it now sent a spark of loneliness through Honour that she pushed down as she filled the kettle and set it on the stove. Turning back to her friends, Honour sat opposite them. 'So, tell me. Are you two all right?'

22

Scott's mouth was dipping as he nodded. 'Aye, we're fine, Honour. But we've something to tell you.'

Bridie tugged at the sleeve of her collarless shirt, the soft aqua-coloured linen making her eyes seem surreally blue. Honour studied them, and there was pain there, a burden that Bridie seemed to want to share, and yet, she was still not speaking. Flooded with affection, and understanding of the need to share and yet hold onto things that hurt to speak about, Honour covered Bridie's hand with hers. 'Whatever it is, I want to help.' Honour patted her fingers and sat back, as Bridie took a moment, then leaned forward on her elbows.

'Honour, I know we shouldn't barge in like this, or force a confidence, but we think we know what's going on with Tara.'

Honour was taken aback, instantly trying to figure out how they had found out. It wasn't her neighbours who had something difficult to share, after all, but Honour herself, and it was clear that she now had no choice but to talk once again about what was keeping her awake every night.

Her decision not to tell anyone other than her parents, and Lorna, had made sense when she'd taken it. By saying it out loud, Honour was giving what was happening to her daughter more power, which was the last thing she wanted.

Bridie was staring at Honour, her fingers now knotted tightly in Scott's. As always happened when Bridie came into the cottage, the scent of lavender had floated in with her. 'I'm sorry. Scott told me to stay out of it, but I just couldn't. You know how much we care about you all, and now, with Kenny gone, you're coping with so much.' She paused. 'This is just too cruel, Honour.' A single tear bubbled over her bottom lid.

Honour's heart contracted. She felt bad for keeping Bridie and Scott in the dark, but she was conflicted, as she believed that the more people who knew about Tara, the more ground cancer gained. 'I'm sorry I didn't tell you both. It's just been such a whirlwind since we found out. Things have moved so quickly, which, of course, we're grateful for, in a sense, but I've not been able to catch my breath.' She stood up to turn off the whistling kettle, then, seeing the pallor in Bridie's face, Honour wanted to offer her some comfort. 'How about something stronger?'

Bridie took a moment, then nodded. 'A wee tot wouldn't go amiss.' She eyed Honour, then wiped her cheeks with a cotton hanky she dragged from her sleeve.

'Scott?' Honour saw the tiny smile on his weather-beaten face.

'Aye, why not.'

'We should be the ones getting you a drink,' Bridie huffed as Honour passed her, went into the living room, and opened the cabinet where they stored the limited selection of spirits they kept for guests. At the front was a bottle of Glenmorangie that had never been opened. Someone had brought it as a gift one Burns Night and Kenny had thanked them profusely before toasting the bard, Robert Burns, with Irn-Bru.

Pouring them all a single measure, in the heavy crystal tumblers that were rarely used, Honour returned to the kitchen to find Bridie standing at the window, looking out at the garden. The late-afternoon sky was clear of clouds and a flock of starlings were performing their acrobatics, thousands of birds, seething and pulsing across the sky as if being controlled, and connected by a single thread.

Honour set a glass on the counter next to Bridie, then handed one to Scott. 'There you go.'

Bridie lifted the glass and held it under her nose. 'You know, Tara kicking the football against the back of the house used to drive me bonkers.' She glanced over at Honour, whose mouth fell slack.

'Why didn't you say anything?'

'Because I got so used to it that eventually it was comforting.' Bridie shrugged sadly, then took a sip of whisky.

'I'm sorry, Bridie. I should've thought about it disturbing you.' Honour set her own glass down, the smell of the smoky whisky suddenly making her queasy.

Bridie shook her head. 'No, love. That's how I worked out that something was wrong. She hasn't been out there in a few weeks. At first, I thought maybe she was just too sad to play, missing her dad – you know. But then it began to bother me.' Bridie set her glass down and turned to face Honour. 'I said to Scott, something's up. But he told me to keep my nose out.' She shrugged as Scott nodded, sipping a little whisky. 'Not my strong point, as you know.'

Honour gave a half-smile and sat back down. 'So how did you find out?'

Bridie joined them at the table, looking pointedly at Scott.

He took a moment, then said, 'I was over at the Victoria last month, for some physio on my shoulder. I saw you and Tara there, in the orthopaedic ward, then last week I went to visit an old navy friend who's in there with liver cancer, and well...' He shrugged. 'It's not that big a place and when I saw Lorna come out of one of the treatment rooms, then you followed her into the corridor and looked upset, I put two and two together.'

Honour could picture how it had happened, imagining sweet, thoughtful Scott, spying her but having the discretion to say nothing, and to respect her privacy. 'It's just so hard to accept that this is happening. I've wanted to keep it as private as possible, thinking that the fewer people who know, the better.'

Bridie nodded. 'I understand, but, Honour, you must need help. I know you have your mum and dad, but, day to day, some support could take a bit of the weight off your shoulders.' She eyed Honour. 'If you decided to open up a bit about it, let the community know...'

Honour shook her head. 'No, Bridie. I can't have people thinking I can't cope.'

'Let me finish, lass,' Bridie chided her softly. 'If you do decide to let people in, it's a show of strength. Asking for help is not you saying I can't cope. Quite the opposite.' She sipped her whisky.

Scott drained his glass, keeping his eyes on Honour's. 'How many times have you and Kenny helped your friends and neighbours since you moved in here? I bet you can't even count.'

Honour leaned back in the chair and let herself remember some of the things she and Kenny had done for people they cared about. They'd paid Gregor for two months that he couldn't work when he'd broken his wrist falling on some ice. Honour had cleaned and done Bridie's shopping for weeks when she'd had shingles, two years earlier. A year after that, they'd delivered numerous packages of blankets and clothes, bottled water and groceries to three families whose houses had been badly burned in a fire near Marketgate. Recalling what she considered to be these and other minor acts of kindness, she could see Bridie begin to smile.

'So, what do you say? If you give me permission to activate

the phone tree, so to speak, as in tell Craig and his parents at Green's, the word will spread.'

Scott leaned forward on his elbows. 'Folk will want to pitch in, Honour, even if it's just to take your bins out, or save you cooking a night or two when you've been at the hospital all afternoon.' He tipped his big head to the side. 'Just think about it, love. Crailers take care of their own and you are family to many more people than you think. Your in-laws were an institution around here, and now, you and the kids are.' He smiled.

Bridie was nodding enthusiastically. 'We won't intrude, just lighten the load a little, if you'll let us.'

Honour thought about how nice it would be to come home to a home-cooked meal after hours at the hospital. To have her plants watered if she forgot, or to have her washing taken in if it started to rain while she was out. These small things had the potential to make a difference to her feeling overwhelmed, or strong, so perhaps she'd been wrong. By keeping people out, people who cared about them all, Honour had isolated herself, leaving her struggling with the fallout of her own stubborn silence.

As she took in Scott and Bridie's faces, both with such gentle eyes, and kind hearts, Honour felt undone. How fortunate they were to live in a place where there was such a sense of community. It seemed like an increasingly rare thing these days, and as Honour felt her walls coming down, so she instantly felt lighter, nimbler, simply thinking about friends rallying around when she was stretched to breaking point. 'Honestly, I *could* do with a little help, here and there.'

Bridie pressed her palms together. 'Good – good decision. I'll make sure that people know not to intrude, and I'll check with you before anyone does anything major.' She paused. 'What would be the most help to you, right now?'

Honour took only a moment to say, 'Shopping. Sometimes I'm just so wiped out at the end of the day that I can't make it to

Green's. We've had more fish and chips lately than we should in a lifetime.' She laughed softly as Bridie nodded decisively.

'Right. All I'll need is a list of the basic things you get weekly, and then we can check every few days for whatever else you need.'

Scott jumped in. 'Gregor was asking me the other day if he could do any odd jobs for you, too. He's afraid to tell you that he's fishing with Tom Flint now, over in Anstruther.' He shrugged. 'I told him to stop being such a silly beggar and to come and see you.'

Honour nodded, sad that Kenny's old fishing partner still felt as if he should stay away. 'Tell him I'll find him some jobs, no problem. The washing line needs to be replaced and there's a tile loose on the roof that rattles whenever it's windy.'

'See?' Bridie stood up, tucking her shirt back in behind her trousers. 'I bet there are lots of bits and bobs like that we can sort out.' She circled the table and put her arm around Honour's shoulder. 'These shoulders are broad, and strong, but you're not Atlas, Honour. I'm proud of you for doing this, and I'm sure your parents would feel the same.'

As Tara's last week of treatment had commenced, the community had come together, helpful but not intrusive, just as Bridie had promised. Scott had taken over caring for the garden, and Craig from Green's was delivering her shopping to the front door. Bridie would take it into the cottage and put it all away before Honour and the children got home. Craig had included a bunch of sunflowers the first time, which had made Honour well up, the thoughtful gesture just the beginning of a flow of kindness that, at times, took her breath away.

On the final day of treatment, Honour came home to find Gregor on her roof, a bag of tools around his waist and a paint-spattered ladder propped up against the side of the cottage. He looked down at her, a sheepish smile on his leathery face. 'Scott told me.' He jabbed a thumb at the roof. 'Thought I'd sort it for you.'

Honour was so pleased to see him, after weeks of absence, that she clapped her hands together. 'You're an angel, Gregor. Thank you. That bloody thing's been driving me mad for ages.' She gave him a thumbs up. 'Let me get the kids inside and I'll make you a cuppa.'

Going to get the milk, she spotted a bag of prawns in the fridge, a gift from Gregor, with a smiley face on a Post-it attached to it. Touched, she opened the bag and the musty smell brought her eyes closed. They hadn't had prawns in the house since Kenny had last brought them home, and while it shook her, it also felt like another hurdle that it was time she crossed.

Today being the last day of treatment, Honour had intended on cooking a special dinner, so when she found a plate of lamb chops, already cooked, in the fridge, she smiled gratefully, knowing it was Bridie. Relieved that even this small task had been completed for her, Honour walked back into the living room, where she saw the laundry basket sitting by Kenny's chair, all the sheets and towels she'd pinned out on the line that morning folded and stacked neatly inside it.

Tara was lying on the sofa and had dragged the tartan blanket over herself, while Callum was sitting on the floor, channel-surfing. 'What do you want to watch?' He turned to his sister.

'I don't care.' Tara's voice was brittle. 'Anything you want.' She was as pale as milk and her eyelids looked heavy. 'Just not *Star Trek* again.'

Callum tutted. 'That's the only thing good on.' He flicked between several channels before getting up and handing the remote to Tara. 'You choose. I can't be arsed.'

Honour's eyebrows jumped. 'Callum MacLeod. Language.'

He looked over at her, his glasses perched on the end of his

nose and his eyes wide behind the lenses. The haircut that
Malcolm, Bridie and Scott's son, had taken him for the day
before made him look older than his years and his jeans were
getting snug around his waist, accentuating the emerging triangular shape that reminded Honour of his father's slender frame.

'What? Lorna says it all the time.' He shrugged, a cheeky
twinkle in his eyes.

'Well, I'll be having words with Miss Lorna, then.' Honour
mocked annoyance.

He snorted softly, then flopped down next to Tara, dragging
some of the blanket over his knees.

'Oi, get off, Call-umpty-dumpty,' Tara huffed. 'You weigh a
ton.'

He pulled a face at her. 'Oh, shut your cakehole.'

'Callum,' Honour warned, as he grimaced comically.

'Sorry.'

Just as Honour started to cross the room to pick up the
laundry basket and take it upstairs, her phone rang in her back
pocket. Fishing it out, it took her a moment or two to register
who was calling. Seeing the two initials, a wave of panic hit her,
shaking her fragile world, once again.

23

Out in the back garden, the early-evening sky was overcast, and the smell of vinegar floated up from Bailey's on Shoregate, which happened when the wind was coming in from the south. Honour was perched on the edge of the wooden planter box, where her neglected herbs and lavender were slowly coming back to life, thanks to Scott's regular ministrations. She looked at the phone and counted the fourth ring, usually the last but one before a call would go to voicemail. But deciding that she was done hiding from Jack, she answered.

'Honour, it's Jack.' His voice sparked a slew of uncomfortable memories, making her cross her arms protectively around her middle.

'Yes, I know. What do you want, Jack?' She'd let irritation seep into her voice, so she took a moment to regroup, and sat up straighter.

'Look, I know you don't want to hear from me, but I heard about Tara.'

Honour was rocked, this being the last thing she expected. Her pulse began to race as she stood up and carefully closed the back door. 'Who told you?' There was no point pretending she didn't know what he meant. She didn't have time for those games anymore.

'Malcolm phoned me. He thought I'd know, so...' His voice faded, a trace of uncertainty creeping in. 'Don't be angry with him.'

Honour struggled to find words, to gain clarity about how she should handle this, and as she paced back and forth along the gravel path, an image of Kenny's face flashed in her mind. She saw the hurt, the profound sadness, and then his request of her to cut Jack off, as Kenny felt he had been cut off, and Honour was flooded with her old friend guilt – guilt at breaking more than just her word, or at letting his hand slip away. 'I'm not angry with Malcolm, I'm just surprised.' She glanced at the door, checking that the children were still safely inside, and out of earshot.

'I don't know if there's anything I can do, Honour, but I want you to know that I'm here. If you need help, please tell me.'

The idea of him helping her was so beyond her imagination that Honour laughed. It was a short, harsh kind of sound and as she heard it, she flinched. Despite everything that had gone on between her husband and his brother, and her honouring Kenny's wishes in keeping Jack out of their lives, she was not a cruel person, and that laugh had smacked of cruelty. 'Listen, Jack. I appreciate the offer, but we are fine.' She saw a shadow move in the kitchen and squinted as Tara's shape came into focus, getting a glass of water at the sink. 'I've got to go.'

There was a moment of silence and then Jack sighed. 'OK. Well, you know where to reach me. I really want to say how sorry I am that this is happening to you, Honour.'

Honour forced a swallow. 'It's happening to Tara, Jack. She's the priority now.'

'I know, I just meant...' He stopped himself. 'Well, I'll let you go. Give my love to the kids, will you?'

Honour frowned, wondering if never having met him, the children would even register who Uncle Jack was, after all this time. Shaking her head, she said, 'Bye, Jack.'

'Bye, Honour.'

Honour ended the call, her heart beating like a drum as she shoved the phone away, smoothed her hair and took a moment to gather herself. After more than a decade of not seeing or having any contact with him, believing that he was out of their lives forever, that hearing her brother-in-law's voice could still take the feet from under her was not only disturbing, but frustrating.

Doctor Ford was fiddling with a pen, and the slightly anxious edge to her voice had made Honour's heart rate spike as she pictured Tara and Callum, out on the back lawn where she'd left them, happily playing a game of snap on the old blanket from the shed. Marion was keeping an eye on them and had told Honour not to rush back, that she'd organise a snack if they wanted anything.

'So, Mrs MacLeod, Doctor Hail from the Victoria sent me the report on Tara's post-chemotherapy scans.' She studied Honour's face.

Honour was holding her breath and, on her lap, out of sight of the doctor, her fingers were crossed on both hands. 'Right,' she croaked.

'It appears that the tumour hasn't shrunk, so he is recommending surgery to remove it. Then, depending on how surgery goes, a possible second course of chemotherapy.' She set the pen down and linked her fingers together. 'I know this isn't the news you were hoping for, Mrs MacLeod, but there's reason to hope that it has remained localised.'

Having come into the room, her every fibre focused on receiving good news, Honour's mind was instantly awash with images of operating rooms, scalpels, her daughter's knee open to the surgeon's hands and, inside it, an uninvited cluster of cells eating away at Tara's joint. As Honour fought to banish the gruesome pictures she'd conjured, focus on Doctor Ford's words, and find the light inside them, it felt as if the room was swaying. Gripping the arms of the chair, she willed the swoop of fear that sucked at her core to allow her to speak.

'Mrs MacLeod?' The doctor leaned forward, her wavy hair falling over her shoulder, and her eyes more green than turquoise today. 'Are you all right?'

Honour wanted to scream. Of course she wasn't all right. Her worst fears were coming to life and there was nothing she could do to change that. Taking a moment, she nodded. 'So, what if the surgery doesn't go well? Or if they find that it's spread?' She swallowed over the lump in her throat. 'What then?'

Doctor Ford sat back again. 'Well, I don't like to speculate.' She pressed her lips together as if shutting whatever else she knew inside.

Honour felt her self-control seeping away, her determination to see the positive in this mess going with it. 'Please just indulge me, then. What are all the potential outcomes we should prepare for? I need to know.'

Fiona Ford looked taken aback at Honour's tone, but Honour held her gaze steady, needing to know everything – however frightening – that her amazing, brave, girl could be facing.

'Once the surgeon is in there, they'll find out whether the tumour has metastasised, also how much damage has been done to the knee joint. At this point, it's what is called limb-sparing surgery.' She paused, as Honour frowned at the term, its meaning all too clear.

'And if it's not possible to remove it all, what then?'

Doctor Ford hesitated. 'In certain cases, the joint is affected to the point where the patient might need a bone graft, or even a full joint replacement.'

Honour closed her eyes briefly and tried to picture Tara with a titanium knee joint, ugly scars on her creamy skin, and enduring the months of rehabilitation and physiotherapy she'd likely need to function normally, never mind play football, if she ever wanted to, again.

'If the joint is too damaged to sustain a replacement, or if the tumour is large or has a high potential to recur, then, worst case, amputation would be another course of action to consider.' Seeing Honour pale, Doctor Ford patted the air. 'Now, I'm not saying that's the case for Tara, but it is a possibility if limb-sparing is not an option.'

There was a buzzing in Honour's ears, as if a thousand bees were circling her head. Her tongue felt as if it had doubled in size as she tried to process what she'd just heard. *Amputation.* It wasn't possible that that word and her precious daughter's name had been used in the same context.

'Children do particularly well in those situations, as they adapt to prosthetic limbs more quickly than adults.' Doctor Ford's eyes were swimming with concern. 'Mrs MacLeod, it's important that we take one step at a time. It's not helpful to you, or Tara, to start worrying about scenarios that may not come about.'

Honour could hear her pulse now, her face burning and seeming to throb in time with the thumping of her heart. While this was already too much to absorb, she needed to know everything. Knowledge was power, and whatever else she learned from here, being fully informed was the only way she'd not drown. She could handle most things, but she'd had enough of the unexpected for a lifetime. 'I understand what you're saying, but this is how I cope. I think through every scenario so that I can plan, make contingencies. I need to find ways to help my daughter navigate all of this, the only way I know how to.' She blinked rapidly as the press of new tears threatened to blind her. 'If all of that doesn't work, what are our options?'

Doctor Ford frowned, her eyes flicking from Honour's to the door. 'As I say, it's speculation at this point, and Doctor Hail will give you more detail, but if surgery, chemotherapy or an amputation are not effective, and if the bone marrow is compromised, in some cases bone marrow transplants are performed.'

Honour stared ahead, the window behind the doctor seeming to ripple as the late-August light filtered through the textured glass. The room smelled of menthol and sanitiser, and as she mentally sifted through the questions that she still had, her mind spinning wildly, Honour suddenly needed fresh air to clear her head.

Standing up, she slung her bag over her shoulder and gripped the back of the chair. 'Thank you for being honest with me.' She studied Fiona's face, seeing relief ease the tension in her jaw. 'If I have any more questions, can I phone you?'

'Of course.' The doctor stood up. 'We'll be in touch as soon as we have a surgery date. It could be as soon as next month.'

Honour felt the air leave her in a rush. The idea of waiting for any length of time was nightmarish, and yet she needed time to prepare Tara, and Callum, and her parents, for this next step. 'OK. Thanks.' She opened the heavy door, hearing laughter coming from the waiting room. The joyful sound that once would have made her smile now felt like an insult she must accept.

Shaking the doctor's hand, she turned and walked into the hall, wondering how she was going to hold it together enough to tell her daughter that not only must she have surgery soon, but that might not be the end of this ghastly journey.

Tara stared at Honour, her eyes filled not with fear, but with anger. 'Why is this happening to me? It's not bloody fair.' Her chin began to tremble.

'Can she say that?' Next to Tara, Callum was pale, having had a flare of his Ménière's disease that had left him dizzy and nauseated, and taking up residence on the couch for the past two days. His flare-up was heightening Honour's sadness, seeing both her children struggling simultaneously, another cruel blow.

Honour looked at them both, wondering how she had failed them so badly. 'Today she can, Cal. And it's *not* bloody fair, my love. There's no other way to put it.' Honour eased herself in between her children, planting her bare feet firmly on the silky rug beneath the old chest.

Her mother sat across the room, in Kenny's chair, her eyes bright and an odd smile frozen on her face. Honour had brought her up to speed as soon as she'd got home from the doctor's office, before asking her mother to stay with her while she talked to the children. This time, Honour needed the calm support her mother always offered, a dusting of optimism on the grim news Honour had just shared with Tara.

'So, they take the tumour out, then I have more chemo?' Tara's shoulders were slumped forward, and Honour was shaken to see Tara's vertebrae clearly visible under her Dundee United T-shirt.

'Yes, that's the plan.' Honour gently rubbed Tara's back, feeling her lean into the circular strokes.

'When is the operation?'

'I'm not sure yet, love. We'll have to wait and see when the hospital sends an appointment.'

At this, Marion's eyes seemed to come alive.

'Honour, how about we make some tea?' She stood up, tucking the hair behind her ears.

Puzzled, Honour frowned. 'Now?'

'Yes, I'm parched.' Marion widened her eyes, a sure sign that she needed a private chat.

Aware that her mother wouldn't do this unless she had something important to say, Honour hugged the children to her, then stood up. 'We'll be back in a few. Do you two want a drink?'

Tara shook her head as Callum nodded. 'Chocolate milk, please.'

'Fine.' Honour ruffled his hair and then followed her mother into the kitchen. Marion stood by the back door, her hands clasped in front of her chest as if she were praying. 'What's going on?' Honour pulled the kitchen door almost to and faced her mother.

'I think you should go private for the surgery. It could be weeks before she gets an appointment on the NHS and who knows what could happen in that time.' Marion's face was flushed.

Honour was taken aback, this not having entered her head as an option. 'I can't afford it, Mum.' She shook her head. 'I mean, I doubt I could.' The insurance payment had finally come through for the *Lila Rose* just a week earlier, but Honour was still worried about money, and making it last as long as possible.

Marion moved in closer and lowered her voice to a whisper. 'We can probably afford it. Your dad and me. We've been desperate to help you somehow, and this is something we can finally do.' She eyed Honour. 'From what I've read, timing is everything with cancer, and the longer you wait...' She shrugged. 'Please let us help Tara, Honour. At least let's look into it, see how much it'd be.'

Honour soaked in her mother's features, the soft wrinkles at the edges of the gentle eyes that took on a particular glow whenever she was with her grandchildren. Honour tried to picture a time when her parents had not been there for her, or her family, knowing that none existed, and her gratitude left her unsteady on her feet. As she wrapped her arms around her mother, breathing in the familiar lily-of-the-valley scent and feeling the sheer maternal force of Marion's arms around her, Honour gave way to tears.

'I just want her through this as soon as possible, Mum. So, yes. Let's find out how much it is, and then I can talk to the hospital. See if they'd take her as a private patient. I like Doctor Hail, so I want her to stay with him.' Honour let her mother rock her gently, as the tears trickled down Honour's face and darkened the shoulder of Marion's shirt. 'Thank you for thinking about it, and for offering. I'll pay you back, of course.'

Leaning back from her, Marion smiled. This time, a genuine smile, filled with relief, and palpable positivity. 'Don't think about that now. We'll make this happen. You'll see. And then the wee lamb can start to recover, whether that's with a new knee, or not.' Marion halted, obviously unprepared to go beyond the best-case outcome she was working hard to manifest for them all.

Unable to see beyond it either, Honour nodded. *Please, let this be the last challenge my girl has to face. Surely, as a kind and loving young person, who has never hurt another living being, she deserves that grace?*

24

Less than two weeks had passed since they'd seen Doctor Hail, who had said that he would be able to take Tara on as a private patient. Events had then moved so quickly that Honour had felt as if she were floating through the days leading up to surgery – as if she were being controlled by a celestial puppeteer with a twisted sense of humour. While she'd resented the feeling of helplessness that created, one bright spot in the unnerving mayhem had been that Tara had begun to smile again, having a date for surgery giving her an end point to focus on.

Honour's parents, Lorna, Bridie, Scott, Gregor, Craig, and the rest of the community had continued their support as Honour prepared her little family for this day. Now, as she paced along the overly warm corridor in the Victoria Hospital surgical wing, counting her steps to help pass the time, Marion and Kirk were at home, waiting for Callum to come home from school.

He had protested, saying that he wanted to go with them to the hospital, but Honour had told him the best way he could help would be to make sure that Grandma and Grandpa were OK, and not worrying too much. She knew by the way he'd squinted at her that he wasn't buying the placatory logic, but the gentle sage in him had come to the fore and he'd simply nodded.

Kirk had downloaded *Apollo 13* and Marion had told Callum he could have whatever he wanted for dinner. Earlier that morning, as Honour had hugged her parents goodbye, seeing their eyes fill as they'd kissed Tara's cheeks – Honour had felt as if her heart might implode. A mixture of pride in her amazingly strong children, gratitude for her supportive parents, and the way that her friends and neighbours had rallied around them was literally filling her up to bursting, keeping the fear at bay. Determined to hold steady, steer them all to a positive endpoint, she'd smiled at her parents and Callum, as her heart had thundered in her chest, every beat a reminder of how hard they all were working to move through this, together.

Now Tara had been in surgery for over five hours and there was only so much watery coffee Honour could drink. The smell of bleach filled her head as with each step, her shoes squeaked conspicuously on the highly polished floors. She tried to quiet them as she walked past the nurses' station, for the umpteenth time, as her eyes strayed to the monitor on the desk. There was a spreadsheet of patient names and surgeries flickering on the screen and as she halted her progress, she guiltily scanned the list, looking for Tara's name. Knowing that she shouldn't be snooping, a tap on her shoulder made her jump.

'Mrs MacLeod?'

'Oh, yes.' She spun around and pressed her palm to her chest.

'Tara's out of surgery and in the recovery room.' Bright blue eyes behind a surgical mask held her gaze. Doctor Hail was in his mid-fifties, a tall, lean man with long, elegant fingers – fingers that Honour had thought fitting for a surgeon, especially one who would be cutting into her daughter's body. Throughout the entire process, he had been patient and infor-

mative, answering all her questions without a trace of conde-
scension, and now, as he removed his mask and rubbed his palm
over the crown of his sand-coloured head, Honour caught a tell-
tale shadow pass behind his eyes.

'Is everything OK?' She winced at the banality of her question, watching as he pointed to a row of plastic chairs, set
against the wall.

'She did very well. Let's sit.' He held his hand out, as if to
lead her there. The gesture instantly sent alarm bells ringing as
Honour followed him on unsteady legs.

As she sat on the edge of a chair and he perched across from
her, Honour was struggling to keep from screaming, *Tell me
what's going on, for God's sake.*

'We were able to remove the tumour, but it was larger than
originally indicated, so we replaced her knee joint with an
internal prosthesis.' He paused, as Honour held her breath. His
next words could potentially change her, and Tara's, life
forever, and while Honour was desperate to hear what he had to
say, it also terrified her.

'A knee replacement?' she whispered.

'Yes. We used a modifiable device that can be adjusted as
Tara grows.' He gave a single nod, then continued, 'But based
on the size and nature of the tumour, there is a high potential
for recurrence.' He kept his voice steady, his eyes on hers.
'Depending on the next scan results, and the blood tests we do
post-operatively, we may need to look at further intervention.'

Honour was working hard to process what he was saying,
the words recurrence and intervention bringing her to the very
edge of the seat. 'What kind of intervention? More surgery? Or
chemo?'

Doctor Hail pursed his lips, his eyes flicking to the nurses'
station behind them. 'Dependent on the scans and blood test
results, more chemo might not be the best course of action. If
Tara's bone marrow has been compromised by the chemo-

therapy she's already had, which is not uncommon, we could be looking at amputation.'

Honour felt as if he had sliced her open, her resolve to be strong leaking out and forming an ugly puddle on the floor under her chair. 'Oh, my God,' she croaked, her hands curling into fists in her lap. Flooded with images of her girl in a wheelchair, her left leg terminating above the knee in a bandaged stump that she would later have to fit into a prosthetic limb, Honour felt as if she might pass out.

'We're going to do our absolute best for Tara, Mrs MacLeod. Rest assured, we won't recommend anything that isn't essential.' He leaned forward, his fingers gripping his angular knees. 'The sooner we can get the post-op tests done, the better, then we'll develop an ongoing treatment plan.' He paused. 'There's also a bone marrow transplant to consider.'

Honour scanned his face, the eyes now shrouded in professional calm, something she needed but wasn't sure what to do with. 'How long until we know which direction we're going?' Unable to sit any longer, she stood up, steadying herself by pressing her calf into the edge of the plastic chair behind her. It gave beneath the pressure as Honour heard the crackle of an intercom, and the hum of conversation from a room down the hall. The noises were not particularly loud, or offensive, but in this moment, they felt like claxons blaring, shattering the delicate film that had formed over her question.

'We'll move things along as quickly as possible. My best guess is that we'll have a clear picture by the end of next week.'

Honour mentally calculated what that meant, September usually being a busy time with the children back in school, and Honour taking on more shifts at the care home. Kenny loved September, as the shrimp, lobster and crab haul would begin to tail off, meaning he had slightly shorter days at sea and more time to spend with the family. Picturing his eyes, particularly the tiny gold flecks that caught the light when he looked into the sun, Honour craved his presence more now than she had since he'd been gone – the force of strength that would flow from his body to hers, like osmosis, feeding her what she lacked.

Battling to focus on the doctor's face, she felt paralysed by all that they didn't know. Amputation had been talked about as a worst-case scenario, but even with her limited understanding of the case, she knew exactly what recurrence meant, for Tara. More pain. More surgeries. More chemo – if her system could take it. A bone marrow transplant had been mentioned, too, but that had seemed like a last resort, so to hear him say it now was startling.

Doctor Hail stood up. 'I'll be in touch when we have results. Tara will stay here for a week or so and then we'll begin her physiotherapy. We'll manage her pain and help her adjust to the new knee before she comes home.' He smiled, his eyes filled with compassion. 'Any questions?'

Honour had to fight a nervous impulse to laugh. 'Um, yes. What situation would make a bone marrow transplant necessary? It can be brutal on the patient, from what I understand.' She swept the hair away from her forehead, the skin clammy under her fingertips.

He nodded slowly, acknowledging the gravity of the question. 'In Tara's case, the chemotherapy didn't have the effect we were hoping for, in terms of shrinking the tumour. So, in the situation where it recurs or has metastasised, further chemo wouldn't be the best course of action. Her bone marrow is already weakened, so a transplant would be the better option.'

Honour nodded, compelled to push a little further. 'Can I get tested now, so that if she needs that, we're ready?' She held his gaze.

'Well, you could be tested, but parents generally are only a half-match for their children and a full match is what we'd be looking for.' He paused. 'A sibling would be the best chance for a full match.'

Honour felt her heart contract. She should have done more research – known that she more than likely wouldn't be a sufficient match. As she let the information sink in, Callum's face flashed behind her eyes. As fate would have it, her sweet, gentle boy had a better chance of being able to donate his marrow to save Tara than Honour did, but with his Ménière's disease, surely he would be at risk for complications? Needing to know all the implications, Honour said, 'You know we have a son, Callum.'

Doctor Hail nodded.

'He is nearly nine, but has Ménière's disease, so he's immune compromised.' The knot in her throat began to tighten. 'If he was a full match, what risks would he be facing as a donor?'

'Well, bone marrow harvesting calls for a needle to be placed into the soft centre of the bone, usually in the hip or sternum.' He tapped his chest. 'The procedure is done in an operating room under anaesthesia, so there are some inherent risks with the anaesthesia itself, and for infection. Donors can also experience back or hip pain, fatigue, muscle pain, headache or bruising at the incision site.' He paused as Honour tried to imagine her fragile boy on an operating table. 'In your son's case, I'd say the highest risk factor would be for infection. Despite our best efforts, though extremely rarely, it can happen.'

Honour stared at him, the words she needed evading her. Was it possible that if Tara needed a transplant, and Callum was a full match, that she could put her vulnerable son's health at risk to save her daughter?

25

After her spending an hour with Tara, as she slipped in and out of sleep, the nurse had told Honour to go home and get some rest, then come back for evening visiting hours. Seeing her reluctance to leave, the nurse had assured Honour that Tara would not be left alone and that they'd phone if she woke up fully.

Honour now drove home from Kirkcaldy on autopilot, the beauty of the Fife coast villages she passed on her right slithering past unnoticed. The water looked angry, long white curls topping the parade of waves rippling across the surface, and the sky had taken on a purple hue, usually a portent for storms to come.

The doctor had said that blood relatives would be the first they would test to find a match, and as she thought through the tiny group that she might now call upon, Honour's eyes filled. Her parents would insist on being tested, she knew that without question. She would be tested herself immediately, too, though Doctor Hail had said that, at best, they'd all be half-matches. She was reluctant to put Callum through the process due to the risks associated with that, in his case, and she was wrestling with the onerous decision that had raised its head – whether she could potentially jeopardise his health to help his sister.

With Kenny and his parents all gone, there was no one else to ask, and the sad reality of the reduced size of her family took Honour by surprise.

Not something she'd given much thought to until this very moment, she was struck by thoughts of her own mortality and if, God forbid, something happened to her, what would become of her children?

She parked the car near the harbour as the wind picked up, bringing the musk of seaweed mixed with the salt-and-vinegar combination that floated around Bailey's fish shop. As she took her bag from the car and locked it, going straight back to the cottage suddenly felt claustrophobic.

She'd phoned from the hospital to tell her parents that Tara was through surgery and her mother had said not to rush back, as Callum was fine, had eaten a massive lunch and was now playing Monopoly with his grandpa. Knowing that her son was safe, and calm, gave Honour the licence she needed to take a few minutes to herself before she went home and had to find a brave smile, tell them all the positives of Tara's situation, knowing that soon after she'd have to share what Doctor Hail had told her about the prognosis.

Turning towards Castle Promenade, Honour pulled her leather jacket tighter around her and walked past the handful of shopfronts, keeping her head down – hoping to get to the end of Shoregate without meeting anyone she knew. The fates were on her side, delivering her safely to the old castle wall, and along to where the sundial stood. She looked down at the stone face, her hair whipping around her neck like a scarf as two gulls screeched overhead. She tipped her head back, watched them bank in the wind, seeming to hang, motionless in the strong updraught.

As the image of Tara's wan face flickered behind Honour's

eyes, she stepped forward, touched the stone pedestal of the dial, and then kissed her fist. Pressing her mouth into her curled fingers, she muttered, 'Kenny, I need your help. Tara is in trouble, and I'm scared.' She blinked her vision clear. 'She needs your strength to get through this. She depended on you for so much. I'm doing my best, but she misses you terribly.' Honour gulped, a surge of self-pity making her shake her head defiantly and push her shoulders back. 'I'm not going to bloody well cry anymore. Just please be here for us, Kenny. In whatever way you can.'

Honour turned her back on the sundial and looked along the castle wall, when something inside her shifted. Earlier, as she'd been thinking through all the family members that could be tested as donors, one person had not made the list. Kenny's brother, Jack. He was the only other blood relative who might be a match, albeit a remote chance, and as Honour stopped in her tracks, the idea of contacting him to ask this of him felt unthinkable.

After her promise to Kenny, and the way she'd dismissed Jack when he'd phoned, the painful memories that she had buried for so many years once again threatened to overwhelm her. She turned and leaned her back against the wall and forced herself to think of bright things – the smell of the pots of lavender on her front steps, the sound of Tara laughing, of Callum and her bickering then ending up giggling together, feeling the strength of her mother and father's arms around her – until, eventually, her heart rate returned to normal.

Whatever happened next, she would keep Jack at arm's length unless there were no other viable options. She owed that to Kenny's memory, at the very least.

Tara lay on her back, her head turned towards the window and her leg supported by a pillow under the knee. She looked fragile, as if her lean body were sinking into the mattress, the blanket barely rising above the surface of the bed, other than over her raised knee. Her thinning hair had been brushed and was in a low ponytail that fanned scarlet across the pillow, and as Honour walked slowly into the room, unsure whether her daughter was awake or not, Tara turned and looked at her mother.

Honour instantly saw the wet tracks on Tara's cheeks, the familiar flush to her face and across her nose. Honour's heart lurched as she perched on the edge of the bed and lifted Tara's hand. 'You're awake, darling girl. How are you feeling?' She gently thumbed away a tear that hung under Tara's jaw. 'Are you in pain?'

Tara shook her head. 'Only a little. It's dull, but deep inside.' She laid her hand on her knee, the gesture making Honour wince.

'Careful, love.' She tucked a wisp of hair behind Tara's ear.

'I can't really feel it.' Tara lightly tapped her knee. 'The bandages make it sort of numb.'

Grateful for that small mercy, Honour shifted off the bed, dragged the plastic chair closer and sat on the edge of it. Honour could see the sadness cloaking Tara's fine features, a face that she knew better than her own. 'What's wrong, sweetheart? You can tell or ask me anything.'

Tara took a few moments, her eyes flicking between the window and Honour's face, then she shifted a little higher up the bed. 'Is the cancer gone?'

The simplicity of the question was not unexpected, nor the directness of her daughter's manner, but Honour took a few seconds to gather herself.

'Doctor Hail said the operation went well. They replaced your knee joint to make sure they got rid of it all.' She nodded as Tara's eyes bored into hers.

'Do I have to do more chemo?'

Honour shook her head. 'Not at the moment. In fact, you might not need to again.'

Tara nodded, her fingers going to her mouth as fresh tears began to trickle down her cheeks.

'Oh, Tara love. Talk to me. What are you feeling, or worrying about?' Honour leaned her elbows on the bed and gripped Tara's hand tighter.

'I have to tell you something.' Tara licked her lips. 'Don't be cross, OK?'

Honour frowned, convinced that there wasn't anything Tara could confess that would make her cross, ever again. 'Of course not.'

Tara swallowed, then whispered, 'I lied about not wanting to play football anymore. It felt bad to want to play when Dad couldn't be there.' She shrugged miserably. 'So, when you asked me, I lied.'

Honour tried to smile at her daughter, her insides crumbling not only at Tara talking about Kenny this way, but at the real reason for Tara's change of heart proving to be what Honour had suspected. 'That's OK, love. I understand, I really do.'

Tara's chin trembled as she continued, 'I'll never play for Scotland, now.' She tapped her knee again. 'Dad said I was good enough to.'

Feeling as if the sky had dropped to just inches above her head at her daughter's despair, Honour took a moment, then said, 'You were good enough, Tara. Dad was right.' No sooner had she said it than Honour bit down on her lip. She had used the past tense when referring to Tara's capabilities and, suddenly, all Honour could think about was righting that wrong. 'You might still be able to play, though. People do a lot after joint replacements. We'll ask Doctor Hail and see what he says. Don't write yourself off just yet.'

Tara covered her face with her hands, her arms quivering. 'I miss Dad. Why is all this happening?'

Unable to bear the remaining distance between them, Honour moved onto the bed, careful not to disturb Tara's knee as she lay next to her and wrapped her arms around her daughter. 'We will get through this, Tara. You have so much living to do, and so much to give this world. If it's not professional football, then you'll find a new passion. You're too clever, and kind, and positive, not to.'

Tara leaned into her mother, her voice hitching. 'I hate frigging cancer.'

Honour closed her eyes and began to rock Tara gently, the way she had when she'd been a baby. 'I hate it much more, my love. Believe me.'

As she rocked Tara and waited for her to stop crying, Honour wished for the umpteenth time that this invasive, cruel condition had come for her, not her darling girl. Why did the universe seem to be punishing Tara – an innocent – for the mistakes of her parents?

26

Tara had been home for a week, her spirits gradually improving as she navigated the cottage on her crutches and made slow but steady progress with her physiotherapy. Her ingrained determination had kicked in as she pushed through pain, and the fear of uncertainty about her new knee, and, watching from the other side of the room while she battled on with her therapist, Honour's heart had taken up permanent residence in her mouth.

She'd been trying not to tiptoe around Tara, fuss her too much or make her feel more vulnerable than she already was, but it was the hardest thing her daughter had ever faced, and Honour hated the helplessness of being reduced to an observer. This was the first serious thing that had happened that she couldn't fix for Tara, and it was torturous.

Callum had been nothing short of amazing since Tara had been home, bringing her glasses of milk, letting her choose what they watched on TV and carefully carrying her tray into the kitchen when she'd finished her meals. Only once had he complained, when, on the first night, Honour had said that Tara needed to sleep on the couch for a few days, to avoid using the stairs.

Honour had dragged the old air mattress out for herself and, seeing it, Callum had said, 'I can sleep down here, too. Tara and me can do a tickly-feet bed.' Honour had told him no, that he and Tara sleeping at opposite ends of the couch, as they liked to do sometimes, wasn't a good idea. When he'd resisted, and she'd reiterated that he needed to go up to his own bed, he'd crossed his arms tightly around himself and pouted, saying, 'That's not fair. You'll probably have fun down here without me.'

As soon as Honour had taken him aside and explained that she was worried that he might kick or hurt Tara by mistake in the night, he'd grudgingly agreed to sleep upstairs on the condition that he could stay up half an hour later than usual, even on school nights. Amused at his negotiating skills, and not wanting him to feel any more excluded from what was happening to his sister, Honour had agreed.

Now, Callum and Dougie were up in his room playing with his telescope, while Tara lay on the sofa watching TV. It being a Saturday, Lorna had brought lunch for them all, and their empty plates were now stacked in the sink.

Honour and Lorna sat at the kitchen table, a pot of coffee between them, along with the remains of a raspberry cheesecake that Bridie had dropped in that morning that they were both picking at with forks.

'So, you'll know soon.' Lorna put a chunk of cheesecake into her mouth.

'Doctor Hail said next week, but he'd phone if the results came back sooner.' Honour set her fork down, her appetite not what it used to be. Eating had been one of her favourite things to do, something they especially enjoyed as a family, but now it felt like a function of survival rather than a pleasurable experience.

'Doc Hail's a gem. When there's any info, he'll be in touch.'

Lorna cut another sliver off the cheesecake, letting the loaded fork hang in front of her mouth. 'Tell me your fears.' She eyed Honour. 'Your worst fears. If you say them out loud, they lose their power.' She popped the cheesecake into her mouth.

Honour took a moment, then shook her head. 'It's not like talking about a bad dream, Lorna. If I say the words out loud, it makes them a possibility, like I'm giving them room to grow.'

Lorna frowned. 'Hm, well tell me something else. How's Callum coping? He seems to be doing all right, whenever he's over with us.'

'He's amazing. Honestly, sometimes I feel like he's the grown-up and I'm the child.' Honour nodded sadly. 'He's wise beyond his years – at least most of the time – so I haven't sheltered him from what's happening. It helps him to have the facts, so he's pretty much up to date with everything, except the donation thing.'

Lorna stopped chewing and put her fork down. 'So, what are you thinking about that?'

'At the moment, I'm not having him tested, not until we know that none of the rest of us are a match. I can't put him through that if it's not absolutely necessary, and even then, with his Ménière's, I'm not sure I can risk him getting an infection, or something worse happening. He's vulnerable enough as it is.' Honour's throat began to tighten as, once again, she considered the dilemma that left her staring at the ceiling in the dead of night, tears leaking from the edges of her eyes and trickling onto her pillowcase. Pitting one child against the other in a freakish game of health roulette was undoubtedly the hardest decision Honour could ever have to face, and she dreaded the day that she might have no choice.

Lorna extended her hand across the table to Honour, who gripped her friend's slender fingers. 'Honour, you might not even have to go there. Once the results are in on Tara's scans and bloods, whatever further treatment she needs will be clear.

Let's try to focus on the now, how well she's doing with the new knee, how determined she is to get better, and the bright future she's going to have when all this is behind her.'

Honour took in Lorna's face, the moss-green eyes, the long, fair hair caught up at the crown with a pincer-like clip and the dusting of freckles across the slender nose, and despite the kind intention of her words, Honour wanted to snatch her hand back, shout at Lorna that if she was able to focus on the positives in this hellish scenario, that was only because it wasn't her baby going through it. As Honour fought the power of the anger that surged through her, unwilling to take her fear out on her friend, she simply nodded.

As if reading her mind, Lorna gave a soft sigh. 'Look, I didn't mean to sound like I'm discounting how serious this is. You know I love you and your kids like my own. It's an annoying habit of mine to quote the cheesy, inspirational calendar that's up in the staff canteen whenever I'm worried.' She grimaced, then tightened her grip on Honour's fingers. 'Whatever happens, you are not alone.'

Honour let out a strangled laugh, picturing the calendar. 'I don't know how to thank you for everything you've done and are doing for us all,' she gulped. 'It's so good to know you're on our side.'

Lorna's eyes filled as she sat back, lifted her fork and scooped up a huge piece of cheesecake. Sniffing, she stuffed it into her mouth, where, almost imperceptibly, her chin was quivering. Seeing it, Honour stood up and circled the table, then, standing behind Lorna's chair, she wrapped her arms around Lorna's petite shoulders.

'It's OK to let me know you're scared, Lorna. I tell you all the time.' Honour caught the earthy scent of sandalwood that lingered on Lorna's skin just as Honour's phone buzzed on the table next to her plate. Her heart leaping as it always did now whenever the phone rang, Honour released her friend and walked quickly to her place, picking up the phone.

Lorna wiped her nose on a paper napkin, stood up and lifted their plates, heading for the sink. 'Who's that?' she mouthed, as she set the plates on top of the pile in the sink.

Honour's pulse was racing as she looked at the screen, the number for the Victoria Hospital before her. 'It's the hospital.' She frowned at Lorna, whose eyes widened. 'On a Saturday?'

'I'll wait in there, with Tara,' Lorna whispered, giving Honour a thumbs up as she walked into the hall.

27

Honour's hands were shaking as she swiped the screen a couple of times before successfully answering the call. 'Hello?'

'Mrs MacLeod, it's Doctor Hail. I wanted to catch you as soon as the results came in. Is this a bad time?'

Honour shook her head. 'Not at all. What's going on?'

The next moments that passed seemed elongated, like chewing gum was stretched between each one, until Honour was almost ready to ask her question again.

'Tara's blood tests show that there's an elevated ALP level – that's alkaline phosphate. It's a chemical that is a measure of bone activity – indicating that the level of activity is higher than normal.'

Honour sat down hard at the table, feeling her face begin to tingle. She might not fully understand this, but she remembered that term from the very start of this nightmare and she'd surmised enough from his guarded tone to know it wasn't good. 'So, what now?'

'The high number is generally a marker for cancer, so it's likely that Tara's tumour has metastasised. She also has a low white blood cell count, which, as we discussed last week, means that her bone marrow has been compromised by the chemo-therapy. Her neutrophil count is low, too, so she's highly suscep-tible to infection, which, should that happen, she'd struggle to fight off. We must do everything we can to protect her from that happening, Mrs MacLeod, so I'd recommend we bring her back into the hospital, where the environment is more controlled.'

Honour closed her eyes, the idea of not having Tara at home so painful, she could hardly breathe. 'Are you sure? I mean about it spreading?' She stared out of the window, where on the adjoining wall with Bridie and Scott's house, the leaves on the clematis were turning brown – the vine shrivelling as the year began to wane. The wind was buffeting the wooden trellis, making it look as if it might break loose from the wall and collapse onto the grass, just as Honour felt she might collapse onto the floor and let her pain ooze out onto the tiles like a bloodletting.

'The blood tests are an accurate gauge, Mrs MacLeod, so we need to move forward with a treatment plan.'

Honour forced herself to focus, ask pertinent questions, rather than let her anxiety make her mute. 'So, what's the next step?'

'Well, at this point, I'd say that a bone marrow transplant would be Tara's best chance of beating this.'

Honour nodded, the concept one that she'd been subcon-sciously readying herself for ever since he'd first mentioned it as an option. All she could think about now was how quickly they could proceed with the testing, so she said, 'I want to get tested now. And so do my parents.'

'Right. I understand you wanting to do that, but, as we discussed, it's highly likely that none of you will be a full match.'

She sucked in her bottom lip. 'I know, but how soon can we have the tests?'

It seemed he was hesitating to answer, as she pictured him

looking in a giant ledger, as if he kept things like that written down somewhere. 'We can arrange them for this coming week, if that's convenient.'

'It is. Just tell me where and when, and we'll all be there.' She stood up, feeling as if her knees might lock.

'And have you thought any more about having your son tested? I do understand your concerns about his Ménière's disease, but there is a much higher chance of a sibling being a full match.'

Honour walked to the sink, watching the autumn sky fill with starlings, a bubble of movement sliding away towards the horizon, fluid, graceful and a painfully beautiful sight at such an ugly moment. 'Not yet. I don't want to subject him to anything risky or distressing unless we have no other options.' She heard the floorboards overhead squeak, Callum and Dougie's laughter filtering through the floor filling her with doubt about her decision.

Was she risking Tara's life to keep Callum out of danger?

Lorna had taken Dougie home soon after Honour had told her what the doctor had said, and now, Honour sat with her two children on the sofa, one on either side of her. Explaining about the bone marrow transplant process in a way that would make them feel empowered rather than afraid had tested Honour, but knowing her children and how they processed information, she felt that they had taken it in, in the best way possible.

Callum was leaning forward, chewing the sleeve of his sweatshirt, his eyes firmly on Tara, who was staring into the empty fireplace. 'So, you understand that Grandma, Grandpa and I will be tested to see if we can be your donor, Tara?' She took in Tara's profile, the high forehead, the slender nose, the now stringy hair that coated her back.

'Yes. I get it.' Tara nodded, then looked over at her mother.

'What if none of you can be the donor, though? Will we get bone marrow from someone else?'

'Yes. There's a national donor registry where people sign up to be donors. Their blood and DNA is all tested in advance, so Doctor Hail will find us the perfect match.' She paused, nervous to make promises like this when she couldn't guarantee they were possible.

'So, when we have a donor, we'll do the operation to give me their bone marrow, then my system will be strong enough to fight off the cancer? Is that how it works?' Tara shifted so she was facing Honour, her finger absently tracing the outer seam of Honour's jeans.

'Exactly. It's like your immune system will get a battery recharge.' Honour nodded, discreetly scooping a few strands of hair from Tara's back and twisting them into a ball in her palm.

Callum shifted closer, his breath smelling of the chocolate ice cream he'd had after lunch. His navy-blue Space Camp sweatshirt was riding up his back and his bare feet dangled over the edge of the sofa. 'Will my marrow be tested, too?' He frowned, once again sucking in the end of his sleeve.

Honour gently removed the cotton from his mouth and took a moment to form her answer. It was critical that he not feel bad about anything that was about to happen, so she picked her words carefully, and gave herself licence to lie as needed. 'Actually, Cal, they need an adult to be the donor. It will be better for Tara that way.' She eyed him, readying herself for his rebuttal.

Callum considered what she'd said, then shifted forward and planked his feet on the floor. 'I'm not a baby, Mum. And even if I'm not a grown-up, my marrow could be better than a stranger's.' He paused, as if having a series of revelations. 'What if the stranger is a weirdo, or ill with something, or smokes cigarettes? What if they aren't kind and say they won't help Tara? What if...' He stopped, seeing Honour's expression as she absorbed the sometimes eerie wisdom her young son displayed.

Honour sat back and opened her arms, drawing a child in on each side. 'Doc Hail will only use the best donor he can find. Nothing else will do for our Tara.' She hugged her children closer. 'I trust him, and he is the top doctor for this kind of thing that there is. He won't let us down. Believe me.' Hearing the words float from her mouth, she willed them to be true.

'OK.' Callum sounded dubious. 'When will he find out who is the best?'

Honour shifted forward, releasing them from her arms. 'Hopefully soon. We're going to be tested next week and then, once Tara is in the hospital and we know who is going to donate, we'll get ready.'

Tara tugged her sweater down at the front; with the movement, the striking footballer on the front appeared to be shooting the ball. 'Why can't I stay here until then, though? I get it about infections and stuff, but I don't really see anyone to catch anything from except you and Cal, and sometimes Jenna, or Lorna and Dougie. I suppose Bridie comes in too, and then Grandma and Grandpa, but I could stay up in my room. Wear a mask, and wash my hands all the time, and all that.' Her eyes seemed an unreal shade of blue, awash with pleading as Honour stood up and forced a swallow.

'I want you to stay here too, Tara, but Doc Hail knows best. It's just for a couple of weeks or so, and once the transplant is done, you'll soon be able to come home.' Honour wished with all her might that this was the true course of events, but deep inside, she doubted that it would be this straightforward. Nothing about cancer could be considered straightforward, and that was perhaps the only fact she *was* certain of.

Tara lay on her side in her bed, Taylor Swift singing quietly on the iPad next to her as Honour stroked her daughter's back. Searching for any kind of comfort she could offer her brave girl,

Honour began to think of ways to keep Tara looking forward, focusing on the after in this next, frightening phase of her illness. Honour sifted through some ideas of things that Tara liked to do, gently rolled Tara onto her back, and tucked the duvet tightly down her sides, as Tara used to ask her to do as a little girl.

'There. Just like a big, fat sausage roll.' Honour smiled at her daughter, seeing the beginning of a smile tug at Tara's lip.

'I'm a bit too old for that now, Mum.' Tara's mouth twitched again, lifting Honour's spirits. Hopeful that Tara's inherent optimism would come to the fore, as it always had in the past, Honour went on. 'Is there something special you'd like to do when you get back home? Anything that you've always dreamed about?' Honour held Tara's gaze as the trace of a smile disappeared and Tara shifted up higher on her pillows.

'Why are you asking me that? Is it like a last wish, or something? Am I going to die, Mum?' She set her chin in the same way that Honour did herself when she didn't like the look of whatever she was faced with.

Honour instantly wanted to kick herself for missing the mark so badly. 'God, no. I just want you to have some fun stuff to look forward to when you're home again.' She took Tara's hand in hers, noting the warmth of Tara's skin. Instantly sucked into the worrying possibility that Tara might have a temperature, Honour took a second to continue. 'How about us all going to a concert? Or maybe we can get Grandma and Grandpa to take care of Frodo for a few days and we could go camping, on Skye or Lewis?'

Honour tried to picture them lying next to one another under the old canvas tent that Kenny had insisted was perfectly adequate the one time they'd gone camping in the Cairngorms, two years earlier. On the first night, the heavens had opened, and the tent had leaked so badly that they'd packed up and moved into a nearby hotel, where they'd eaten huge plates of shepherd's pie that Kenny had said wasn't nearly as good as Honour's, before watching a Harry Potter film in their room.

Tara had been delighted, saying it was the best camping trip ever, except for her having to sleep in beside Callum, in the other double bed. Honour had laughed, saying that if they wanted to camp again, they'd need to buy a decent tent. Kenny had pulled the covers over her head and chuckled as she struggled to get out, saying, 'You're a bunch of spoiled beggars. A wee bit of rain has never killed a MacLeod, yet.'

As the happy memory floated into her heart, Honour sighed. 'Honestly, Tara. Have a think about it and let me know. We can plan while you're recovering.' She smiled again, seeing Tara's brow smooth of the deep frown. 'Now, get some sleep. I'll check on you before I go to bed and give you your last painkillers, OK?'

Tara nodded, then, as Honour made to leave, she grabbed her hand. 'Are you scared, Mum?'

Caught off guard, Honour went into super-mother mode and shook her head vigorously. 'Not even a little. I know you, Tara MacLeod, and we've never come across any challenge you couldn't take in your stride. This will be no different.' She smoothed Tara's brow, again noting the heat coming from her skin. Tara nodded against the pillow as Honour placed the back of her hand on Tara's forehead. 'I'm going to take your temperature before you go to sleep. Just to be extra careful, OK?'

Tara sighed. 'OK. I feel fine, though.'

Honour cupped her cheek. 'That's good. This is just me being super-careful.' She paused. 'You know how much I love you, right?'

Tara's eyes widened as she nodded. 'Yes, Muuum.'

'Good. Close your eyes and I'll be back in a sec.'

Tara's eyelids looked heavy as she turned onto her side to face the window. Honour stood still, watching her daughter's ribcage instantly begin to move rhythmically like a bony bellows, as if sleep had already claimed her.

Honour tiptoed out into the hall, heading for the bathroom to find the thermometer, praying that her concern over Tara feeling hot was unfounded. All Honour had to do was keep Tara healthy until she went back into the hospital.

28

Tara's temperature had been very slightly high when Honour had checked it at 10 p.m. She'd given her some aspirin and checked her again at 11 p.m., by which time it was back to normal, but by 2 a.m., unable to sleep, Honour had padded into Tara's room and taken her temperature again. This time, it was 101 degrees and panic began to seep in.

She phoned and left a message for Doctor Hail, on the after-hours line, helped Tara into the bath and sponged her neck, face and back with cool water. After an hour, around 3.15 a.m., when Tara's temperature rose to 102 degrees, Honour phoned for an ambulance, then called her mother. 'Her temperature won't come down, Mum. She's droopy, and her eyes are kind of out of focus.'

Marion immediately said, 'Dad and I will be on our way in ten minutes. If they get to you before we do, ask Bridie to come in and watch Callum.'

Honour's relief came in a rush. 'Thanks, Mum. I'll phone you as soon as I know what's happening.'

She checked on Callum, who was sleeping soundly, then helped Tara change her pyjamas and tucked her under a blanket on the sofa, when there was a knock at the front door. Glancing at the clock, she deduced that it was too soon for the ambulance to have reached them, so she squinted through the glass panel. Seeing the flash of silvery hair, Bridie's profile came to life, so Honour opened the door. 'Bridie, hi.'

Bridie was wearing a thick, purple dressing gown over her nightgown; her feet were in faded green wellingtons and she carried a bulging plastic bag from Green's. 'Hi, love. I couldn't sleep, then I saw all your lights come on, so thought I'd pop over and see if everything was OK.' She craned her neck, looking into the living room behind Honour.

Touched by Bridie's concern, Honour said, 'Actually, things are not great. Tara's got a very high temperature and I'm waiting for the ambulance to arrive. Mum and Dad are coming over, but I'm not sure how long they'll be.' She stepped back and beckoned to Bridie. 'Come in out of the cold.'

Bridie stepped inside the room and closed the door behind herself. 'What can I do?' She set the plastic bag on the ground by the door. 'I brought my knitting just in case you wanted some company.'

Honour pressed her forefinger to her lips, and whispered, 'Tara's nodded off on the sofa, and Cal's sound asleep upstairs. If the ambulance gets here before Mum and Dad...' She halted as Bridie nodded vigorously.

'I'll stay here with Callum for as long as you need me to.'

Overcome with gratitude, Honour squeezed Bridie's hand. 'Thank you. That would be such a help.'

Bridie nodded, sliding off her boots and setting them by the door. 'I'll put the kettle on while you finish getting ready.' She gestured towards the kitchen.

'OK.' Honour nodded, just as she saw the flash of a blue light coming from outside the window. 'I think they're here.' She dashed back to the door and opened it, a trace of musk floating in from the water below as her face was coated with the cold mist that had settled over the lane.

Tara was limp, her cheeks florid and her mouth curling around silent words. Honour's heart was clattering under her breastbone, her mind spiralling down all the terrifying tangents she'd been keeping at bay daily. Honour robotically answered the questions the medics were asking, reeling off facts about Tara's medical history, how long she'd had a temperature, what she'd eaten that day, who was her GP, her mouth feeling disconnected from her brain.

'Mrs MacLeod?' The taller medic touched her arm, his hand gentle but firm. She made eye contact with him for the first time, noticing that he had unusual, grey eyes, a silvery colour that reminded her of the sea off the coast of St Andrews, where she'd grown up. 'Mrs MacLeod?' he repeated her name, tugging her back to the moment.

'Yes, sorry.'

'Do you want to come in the ambulance with your daughter, or follow us in the car?'

Honour swallowed, the idea of not being with Tara every second gut-wrenching. 'I'll go with her. My friend is going to stay here with my son until my parents get here.' She gestured towards Bridie, who was standing in the kitchen doorway.

'Right. We'll bring a gurney up to the house in a few minutes and get Tara safely into the ambulance.' He held Honour's gaze. 'We'll give her fluids and let the Victoria know we're coming in.'

Honour nodded, scanning the room for her handbag.

Bridie, seeming to read her mind, brought the holdall from the kitchen, Honour's handbag, and a smaller canvas bag into the living room. 'Here are your things, and I've packed some sandwiches and a flask of tea for you.' She handed the bags to Honour, who took them blindly, then turned towards the door.

Setting the bags down while she dragged her coat on, Honour found her voice. 'Bridie, I...' She gulped. 'Thank you.'

Bridie patted the air. 'It's nothing. Just give me a ring later when Tara's settled and let me know how you both are.'

By 6.30 a.m., Tara was on fluids and intravenous antibiotics. Her fever was gradually coming down and Doctor Hail had made an early drop-in to her room, to talk to Honour.

They'd done a blood panel and an MRI and found that Tara's knee was infected, and as Honour sat next to the bed listening to the doctor speak, she focused on his mouth, afraid she might miss any tiny detail that could give her hope to hold on to.

'We need to monitor Tara closely and keep her on IV antibiotics for the next few days.'

Honour nodded. 'Right. But for now, is she stable, at least?'

He held her gaze. 'I won't mince words, Mrs MacLeod, she isn't out of the woods just yet.'

Honour felt her leaky heart take on more water. 'So, what else can we do?'

He glanced at his shoes briefly, then back at Honour. 'My best advice would be that we move towards finding a bone marrow donor.'

Honour stood up, letting go of Tara's hand, then covering her arm with the light blanket, its surface like a waffle cone, some thin threads having worked loose from the light-blue cotton. 'Let's get the tests done. My parents and I are ready.' She walked to the window that overlooked the car park below, seeing a large white van pulling up with the words Universal Laundry on the side.

'I took the liberty of activating Tara's case on the national registry, and we can get your testing done in a few days.' He tipped his head to the side. 'It's just you and your parents, at this stage?'

Honour nodded. 'Yes, at the moment.' Her heart was cramping painfully, so she pressed her palm to her chest. 'I'll think more about Callum being tested, but not yet.'

'I respect your decision, Mrs MacLeod. If we don't find a full match soon, though, you might want to reconsider.' Honour held his gaze, the clear blue eyes giving away his concern. 'I'll have my office phone you later today with appointment times and then we'll take it from there.'

Honour walked back to the bed, where Tara was now stirring. Her hair was spread out behind her head like a delicate scarlet crochet and her face was less flushed than a few hours ago.

'Mum?' She opened her eyes, scanning the room for something familiar to land on. Seeing Honour, Tara's face crumpled. 'I'm in the hospital again.'

Honour perched on the edge of the bed and smoothed the hair from Tara's forehead, relieved that it felt significantly cooler than it had in the night. 'Yes, my love. For now. You have an infection, so this is antibiotics.' She pointed at the IV that was taped to Tara's arm. 'It's the fastest way to get them into your system, Tara, and your temperature is already coming down.' She smiled at Tara, who swiped at her nose with the back of her hand.

'OK.' Tara sniffed.

Doctor Hail stepped forward and handed Tara a clean tissue. 'It's good to see you, Tara.' He smiled. 'We've got you on the good stuff.' He winked and gestured at the plastic bag hanging on a hook by the bed. 'I don't give this magic juice to just anyone, you know.'

Honour watched Tara take in what he'd said, and instantly knew, by her expression, that her clever daughter was in no mood for friendly banter. Before Tara could say anything snippy that might offend the doctor, Honour stood up. 'Would you like a cold drink, sweetheart?' She turned to Doctor Hail. 'Is that OK?'

Seeming unfazed by Honour diverting the conversation, he nodded. 'Perfectly fine.'

'Tara?' Honour smiled at her daughter.

Tara nodded, then shifted up higher against the pillows, careful not to tug on the IV in her arm.

Honour nodded, turned towards the door and gave the doctor a look that spoke volumes. Picking up on her signal, Doctor Hail said, 'I'll pop in later to see how you are, Tara. Just rest for now.' He smiled at her, then followed Honour out into the corridor.

Outside the room, Honour turned to face him, her heart racing. 'What are the chances of finding a full match on the registry?'

He hesitated, then took the stethoscope from around his neck, folded it awkwardly and put it in his pocket. 'There's no way to know precisely, but currently there are thousands of donors registered, with more joining all the time.' He eyed her. 'I can't put a precise timeframe around it, though, I'm afraid.'

She nodded, her insides seeming to collapse. 'How long can she wait, though?'

He shifted his feet, apparently reluctant to put a number on this, too. 'If we get the infection under control, and stabilise her, we can do further tests.' He flicked his eyes to the corridor behind her, where two nurses were talking animatedly. When they saw him, they lowered their voices and walked quickly behind the nurses' station. 'Tara needs rest and to get her strength back before we do anything more invasive.'

The word brought Honour's chin up with a snap. 'Invasive?'

He hesitated, then, seeing Honour's expression of despair, took her arm and led her to a chair that sat against the wall. 'We're not there yet, but if we don't find a donor, and the infection lingers it will drain Tara's resources. She's already vulnerable to a recurrence based on the nature of the tumour, so we do have to consider amputation as an option.'

Honour felt his hand under her arm, the strong fingers feeling alien and yet welcome, remembering how long it had been since she'd been touched other than by her family, or friends offering comfort. With everything that she was managing – Tara's needs, Callum and his concerns, her parents, even the community that had rallied around her – Honour had put her own needs at the end of the list, and now, having Doctor Hail be kind in this way seemed to drain the remaining composure that she had been holding in reserve.

As she sank onto the hard plastic chair, she pressed her eyes closed, trying to banish the image of Tara's truncated leg. Feeling as if she might vomit, Honour sat back and leaned her head against the wall. 'I know we have to consider it. But surely that's a last resort?'

'Let's focus on the transplant testing for now, and once we see how Tara responds to the antibiotics, we'll talk again.' He stood back and shoved his hands into the pockets of his white coat. 'Is there anyone we can phone to be here with you? Perhaps take a shift with Tara so you can get some rest?'

Honour shook her head. 'No. I'm fine.' She pulled her legs under her and stood up. 'Just please get us in for the tests as soon as possible. I need to feel that I'm doing something practical to help.' She swallowed hard. 'At least trying to.'

He nodded and extended a hand. Gripping it, Honour tried to smile her gratitude as her voice failed her.

'Understood.' He smiled. 'We'll be in touch.'

She watched him leave, his long strides purposeful and swift as she wished him away, to move them on to the next stage and, hopefully, towards a solution for Tara that wasn't the stuff of Honour's nightmares.

29

All the way home in the car, Honour had replayed her conversation with Tara. She'd been watching the small TV mounted high on the wall across from the bed and her colour, while pale, was much improved.

Honour had been stretching out her stiff back, catching a musky whiff of herself – the result of two days without a shower – as Tara had turned off the TV and turned to face her mother. 'You can go home, you know. I'm OK.'

Honour had instantly pictured herself standing under the hot water at home, soaping herself clean of all the hospital smells, the foamy suds taking the discomfort of the past two days away. But thinking about easing her own discomfort had instantly made her feel guilty, and she'd said, 'No. I'm fine, love.'

'Actually, Mum, you're not fine.' Tara's eyes had sparkled with mischief.

'What do you mean?' Honour had frowned.

'You smell like old socks, or cabbage or something.' Tara had pinched her nose and comically puffed out her cheeks, instantly lifting Honour's bruised heart.

'Excuse me?' She'd feigned offence.

Tara had leaned her head back against the pillows, a smile tugging at her mouth. 'Seriously, Mum, go home for a while. See Cal. Have a bath, or something. I'll still be here when you get back.' She'd spread her arms wide, then she'd flapped her hand under her nose. 'Seriously stinky.'

For a second, Honour had wanted to grab her daughter up into her arms, hold her close to her body and bolt out the door, sprint along the corridor and out into the murky twilight, not stopping until she'd bundled Tara into the Audi and driven her home. Then she'd pull the curtains and lock the doors, stop anyone or anything ever hurting Tara again. The crazy image playing out in her mind, Honour had found a smile.

'OK. But is there anything you want, love?' She'd crossed the room and picked up her bag from near the door.

Tara had taken a second, then shaken her head. 'Nope. Unless you've got a spare left leg lying around somewhere. One that isn't mangled.' She'd let her palm rest on her thigh, her characteristic attempt at humour in a dark situation making Honour so proud that her throat had knotted tightly as Tara had continued, 'You don't have to come back tonight, either. Just come in the morning.' She had looked over at the darkening window, where, outside, the rain was pattering on the glass, beyond it, the night sky turning from indigo to navy blue. Then, a shadow had seemed to cloud Tara's eyes.

'What is it, love?' Honour had let her bag drop to the floor.

'I'll never play again, will I?' Tara had gestured at her leg. 'Maybe I should start learning about the stars so I can go to the moon, with Cal.' She'd shrugged miserably. 'He'll probably go, you know.'

Her comment driving a spike directly into Honour's heart, she'd taken Tara's hand. 'We're not saying never, Tara. We don't know that.' She'd kept her voice steady as Tara's mouth dipped.

'I'm not stupid, Mum. I know what's happening to me.' Her eyes had been clear as she'd studied Honour's face. 'I'm not scared, really. I'm just angry, and fed up, and stuff.' She'd blinked several times as Honour had desperately searched for the right thing to say, words failing her.

That night, as soon as she got home, Honour stood under the shower for fifteen minutes letting the stingingly hot water soothe her aching back. The privacy of the bathroom was a welcome respite from the constant flow of medical staff through Tara's room, and as Honour stepped out of the shower and swiped the steam off the mirror, she was shocked at how drawn she looked. It wasn't the first time she'd seen her reflection over the past few days, but it was, she realised, the first time she'd really looked at herself for quite a while.

Placing her hands on her cheeks, she pulled her skin back to smooth out the webs of new wrinkles that occupied the edges of her eyes, and the two deeply etched lines that now bracketed her mouth. In the past, she'd been told that she didn't look her age, but after the events of the past four months, she looked every inch of her thirty-nine years, and then some.

As she took in her eyes, usually bright and optimistic but now dull and slightly hooded, and her cheeks – sunken due to her recent weight loss – Honour softly sighed. But rather than be disappointed by the changes she saw, evidence of the creep of age and experience, she was filled with gratitude for the privilege of living, and then, just as quickly, overwhelming sadness took over.

What if Tara wasn't given the same privilege, of seeing wrinkles begin to form, of watching her own face change with time – showing the fingerprints of the life that she'd led? What if Tara's life was cruelly cut short and she didn't get the chance to experience first love, a career she could flourish in, a life partner, or maybe having children of her own? Honour closed her eyes as tears washed her cheeks, silent sobs coursing through her as she gripped the sink.

It took her ten minutes to gather herself, splash cold water on her flushed face and pull on a clean tracksuit before emerging from the bathroom and going downstairs.

In the living room, Callum was sitting next to his grandpa on the sofa, Callum softly narrating over an episode of his favourite programme, *Universe*, on the BBC. Seeing his tawny head leaning in towards Kirk's, Callum's voice low and metered as if every word was loaded with significance that he didn't want his grandfather to miss, Honour pulled her damp hair into a ponytail and wound a band around it. She knew she needed to tell Callum something that would satisfy his probing questions about Tara, but, as yet, she hadn't decided what, exactly.

When she'd first got back from the hospital, she had taken her mother into the kitchen and whispered to her about the testing the following day. 'It's just a simple cheek swab to get a sample of your DNA, Mum. If you are a basic match, then you'll have additional blood tests, et cetera.'

Marion had nodded, saying, 'Fine. What about Cal?'

'I'm not going to tell him. At least not yet.' Honour had chewed at the cuticle around her thumb until her mother had gently moved her hand away from her mouth. 'I mean, he knows about bone marrow transplants, in principle. Just not that we're there yet.'

'I think that's the right approach, Honour. Let's see what these tests show first.'

Relieved that her mother agreed with her thinking, Honour had hugged her tightly, Marion's breath warm and minty as she'd kissed Honour's cheek before shooing her upstairs to shower.

Now, behind her, Marion was setting the kitchen table for dinner. The fridge had various provisions in it that Craig had dropped off from Green's that morning, and Marion had assessed them and was planning to put together a risotto, with some fresh asparagus. Honour began to help her mother, putting some mushrooms into the sink to wash them, when the doorbell rang. Her insides sinking at the prospect of having to face anyone other than the trusted people already inside her home, Honour sighed. 'God, who's that?'

Marion dropped the tea towel she held. 'I'll go. Just finish setting the table.'

Honour watched her mother walk out of the kitchen, then Honour set four glasses on the table, the sight of Tara's empty place robbing Honour of her breath.

Just as she put the salt and pepper at the centre of the table, Marion walked in, followed closely by Bridie, carrying a large casserole covered in tin foil. 'Look who I found on the doorstep.'

Bridie carefully put the casserole on a metal trivet at the side of the Aga and, without saying a word, pulled Honour into a hug. Relieved that it was Bridie, and that no false bravery, or explanations were needed, Honour hugged her back, feeling the wiry ribs flexing beneath her forearms. After a few second, Bridie pulled back.

'It's fisherman's pie. I left out the mussels as I know Callum's not keen.' She nodded towards the living room. 'They look relaxed in there.'

'Yes, Dad's great with him. And thank you for the pie, Bridie. You're a gem.' Honour smiled at her. 'We were just going to crack a bottle of something to have with dinner. Fancy a tot?' Honour surprised herself, issuing an invitation for Bridie to stay, but quickly turned towards the French dresser and took out three glasses from the bottom cupboard.

'Well, maybe a quick one. Scott's watching the match, so he won't miss me for a bit. Or at all.' Bridie laughed softly as Honour opened a bottle of Sauvignon that she'd been keeping in the fridge since Lorna had brought it over the previous week. 'I wonder if Tara can watch it at the hospital.'

Honour tried to picture Tara, lying in her bed watching the game that she'd dreamt of playing professionally one day. The image too painful to witness, Honour hoped that, by now, Tara was fast asleep and avoiding that particular brand of torture.

The three women sat at the table and touched glasses before each leaned back in their chairs. Bridie's hair was in an intricate, plaited rope across the top of her head that made her look like a Swiss schoolgirl, and Marion's fluffy curls were halo-like – the gilded light from the living room shining behind her. Honour watched them lock eyes across the table and, knowing that it was safe to share what was happening with Bridie, she said softly, 'So, the infection looks like it's responding to the antibiotics, but Tara's pretty weak, and Doc Hail wants to let her recover some strength before we decide if they need to do more surgery.'

Bridie put her glass down and nodded. 'Right.'

'He thinks that we should move forward with a bone marrow transplant, if we can find a match.' Honour sipped some wine, aware that she wasn't really tasting it. Much as the light had recently faded in her life, so all her senses had followed suit, dulled by worry, sleeplessness and the ongoing battle with fear that was draining her daily.

Bridie sat forward, leaning on her slender elbows. 'So, who can be a donor?'

'Immediate family are the best bet for a match, so Mum, Dad and I are getting tested tomorrow.'

Marion nodded. 'We're going in in the morning. It should be straightforward. Kirk was researching it online last night.'

Bridie blinked several times, then frowned. 'Could Scott, Malc and I be tested? I know it's probably unlikely, but stranger things have happened.' She shrugged.

'Bless you, Bridie, thanks, but for now we're going to stick to family.' Honour paused. 'It's a very small pool to draw from these days, but it's the best chance for a match.'

Bridie eyed Marion, who appeared to be giving her an unspoken warning of some kind. Unsure what her mother was afraid of Bridie saying, Honour sipped some more wine.

Bridie shifted in her chair as if sitting on something uncomfortable, then her eyes widened – like she could hold back no longer. Honour put her glass down as Bridie blurted, 'What about Jack? He's family. Is he being tested, too?'

Hearing Bridie speak Jack's name out loud felt like witnessing an evil genie being released from a bottle, so Honour flinched. Not having thought about him for weeks, she stammered, 'Um, no. He doesn't know about this.' She met her mother's gaze, Marion looking somewhat quizzically at her.

'Could an uncle be a possible match though, Honour?' Marion's eyes widened. 'I know Jack's been a huge disappointment over the years, but maybe, now...' She halted at the sight of Honour's expression. The entire village had been aware of Jack's mysterious disappearance, during Allen's illness, and Kenny's hurt over it all, so Marion and Kirk had known about it too, added to which, Honour had talked to them about Kenny's sense of abandonment.

What her parents didn't know about was her promise to Kenny, never to have any contact with Jack again, or what her own role had been in his leaving – both of which weighed heavier on Honour now than when it had happened all those years ago.

'I don't know, but I doubt it.' Honour stood up, tipping her remaining wine down the drain.

'Perhaps it'd be worth talking to him? Do you know how to contact him?' Marion's voice was tentative, her words settling on Honour's back like an unwelcome shawl.

'Let's just focus on us for now, Mum, OK?' She turned to face her mother, and Bridie, who were both frowning.

Marion took a second, then nodded, watching Bridie, who had also stood up, obviously sensing that she had inadvertently taken the conversation to an uncomfortable place. 'Well, I'd better be off before half-time.' She jabbed a thumb over her shoulder. 'Do you need any help with Callum tomorrow?'

Honour shook her head, relieved that they could move on. 'No, but thanks. Lorna's coming to get him and take him to school, and we'll be back well before he's finished, so I'll pick him up.'

Bridie nodded and put her empty glass in the sink. 'Well, you know where we are if anything changes.' She smiled kindly at Honour, whose heart was slowly returning to a normal pace. 'Enjoy the pie and I hope you all get some sleep tonight.'

Marion hugged Bridie, then followed her to the front door, leaving Honour in the kitchen. As she slid the pie into the fridge, her mother was soon back behind her. Honour immediately sensed that the subject of Jack was not closed, as she had hoped, and she turned to see Marion carefully push the kitchen door shut. Alarmed, Honour avoided her mother's eyes and busied herself with washing the glasses in the sink.

'Can I ask you something?' Marion lifted a tea towel and began drying the glasses.

'Uh-huh.' Honour dried her foamy hands on a piece of kitchen paper and tossed it into the bin.

'Is there anything other than the obvious – i.e., Jack buggering off to Edinburgh – that is bothering you? Not that he's come up much over the years, but whenever he has, you seem to shut down.'

Honour felt as trapped as a lab rat in a maze. Her mother had a way of looking directly into her soul, divining secrets that Honour worked to bury. But this time, what she was hiding was too ugly, too unforgivable to reveal, and no matter what else happened, Honour could not tell her mother the whole truth of why she clammed up when Jack's name was mentioned.

I made a promise to Kenny. Just let me keep this one promise, please.

30

The next morning, Honour saw Callum off to school with Lorna, hugging her friend tighter than usual. Lorna returned the pressure and whispered in her ear, 'I have a good feeling. There's going to be a match.'

Honour found a smile. 'From your mouth to...' She pointed at the ceiling as Callum said a cheery, 'Bye, Mum', then followed Lorna outside.

Turning her back on the door, Honour gathered her mane of hair away from the back of her neck. Today was possibly the first step towards a new future for Tara, and whatever role Honour could play in that, minor or otherwise, felt like a giant positive. Smiling to herself, she darted up the stairs, two at a time, and headed for the shower.

The testing had taken only minutes, but before they'd each been taken into the procedure room, Honour had sat next to her parents in the stuffy waiting area. They'd been quiet, exchanging smiles and nods, as if speaking might upset the delicate balance of things, tipping them towards the negative rather than keeping them all focused on this process of producing the results they needed. Her father had sat between her mother and her, holding one of each of their hands, and the gentle pressure of his fingers had stopped Honour from fidgeting, just as it had when she'd been a child.

Now, outside the hospital entrance, the rain was bouncing off the surface of the car park as they huddled under the canopy over the front doors. 'God, the heavens have opened, right enough.' Marion hooked her arm through Kirk's as Honour pulled the collar of her jacket up around her chin. 'Shall we make a run for it?'

Honour checked her watch, seeing it was just 8.58 a.m. They'd been here for less than an hour, but those fifty-eight minutes had the potential to change everything. As soon as she'd seen her parents off, she was going back inside to see Tara, and hopefully encourage her to have some breakfast. The nurses had told Honour that they'd been struggling to get Tara to eat, so Honour had brought in her favourite – toasted bacon rolls – to coax her with.

'I'll go and get the car. You stay here, love.' Kirk kissed the top of Marion's head.

Smiling at her parents' customary, gentle affection with one another, Honour stepped forwards. 'I'll say goodbye now, then.' She hugged her father's neck. 'Thanks for everything, Dad.'

'Just stay positive, love. And let us know how Tara is feeling today.' He smiled at her, then turned and walked quickly away into the pounding rain.

Honour draped her arm around her mother's shoulder, noticing that Marion's head felt lower against her collarbone than usual. 'I think you're shrinking, Mum.' She hugged her tightly.

Marion laughed softly. 'Yes, age brings such precious gifts.'

Honour's insides lurched at the notion that her mother was ageing, and while it did bring challenges, it was a privilege that she was still afraid that Tara might not be gifted. Honour took a moment to rearrange her thoughts, as, typically, Marion read them.

'She's going to get through this, Honour. I believe it, and so must you.'

Honour swallowed hard and nodded. 'I'll phone you later.' She dropped a kiss on her mother's cheek. 'I love you.'

'Give Tara a hug from us.' Marion walked towards the Volvo station wagon that drew up to the door, where, inside, Kirk was waving.

As she waved back, Honour's phone buzzed in her pocket and, turning back to the door, she saw Doctor Hail's name on the screen. Walking inside the hospital, feeling the wall of overly warm air bathe her face, she heard his voice, brusquer than usual.

'Mrs MacLeod. Are you still in the hospital?'

'Yes, I'm down in reception. I was just seeing my parents off.' A metallic crash made her jump as she passed the front desk and headed for the lifts. 'I'm on my way up to Tara's room.' She waited for the doors to open, her heart rate beginning to pick up. 'Is everything OK?'

Doctor Hail hesitated, then said, 'I'll meet you at her room.'

Honour's insides contracted just as the metallic doors squeezed open, and she waited for a smiling health worker to push an elderly man in a wheelchair out into the lobby. Inside the lift, Honour pressed the button three times, willing the sluggish doors to close faster. 'I'll be there in five minutes.' The doors slid closed, seeming to expel all the available air in the elevator, leaving Honour panicked as she ran through all the scenarios they'd discussed in her mind, trying to imagine what else could have gone wrong.

Outside Tara's room, Doctor Hail was looking at a tablet, his stethoscope slung around his long neck. As Honour approached, he handed the tablet to the nurse next to him and watched her walk away down the corridor. Something in the curve of his shoulders set alarm bells off inside Honour, and she picked up her pace.

'Good morning.' He smiled, but it was guarded, a little too practised.

'What's happening?' Honour looked behind him at the closed door. 'Why's the door closed?'

He gestured towards the two plastic chairs against the opposite wall, and the familiar delaying tactic sent Honour's quickening heart into overdrive. 'She's sleeping, which is a good thing. Tara's temperature spiked again this morning, so we've switched her to a different antibiotic. We've used some cool packs to help bring her temperature down and we're observing her closely.'

Honour heard a buzzing in her ears, a warning sign she'd learned from both of her pregnancies indicating that she might pass out, so she sat and leaned forward – her elbows on her knees. She focused on the linoleum floor, the smell of cleaning fluids filling her head. There was a gentle hum of conversation coming from the room directly opposite Tara's and then laughter, the lilting sound of relief that made envy bloom in Honour's chest.

'Mrs MacLeod?' Doctor Hail sat next to her. 'Are you all right?'

Honour nodded, swallowing over a nut of despair.

'Your tests are underway, and we've activated the donor register.' Doctor Hail paused. 'We're covering all the bases, so to speak.'

Honour sat back, her top lip clammy and her fingers beginning to tingle. 'Can I see her?'

'Of course. Just try not to wake her, for now.' He stood up, taking off his glasses and slipping them into the top pocket of his crisply ironed shirt. 'We've put a rush request on the swab tests, and I'll contact you as soon as we hear from the lab.'

She stood up, feeling the blood rushing back to her numb feet. 'Thanks.'

'Phone me if you have any concerns or questions.' He extended a hand as if to lead her back to Tara's room.

Not wanting his touch today, Honour stepped back. 'I will.'

She made her way over to Tara's room, then took a few moments, letting her hand rest on the door handle. Behind this door, her daughter slept while medication did battle with infection, much as Honour was fighting her own sense of helplessness.

With Tara fractious, and slipping in and out of sleep, Honour couldn't bring herself to leave her, so she'd phoned her mother and asked her to pick up the overnight bag that Bridie had packed for her and bring it to the hospital.

Marion had stayed only a few minutes, sensing that Honour needed quiet – time to focus one hundred per cent of her energy on Tara – and as Marion had been leaving, Honour had clung to her mother, grateful that she didn't have to explain herself.

'We've taken a few things to the cottage, and we'll stay there as long as needed, Honour. You just concentrate on Tara, and we'll take care of Callum and everything else.'

'Thanks, Mum. I don't know what I'd do without you both.' She'd felt tears prickle behind her eyes. 'If we hadn't gone private, I just don't know what would've happened. How long all this would've taken.' Honour had tried to stop calculating how much she must owe her parents now, but every time they told her to stop worrying about it, she couldn't put the thought away. Someday she'd find a way to pay them back. She had no idea how, but she'd find a way.

. . .

The following afternoon, Tara had rallied, and Honour had made it home to shower and change, thanks to Lorna staying with Tara for a couple of hours.

Feeling somewhat refreshed, Honour was back at the hospital, and standing at the end of Tara's bed. 'What can I get you to drink, sweetheart?'

Tara's cheeks were flushed, but her temperature was coming down. 'Lemonade or apple juice.' She licked her lips, the skin dry and chapped.

Honour dug around in her bag and found a ChapStick, handing it to Tara. 'Put some of this on while I nip to the cafeteria.'

Tara took the ChapStick and smeared it on her lips. 'Ugh, its cherry-flavoured.' She grimaced. 'Gross.'

Honour took it back and tossed it into her bag. 'Sorry. It's all I have.'

Tara sat upright; a stack of pillows piled behind her. 'Can I have some crisps?'

Honour nodded, delighted. 'Of course. Salt and vinegar?'

'What else.' She smiled at her mother. 'I'm not Cal, eating prawn cocktail or stinky cheese and onion.'

Honour laughed softly as she tucked her credit card into her pocket. 'Hey now. He's really missed you.'

'I bet he has.' Tara rolled her eyes. 'I bet he's hardly noticed I'm not there.'

'Not true.' Honour gave Tara a disapproving look. 'You are a bit hard on him at times, Tara, but he adores you.'

'If you say so.' She gave a cheeky smile, then continued, 'He's all right as little brothers go, I suppose.'

'I'll be back in a tick.' Honour walked out into the corridor and was overcome by the smell of steamed vegetables. Realising that it was after lunchtime, and she had not eaten since the previous afternoon, her stomach rumbled loudly. Pressing her palm into her middle, she made her way towards the lift, but before she could step inside, her phone rang in her back pocket again. It was Doctor Hail, so stepping away from the lift, she answered it.

'Hello, Mrs MacLeod.' He sounded distracted. 'We've just had the results of the swab tests.'

Honour's stomach flip-flopped as she closed her eyes and waited.

31

Honour pressed her back against the wall, her heart clattering in her chest. The next few seconds passed as slowly as treacle trickling off a spoon, then Doctor Hail said quietly, 'As we suspected, we don't have a full match with either of your parents, or you.'

Honour closed her eyes as flashes of red crept across the insides of her eyelids. 'Oh, God.'

'We're monitoring the registry constantly, but I must ask you if you've given any more thought to testing your son. The chances are far higher that, as Tara's sibling, he'd be a match.'

As her mind flooded with all the potential risks involved for Callum with being a donor, Honour slid down the wall, pulling her knees up to her chest. If there was a chance that he could save his sister, she knew that Callum would want to, but could she, as a parent, knowingly put his health at risk? How was any mother supposed to make a decision like this, juggling priorities this way, playing God between her children's health, and needs?

Feeling trapped inside paralysing indecision, Kenny's voice

suddenly filled her head. '*Don't doubt yourself, Red. Follow your gut. You know what to do.*'

Letting the words sink in, she pushed herself up from the floor and cleared her throat. 'Give me a little time, Doctor Hail, and I'll get back to you.'

The more research Honour did on the donation procedure, the more her concern grew for Callum, but when she slowed her racing mind down, she knew that she was letting fear cloud her vision. No matter how much she resisted it, the fact was that Callum was the last hope for a familial, full match, and even with her concerns mounting, there was no way to avoid, at the very least, finding out if it was possible. If there was a way to save Tara that she did not explore, Honour knew she would never be able to forgive herself.

Callum was due back from school in a couple of hours and Lorna was dropping him off. Honour busied herself with laundry, watering the pots on the front step, then she cut all the dried-up lavender spears and was careful to strip them into a cotton bag that she kept for the purpose. The scent of the greyish kernels lingered on her fingers as she leaned against the sink and breathed it in. Feeling the taut muscles of her neck relax a little, her phone rang on the table behind her. Thinking it might be her mother, she grabbed it up.

The letters JM shone starkly on the screen and, seeing them, Honour clamped her hand over her mouth. She tried to calculate how long it had been since Jack had last called her, her hands beginning to shake. By the fourth ring, she was perched on a chair at the table, her finger lingering over the button to accept the call, but as she was about to answer it, it diverted to voicemail and Honour slumped back in the chair, a mixture of adrenaline and relief making her exhale.

Waiting the few moments for the voice message to register,

she paced in front of the sink, looking out at the overcast afternoon sky, spotting the brown stems of the clematis badly needing to be cut back. Finally, seeing the envelope symbol appear on the screen, she listened to the message.

His deep voice was strained as he spoke in an earnest tone that made her frown. 'Honour, it's Jack. Well, you probably know that already.' He sounded embarrassed. 'Look, I know you don't want to talk to me, and I don't blame you, but I had to phone. I was talking to Malcolm again yesterday and he told me how ill Tara's been, and about the transplant and stuff. I just wanted to say how sorry I am.'

His words sent Honour back to the table, where she flopped down into her chair, feeling entirely exposed, her family's life laid bare once more. How could Bridie and Scott's hapless son have told Jack what was going on in their lives? Did he think that was acceptable? Honour switched the phone to her other ear as Jack continued to talk.

'After everything that's happened, with you, and with Kenny, I need to do something. To help if I can. You know where to reach me if you need anything at all. I'll go now. OK. Phone me any time. Bye, then.'

As she laid the phone face down on the table, Honour leaned back against the wooden slats of the chair, suddenly exhausted.

Marion had offered to come and stay at the cottage for a while and take care of Cal to let Honour go back to work. She hadn't been into the care home since Tara had been taken into hospital, and her fear of losing her job when it was their only steady income was growing. Tilda had assured her that she would not lose her place there, but Honour couldn't afford to risk it, so she'd accepted her mother's offer.

Bridie had continued to be an angel, dropping off food, and

magazines for Tara, doing laundry, feeding Frodo, taking Callum out for walks on the beach, while Scott had been working in Honour's back garden, pruning the dried-out shrubs, weeding, and even aerating and feeding the sad patch of lawn.

This evening, when Honour had got back from seeing Tara, Marion was asleep on the sofa, her fair hair fanning across the back of the leather cushion like a silver doily.

'Hello,' Honour whispered to Callum, who was sitting in Kenny's chair. 'Are you all right?'

He nodded.

'How long has Grandma been asleep?'

He looked at his grandmother and smiled. 'Dunno. Bridie's washing up.'

A clattering sound came from the kitchen as if to underline Callum's statement, and Honour jumped, then she dropped her bag near the door and walked into the kitchen.

Bridie was at the sink, her sleeves rolled up and the draining board full of plates and mugs. 'You don't have to do that, Bridie.' Honour touched her neighbour's shoulder.

'Och, it's no trouble. Your mum was a wee bitty tired today, so I offered.' Bridie's long plait split her lithe back in two, her pale green sweater hanging well below her hips. 'There's a chicken stew in the fridge, and a trifle. And I've put another container of soup in the freezer.' She dried her hands on the tea towel Honour held out to her, then hung it neatly on the handle of the Aga.

'You're an angel.' Honour pulled a chair out and sat down. 'Mum's been fabulous this week, but I feel bad how much this is taking out of her. Running my household is not exactly a picnic, you know.' She gave a gentle laugh. 'How's Cal been today?'

Bridie sat opposite her, rolling her sleeves back over her wrists. 'Fine, I think.'

Honour nodded, her body beginning to release the tension

that had held her upright all day. 'Have you been here all afternoon, then?'

Bridie nodded. 'From about one. I went into my studio this morning and worked for a few hours, then I popped in to drop the food off and your mum and I had a cuppa. I just stayed to keep her company.' She smiled. 'Don't worry about her, Honour. She's stronger than she looks.'

Honour nodded. 'She is my hero. Truly.'

Honour stood up and stretched out her taut back, just as Callum padded into the kitchen behind her. His headphones were around his neck and his glasses were perched on the tip of his nose, the lenses thickly smudged as always.

He walked over and leaned in to her side.

'Hi, love. Everything OK?'

He shrugged. 'Yeah. I'm OK. Bored, but OK. School was boring.'

Honour laughed softly, gently moving his glasses further up his nose. 'Everything is boring at the moment, eh Cal?'

He took a moment, then his shoulders jumped. 'Yes, a bit.' He surveyed her face then he added, 'But I found something good today.'

Honour drew him closer to her side. 'Oh, yes? What was that?'

He lifted the iPad and stroked the surface, the screen coming to life. 'There's a website where you can buy a star. You can call it whatever you want, and you get a certificate to say it's yours, and a map of where it is in the sky.'

Familiar with this concept, Honour nodded. 'Yes, I've heard of that.'

Callum eased himself away from her and slid onto his usual chair at the table. 'Can we buy one for Tara, for Christmas?'

Honour's heart twinged as she took in his earnest face, the guileless hazel eyes, and the wide mouth, so reminiscent of his father's, twitching as it did when he was excited about something. 'I think that's a brilliant idea.' She moved over to him and leaned in, looking at the screen more closely. Catching Bridie watching them, she smiled as Bridie surreptitiously wiped her eyes. 'What shall we call it?' Honour asked.

Callum's mouth dipped, then he said, 'Tara's star. Can't really call it Tara-dactyl.' He grinned, his eyes going to Bridie, who had snorted. 'But what if we got more stars, like a family constellation? Then we can have one for Dad, one for Tara, and you, and me? That way, we'll always be together in the sky.'

Honour was now battling the tears that were clogging her throat. 'Callum, I love that idea.'

She kissed the top of his head just as he said, 'We can get them for Grandma, and Grandpa, too, and one for Uncle Jack, if you want.'

Honour's heart lurched. The few times they had talked about Jack during Callum's short life were long ago, and his mentioning him now was utterly shocking. Unsure how to respond, she looked at the door to the living room, where Marion now stood, her eyes wide.

'What's all this?' She walked to the table and touched Honour's arm. 'What did I miss?'

Callum smiled. 'Don't tell Tara. It's a surprise.'

Honour was still unable to form words, so she walked into the hall, then beckoned to her mother, while Callum started to show Bridie the website. Taking Marion to the far side of the living room, Honour whispered, 'Why is he talking about Jack? What brought that on?'

Marion shrugged. 'I think he maybe overheard Bridie telling Malcom off earlier. Callum was in the back garden with Scott, helping him with the grass, and Bridie and Malcom were out in her garden at the same time. She was having a go at him for talking to Jack about Tara, so Cal must've heard.'

Honour tried to picture the scene, Callum hearing the name of someone who had never featured in his life, and yet whom he knew to be part of his family – enough to be included in their constellation. That he was thinking about family in this way, a collective that needed to be kept together, taking up a permanent place in the sky, was heartbreaking. It was clear that Callum was worrying about losing Tara, as he had his father, and this gesture was about securing the family he had left, in the only way he could think of.

'Bless his heart,' Honour sputtered. 'I think I've made a mistake, not letting him be tested, Mum. He is so clever, so intuitive. I think it's time.'

Marion nodded, then cupped Honour's cheek. 'I think you're right. There's no harm in getting that done, and then you can make an informed decision, if he is a match.'

Honour took in her mother's face, the gentle eyes that had carried her through many a crisis in her life. 'It's going to be all right, isn't it, Mum?' Honour hugged her mother, the familiar lily-of-the-valley scent lingering at her neck.

'Yes. It is.' Marion's voice was thick. 'And let Cal do the star thing. It's important to him.'

Honour pulled back from her mother's arms, taking in the shadow of an unanswered question in Marion's eyes. 'I will. And he can even get one for Jack if it makes him feel safer.'

Marion smiled. 'Good. Now, let's get you some dinner. You looked exhausted.'

Honour let her mother lead her back to the kitchen, where Bridie was asking Callum about the planets, smiling as he chattered about Venus being closer to the sun than the earth is. Honour listened to him, marvelling at his passion, and depth of knowledge about the universe, as she tried to picture their family constellation, a handful of stars that would always be connected, even if life had done all it could to tear them apart, and even if that constellation included Jack.

32

As October drew to a close, and with Callum's ninth birthday behind them, Tara had become much weaker. Her blood counts were low, her appetite non-existent, and she was having pain above her knee joint that radiated up into her hip. Honour was waiting for, and at the same time dreading, the latest scan results, but with no matches coming up on the national register, it was now critical that they find a donor.

Honour had made an appointment for Callum to be tested that morning. Now, as she watched him cleaning his teeth, his eyes flicking to hers as she busied herself straightening the damp towels on the heated rail, as always happened with Callum, she sensed a question coming.

She tried to keep her face impassive as he spat his mouthful of foam into the sink, and rinsed his mouth out, sliding his toothbrush back into the ceramic jar where three brushes still stood. Kenny's purple toothbrush was slightly taller than the others, the bristles splayed out from his vigorous scrubbing. Honour would tease him, telling him that he'd wear his enamel away, but Kenny would just laugh, foam trickling onto his chin as he flicked water at her as she'd laugh loudly at his antics.

Seeing the toothbrush made her eyes burn, so she focused back on Callum, who was now tucking in the top of his new pyjamas, that were navy blue and covered in shooting stars and comets. He'd had a bad couple of days with his Ménière's, leaving him dizzy and nauseated. Thankfully, this morning, he had begun to look more like himself again and had even been keen to go back to school, much to Honour's relief.

'So, there's not a needle or anything. Just like a Q-tip?' His question startled her back to the moment.

'No needles.' She drew a cross over her heart. 'Painless, and over in seconds.'

He nodded, his hand going to his hips. 'And then, if it works, I can help Tara get better?'

Honour smiled. 'That's the hope.'

Callum kicked the bathmat, his bare feet seeming to have stretched in just the last few weeks. 'I wish Dad was here. He'd get everything fixed.'

Honour winced as she nodded, aware that his comment was not meant as a slight, just as testament to his faith in his father's ability to find the cure for all their ills. She had thought this about her own father, all her childhood, and the memory of the sense of comfort it gave her made her smile. 'Yes, he would.'

Callum surveyed her face, then dipped his chin, his voice little more than a whisper. 'What if it doesn't work?'

Honour stepped forward and drew him in to her front, his head now level with her diaphragm. 'We'll think positive thoughts, Cal, and whatever happens, we'll keep Tara's chin up.' She smoothed a tuft of damp hair that stubbornly sat upright at the back of his head. 'We're a team, and what do we MacLeods always say?'

He looked up at her, his eyes glittering. 'Hold fast.' He repeated the clan motto that Kenny would pull out of the bag whenever they faced challenges.

'Exactly.' She made a fist and punched it towards the ceiling, another of Kenny's quirks whenever the motto was mentioned. 'Hold fast.'

Callum had been a champion at the hospital, partly chuffed that he'd got to miss school again but also genuinely pleased that, after his appointment, he would be able to see Tara, having been kept away to minimise the risk of infection. Now, he was sitting at her bedside, his elbows propped on the mattress as she flipped TV channels with the remote. 'Can't we watch something interesting?' he grumbled. 'This is all girls' stuff.'

Tara tutted, her mouth seeming to take up much more of her face due to her recent weight loss. 'Cal, it's the middle of the day. All that's on are chat shows and old films.' She continued to flip through the channels. 'How about this?' She stopped at a nature programme where a pride of lions was pacing across an African plain.

'Suppose so.' He huffed, then stood up, and made to climb onto the bed next to her. Honour was instantly anxious, afraid this was too close, that he might be the unwitting harbinger of germs, passing on a new infection that could bring Tara to her knees again.

'Cal, can you just sit on the chair, love?' Honour moved across the room, lifting Cal's jacket from where he'd dumped it on the floor. She then folded it over the back of the chair by the window.

'It's a better view from here.' He was already half on the bed.

'Cal.' Honour's voice was brittle now, her stress leaking into it. 'Please.'

Tara caught her eye and almost imperceptibly shook her head. 'It's OK, Mum. He's wearing a mask.' She tipped her head to the side, her eyes full of mischief, a sight that made Honour's tattered heart warm. 'Which is just as well, because he stinks of cheese and onion crisps.'

Callum snorted, shifting in closer to his sister as he shoved his glasses further up over the mask. 'Shut up. I do not.' He batted her leg playfully. 'Anyway, it's better than smelling like Marmite.' He grimaced behind the mask. 'That makes me puke.'

Honour tutted. 'Hey. That's enough.' She smiled at them fondly, the new, more gentle nature of their teasing still a welcome change. 'Lorna is going to pop in and see you both in a while, so, Cal, stay here and don't wander off anywhere while I go and get some coffee.'

He nodded, his head tipping closer to Tara's shoulder. 'OK.'

Honour took another second to soak in the scene, Tara allowing her little brother to make contact with her shoulder rather than shove him off as she would have a few months ago. Smiling her gratitude at Tara, who widened her eyes theatrically, Honour walked out into the corridor just as Lorna was coming towards her.

'Hey. Sorry it took me a while. I got pulled back in to help in paediatrics.' Lorna smiled, her fair hair in a tight ponytail, and her petite frame made even smaller by the loose scrubs she wore. 'How's the patient today?'

Honour nodded, picturing Tara's wan complexion, the way her eyes seemed to take over her thin face, the image soul-destroying. 'Her spirits are good, she's just so thin, Lorna. I feel like she'll snap when I hug her.' Honour felt her throat clogging up, so she cleared it. 'Cal's in with her now. They're so sweet together these days. It's like they actually like one another.' She smiled at her friend, seeing Lorna assessing her.

'Don't hold your breath. As soon as Tara's well, they'll go back to hating each other.' Lorna gave a little snort, her words making Honour's chin lift. Lorna's certainty that Tara would get well was reassuring and exactly what Honour needed from her friend, but Honour couldn't fight the voice deep inside, the one that whispered to her when no one was around that there was no such thing as certainty in all this, and that despite her efforts to control the outcome, her daughter's fate was out of her hands – something unbearable for any mother.

Seeming to read her mind, Lorna hooked her arm through Honour's. 'If they're happy in there, let's sneak off for a coffee. We haven't had a decent, kid-free chat for weeks, and then I'll pop in on them on the way back.'

Grateful for the break, Honour nodded. 'Sounds good. We can't be too long, though.'

'Trust me. I can't ever be too long. My breaks are few and far between and last just about long enough for me to pee.' Lorna tugged Honour closer. 'Now, talk. What's going on in that head of yours?'

Honour followed Lorna up the stairs to the floor above, where the brightly lit café was half-empty. With two steaming cups of coffee and a slightly curled-up sandwich that Lorna had grabbed, they sat at a table near the window overlooking the car park. Honour sipped her coffee and, gradually, the bitter brew seemed to unlock her taut throat, letting all the frayed thoughts that kept her awake at night flow out. All the while, Lorna just nodded, chewing her sandwich until she popped the last piece of bread into her mouth.

Honour sat back, feeling as if she'd shed a giant anvil of worry from across her back. 'God, sorry. I am such a friggin' downer these days.'

Lorna shoved her plate away, brushing crumbs off her lap. 'For God's sake, Honour. I'm amazed that you can keep functioning at all, be super-mum for Tara, keep up with Callum, work, never mind just cope with daily life without Kenny.' She huffed. 'I'd be curled up in the foetal position in a cupboard, and Dougie would have starved to death.' The laughter that followed was more relief than amusement, and Honour let the salve of that soothe her troubled heart.

After a few moments, she checked her watch, seeing that they'd been away for almost half an hour. 'Gosh, we better get back.'

Lorna clapped her hand over her forehead. 'God, I almost forgot to tell you. Doctor Hail has put a rush on Callum's testing. He said to tell you that the results should be back in a couple of days.'

'Oh, that's great. Thanks.'

'Right, let's go and see your lovely kids.' Lorna cocked her arm. 'Madam.'

Honour looped her arm through her friend's, and they headed for the lifts.

Honour had worked a morning shift the following day and had enjoyed spending a quiet half-hour with Professor Payne. She felt bad that she'd been neglecting him lately but as often happens in a village, he had learned of her troubles and had greeted her with a hug and a box of Roses chocolates that he'd asked his son to buy. 'Honour, my dear. I am so very sorry for everything you are going through.' His pale eyes had been filmy. 'If there's anything an old duffer like me can do, please don't hesitate to ask.' He'd held a wizened hand out to her, and she'd clasped it in hers, his skin feeling papery and fragile.

'Thank you so much, Professor. We'll enjoy these at the weekend when, hopefully, Tara will be home.' Honour crossed her fingers and planted a light kiss on his head.

'Ah, stop that, now. You'll turn me soft, lass.' He'd chuckled, the throaty sound quickly turning into a rattly cough.

She'd changed the dressings on his legs, happy to see that

the ulcers were beginning to heal, thanks to her suggestion to the nurses that they persevere with the honey treatments. Then she had made him a cup of tea and stayed with him until he'd settled in for a nap in his chair. After tucking a blanket over his knees, she had tiptoed out of the room.

Having been home only half an hour, taken in the washing that she'd hung out that morning, Honour sat in the living room with her feet up on the trunk, and a mug of hot coffee balanced on her thigh. The warmth of the room began to ease her coiled insides as she looked at the empty grate, deciding that tonight she'd light the fire when she got back from seeing Tara.

The first November nights were drawing in, both with early darkness and the wall of cold that signalled the true beginning of winter. Honour closed her eyes and let her mind wander to winters past, when all four of them had huddled in front of the fire during power cuts toasting bread and crumpets by candle-light and playing Monopoly or Yahtzee until the fire had begun to dim, then Honour felt herself drift towards sleep. As she recognised a tingle of worry at possibly sleeping beyond Callum's pick-up time, her phone chirped from the kitchen where she'd left it on the table.

Her heart leaping, as it always did now when she heard this sound, she jumped, sloshing hot coffee over her thigh. 'Shit.' She stood up, lifting the soaked scrub away from her leg that was already tingling. 'Double shit.' She walked quickly into the kitchen, simultaneously lifting her phone, and dumping the dripping mug into the sink.

Doctor Hail's name lit up the screen. 'Hello, Mrs MacLeod?'

'Yes. Hi, Doctor Hail.' She grabbed a cloth from the sink and dabbed at her damp trouser leg.

'I'll get right to it. We got Callum's lab results back and I'm afraid he's not a full match.' He paused, as Honour's insides somersaulted. How could this be? Doc Hail had said that a

sibling would be the best chance at a full match. 'I don't understand. I thought he was our best bet.'

Doctor Hail's voice was metered, his next words obviously
carefully curated. 'Yes, a full sibling would have a very high
chance of being a full match. But I'm afraid with a half-sibling,
it's almost unheard of.'

33

Honour slumped down in a chair, her elbows smacking onto the tabletop. 'What do you mean, a half-sibling?' As soon as she'd said it, she wanted to snatch her question back.

What Doctor Hail was saying was clear; the tests showed that Callum was not a full sibling, and so, Kenny wasn't Tara's biological father. Honour's head spun out of control, and as she tried to grasp what she had just heard, the doctor was discreet. Rather than ask any questions, he calmly said they'd keep searching the register and do all they could to care for Tara in the meantime.

Shattered, unable to continue the conversation, Honour croaked a goodbye, then let the phone drop to the table. Tears flooded her eyes as the painful memory that she'd fought to squash for over a decade flashed to life.

It was twelve years ago, on a rainy Thursday night in July, around 11.30 p.m. Honour had been at home alone since getting back from work at 4.30 p.m., and Kenny and Jack had been propping up the bar at the local pub since before dusk.

Honour left two messages on Kenny's voicemail asking him when he'd be home, and not having heard from him by 11.15 p.m., she slammed around in the bathroom, brutally scrubbing her teeth until her gums bled, then slapping night cream on her face as hot tears merged with the oily serum, making her eyes sting.

With her pyjamas on under a heavy robe, she went downstairs, determined that this time she was going to lock him out, make him realise that she'd been serious when she'd told him that the binge drinking had to stop. She wanted to blame Jack, who was older, supposedly wiser, and could hold his drink better, but in her heart, she knew that Kenny was the one who never wanted to leave the bar once his friends began to gather there.

As she switched off the lights in the kitchen and crossed the living room, heading for the front door, it flew open, startling her, and letting a gust of briny wind in, along with a spray of rain that misted around the two men standing there.

Jack was holding Kenny firmly under his left arm, Kenny's head lolling to the side and a dark stain on his jacket that, within seconds, Honour could smell was vomit.

'For God's sake,' she grumbled. 'What the hell, Kenny?'

Jack hefted Kenny into the room and Honour grimaced at the sour smell of her husband as she closed the door behind them and watched her brother-in-law guide Kenny towards the stairs.

'Hi, Hon. Sorry about this. He wouldn't be moved tonight.' Jack at least had the decency to look embarrassed at the state of his brother, Jack seeming not to be nearly as inebriated himself.

'Too little too late, Jack,' Honour snapped as Kenny stumbled at the bottom of the stairs, banging down onto his knees on the first step.

Jack hauled him up again, gripping him under the armpits. 'Come on, wee brother. Up to bed with you.'

Honour grabbed the back of Jack's wet jacket. 'No. He's not sleeping upstairs in that state.' She yanked Jack back from the stairs. 'Put him on the couch.'

Jack looked surprised but made to guide Kenny towards the sofa, when Kenny lifted his chin, locking eyes with Honour. 'No' the couch. I wanna go to ma bed.'

Honour jammed her hands into the pockets of her robe, her face on fire, determined not to cry this time. 'No way. You'll sleep down here. You promised me you'd stop this, Kenny. I can't bloody take it anymore.' Her voice rang out, brittle, and louder than she intended, making Jack's eyebrows jump.

Kenny shouted at her, his words slurred, 'Don' tell me wha' to do, wooman.'

Jack tried to keep hold of his brother, but Kenny jerked himself out of Jack's grip and lunged to the side, probably aiming for the stairs again but instead falling backwards into the space between the couch and the old trunk.

Honour instinctively stepped forward to catch him, break his fall, and when his elbow smacked into her top lip, she yelped in shock. The pain began as a tingling that made her eyes water as she clamped her hand over her mouth, while Kenny seemed to melt into a damp heap on the rug, laughing like an idiot as Honour began to cry. Her face started to throb, and the tang of blood crept into her mouth, making her gag.

Seeing her bleeding, Jack seemed to sober up instantly. 'Jesus, Kenny. Look what you've done.' He pulled Kenny up onto his feet as if he weighed no more than a basket of fish, then, bending down, Jack folded Kenny's body over his shoulder – like a bedraggled ragdoll. 'I'll get him up to bed, then I'll clean him up.'

Losing the will to argue, Honour dashed into the kitchen and pulled off some sheets of kitchen roll, wetting them and dabbing at her lip. The blood seemed like a lot as she flopped into a chair, put her head back and let the tears come, tears that she'd hidden numerous times from Kenny when this kind of drunken debacle had happened before. She'd been horrified by this behaviour for months, dreading the nights when he'd tell her he was popping into the Harbour Arms for a quick pint, as it was never quick, and it was never just one.

She stood up and walked into the hall, the damp paper pressed against her lip. A few moments later, Jack met her coming down the stairs. 'God, Honour. Let me have a look.' He led her to the sofa and helped her sit.

'What about him?' She nodded towards the stairs, unable to say Kenny's name, her voice gruff with tears.

'He's fine. I took his coat and shoes off and put him on his side, in the bed in the spare room. He'll sleep it off.'

Honour pictured Kenny, half-dressed, filling the narrow single bed they'd been given by his parents when they'd moved into the cottage. 'I should go and see to him.' She tried to stand up, but Jack's hands were firm on her shoulders.

'Sit still. Let me see.' He eased the wad of bloody paper away from her mouth, wincing as he caught sight of the mess his brother had created. 'It's colourful, but I don't think it's deep.' He took the paper from her and carefully dabbed her lip, checking periodically to see if the bleeding had stopped. 'It's slowing down.'

Honour let him guide her hand away from her face. Let him take the paper. Let him help her, which was more than her husband was capable of, and as she began to cry again, she slumped onto Jack's shoulder, feeling the rough wool of his jacket against her cheek, and catching a whiff of beer from his breath. As her body shook with sobs, she gasped, 'I don't know that person upstairs, Jack. He's not the man I married.'

Jack rubbed her back, letting her cry it out, then, as her sobs abated, he eased her upright and gently swept the long ponytail behind her shoulder. He put his forefinger under her chin and turned her face towards his, scrutinising the cut on her lip.

Concern filled his mossy eyes, and he tutted softly as he once again dabbed her lip with the paper. Honour was heartbroken, exhausted, afraid that her marriage was on the brink, and she craved kindness, comfort, exactly what she was being offered – not by her husband, but by his brother. Jack's gentle ministrations began to soothe her pain, and Honour craved more – more of the feeling of safety his large hands provided, more of the sense of being cared for rather than being the carer – so when Jack lifted her chin again and locked eyes with her, she didn't resist when he leaned in and kissed her lightly on the lips.

The pressure of his mouth against hers created a mixture of pain and fierce desire to have him kiss her more deeply, to take her away from the reality of her life that had gone so badly wrong.

Before she could stop herself, she responded to the kiss, wrapping her arms around Jack's neck.

He mumbled, 'Oh, God. I've dreamed of this. It's always been you, Honour.'

Hearing the words was like a bolt of lightning sparking through her, shocking, and yet warming her empty insides, and Honour let go of that shock and let her need to be loved take over.

When they woke up in the middle of the night, like two spoons on the sofa, Honour was instantly mortified, certain that she'd just made the worst mistake of her life. Jack roused himself, pulling on his jeans and awkwardly raking the mass of dark hair away from his angular face.

Trembling, Honour spoke quietly but leaving no room for misinterpretation. 'This should never have happened and can never happen again. It was a mistake. A terrible mistake.' His strong jaw sagged and the sadness that filled his eyes was painful to see. But awash with guilt, and red-hot shame, she continued, 'We can't be around each other, Jack. We just can't do this to Kenny.'

'I never meant to get in between you and him. But you can't deny that we feel something for each other, Honour. Ever since he first brought you home, I...' He shrugged, obviously conflicted – torn between what he wanted and what he knew was the right thing to do.

She moved away, putting the sofa between them, 'We don't feel anything real for each other, Jack. That, tonight, was pure sadness. Desperation and nothing more.' She saw him take in her words, then drop his chin in defeat.

'What can I do?' He lifted his jacket from the floor and slipped it on.

'Nothing.'

He eyed her then, and she was shocked when he nodded. 'OK. I'll stay away.'

Honour grabbed onto his statement as a drowning man might a life raft, saying, 'That'll be best, Jack. At least for a while.'

When he'd left within a week, never to return – even to see his dying father – she had kept everything that had happened to herself, but her guilt, and shame, at allowing his family and friends to judge him without knowing the truth had burrowed deep inside her, leaving a scar that would never heal. She had never meant for Jack to leave forever, and, over time, she had convinced herself that his decision wasn't only about her. But she had never been able to bring herself to tell Kenny what had happened, to pull their marriage apart, too.

Within a week of Jack leaving, she and Kenny had reconciled. He'd sworn to change his ways, had joined AA and had never touched another drop of alcohol since that night. Seven weeks later, Honour had discovered that she was pregnant – an unexpected gift that she and Kenny had gratefully received, diverting their focus to the future, and letting them put the dark days they'd survived behind them.

Now, Honour stood up and filled a glass with water at the sink, and as she drank it down in several long gulps, Jack's words came back to her. '*After everything that's happened, with you, and with Kenny, I need to do something to make amends.*' They reverberated inside her aching head, until the lingering question she had not allowed herself to address, for over a decade, surfaced once again. What if the thing she had feared, and pushed down every time she thought of Jack, was true?

If he was Tara's biological father, could he now potentially save their daughter? The idea was too shocking to contemplate, and yet, Honour was suddenly filled with a sense of such certainty that she couldn't move. The very last person she wanted to call on could now be her daughter's last chance.

Once Callum had gone to bed, Honour poured herself a large whisky, dribbled some water in it and headed for the bathroom. She filled the tub and added lavender oil, sank into the steamy water, and stuffed a towel behind her head. Her phone sat on the tiled shelf behind the bath and as she stared at it, knowing that she had no other options left, she took a gulp of whisky, letting the smoky burn linger on the back of her tongue.

Once the ache in her back had finally begun to ease, she sighed, heaved herself out of the water, dried herself and slipped on her thick robe. Then, pulling her shoulders back, she picked up the phone. If there was any other way, she'd have taken it, but as she searched for the number she needed, her heart was clawing its way up the back of her throat.

It rang only twice and then she heard his voice. The way he said her name, rolling the last letter longer than necessary, made the hairs on her arms stand up. Putting her reaction to him aside, she took a moment to gather herself, then said firmly, 'Jack, it's me. I need your help.'

34

Within a week, Jack had an appointment at the Victoria to be tested and had asked if he could stop by the cottage afterwards, before heading back to Edinburgh. Honour had let her gratitude towards him sway her, and she had agreed, and now, as the watery midday sun battled with the veil of heavy cloud rolling in from the west, she stood at the kitchen sink, her stomach fluttering.

Wanting to feel as together as she could, she'd dressed carefully. She'd chosen to wear her jeans, a creamy Arran sweater, and her new sheepskin slippers, and she'd scraped her hair into a high bun, securing it with one of Tara's velvety bands. Make-up-less, except for a sweep or two of mascara, her hands were shaking as, after washing up the breakfast dishes, she slipped her wedding ring back on.

Checking her reflection in the window, she was annoyed that she was nervous, so she tried to dig deep, to find the cool resolve she'd need to see him again, face to face, after all these years. As she looked at the outline of her face, her features indistinct in the glass, she wondered if he'd think her very altered, less attractive, and as the thought surfaced, so she hissed, 'For God's sake, Honour. What does it matter what he thinks?'

Turning her back on the sink, she looked through the open door towards the living room just as the doorbell rang. Taking a moment to compose herself, she walked through and opened the door, her face a mask of calm – the furthest thing from what she was feeling inside.

'Hi, Hon.' He used the contracted version of her name that only he had ever used. 'Long time.' The impossibly green eyes were edged with fans of shallow wrinkles, the razor-sharp jawline slightly softened by time, and perhaps a few more pounds than he'd once carried. His dark-brown hair was peppered with grey at the temples and the tan suede jacket he wore over black jeans and a light-blue shirt screamed sophisticated city to her simple village. For some strange reason, while he hovered awkwardly on the doorstep, she calculated his age, realising that he was now forty-five, three years older than Kenny would have been, and seven older than her.

Seeing his discomfort, she opened the door wider. 'Sorry. Yes, it's been a long time.' She gave a half-smile and stepped back. 'Come in.'

He carefully wiped his leather boots on the mat and walked into the room, nervously scanning it as if checking for snipers, or for his dead brother to jump out at him with a machete.

Honour let him swim in his discomfort for a few seconds, the reason for him being here rematerialising, then she pushed out a breath, closing the door behind her. 'I'll put the kettle on.' She walked past him, aware of the size of him, compared to his brother. Jack took up more space in the room than Kenny had, but not only with his physicality. He also took up more of the oxygen, leaving her feeling slightly light-headed as she walked into the kitchen.

He followed her, then sheepishly stood behind one of the chairs across the table from her. 'You look well.'

'You need your eyes tested,' she quipped as she set the kettle on the Aga. Turning to face him, the trace of anxiety she saw in his eyes softened her determination to be cool with him. 'Sit, for goodness' sake.'

He drew out the chair and sat down, his broad shoulders and barrel chest an odd sight across the table. Honour had become used to it being just her and the children now, so his presence put her on edge, but for more reasons than just his size.

'How are you?' She sat opposite him and moved the salt and pepper shakers closer together, her stomach knotting tightly under her sweater.

'I'm OK. Getting on with things.' He shrugged. 'How's Tara?'

Honour sighed. 'She's remarkably strong in many ways, but so young, and vulnerable at the same time. She keeps her chin up despite feeling like hell, most of the time.' She was on the point of saying that Tara had Kenny's iron-willed determination, but just before the words tumbled out of her mouth, Honour sucked in her lower lip. If what she believed to be true were true, then Tara's determination came from two potential sources – herself or Jack – and poor, unsuspecting Kenny had no part to play in it. Conflicted, but unwilling to share her suspicions yet, to give Jack that much power over her or her daughter until she knew his intentions, Honour regrouped. 'Thank you for doing that today, Jack. It means a lot.'

'My pleasure. Well, not a pleasure, but I mean... of course.' His cheeks coloured slightly, surprising her. He had never been a bashful man. Quite the contrary – full of laughter and confidence, at times verging on what Honour had thought was arrogance. She'd sometimes felt superfluous, even belittled, by the way he'd talk over her after a few pints, so seeing him squirming in her company gave her a sense of the shift in balance between them. It was as if the tables had turned after what had happened, their one night together passing the baton of control firmly to Honour. Her burly, loud, domineering brother-in-law was in her domain now, and while it felt safer than before, it also made Honour incredibly sad – the reason for him reappearing in her life as miserable as she'd felt this past few months.

'The test results have only been taking a day or so. Doc Hail is a miracle worker.' She tried to smile. 'He's great with Tara, too.'

'That's good.' Jack nodded, leaning forwards, and slipping his arms out of his jacket. The movement instantly made Honour anxious. Was he planning on staying longer than she was comfortable having him here? 'I don't want to overstep, Hon, but are you OK? I mean, do you need anything?' He scanned the room as if looking for signs that the house was falling into rack and ruin without his brother's presence.

Unsure what he was getting at, Honour frowned. 'Like what?'

He draped his jacket over the back of the chair and leaned forward on his elbows, just like Kenny used to when he had something important to say. 'I know you said you were all right, but are you sure you're coping OK, money wise?'

Taken aback at the implication, Honour's frown deepened. 'I'm fine, but that's really none of your concern, Jack.'

He sat back, his eyes closing slightly. 'Look, I didn't mean to offend you. I was just thinking that without the income from the boat, and—'

Honour stood up abruptly. 'I didn't ask you for anything other than to be tested, Jack. The kids and I are totally fine. We're not alone, you know. We have family to support us.'

His face seemed to droop at the word *family*, and as he watched her move to the stove and lift the now steaming kettle off the top, he stood up and pulled his jacket on. 'Don't bother with the tea. This was a mistake.' He paused. 'I just wanted to try to help Tara and see if you and I could move on. Put the past behind us. But I was obviously barking up the wrong tree.'

She set the kettle on a trivet and met his eyes, and seeing the profound pain there, Honour had a shocking revelation. His decision to leave the village had not only given her the space she'd asked for, but it had also caused him to give up his father, and Kenny, the only remaining family that he had. Her fear of discovery had damaged them both, her internally as the guilt ate away at her over the years, and him equally as intensely – by isolating him from everyone he loved. She took in his expression, and she wondered which of them had suffered the most.

Empathy flooding her heart, and shame at her part in his punishment, Honour wanted to give him something back. 'Look. I'm sorry, Jack. I didn't mean to be cruel. Sit and have some tea.' She saw his eyebrows lift as she filled the teapot, her hand shaking slightly. 'I know what all this has done to you.' She drew a line between them in the air. 'I was so young and scared. Terrified of what we did, and what it would do to Kenny if he ever found out.' She took a moment to get the next part just right. The words feeling as important as any she had uttered in her thirty-eight years. 'We both made a mistake that night, and we've paid for it differently, but in our own way.' She saw him nod as she set a steaming mug in front of him.

'I took advantage, Hon. I knew you were in pain. In a bad place with Kenny.' He closed his eyes. 'I saw an opportunity, and I took it, even though I knew better.'

The sincerity of his words was ringing in Honour's ears, his willingness to share the blame more than she could have hoped for, and more than she felt she deserved.

'The thing is, Jack, that all seems so small now, in the face of what's happening to Tara. After losing Kenny, I just can't take another loss. It will end me. Do you understand that?' She felt tears behind her eyes, but determined not to let them win this time, she blinked them away. 'If your tests come back and you're a match, will you be Tara's donor? I know it's a big ask, but I need this, Jack. I need it more than life itself.' She gripped the back of the chair, watching his jaw twitching.

'You don't have to ask.' He looked suddenly exhausted. 'Of course, I will.'

She walked around the table and, without thinking, relief sent her arms around his neck. 'Thank you,' she whispered, catching a faint cedar-like scent coming from his skin that made her take a step back, the memories it invoked too painful to access again.

They sat together for a few minutes, their delicate truce feeling new and unsettling to Honour, so she was relieved when he eventually drained his mug and stood up. She followed suit, and moving towards the door, she found a smile. 'Thanks again for today, and as for the past, let's bury it, Jack. Let's forgive each other because there are bigger things to focus on now.'

He took a moment, then gave a small smile that lifted only the right side of his mouth, but she saw the relief behind it. 'Deal.'

She walked into the hall, knowing that, for now, this was the best they could hope for. Their truce brought with it a promise of some peace for them both, after far too long. At least until his test results came back. Then if what she suspected was confirmed, they'd be having a very different conversation.

35

Two days later, Jack phoned while Honour was at work. She had a morning shift and was planning on going straight to the hospital to see Tara as soon as she finished at noon. She had just left Professor Payne's room when her phone rang, so she darted along the hall to the staffroom, glad to see it was empty. 'Hi, Jack.'

'Hi.' He sounded odd, as if he had a cold.

'What's going on? Are you OK?' She closed the door to the staffroom and walked to the window, looking out over Market-gate. In the street below, some last vendors were taking down their stalls from the farmer's market, stacking empty crates where locally grown produce including potatoes, leafy cabbages and blood-red beetroots had been displayed earlier that morning.

'I got the results. They just phoned.'

Honour's heart leapt, but he sounded flat, so just as quickly it dipped again. 'And?' She gripped the phone tighter, pressing her hips against the windowsill.

'Hon, I'm a match. A full match.'

'Oh, my God.' She covered her eyes with her palm, tears instantly flooding in. 'Oh, Jack.'

'Honour, there's something else.'

She was trembling so badly that she stumbled across the room and sank into the sagging armchair, next to the ancient vending machine. She knew exactly what he was going to say next, but she didn't have the energy to stop him. To tell him that she already knew.

'Doctor Hail told me that these are called haploid-identical matches, which apparently are really rare.' He stopped for a moment. 'They happen when the donor is a parent, and the genetic match is at least half identical to the recipient.'

Honour heard a high-pitched tone in her ears which threatened to drown him out completely. She forced herself to focus on the door frame across the room, and let his words in.

'Are you there?'

'Yes.' It was all she could manage.

'Hon, this means that I'm Tara's biological father.'

Hearing him say it out loud was like a dam bursting, all the years of pain, of guilt, shame, and of hiding what she'd done from the people she loved crashing over her in waves. She bent forward, her chest meeting her knees, a release of such magnitude following that she opened her mouth in a silent scream, imagining all the hurt rushing out of her, and, in its place, forgiveness rushing in.

She needed to forgive herself. To forgive him. And she wanted nothing more than to have Kenny's forgiveness, but knowing that last fragment of peace would never come now brought her upright in the chair.

'Honour?' Jack's voice was loaded with concern. 'Are you still there?'

She nodded, then whispered, 'Yes. I'm here.'

A few moments passed, then he said, 'Did you have any idea?'

She pushed herself up from the chair and went back to the window, the need to see the sky, to relate to the world outside her head, overwhelming. 'I suspected, but only very recently.'

'Why didn't you tell me?'

She leaned forward, her temple meeting the cool glass, sending a shiver down her neck. 'I didn't know for sure until just now, Jack, but I'm really sorry you had to hear it from the doctor. I didn't know what to do for the best, but I couldn't say anything until it was confirmed.'

'By these tests.' It was a statement, not a question, so she stayed silent. 'I get it.'

Unsure what he wanted to hear, Honour took a shallow breath. 'You'll help her, won't you?'

'I told you I would, even before...' He halted, she guessed to fully absorb the gravity of his next sentence. 'Before I knew she was my daughter. So, of course I'll do whatever she needs. Whatever *you* need me to do.' He hesitated, then spoke so quietly that she almost missed it when he said, 'I always have.'

He continued to talk about the procedure, the small percentages of donations that involved marrow as opposed to stem cells, how they'd take his liquid marrow from the back of his pelvic bone, through a needle while he was under anaesthetic. As he talked on, Honour stared out at the street, her mind reeling forwards in time to the day that Tara would come home after the transplant, her cheeks pink with health and her eyes flashing brightly again.

Honour then pictured them sitting around the Christmas tree, for the first time without Kenny, and as she heard Jack say her name again, she was suddenly struck with the reality of what was going to happen. Jack was going to give of himself in a way that even she couldn't, to save her daughter – *their* daughter – and Honour didn't know if there would ever be a way that she could repay him.

She tried to imagine him perhaps seeing Tara in the hospital, talking to her, knowing what he now knew, and her skin grew clammy. Tara had asked about her uncle only a handful of times over the years, but she had accepted his absence as normal, as she'd never known anything else. To have him suddenly show up – essentially a stranger – but a stranger in a superhero cape ready to save her life, would inevitably spark questions from Tara that Honour would need watertight answers to.

Tara was too intelligent, too intuitive to placate with half-truths, but if she found out that Kenny wasn't her father because her mother was fallible, and weak, the damage that could do to Tara's psyche, her innocent, trusting heart, and her relationship with Honour was unthinkable. Tara had been through so much already, in her eleven tender years, that Honour couldn't pile anything more on her emotional plate. *When she was better, stronger, older, and I'm brave enough to tell her, will Tara ever forgive me, ever understand?*

As for Marion and Kirk, despite her fear of their reaction to her fall from grace, Honour would figure out a way to tell them the truth, one day. She owed them that much – just not now.

Jack's voice began to trail away as Honour readied herself for yet another hurdle. Another promise that she needed him to make her. And the prospect of asking it, in the face of everything he was already doing, was excruciating.

'Jack. I have one more request.' She steadied her voice. 'I know I've asked so much of you already, but this is critical.'

'What is it?' He sounded cautious.

'Tara can't know the truth about you. Who you are. At least not yet.' She forced a swallow. 'She adored her dad, and shattering that connection, negating those precious memories, would be cruel beyond words. Maybe when she's older...' She waited, willing him to say that he understood, her heart threatening to burst through her ribs.

After what seemed like an eternity, he said, 'I agree. She

doesn't need to know at the moment. I've missed out on her entire life, so I have no right to disrupt it now, or to tarnish her memories of Kenny. For what? To make myself feel better?' He halted, as Honour closed her eyes, relief sweeping through her like the incoming tide. 'She'll not hear it from me, Hon. You have my word. I owe you, her, and Kenny's memory that much.'

'Thank you, Jack.' She swiped away a tear from under her eye. 'I seem to be saying that a lot to you over the past few days.'

He gave a deep laugh. 'Yeah, well it's better than bugger off, I suppose.'

She laughed, a spurt of relief, gratitude and sadness all rolled into one slightly odd sound that carried her emotions into the silence of the room. She hoped he appreciated how much this meant to her, because thank you seemed wholly inadequate. 'Yes. It's definitely better than that.'

Lorna's mouth was semi-open, her chin pulled back. When Honour had texted her the next day, saying she needed to talk on Lorna's next break, they'd met in the lobby and gone out of the hospital to a small coffee shop across the street. Honour was anxious that they'd be overheard inside the Victoria, and she knew so many of the nurses and staff now that privacy was hard to come by. What she had to tell her best friend was nerve-racking, and even though she felt she knew Lorna better than any friend she'd ever had, Honour was still apprehensive about her confession damaging Lorna's opinion of her and, consequently, their friendship.

Now, sitting opposite Honour, Lorna's eyelids were flickering as if she was resisting blinking, in case she missed something, 'OK. Just so I am clear. You had a thing with Jack?'

'Not a thing, thing. A one-time thing.' Honour felt her face warming at the ridiculousness of what she'd just said. 'We were together once. One time, on a night when Kenny was drinking.

He came home absolutely blotto, and Jack put him to bed.' She fingered her lip as a memory of that night filtered back. 'Kenny hurt me, and—'

Lorna gasped. 'That bastard.'

'No. It wasn't like that, Lorna. He was falling all over the place, just floppy drunk, and he banged my lip. It was one hundred per cent an accident.' She held Lorna's gaze, the importance of her point being heard, paramount. The last thing Honour wanted was to tarnish Lorna's perception of Kenny. 'After Jack got Kenny into bed, he helped clean me up. I was so heartbroken, miserable, and lonely, it was a moment of weakness. Jack was there, calm, caring, sensible – everything that Kenny wasn't, at that time.' She forced herself not to drop her eyes to the tabletop. 'It was the worst mistake I've ever made, but, Lorna, it gave me Tara. And when I look at her now, see the amazing young woman she is becoming, it's hard to regret everything about how she came to be.' Honour felt a tear bubble over her lower lid, so she swiped it away. 'I'm deeply ashamed of what I did. What we did to Kenny. But if it meant that Tara wasn't in my life...' She couldn't continue without losing control of her voice completely.

Lorna leaned forward; her eyes piercingly clear as she reached for Honour's hand across the table. 'Look. Kenny was in a bad place back then. I knew there were problems, but you didn't really tell me everything that was going on, because you always protected him.' She squeezed Honour's fingers, then sat back. 'I'm sorry I didn't know how bad it was. I should've been there for you more.' Lorna's eyes were glittering.

'Don't, Lorna. You were always there for me. I chose to hide things because I felt it was my failure, too.' She swallowed hard. 'I used to think that if he needed to be blind drunk to come home, then I must've been doing something terribly wrong.'

Lorna shook her head, tucking a tendril of hair behind her

ear. 'We always blame ourselves, don't we? It's the female condition.'

Honour shrugged. 'Anyway, here we are. Jack wanted to be tested as a donor and now we know.' She paused. 'To be honest, there's been a part of me that always wondered... you know, with the timing of the pregnancy and everything. But I put it out of my head because I wanted to believe she was Kenny's.' Honour's ragged voice broke his name in two. 'He was the love of my life, Lorna. And if I can't save Tara, all the shame and guilt that I've buried over the years will feel like it was for nothing. I need to be the best mother I can to her, to make up for all the ways I've failed her. And Kenny.' Tears were tracking down her cheeks now as Lorna dug into her bag and handed Honour a tissue.

'Listen to me. You are the best mother I know. You put those kids first without fail, and you always have. You can't dump all that guilt on yourself.' Lorna dipped her chin as a mother might when talking to her child. 'It's not your fault that Tara is ill, Honour. There's no failing on anyone's part in that respect. Cancer is a beast of a disease that has no compassion, takes no amount of love or care or innocence into account when it strikes. It's ruthless and we all do whatever we can to fight back. Now, you have the golden goose in Jack, so leave the past behind and look at it this way. If you hadn't shagged him, Tara would be Kenny's and we might still be looking for the perfect match.' Lorna held her palms facing up as Honour's middle twitched – a strangled laugh at her friend's logic escaping her.

'God, Lorna.' She shook her head. 'You are the limit.'

'Well, I'm serious. Everything happens for a reason. You know I believe that. So, if Jack wasn't her biological father, who knows what might have happened, when a donor would have shown up, or how sick she'd have been by then.'

Honour took in Lorna's earnest expression, the high forehead, the wide-set eyes, the way her mouth curved upwards at the edges, as if she were always about to smile, and wanting to accept this justification, more than anything, Honour nodded. 'I want to believe that, but it feels too easy. Like a get-out-of-jail-card that I don't deserve.'

Lorna frowned. 'If anyone deserves one of those, it's you. You need to let it go. Yes, it was a mistake. But honestly, Kenny played a part in it happening, too. You now need to focus on the silver lining. Jack can help Tara, and that's the priority. Stop wallowing in guilt and look to the future.'

Honour looked out of the window, seeing a young woman pushing a stroller with twins in it past the café. The children were dressed, one in pink and one in blue. Honour stared at them, trying to picture her life without her own precious children, and regardless of how they came to *be* in it, she couldn't imagine it. They were her everything, and now, with Kenny gone, Lorna was right. It was time to forgive herself once and for all and focus on getting Tara well.

'Do your parents know about Jack donating?' Lorna pulled a note from her purse and signalled to the waitress for the bill.

'No. I can't tell them. At least not yet.' Honour slipped her jacket on. 'I can't shatter their illusion of me as the daughter they deserve.'

Lorna gave her a look loaded with disapproval. 'They wouldn't condemn you, Honour. They might be shocked, even a little disappointed, but I'm sure they'd understand. They weren't blind to you two having problems back then.'

Honour shook her head. 'Maybe, but I can't cope with their disappointment while Tara is going through all this. They're worried enough about her without me adding that little gem to their plates.'

The two friends stood up, lifting their bags, and heading out the glass-paned door to the street. Outside, the breeze was loaded with the smell of freshly baked bread from the baker next door, and the afternoon sky was a mash-up of grey and blue. A siren sounded nearby, and Honour pictured someone in the back of an ambulance, heading to the Victoria.

'Lorna, thanks for not judging me. I was scared to tell you in case you thought less of me.'

Lorna slid her arm through Honour's and smiled at her. 'I'd never let anything change my opinion of you. You have no idea about some of the stupid things I've done over the years. Once Tara is home, and life is getting back to normal, we'll palm the kids off on your parents, have a sleepover at my place and I'll shock the socks off you.' She gave a cheeky wink.

'What are you on about?' Honour frowned, trying to imagine what Lorna might have done that she wouldn't approve of.

'No. We'll save it for later. Just know that you are not the only one who makes mistakes. You are human, Honour. We all are. All we can do is try to learn from them, and not make the same ones over again.'

Honour laughed softly. 'Believe me. That's never going to happen.'

'Good. Right. So, we move on.' Lorna gently tugged Honour along the pavement.

Honour's heart felt lightened, not just from finally sharing her burden of guilt, but at being loved so unconditionally. Lorna was a ray of light in a murky phase of her life, and Honour hugged her close, sending out a silent thank you for the people who surrounded her right now, when she needed them the most.

Even the one person she had worked to keep out of her life for so long.

Even Jack.

36

The wheels moved quickly with Jack's pre-transplant testing, while Tara remained stable in hospital, protected from infection.

Just days after her conversation with Jack, Honour was so excited and nervous about going in to tell Tara that they'd found a match for her that she'd dashed to the ladies' room at the end of the stuffy corridor in the Victoria and thrown up. She'd taken a few minutes to splash water on her face, chew a mint and smooth her hair before emerging. Now, she was in Tara's room, rearranging the few personal items she had on the bedside cabinet, Honour's breathing shallow behind her mask.

They weren't permitted to have fresh flowers in the room, so Honour had found some silk sunflowers in St Andrews that she'd put in her best, emerald-green vase and sat on the windowsill where Tara could see them. All Tara's cards from Jenna, her friends at school and the football team were stacked in a little woven basket next to the vase.

Honour shuffled the items on the cabinet again, and Tara huffed, 'Mum, leave it. I could reach it all the way it was.' Her cheeks were carrying more colour than in the previous days.

Her appetite had improved a little and she'd eaten two small rolls with bacon that Honour had brought in for her that lunchtime.

'Sorry. I was just thinking I'd clean it with an antibacterial wipe.' Honour was stalling, and as she looked at Tara, it was obvious that she was suspicious of her mother's behaviour.

'They did that this morning.' Tara thumped the pillow behind her. 'They do it every day. It's fine.'

Honour nodded, dragging the plastic chair closer to the bed. The moment had come, and she couldn't delay this conversation any longer. All she could hope was that it went smoothly.

After dropping Callum at school, she'd written herself some notes, practised it in the mirror, but still unsure how to position the information that Jack was the donor with her parents, she was certain that her decision not to tell them yet was right. She knew that with her mother's mastery of internet research, as soon as she told them it was him, Marion would likely put two and two together. Honour wasn't ready to fall on her sword, face the looks of shock, or disappointment that she knew she'd see in their eyes, so for now all they knew was that a donor had been found, and the transplant was going ahead. Marion had been tearful on the phone, and Kirk had sounded gruff – a sure sign that he was suppressing tears, too.

Tara was still watching her, her fingers laced delicately over her stomach. 'Are you OK, Mum?'

Honour smiled behind her mask, hoping that her eyes would convey reassurance. 'Yes. And I have some amazing news.' She lifted one of Tara's hands in hers.

'They've found a cure for cancer?' Tara widened her eyes, the wry insight behind the quip breathtaking.

'I wish. But no. Not as far as I'm aware.' Honour paused. 'However, we have found a full match for you, so you're going to have a bone marrow transplant.'

Tara's eyes widened, this time with genuine surprise. 'Really? Who is it?'

The inevitable question had come, just sooner than Honour had anticipated.

'That's what I want to talk to you about. You know that Grandma, Grandpa, Cal, and I were all tested, and none of us were a match?'

Tara nodded. 'Yep.'

'Well, do you remember us talking about your Uncle Jack? Your dad's older brother?' Honour's pulse thrummed as she released Tara's hand and sat back in the chair.

'Yeah.' Tara frowned. 'The one we've never met?'

Honour nodded. 'Yes. He lives in Edinburgh, and he's a few years older than your dad was.' She took a moment, then continued. 'Well, he found out how ill you'd been, and I asked if he'd be tested as a donor. He immediately agreed.'

Tara sat forward and pulled her knees up to her chest, her thin arms hugging them close over the blanket. 'Why would he do that? He doesn't even know me.'

Tara's question was exactly as anticipated, so Honour reran in her mind the lines she'd rehearsed that morning in the mirror, then dived in. 'He is family, Tara. However far removed. And he was very sad about your dad, and worried about what's happening to you. He was tested last week, and it turns out that he's a full match. Doc Hail says it's very rare, but it happens sometimes, in families.'

Tara frowned, then looked out of the window. 'It's weird that I've never met him, though. I mean, it's like he's a total stranger.' She turned back to face her mother.

'I know, but think about this. If a donor had been found on the registry, they'd be a total stranger too. Right? This way, it's someone closer to home. Someone we know.'

Tara lay back, pulling the blanket up over her chest. 'What's he like? Does he look like Dad?'

Honour hesitated, this not having been something she'd anticipated. Having to describe Jack brought back their encounters, from a decade ago and from just days before – both equally as unsettling. 'He's quite a bit taller and has dark-brown hair. His eyes are green, and his voice is lower and louder than your dad's.' She paused. 'He's clever and funny, and he cares about you, Tara.'

Tara held Honour's gaze, her mouth pursing as if she were chewing over the information. Then, she leaned her head back against the pillows, and sighed. 'I think it's weird, but I'm glad. If he wants to help me it's good. Do you think Dad would've been happy about it?'

Honour let that thought permeate, imagining Kenny's anger at her letting Jack back into their lives, but then as an image developed of her telling Kenny *why* she had gone back on her word, the chair seemed to become rock-hard beneath her, and so Honour stood up. 'He would have been so glad, and grateful to Uncle Jack. Your dad would have turned the world upside-down to help, and protect you, Tara, any way he could. This is a good thing, love, and we need to see it that way.'

Tara nodded against the pillow, her eyelids beginning to droop. 'It's good I'm getting bone marrow. Maybe I'll get well enough to be able to come home soon.' She looked at Honour, and gave a tiny, and yet hopeful, shrug.

Honour's stomach was knotting as she moved in beside Tara and drew her into her arms. 'That's the plan, sweetheart. We all just want you home.'

Tara nodded, then wound her fingers through Honour's. 'Can I meet him?'

This was another question Honour had anticipated but had hoped would not come up. Now she had to face it. If Tara had asked her to lasso the moon and pull it to earth right now, Honour would have said, of course. 'Yes. If you want to, love. You can meet him.'

Tara sat upright again, then scraped her hair behind her ears. 'I do. I want to say thanks to him. Even if we don't know each other, I want to see him.'

Honour nodded slowly, working to keep her face unreadable. The face mask was helping her to some extent, but Tara knew her too well for Honour to be able to hide all that she was feeling. 'OK. I'll give him a ring and ask him to pop in. He wanted to meet you, too, so I'm sure it'll work out.'

'What will I say to him, at first, I mean? Nice to meet you? Thanks for being my donor? Why haven't you come to visit before? Why didn't you and my dad get on?'

Honour picked up the jab in Tara's last statement and dipped her chin. 'No. You can just say nice to meet you, thank you, et cetera. Keep it polite, and kind.'

'Hm.' Tara shrugged, once again lying back against the pillows. 'But why did Uncle Jack never come to see us?'

'Because he made his life in Edinburgh, and he and your dad were very different. It wasn't that they didn't get on, more that life took them down different paths.'

She waited for Tara to question that, but instead she just sighed.

Seeing Tara's eyelids drooping again, Honour stood up and smoothed the blanket. 'You get some rest, sweetheart. I'll pop home to see Cal, and I'll be back later.'

'OK.'

Honour pressed her lips to Tara's forehead, catching the coconut scent coming from her freshly washed hair. 'Sleep now, my angel.'

Two days later, the date for the bone marrow harvest was set for the following Monday. Honour had spoken to Jack, who had said that he would gladly come in to meet Tara, and today, a Friday, was the day. Honour had suggested that he come to the cottage first, then they drive in together, as she wanted to coach him a little more in how to deal with Tara, if she started to ask too many probing questions. Jack had agreed, and now that they were in her car, heading to Kirkcaldy, he seemed anxious.

'So, what do I say if she asks me why I've not been around?' He twisted in the seat, tugging at the seat belt that was tight across his chest.

'Just say that your work keeps you in Edinburgh, and maybe that you travel a lot, or something.' As she said it, Honour was instantly ashamed that she didn't know what Jack did now. When he'd left the village, he had been working on the boat with Allen and Kenny, a fisherman, and a fisherman's son. Embarrassed at her lack of curiosity, she cleared her throat. 'I never asked you what you've been doing all these years. Sorry.' She focused on the road but felt his eyes on her.

'That's OK. We weren't exactly in the market for small talk.' He paused. 'I'm a financial consultant.'

Honour flicked her eyes to his profile, surprised that he'd taken such a tangential path to that of his father and his seagoing heritage. 'Wow. That's quite a change.'

'Yeah. I help people invest and plan for retirement. I do travel quite a bit, actually.'

'That's great. Good for you.' Honour hoped she sounded genuine in her admiration, but giving him praise still felt so impossibly hard that she diverted the conversation back to Tara. 'So just tell her that.'

He nodded, looking at the road ahead. 'I won't give anything away, Honour. You don't have to worry.'

She glanced at him, struck by the way his chin had dropped, the sudden heaviness in his voice. Once again, she was torn, conflicted by her wish to keep him at a distance and not give him access to her troubled heart, and telling him just how much this meant to her, his willingness to do this for a daughter who couldn't pick him out of a crowd.

He scrubbed a hand over his hair, then leaned his head back against the headrest, as the impulse to tell him everything she feared took over. Seeing the familiar sign for the Cameron Bridge distillery, she checked her mirrors, then pulled the car off the road, parking in front of a row of tidy bungalows that felt like old friends now, due to the number of times she'd passed them on her way to and from the hospital.

He looked at her, frowning. 'What's going on?'

Honour turned off the engine and twisted to face him. 'Jack, I should have said this earlier, made sure you understood.' Her throat began to narrow. 'You doing this for Tara is above and beyond. I can't tell you how grateful I am. There's no way I can ever thank you enough. And you agreeing to keep your identity a secret for now.' Her voice threatened to crack as his face softened, then his giant hand settled over hers on the gearstick, his palm cool and his grip firm.

'You don't owe me any thanks. I want to do this. I should've been here for you before now.' He removed his hand and took a few moments to compose himself. 'When I heard about Kenny, I felt responsible. If I'd stayed. Been here to help him. Work the boat. Maybe I could've done something to stop it happening.' His eyes grew filmy. 'I don't know.'

Honour heard the unfiltered pain in his voice, her last reserves of anxiety at his being here crumbling away. 'You weren't to blame, Jack. If anyone was, it was me. I was the one with him that day.' She swallowed hard at the painful memory. 'I told you to stay away for a while, but when you left for good, I let Kenny, and your dad, and the village believe it was because you were selfish and uncaring. I let that happen even when I knew the truth.' Her heart was racing as she fished a tissue out from her sleeve and wiped her nose. 'You honoured your word, and kept our secret, and let me go on with my life while you gave up everything you loved.' She couldn't control the tide of regret inside her, and tears began to slide down her face. 'I am so, so sorry. For everything. But most of all for being such a coward that I let you sacrifice yourself to vitriol and anger that you didn't deserve.' She swallowed over a nut. 'Can you ever forgive me?'

Jack looked stunned, his mouth slightly open while he blinked repeatedly. 'There's nothing to forgive. I made a choice. We both did that night. I made a life for myself that suited me. I haven't been miserable all these years, Honour. Don't take that on. I've been happy, despite wishing I'd done some things differently. I saw being away from the family as penance and it felt right, somehow.' He paused. 'Fitting.'

Honour stuffed the damp tissue up her sleeve and sniffed. 'Well, I think we've both done enough penance for one lifetime.' She gave him a watery smile. 'What say you we focus on Tara now, and a healthy future for her?'

He nodded, rolling his broad shoulders back. 'Absolutely. I'd give anything to help her. Marrow, a limb, my heart.' His voice was ragged with emotion, so Honour held her hand out, palm up.

'Same here. That's what parents do for their children.'

He covered her hand with his and squeezed her fingers. 'Thanks, Honour. For letting me in.'

She nodded. 'It was time. Beyond time.'

She switched on the engine and pulled back out onto the road, as a new sense of optimism filled her.

'So, tell me about your new life?'

Listening to Jack speak, somehow the frightening tunnel she'd been stuck in recently seemed less dark, the tiny light at the end that she'd been looking at growing in size and magnitude.

Honour hovered near the door, while Jack sat on the chair next to Tara's bed. He'd taken his leather jacket off and his broad-backed bulk made Tara's slender frame look even smaller than usual, making Honour wonder at the lack of similarity in their physiology.

'Hello, Tara.' Jack's voice was mellow. 'It's good to meet you, finally. I've heard lots of good things about you.'

Tara was sitting up, wearing a pale blue tracksuit, and her wispy hair was caught up behind her head, highlighting the new prominence of her cheekbones. 'You too.' She smiled at him, scrutinising his face as if looking for clues as to who he was, that might be etched into his skin.

'I'm sorry you've been so unwell.' He laid a palm on the blanket close to Tara's hand and Honour sucked in an involuntary breath.

'I've had more fun,' Tara quipped, folding her arms across her middle as if creating a boundary between them. 'But I'm feeling a bit better now.'

'That's good to hear.' He leaned back, crossing his long legs at the ankles. 'So, you're a footie star, I hear.'

Again, Honour held her breath, taken aback that he had remembered this from their brief conversation about Tara.

'I was. Hard to play with a naff leg, though.' She lifted her knee under the blanket.

'I've seen professionals come back from joint surgery. Look at Andy Murray.' He shrugged as Honour pictured the world-famous Scottish tennis player and the amazing comeback he'd made after hip surgery. Annoyed that she hadn't come up with that herself when attempting to comfort Tara, she smiled at her daughter, grateful to Jack for thinking of it.

'Yeah, I suppose so.' Tara nodded. 'Tennis is different to football, though.'

Jack laughed softly. 'Oh, right. Those wimpy tennis players need a racket to move the ball.'

At this, Tara laughed too, her face colouring slightly. 'You know what I mean.'

He nodded. 'I do. But they're both high-impact sports that require a ton of strength and coordination. If you're determined enough, I have no doubt that you'll be able to play again, once you're fully well. From what I hear, you're not going to let this stop you.' He nodded at her leg. 'You're a MacLeod, after all.'

Tara looked over at Honour, a smile still tugging at her mouth. 'Yes. I am.'

'Well, never say never, eh? Hold fast.' Jack made a fist.

Hearing those words, Honour suddenly felt comfortable leaving them alone together. Smiling at Tara, Honour walked out into the hall, her vision blurring as she headed for the lift.

37

Within another week, the transplant had taken place, and Tara was still weak, and thin, but improving. Doctor Hail had said they were pleased with the way her blood work was tracking, and the most recent scans were looking stable.

Honour was run ragged, still going back and forth to the hospital daily, and juggling Callum's schedule, work, and life in general, while keeping everyone informed of Tara's progress. Her parents hadn't been able to go to the hospital yet, as Doctor Hail was limiting Tara's visitors until she was less vulnerable to infection, so Marion and Kirk had been video-chatting with Tara each afternoon, something they all looked forward to.

Lorna was dropping in on her whenever she was working, and Dougie had been spending the odd night at the cottage with Callum, that feeling like a tiny way Honour could thank her friend for all her invaluable support.

As the days slid by with no further word from Jack, since he'd returned to Edinburgh, Honour had been able to let her fear of discovery wane, dwarfed by her growing hopes for Tara's recovery. November was drawing to a close, and as Honour planned for Tara's proposed return home, just ten days before

Christmas, for the first time since she'd lost Kenny, she felt the buzz of excitement. She couldn't wait to drag the battered old tree from the attic, get all the decorations out of the cardboard boxes, light the fire and help the children dress the tree.

Callum had been crossing the days until Tara's return off the fishing calendar that Kenny had pinned to the wall by the fridge, each month showing the best catches in different areas of the world, and now Callum chirped, 'Only nineteen days to go.' His backpack was dragging his shoulders back as if it housed an anvil.

'I know. It's going to be great. We'll make mince pies and dumpling and get Grandma to make her special stuffing.' Honour could almost taste the spicy sausage her mother used, the fragrant notes of sage and cinnamon that always spoke of family gatherings, of Christmases and of joy.

'Can we have bread sauce, too? Tara loves that.' His face was alight. 'She always takes most of it.' He chuckled softly, as Honour pulled him to her, smoothing the usual stubborn tuft at the back of his head. 'Cal, you need to clean your glasses, matey. They are so grubby.' She tutted as she slid them off his face. 'How can you see anything through these?'

'They're OK.' He walked to the table and dragged a chair out while Honour washed the glasses under the tap with a little soap, then dried them on a clean tea towel. She handed them back to him, then checked the clock.

'Right, Lorna should be here any minute to take you to school. She'll drop you off this afternoon, then Bridie will be here with you for a while. Once I get back from the hospital, why don't we get fish and chips from Bailey's, as a treat?'

He nodded enthusiastically. 'Oh, yeah.'

'Great.' Honour lifted the small Tupperware she'd put his packed lunch in and pushed it into the overstuffed backpack. Just as she closed the flap, the doorbell rang. 'There's Lorna. Off you go, love.' She hefted him up from the chair. 'Why on earth is it so heavy today?' She tested the weight of the bag by lifting it off his shoulders. 'Have you hidden your telescope in there?' She laughed as he rolled his eyes.

'No, Mum. It's my *Junior Star Gazer* books, from Grandpa. I'm taking them in to show Miss Henderson. She said she wanted to see them.'

Honour pictured the fresh-faced, new class teacher whom Callum was clearly fond of. 'Ah, right. Well, be careful not to lose them, or Grandpa will be annoyed.'

'I won't.' He trudged to the front door and opened it. 'Hi, Lorna.'

Lorna popped her head in the door. 'Morning all. Let's go, Cal. I'm a bit late today.' She grimaced. 'Sorry, Honour. Got held up by a certain young man not being able to find his PE kit.' She jabbed a thumb over her shoulder towards the harbour, where Dougie would be sitting in her car. 'I'll pop in on Tara this morning. I'm in paediatrics today, but I'll sneak away for a few.' Lorna grinned. 'She's coming on so well, Honour.'

Honour nodded. 'Thanks, Lorna. You're a rock star.'

Lorna posed briefly, holding her palms under her chin like a vogue model, then turned and guided Callum down the steps.

Honour closed the door behind them and headed back to the kitchen. She had half an hour before she needed to leave for work so the thought of at least one cup of tea that was still hot by the time she drank it was enticing.

While the kettle boiled and she flipped through some bills to be paid, the doorbell rang again. The previous evening, Bridie had said she'd drop some treacle scones in this morning before taking a batch over to the church for a bake sale, so Honour stood up and made her way to the door. Seeing the familiar, silvery head and long back through the glass panel, Honour smiled.

'Hello, love.' Bridie smiled broadly, carrying a large plate covered with plastic wrap. 'They're a bitty overdone, but slap them thickly with butter and you'll not notice.' She laughed heartily as she handed the plate to Honour. 'I should stick to painting, really. Or so Scott says.'

'Well, I'm sure he enjoys eating them, regardless. And I know we certainly will. Thank you.' Honour took the plate from Bridie, seeing a flash of the bright blue nail varnish she'd taken to wearing recently.

'He does, the gannet,' Bridie tutted. 'Malc's coming home this weekend, too. So the tins won't be full for long.' She eyed Honour, who sensed that Bridie was still somewhat anxious over the role Malcolm had played in Jack finding out about Tara.

Honour had still not told her parents, or Bridie and Scott, that Jack had been Tara's donor. The right time would come along, but for now, it didn't need to come out. As for Malcolm, Honour wanted Bridie to stop worrying about any possible resentment towards him, so she smiled and said, 'You, Scott and Malc should come in for a drink while he's home. It'll be good to see him.'

Bridie's momentary, anxious expression evaporated. 'Oh, that'd be lovely.'

'Good. It's a date then. I'm just making a quick cuppa before I head into work. Want to join me?'

Bridie shook her head. 'I'd love to, but I've got another batch of those in the oven, and I need to get them over to the church before I go to the studio. I'm working on a new commission, of Pittenweem harbour, for an American couple. Nice people who came into the gallery a few weeks ago.'

'Oh, lovely.' Honour smiled. 'You're so talented, Bridie.' She glanced up at the family portrait hanging above the fire. 'That brings me so much joy when I look at it.'

Bridie gave a sad smile. 'I'm glad. You're a beautiful family.'

Her use of the present tense made Honour's heart contract. That Kenny was gone still felt surreal, the expectation that he'd walk in the door, while happening less often, still sometimes catching Honour off guard.

'Right. I'm off. Have a good day and I'll be here for when the boys get back.' Bridie touched her forehead as if saluting, her long beige sweater tipping her denim-clad thighs under the ubiquitous waxed jacket. 'Bye for now.'

'Bye, Bridie.' Honour closed the door, just as the kettle began to whistle.

In the kitchen, she set the scones on the table and carefully filled her mug with steaming water. Just as she put the kettle back on the stove, the doorbell rang again.

'My God. It's like Piccadilly Circus in here today,' she huffed as she passed through the kitchen to the living room, expecting to see Bridie behind the glass again, possibly having forgotten to tell her something.

Rather than the familiar, silvery-haired outline of her neighbour, a taller person in a dark coat stood there, with what looked like a baseball cap on. They had turned their back to the door, so even as she leaned in and squinted, Honour couldn't make out who it was. Craig from Green's wasn't due to deliver anything until the following day, and Gregor, Kenny's former mate, would be at sea for the next few hours. Whomever it was wasn't tall enough to be Jack, and as she hesitated, her hand on the latch, slightly anxious to open the door, which never happened in Crail, Honour's skin began to tingle. There was something about the way the back curved, the thickness of the neck, and the distinct, steep slant of the shoulders that sent a shiver down her spine.

38

Honour slowly twisted the latch and pulled the door open a few inches, as cold air flooded her lungs – as if forced in by a giant bellows. 'Oh, my God.' Both hands flew up to cover her mouth as the man, head dipped and hands shoved deep in his pockets, remained still. Her legs began to tremble as he gradually lifted his chin, his face partially obscured by a dark bandana, worn under the cap, and covering his left temple and much of his left cheek. She stood, frozen to the spot, and stared at him, as time slowed to a crawl, her mind taking flight – question after question piling in and nothing about what she was seeing making sense.

A pair of seagulls hung high up in the air behind him, their wings curved in the updraught. An electronic beep floated up from the harbour as a vehicle reversed, and the sea breeze coated Honour's face with a salty mist that she could taste. Her eyes beginning to burn, she closed them momentarily and licked her parched lips.

She opened her eyes, half expecting him to be gone, but the man stared directly into her soul, the way only one person had ever been able to do. Honour felt the room tilt. Her skin fizzed as if a thousand ants were marching over her arms and legs as she tried to focus on the deep-set hazel eyes. One was more oval than round now, and the long, aquiline nose was crooked – a zigzag of angry pink skin creating a track under the left eye that connected the bridge of the nose with what she could see of the left cheekbone.

Her pulse thumped wildly in her ears as he took a step forward, his one hand emerging from his pocket to form a fist. He looked different. Smaller. Wirier. It couldn't possibly be him, could it? As she remained frozen to the spot, she still doubted the evidence of her own eyes, but if he spoke, if she could hear his voice, then she'd know. She squinted again at the damaged face, still partly hidden from view, then she dropped her hands to her sides and gasped as he said softly, 'Hello, Red.'

Kenny stood just outside the open door, his hands back in his pockets. Honour was shaking so violently now that she clamped her arms around her middle to hold herself upright, her impulse to grab him stunted by her shock.

He wouldn't look at her straight on, keeping his face turned to the left, and as she gradually released her arms and took a step forward, he held a hand up as if to stop her. 'Kenny?' she whispered.

He lifted his chin and turned face on, the bandana shielding a good part of the left side of his head. 'Hello, love.' The eyes softened then, the familiar twinkle occupying the right one as they locked on hers. The left eye seemed dull, as if the light wasn't getting in anymore, and as Honour stared at him, her shock turned to disbelief.

'What... But where have...? I thought... We thought...' She gulped. 'Where have you been? How are you here?' Her legs were trembling as she took another step forward, and despite seeing him flinch, she could hold back no longer. She lunged at him, and her arms went around his neck, her face smashing into his collarbone. He smelled of coffee and dust, of menthol and, most of all, of home. 'Oh, Kenny.'

His arms were around her back, the pressure a longed-for solace that Honour leaned into. She held him tight, afraid to let go in case he evaporated – or she woke from this dream to be faced with the stark reality that he was gone again.

He whispered above her head, 'God, I've missed you.'

Honour soaked him in, the force of his hug seeming to keep her on her feet rather than collapsing to her knees with the mixture of relief and confusion filling her. Tears soaked her face, dampening the shoulder of his jacket, as they stood on the doorstep, locked together.

After a few moments, Kenny began to rock her gently, as he always had when she was upset, and the motion brought Honour's paralysed body back to life. She lifted her head from his shoulder and leaned back, taking in the face that she knew so well. It was undeniably altered, and yet he was entirely the same – her Kenny. Her husband. She stared at him, seeing anxiety wash over him, as his hand went up to the bandana, checking that it was still in place.

Honour reached out to touch it, but he pulled back. 'Don't.'

Shocked at the recoil, Honour in turn stepped backwards, then, realising that they were standing out on the cold doorstep, where anyone could see them, she pushed the door open wider. 'Come inside.'

He followed her inside, stopping at the back of the sofa to take in the living room. As she waited for him to speak, to explain how this had come to be, how he'd walked back into her life straight from the grave, his eyes landed on the painting above the fireplace. 'She finished it, then.' He glanced at Honour, who was now standing in the doorway to the kitchen, then back at the painting.

She prepared to tell him about Bridie giving her the painting, not long after he'd drowned, but the absurdity of the situation made her shake her head. Before she could rationalise it, her shock turned to anger. 'You walk in here after nearly nine months of me thinking you were dead, and you want to talk about a bloody painting?' Her voice was brittle. 'Seriously? What the hell happened, Kenny. Where on God's green earth have you been all this time? Why didn't you let me know you were alive? We've been in purgatory here.' Her salty tears had tightened the skin on her face, so she rubbed her eyes, feeling the grittiness that followed crying.

He walked towards her, then past her, into the kitchen, the baseball cap and bandana appearing more incongruous inside the cottage than they had out on the step. 'I'm so sorry, Honour. I know I owe you an explanation. Can we sit?' He gestured towards the chair that she'd left pulled out from the table. The place he had always sat.

Honour surveyed him, seeing the new sharp angles of his bony shoulders, the way the jeans he wore wrinkled loosely around his thighs. He had on a flannel shirt she didn't recognise, and heavy work boots that looked too big for him. He stared at her, the odd mismatch of his gentle eyes making her anger begin to defuse, so she nodded. 'Fine. Sit.'

He pulled her usual chair out for her, then sat at his own place, the head of the table, with his back to the kitchen window. He'd always said that he liked this spot because he got to see all the mischief that was going on around the table, but Honour knew it was simply that this view was uninterrupted by distractions, like the sky, when all he wanted was to focus on his family during the precious mealtimes they spent together. He sat back, his hand once again going up to the bandana, then he locked eyes with her. 'There's so much to tell you. To say. I don't know where to begin.'

She leaned forwards on her elbows, lacing her trembling fingers together on the tabletop in case she reached for his hand. If she touched him again, she'd forget about everything else and, at this moment, she wanted to hear every word he had to say. Her life had been nothing short of hell for the past few months, and whatever reason he had for letting her believe he was dead, leaving her terrified and alone, to manage not only her own broken heart but also the children's, it had better be incredible. 'Just tell me what happened. Start at the beginning.'

He nodded, then shrugged off his heavy woollen jacket, draping it around the back of the chair behind him. The familiar movement, the way he made sure its shoulders were evenly hung before sitting back, made Honour's heart falter. She had missed him more than she'd believed possible, trying to survive his loss while coping with a nightmarish situation with Tara. Then, consequently, all the other pieces of their lives had shifted, the very foundation of her family cracking, and here he was, thinner, paler, but glaringly alive. She pressed her lips closed, afraid to say anything else yet, in case she let all the hurt that had accumulated inside her spill out.

'That morning, I'd never seen water like it, Honour. The sea was wild. I know you tried to hold on to me, love, but I knew I was going, and the last thing I remember was seeing your face.' He pressed his eyes closed momentarily, the lids puckering as if he was trying to erase the image. 'Apparently, I got hooked by my lifejacket to a piece of the deck that came away as the *Lila Rose* split. I was unconscious, and floating at sea for over a day when I was picked up by a Norwegian trawler.' He paused, watching her.

Honour remained completely still, her mind teeming with surreal images of him floating in the angry sea, snagged on a piece of decking like flotsam.

'They took me back to Stavanger and I was in a hospital there for a week, with head injuries and brain swelling. I was out of it, Red. Dead to the world.'

His use of the word dead made Honour flinch, as she sat back and let her hands drop to her lap. Through the fog of confusion, she focused on his mouth, the way the lips pursed and released, the way the skin around his chin was darkened, a shadow of a beard beginning to show.

'When I came out of it, they were asking me all these questions, but I didn't know any of the answers. I couldn't tell them my name, or where I was from. I knew that I knew it all, but I just couldn't find the words to tell them.' He shrugged, his fingers fanning out on the table in front of him.

Honour forced a swallow. 'Did you lose your memory?' This seemed like the only acceptable explanation.

He shook his head. 'I don't think so. It was more that I think I buried it. What had happened. Perhaps subconsciously, or maybe consciously. I mean, it was there, but I just couldn't speak about it.'

She recalled having read about certain types of brain injury resulting in a temporary state of amnesia, as if the brain was sheltering the victim from re-experiencing their trauma, and as she looked at his face, the angry scar, the uneven eyes, the haunted look behind the hazel irises she knew so well, Honour tried to clear her mind, breathe through all her pent-up hurt and anger. 'Go on.'

'I stayed for less than a day, after I woke up. They wanted me to stay longer, but I needed to get out of there.' He shook his head. 'It was when they helped me into the bathroom, and I saw myself.' He halted, his chin dropping to his chest. 'I saw myself, Honour.' He met her eyes again. 'My face was wrecked.'

She tried to imagine the rest of the damage the bandana was hiding, the visible section of scar livid and ugly and yet, for her, not affecting the overall landscape of the face she loved. 'So, what did you do?'

'I walked out. Went to the local seaman's mission and stayed there for a while. They were good to me. Gave me clothes, a bed, fed me and stuff.' He blinked rapidly. 'Good people.'

Honour nodded, the picture slowly beginning to come

together, and as she watched him shift in the seat, the phone call she'd received from the coastguard all those months ago flashed back to her. She'd all but forgotten the mysterious man who had been reported as rescued – lying unconscious in a Norwegian hospital. The man she had hoped and yet known in her heart was not her husband. As she replayed the conversation she'd had with the hospital, when they'd told her the man had come around and already left, Honour shook her head.

'They phoned me. The coastguard. Over a week after you... after that day.' She took a second to compose herself. 'They said the man who'd been found had left the hospital against medical advice. But they had no information about his identity, where he was from, or anything.' Her throat began to tighten again, so she stood up, filled a glass at the sink and gulped down half of the icy water. She turned back to face him, her hands gripping the edge of the sink behind her. 'I said to them, there's no way that could be Kenny. He would have moved heaven and earth to get home. He'd have walked on water to get back to his family.' She swallowed over a lump of hurt. 'I just knew in my heart that if you were alive, you'd let me know.' Her voice broke and she walked over and slumped back into the chair.

His eyes were full now, his fingers plucking at a few grains of salt on the table.

'Why didn't you come home, Kenny? Why didn't you at least let me know you were alive? That was cruel. Plain and simple.' Fresh tears tracked down her cheeks as she watched him stand up slowly and walk to the Aga, leaning his hips against the front of it.

'I wanted to, Red. You have no idea how much. But I was a mess. My face...' He halted as she shook her head.

'No. That can't be the reason, Kenny. I just can't believe that would keep you from us. No matter how bad it is.' She pointed at the bandana.

'You haven't seen it, Honour.' His voice was thick. 'The truth is, I was afraid. Afraid that I'd come home, and you'd take one look at me and cringe, back away. Not want me to touch you.' His voice broke and he did something she'd never seen Kenny do. He began to cry.

Before she could stop herself, she was up and crossing the gap between them. 'Kenny, please.'

'No.' Again, he held his hand up. 'I can't let you see it.'

Honour stood in front of him, her hands now steady as she knew categorically what she needed to do. 'Let me see.'

His eyes widened as he made to move past her.

'No, Kenny. Let me.' Her hand went to the bill of the baseball cap, her fingers gripping it tightly.

He didn't move, his breaths becoming shallow and rapid.

She locked eyes with him. 'It's just me.'

She didn't move until he gave an almost imperceptible nod, then she carefully lifted the cap off his head. His unruly hair had been cropped short, military style, the closeness of the tawny stubble making his head look too big for his newly reduced body. She waited for a second or two, then she pointed at the bandana. 'Can I?'

He held her gaze, then he reached behind his head and began untying it. Honour waited, her eyes not moving from his, until the covering fell away from his face. She stood completely still for a moment, then stepped back, taking him in. The left side of his face was puckered, as if the skin had been gathered behind his ear. The scar she'd seen, now in context, cupped his left eye and disappeared across the temple and into the short hair above his left ear. His left eye was more hooded than the right, giving it the oval appearance, but the most significant change was the visible dent above his left eye, a dip in his forehead that looked as if someone had hit him with a wooden bat, leaving a crater that she estimated she could put two fingers in.

When she put all the elements together, his injuries were severe, and even disfiguring, but all Honour could see was Kenny. The man she loved. The father of her children. The person she wanted to wake up to every day for as long as she lived.

She lifted her hand, and, with her index finger, she gingerly touched the scar at his temple, then traced it into his hairline as he winced. He didn't pull away, though, or ask her to stop, so she moved in a little closer and gently ran her fingers over the bumpy skin above his eye. Next, feeling the railway track of marks that stitches had left, running from his temple over the top of his head and ending behind his ear, she leaned in until her forehead was touching his.

He was panting now, his breath heavy with coffee, and the tang of fear, but as he let her stay there, their heads just touching and their eyes locked, he reached for her hand. 'I'm sorry, Red. I know I let you down again.' His cheeks were glistening. 'I should've known how you'd be.'

He cleared his throat as she dropped her chin slightly, her mouth seeking his. Their lips touched, and he groaned, as a starving man might when given a morsel of bread, then Honour felt the pressure of his mouth, the softness of his lips, the gentle tremor in is hand as he held hers up to his chest.

Honour lost track of time, unsure how long they'd stood there, mouths attached, breathing as one, until Kenny slowly pulled back from her. 'I love you, Red.' He stroked the hair away from her forehead. 'Are you sure you can still love me, like this?'

'You're an idiot,' she said softly. 'You are still you. You're my best friend. My love. My partner. I just wish you could have had more faith in me.'

He nodded sadly. 'I know. I'm a fool. But, Honour, the kids. I had nightmares about coming home, them seeing me and being afraid.' He paused. 'I couldn't bear them to be repulsed by me.' A tear crept over his bottom lid, so Honour thumbed it away.

'They will see exactly what I see, Kenny. You. Your heart. Your love. You. You've no idea how much they've missed you.' As she watched his shoulders droop slightly, Honour knew that, aside from his physical injuries, a brain injury could cause hidden scars that he might never heal from, and wanting to reassure him that nothing could get in the way of her love for him, she said, 'Scars or no scars, I love you.'

Kenny smiled, and his expression gave her the strength to continue, a tiny whisper inside her clamouring for more information. *There has to be more to this.*

'Is that the only reason you didn't come home?'

Kenny took a few moments, his eyes flicking between the window and her face. 'Let's sit down, Red. My head aches, and I get tired now.'

She led him to the table, fetched him a glass of water and this time sat in the chair closest to him. 'Want some tea? Something to eat?'

He nodded. 'Tea would be cracking.'

She stood up, put the kettle on and returned to her seat. He reached for her hand, his mouth pinching as tension crept across his face again.

Her nerves jangled at the prospect of something else, something worse than his scars, coming closer. 'What is it?'

He lifted her hand and kissed the back of it, before releasing it and sitting back in the chair. 'I have something else to tell you.'

'OK.' She suppressed the need to close her eyes against whatever was next.

'I was in the mission in Stavanger for about a month. I worked in a bar for a while, just trying to get a little money together so I could get back to Scotland.'

Honour's heart sank at the thought of Kenny in a bar,

surrounded by people drinking – the sick irony of him pulling pints for people while she mourned his death pricking her heart. Before her anger could get a grip again, she saw shame occupy his entire body, causing him to slump forward slightly, his shoulders rounding under the weight of something more that he wasn't telling her. 'Just tell me, Kenny. For God's sake. Help me understand.'

He pulled his shoulders back. 'I was in a bad way, Honour. My head ached like a son of a bitch, twenty-four hours a day. I couldn't sleep because of the pain, and not being able to lie on my back, or this side.' His hand fluttered over his left ear. 'So, one night at work, someone bought me a dram, and...' he stammered. 'I drank it.'

Honour's heart swooped down in her chest. 'Oh, God.'

'It helped with the pain. I slept that night for the first time in weeks. And then the next night, I drank again.'

His eyes were now so haunted that Honour had to look away while she worked through what he'd said. Numb with fear at the prospect of him once again becoming the man she had been married to a decade before, she pressed her fingers to her lips and waited for more.

'I drank every night, more and more, until I couldn't feel anything.' This time, rather than his head, his fingers tapped his heart. 'I drank not to feel. To be numb. To disappear even more than I had already. Then, I kept drinking, to escape my shame, and the disappointment in myself for breaking my promise to you.'

His mouth clamped shut as Honour felt bile rising at the back of her throat.

'I'd broken my word, and I couldn't face myself, never mind you.' His voice cracked again as he dropped his gaze to the tabletop. 'I let you down and I was too scared to come home and tell you. After what happened all those years ago, I couldn't bear to see your disappointment, so I kept on drinking.' He gulped in some air. 'They fired me from the bar, so I left Stavanger, and got a lift across on a boat, to Aberdeen. I wasn't ready to come home, Red, so I went to a seaman's hostel there. It was easy to disappear because no one asked questions. I got a bed, a hot meal a day, and folk left me to my own devices.'

He paused, as if steeling himself for the next part.

'I got bar work again, and drank all my wages every night, for months, until one morning I woke up in the service alley behind the bar. Someone had stolen my boots, and I was covered in bird shit.' He sat up and gave a strangled laugh. 'Bird shit, Red.'

'Oh, Kenny.' She shook her head, trying to imagine the depth of his despair at that moment.

'That day, I made a decision. I got cleaned up and went to an AA meeting in a church hall. I went every day for a month, then I started working again, this time in a supermarket. I packed bags, for peanuts, but I stayed sober. I knew I needed to come home, Red, so I stayed sober so I could get back to you. Ask your forgiveness.' He nodded sadly. 'Can you ever forgive me – for it all?'

Honour stood up slowly, a cocktail of anger, sadness, disappointment and fear coiling inside her. She paced in front of the Aga, wanting with every molecule of her being to wrap her arms around him, tell him that they'd get through this together, just like they had the first time, but she hesitated. Kenny had just bared his soul. Confessed his transgressions and found the courage to face her and take the consequences. She watched him scanning her face for a clue as to either his punishment or acquittal, but then shame flooded in, making her wipe her mouth with her palm. He was asking for her understanding, for her forgiveness, and she wanted to give it. But she could not, in all good conscience, tell him she forgave him when she herself had something to confess.

39

With a fresh pot of tea sitting between them, and Honour having phoned Tilda to say she had an emergency and couldn't make it in today, Honour and Kenny sat at the kitchen table. When she'd hesitated to respond to his question about forgiveness, he'd quietly said he'd like to take a shower, and while he'd been in the bathroom, she had changed out of her scrubs, pulling on jeans and a red cable-knit sweater she knew he liked.

As she'd taken her ponytail down and brushed her hair, checking her reflection in the mirror, she'd heard the water thrumming into the bath. Despite her conflicted feelings about everything he'd told her, the sound of his presence in the house had been such a profound comfort that she had closed her eyes and revelled in it for a while, before going back downstairs.

Now, they sat opposite each other, his face glowing from the shower, and the scars seeming redder across the paleness of his skin. 'I really want to talk about the kids, but, first, do you think that, in time, you can get past what I did, Red?' He sounded nervous, which heightened her trepidation at what she was about to say. Not only did she have to bring him up to date on everything that was going on with Tara, and Callum, but she must now bare her own soul and hope that he could find it in his heart to forgive her.

'Kenny, we have both been through the mill. I believe we can get through anything if we are together and are completely honest with each other. I always have.' She laced her fingers through his. 'I'm trying to understand what you did, and I do want to forgive you, and move on, but there is something you need to know.' She felt him tense under her fingertips, her courage wavering. He studied her, taking in her features as if he were reading a map, so she continued, 'First of all, while you were away, Tara became ill.'

'What do you mean, ill? How ill?' He sat up straighter, his eyes locked on hers.

'Kenny, there's no easy way to say this. She has cancer.'

He sucked in a breath.

The words still felt surreal, the notion that their beloved daughter was less than perfectly healthy, impossible to accept. 'She was having bad leg pain, and when they did scans, and blood tests, they found a tumour in her knee joint. She had a course of chemotherapy and then surgery to remove it, but the cancer was aggressive, and the chemo damaged her bone marrow, so she couldn't fight infections, or the cancer if it recurs, which there is high chance it will.' She watched his face drain of colour.

'Oh, Christ, Honour. What can we do? What can *I* do?'

'Nothing, at the moment. She's in the Victoria Hospital, over in Kirkcaldy, and her doctor is wonderful. He recommended a bone marrow transplant, and we were all tested to be donors – Mum, Dad, even Cal.' She watched him shake his head in disbelief.

'But she is so young. So strong.' He twisted his fingers together in a knot. 'How can she have cancer?'

'I know. I was just as stunned, believe me. But Tara *is* strong, and so determined. She can beat this, Kenny.'

He stared at her, his mouth dipping at the edges. 'I can be tested, too. A parent can donate marrow to a child, right?'

Honour felt the walls closing in on her, her moment to bare her soul materialising. 'We already found a donor, Kenny. In fact, she had the transplant just last week.'

'Really?' She could see the relief in his eyes. 'Oh, thank God.'

'Yes, it was miraculous.' Honour braced herself. 'Kenny, you have to try to stay calm, and understand what I'm going to say to you now. How critical it was that we find a full match for her – which is not easy.'

He frowned. 'Right.'

Honour took a breath, ready to face her demons, terrified of the damage this would cause. 'When he found out how ill Tara was, Jack phoned me.' She saw Kenny flinch at the mention of his brother, his eyebrows lifting as he pushed back in the chair, creating distance even from Jack's name. How was she going to tell Kenny the rest?

'How did *he* find out, and what did it have to do with him?' The familiar edge framed Kenny's voice whenever he talked about his brother.

'Malcolm told him. They've been keeping in touch all these years.' She pictured Malcolm's flushed face and the sheepish expression when she'd last seen him. 'They were friends, Kenny.'

Kenny's frown deepened. 'So, what did Jack want – calling you?'

'He wanted to help.'

Kenny made a huffing sound. 'That doesn't sound like him.'

Honour was being torn between her desire to protect Kenny from any more hurt and her need to come clean, shed the secret that had tortured her for years, but there was nowhere else to go now except forward. 'He wanted to help, so when I asked him to, he got tested and it turned out that he was a match.'

Kenny's eyebrows shot up, the scarred side of his face remaining slightly lower than the other, creating an odd, mask-like expression. 'Wow. What were the chances of that happening?'

Honour's heart ached as if she'd been punched in the chest. 'It's rare, within a family, but it can happen when the donor is a parent.' She let the words hang in the air, their significance creeping slowly over them like an icy fog closing in.

Kenny's eyes seemed to lose focus, his mouth forming a strained line. 'What?'

Honour stood up, the need for space between them overwhelming. 'Kenny, Jack is Tara's biological father.'

His body instantly slammed back in the chair as if she'd hit him. But she was so far in now that she couldn't go back.

'That night, years ago, when Jack brought you home...' She paused, seeing his eyes refocus as he stared at her. 'You remember it, I know. I don't have to remind you.'

He took her in, then nodded silently.

'After Jack put you to bed, he came downstairs to help me. My lip was bleeding pretty badly, and I was really shaken.' She hesitated, seeing him blinking rapidly. 'He cleaned it up, then he was comforting me, and—'

Kenny stood up abruptly, his eyes on fire. 'Comforting you. Is that what we're calling it now?'

Honour felt everything begin to slip away, her composure, her bravery, her hope that by coming clean they could make a fresh start, and now anger filled her up like the incoming tide. A force that could not be stopped – dictated by the pull of the moon. 'Kenny, don't do this. I'm trying to make you understand, and you're hardly in a position to point fingers, or be self-righteous. Your bad decisions put this whole family through months of hell. We mourned you, Kenny. The kids were devastated, thinking they'd lost their father. Do you have any idea what that was like – to see that happening and not be able to take their pain away?'

He kicked the chair out of the way and walked out the door into the living room. Fury compelling her, Honour followed him, preparing for his next verbal assault, but, instead, he stood silent, with his back to the fire, his feet planted wide and his hands on the top of his head. She halted behind the sofa, gripping the soft leather, and willing him to look at her, but he couldn't meet her eyes.

'Are you going to let me tell you why it happened?' She swallowed back the sob that was pressing into her throat, as he waited a moment, then gave a single nod. 'You and I were in a bad place, back then. Your drinking was out of control. I was so unhappy and lonely. I missed the man I'd fallen in love with, the wonderful, funny, kind man I'd married.' She paused. 'That night was an all-time low, for me. I didn't know if you and I would survive, Kenny. Our marriage was teetering on a ledge and then when you hurt me—'

His head snapped up. 'That was an accident, Honour. You know that I'd never have intentionally hurt you.' He looked crushed, his mouth in a miserable half-moon shape as he began pacing in front of the fireplace, his hands scrubbing back and forth across the back of his head.

'I know you didn't mean to, Kenny, but I was at the end of my tether. I was asking myself, what if this was going to be the pattern of my life, forever. What if you got even worse? What if one day you really hurt me? What if we eventually did have children, like we'd talked about, and you got like that around them? I was so scared.'

She walked around the sofa and stopped in front of him, as he stood still and jammed his hands into his pockets again.

'That night, Jack cleaned up your mess, and my face, and when we started to talk, I just fell apart. I was lost, and lonely, and he was kind, and reassuring, and then...' She braced herself.

'He kissed me, and I let it happen. I craved some comfort, and wrongly – so wrongly – I took it where it was offered.'

Kenny clamped his eyes closed, his face rippling with the force of tension coursing through him. 'I can't hear this. I don't want to know.'

Honour stepped closer, knowing that this moment could be the tipping point in her marriage, where everything would implode, or they'd find a middle ground where they could start to rebuild. Tentatively, she touched his shoulder, his eyes snapping open as he recoiled from her. The hurt that shot through her at his reaction was crippling, but she wasn't going to give up. This was her life, and despite his mistakes, this man was her everything. There was nothing he could do or say that would stop her from trying to make things right. 'Kenny. I listened to you. So, hear me out.'

He turned his back on her, staring into the empty grate. His silence was eloquent, and while he didn't say it, she knew he was listening.

'It was just that one time, an act of sheer desperation. Jack and I both knew immediately that it was a terrible mistake, and we agreed that it would never happen again.' Honour recalled the awkwardness of Jack getting dressed in front of the fire, close to where Kenny stood now, and she blinked the image away. 'I told him that we couldn't be around each other and Jack said he'd do whatever I wanted.'

At this, Kenny looked at her over his shoulder, a frown twisting his damaged brow. She knew he was fully engaged now, and the next part of what she had to say was the hardest to admit, harder even than her betrayal.

'I told him to stay away, Kenny. I said it would be for the best.' She saw his eyebrows lift. 'He promised me he would, and within a week, he'd left the village. I never meant for him to leave for good, but that was his choice.'

Kenny turned to face her, his eyes miserable pools. As realisation slowly dawned, he shook his head, once again cupping his temples with his hands as if to control his thoughts. 'Jesus, Honour. I mean, Jesus.' He met her gaze, comprehension clearing the question in his eyes. 'He left because of you.'

Honour nodded miserably, then moved back and sank onto the sofa. 'Yes. Because of what we'd done.' She hiccupped. 'He stayed away because of that, not because he didn't care about you, or your dad, or the business. I was so full of shame, and scared of what we'd done, what it would do to you, and us, if you found out, that I let him be the scapegoat. I wanted to tell you so many times, but I was a coward. I couldn't bear the thought of losing you, of seeing the love go out of your eyes when you looked at me. Just when we'd finally got things back on track.' Her voice gave way, and she dropped her head into her hands. Sobs rippled through her body, years of pain and loss, guilt and fear curdling into a storm of emotion inside her. Her body spasmed, her ribs heaving like bellows, until she felt a hand on her back. Afraid to sit up, to see his hurt, and disappointment, she kept her head buried in her palms. 'I'm sorry, Kenny.' She gulped. 'I'm sorry I let you think your brother didn't care about you. I'm sorry I didn't tell you why he didn't come to your dad's funeral. I'm sorry I was so weak that I let a little comfort lead to betrayal, of the worst kind.' Her voice was raw, her throat on fire. 'I'm so sorry,' she whispered.

Kenny's hands were on her shoulders, easing her upright. Her face was soaked in tears, and as she began to swipe at her cheeks, his fingers were on her skin, wiping with her. 'Stop now.' His voice was low. 'Enough, now.'

Honour's face was on fire as she focused on his eyes. She needed a clue as to where his mind was, if he was comforting her as a kindness before he ripped her heart out, or was he coming back to her, this time, for good? 'Can you forgive me?' she whispered. 'I can't imagine my life without you.'

He moved the hair that was stuck to her cheek, his thumb

rough against her skin. 'Listen, Red. Don't get me wrong, I hate what you just told me, for many reasons, but I'm glad you told me. I caused you a lot of pain, over the years, and I knew it. I thought the good times we had could rub out the bad, and I never told you how sorry I was for putting you through that, with my drinking.' He sat back, then leaned his head against the cushion. 'That it was Jack that gave you what you needed that night turns my stomach, but I know I was failing you.' He sighed, a deep, throaty sound that made Honour shiver. 'If I'm honest with myself about why you were so unhappy that you made that choice, there's only one person to blame.' He laid his palms flat on his chest. 'God, Red. Where do we go from here?'

Honour shifted closer to him, the tiny speck of hope she felt bloom inside her pulling her focus. 'Kenny, I love you more than you'll probably ever know. All I want – all I've ever wanted – is for us to be good together. Have our life the way we built it and enjoy watching our children grow up.' She halted, the truth about Tara now making her last statement sound hollow.

Before she could continue, Kenny sat upright. 'Did you always know that she was his?' His face was unreadable, the new elements to it making it hard for her to gauge whether this was coming from hurt, or another accusation.

'No. I didn't know until Jack was tested.' She took a moment to arrange her thoughts, then went on. 'You and I found out I was pregnant so soon after we sorted things out that I did wonder. Honestly, it was my worst fear.' She shrugged miserably. 'But, over time, I became convinced that she was yours. She was so like you, as a little girl. The same stubborn nature, the things that made her laugh, the way she was so passionate about everything she loved.' She looked at him, seeing his face soften. 'She was so you, and she *is* your daughter.'

'Right.' He sounded less than convinced.

Honour was wrung out, stripped of her strength, her pride,

and her self-respect, but there was something else she needed to ask him. It was now or never. 'Kenny, can we forgive each other and start to heal? Get our life back.' She waited for a response, but he stared straight ahead, lost in thought. 'And do you think you can forgive Jack, too? He deserves to get his family back.'

His head snapped to the left as he scanned her face, his exhaustion dragging his features down. 'Jack betrayed me, and he took advantage. I'm not going to say that he didn't. But it's hard to equate that against what he's done for Tara. For our girl. I'm so tired of being angry, Honour. Angry with him. With myself.' He paused. 'I don't want it anymore.'

Her breath caught. What did he not want? Her? Their life together? She forced herself to probe deeper. 'Want what anymore?'

'The anger. I just want to walk forward. See the sky and the sea. Feel the breeze on my skin. Know that I have a wife who loves me as much as I love her. Sit at that scarred old table in there and talk to our kids about school, the stars at night, the football scores.' He closed his eyes briefly, then lifted her hand from her knee. 'I want us to fix this. Fix our family.'

Honour's heart took flight, her free hand flying up to her mouth as she spoke into her fist. 'Oh, Kenny. I want that too. More than anything.'

He shifted in closer to her, gently easing her head onto his shoulder. 'Then let's fix it. We've always been at our best when we're a team, Red. We can get back there.'

She nodded against his shirt, the flannel soft under her raw cheek. 'I know we can, too.'

They sat there for a long while, silent, and finally in a place of tentative peace. There was no sense of time, or the day passing, so when Kenny eventually shifted his shoulder under her head, Honour started.

Seeing the clock on the mantel, she gasped, 'Oh, my God. It's nearly three o'clock. Cal will be back in less than an hour.'

She looked over at Kenny, the scars seeming less prominent as she saw only the face of the man she loved.

He sat up, then stretched his arms above his head, staring at the painting, before turning to her. 'Do you think I should cover this, when he comes in?' He touched his cheek. 'I'm not that same man.' He gestured towards the family portrait.

'No. I don't think you should cover it. I think Cal will see exactly what I did. His father. His hero.' She smiled now, seeing Kenny's face soften at her words.

'Will I be able to see Tara today?' He pushed himself up from the sofa.

'Of course. You're her dad.' She caught the slight lift of his eyebrows. 'Parents are allowed in, if we wear masks and sterile cover-ups.'

'Will it be bad for her, seeing me? I mean, what if the shock of it...' He halted, a deep frown cutting across his damaged brow.

Honour shook her head. 'It'll be the best medicine in the world, believe me.'

'If you're sure. I don't want to do anything to set her back or, put her at any more risk.' His eyes were glistening. 'She's been through so much already.'

'I'm quite sure.' Honour spoke quietly, her eyes locked on his. 'She will be ecstatic to see her dad.'

Honour's words seemed to float between them, settling on him until he let their message sink in, then he shivered, wrapping his arms across his chest. 'God. It's cold as a witch's tit in here. Shall we light the fire?'

Honour stood up, a soft laugh filling her with such warmth that she thought she'd never feel cold again. 'Yes. Let's. Cal loves to come home to a fire.'

Kenny nodded, then went into the kitchen to get his jacket. She followed him, her stomach rumbling as she realised that she had eaten nothing all day. 'Shall I make us a sandwich?' She opened the fridge, seeing a casserole of stew that Bridie had given her the day before. 'Or there's stew.'

He was behind her, his shoulder close to her back. Unsure whether to turn around, to face him, to offer him a kiss, Honour stood still. 'I'll get some wood in, and a sarny would be great.' He dropped his chin onto her shoulder, pressing it into the taut rope of muscle.

'OK.' She nodded, feeling him move away, so she closed the fridge and looked over at him, standing at the back door. He was smiling, his wide mouth familiar in a way that only a wife could understand.

'Thank you, Honour.' His eyes were suddenly brimming, making her throat narrow.

'For what?'

'For being you. For loving me. For giving me another chance.'

Honour's heart twinged, a surge of love so strong that it hurt, making her sway. 'And to you, for doing the same for me.' She pressed her palm to her chest. 'We'll do better from now on.'

He nodded, took another second to look at her, then walked out into the back garden.

An hour later, when Callum came in the door, he took a few seconds to register what he was seeing. His eyes were enormous as he looked over at Honour, as if asking her if this was real, then, when Kenny said his name, and held his arms out to him, Callum crossed the living room in three bounds and launched himself at his father.

Honour's heart threatened to explode at the unbridled joy on her son's face, and she wiped her eyes and locked the scene into her memory, as something she would never, ever forget.

She joined in the hug, letting Callum's excited questions

surround them. Then, for just a moment, she let go of the weight of everything she'd carried since that shattering day on the boat. There was still much work to be done. Healing, talking and forgiveness would continue to be given over time, but feeling the love surrounding her, she knew that for all the mistakes they'd made, she and Kenny had done so much right, too.

As she thought about Tara seeing Kenny again, the same joy as Callum's lighting up her daughter's face, Honour felt full of renewed hope for the future. For her family, and for all that life had in store for them.

EPILOGUE

TEN MONTHS LATER

The late September sunset was spectacular, the evening sky streaked with pink, and tangerine – a vivid palette – nature's most beautiful offering being reflected in the water moving gently under the boat. The *Tara-Louise* still had the waxy smell of varnish, after the recent repaint, and Kenny had raised the new MacLeod clan flag that now fluttered above them, at the top of the metal post mounted at the stern, behind the winch.

This being her first time on a boat since the *Lila Rose*, and her anxiety bubbling beneath each breath, Honour had insisted they all wear life jackets, but with her distended stomach, hers was open at the front. Callum was hanging on to the siderail next to the cabin, his glasses, clean for once, mirroring the colours in the sky as he watched their progress back towards Crail harbour. Kirk and Marion stood either side of him, their heads inclined towards each other, as always.

They'd been out on the water for less than half an hour, which was Honour's limit, as despite her being in her seventh month, she was still occasionally suffering from nausea, especially in the evenings. Marion had told her that meant they were having a boy, but Honour had been over the moon when Doctor

Ford had told them it was a girl. They'd already decided she would be called Lila, after Kenny's mother, and Marion was busy knitting booties and hats from soft lamb's wool.

Kenny steered the boat towards the harbour, slowed the engine, then turned it off, leaving the *Tara-Louise* to undulate with the swell, the only sound around them now the seagulls above, on their evening foray for food.

Honour watched Callum leave his post at the siderail and walk carefully towards the cabin, heading to his father. Kenny was holding his hand out to Cal and steadied him as they both made their way to the opposite side of the boat, where Honour was waiting.

She picked up the bunch of sunflowers from the basket she'd brought, their heads magnificent golden suns with black-eyed centres that glistened in the muted light. 'Here you go, love.' She handed one to Kenny, then one to Callum. 'Here's yours, Cal.' He took it from her, his glasses obscuring his eyes, which Honour knew were red-rimmed and puffy. 'Mum, Dad.' She held a flower out to her parents, who had moved in next to them.

'Thanks, love.' Kirk's voice was raspy, his free hand tightly clasping Marion's.

Behind them, Jack was hanging back, his life jacket looking too small for his heavy frame as he hunkered down and re-coiled a rope into a pile on the deck. He'd helped Kenny buy the new boat, but they had agreed that he wouldn't re-join the business, his being in Edinburgh suiting both him, and Kenny, better. It had taken time, but the brothers had reached a fragile peace, and as far as Tara had been concerned, her uncle Jack had come back into her life, a cool, fun guy who visited her regularly, and had great stories about when he used to fish, with her dad.

Honour smiled sadly at her brother-in-law, then beckoned to him. 'Come on, Jack. It's time.'

He stood up, looked at the five of them for a few moments, then walked slowly over and joined them. Honour handed him a sunflower, which he accepted, letting it dangle at his thigh.

'Thanks, Hon.' His voice was gruff as he moved in next to his brother at the rail.

Kenny was on Honour's right, wearing sunglasses, and his ever-present baseball cap was pulled down low over his eyes. As she found a smile and leaned into his shoulder, she heard him sniffing softly.

Honour held the last two sunflowers, touching the small, handwritten labels that she had attached back at the cottage that morning. She read them one more time, her vision blurring, and the pain in her heart so sharp that she could barely breathe. Knowing the time had come, she turned to Kenny, 'Do you want to go first?'

He waited only a moment before nodding. 'Aye, OK.' He circled her shoulders with his arm, kissed her softly on the cheek, and then leaned over the rail, the sunflower dangling above the surface of the water. They all watched as he let go of the flower, the heavy head carrying it down onto a wave, where it floated, a splash of gold against the blue-grey of the sea. Kenny had written his own label, and as Honour held Callum's hand tightly, she heard Kenny whisper the words he'd chosen, a gentle, love-filled goodbye that snatched at her heart like a claw.

Next, Callum leaned over the railing, with Kenny holding onto the back of his life jacket. Watching them, her heart in her mouth, Honour tried to slow her breathing. Callum's feet were lifting off the deck as he let go of his sunflower, but instead of a label, a copy of the certificate of purchase for Tara's star was tied to the stem, with a piece of bright red ribbon. Callum watched the flower bob away from the boat, as Kenny gently pulled him backwards until his feet reconnected safely with the deck. Callum then turned and buried his head in Honour's thickened waist, his arms gripping her tightly around her hips.

Kirk nodded to Marion, and together they stood for a few moments, looking at the shore as if they might see their grand-daughter there, running along the sea wall. Then, sighing, Marion took the flower from Kirk and, leaning over the rail, gently let it go. Their whispers were inaudible, but Honour knew the love that her parents felt for Tara was endless and whatever they had said was all it needed to be.

Honour gestured to Jack, who nodded. Then, giving Kenny a quick hug, Jack's big arm lingering around his younger broth-er's back for a few moments, Jack stepped forward and let his sunflower float away on the surface, his lips moving silently.

Passing Callum's hand to Kenny, Honour lifted the first of the remaining sunflowers. She held it up to her face, the petals silky against her lips.

During Tara's last months, when she'd rallied after the transplant and come home to the cottage, Honour had kept a vase of sunflowers in the kitchen. Tara had smiled every time she'd seen them, and then, when the new tumour had been found in her lung, and Tara had deteriorated so quickly, getting her home again had been paramount.

Bridie had painted a stunning landscape – a field of the golden flowers and, at the edge, Tara's profile, her smile peaceful and her hair fluttering in an invisible breeze. They had hung it in Tara's room and Honour would carefully dust it every Friday, as Tara watched her from the bed – that same, gentle smile on her daughter's face.

That she had been able to spend her last days at the cottage, surrounded by everyone she loved, had been a blessing that Honour would always be grateful for. Since the first time he'd walked into her hospital room, and Tara had literally shouted with joy, to the moment she took her last breath, Kenny had rarely left her side, and the renewed bond between father and daughter had been a priceless gift.

Before Honour let the remaining flowers go, she read the

messages one last time, reluctant to make this final gesture, to live out the moment she had been dreading for the past four weeks. Turning over the first label, she whispered the words written on it. 'Darling Tara. My light. My love. My strong, beautiful girl. I will always be grateful for the honour of being your mother. You lived life to the full and the space you leave in our family, and in our hearts, will never be filled. Run free now, my love. Feel the wind at your back and the sun on your face, pain-free and without the boundaries of time or place. Know that you are loved, and always with us. Rest, my angel.' Her throat tightly knotted, Honour leaned over the rail and gently let the sunflower float away on the water, the golden face seeming to smile at her as it bobbed in the waning light.

Last, she lifted the final sunflower, the tiny label fluttering in the breeze that had started coming in from the west. Taking the tissue that Kenny offered her, she dabbed her eyes, and seeing the words clarify, she whispered them softly. 'Dear Tara. I know you would have been the best big sister in the world. I will live life like you did. In full colour.' The last words on the label, *Love, Lila*, seemed to burn their image into Honour's retina.

While nothing could ever replace their precious Tara, the child that Honour carried would help to heal them. She was a gift that had taken Honour and Kenny by surprise, bringing the promise of joy where there was pain, and hope where there was despair. This little person inside her had a future ahead of her, something that had been cruelly taken from Tara, and as Honour stretched her hand over the rail, she looked upwards.

Above them, a sea bird circled, its wings lifted at the tips forming a V-shape against the vivid canvas behind it. She watched the bird hovering, lingering as if it had a message to impart, then Honour let go of the sunflower and watched it undulate away towards the harbour.

After a few moments, Kenny pulled her into a hug, his arm

strong around her as she closed her eyes against the new tears that were pressing in. 'Right, Red. Let's get you home. Bridie and Scott are waiting with a good hot dinner for us all, and Lorna and Dougie are arriving at six, so we'd better not keep them waiting.' He kissed the top of her head, then turned to Callum, who was now holding Jack's hand. 'Ready to return to shore, boys?'

'Aye, let's go.' Jack nodded, his voice thick with emotion.

Smiling sadly at his brother, Kenny walked back to the cabin, as Jack and Callum followed.

Honour hung back, taking one more look at the six golden flowers, separated by the movement of the water and yet still connected in their beauty. As she watched them ease away from the boat, they made her think of the family constellation, the group of stars they'd bought, that Callum had plotted with his telescope. He looked for them every night, and when he found them, he spoke quietly to Tara, as Honour would hover outside his bedroom door, not wanting to intrude.

With one last look behind her, Honour kissed her clenched fist and released the kiss into the evening sky. 'Sleep well, baby girl. Sleep well.'

A LETTER FROM ALISON

Dear reader,

My heartfelt thanks for reading *An Impossible Choice*. I hope you enjoyed it. If you would like to keep up to date with all my latest releases, just sign up at the following link. Your email address will never be shared, and you can unsubscribe at any time.

www.bookouture.com/alison-ragsdale

Honour's story is about loss, impossible choices, the gravity of secrets and their consequences. But it's also about the unshakeable strength of a mother's love in the face of unimaginable challenges. Ultimately, it is a tale of hope that explores the deeply woven bonds of a close family and the love that connects them so profoundly.

Thanks for choosing to read *An Impossible Choice*. If you enjoyed it, I'd be truly grateful if you would take a moment to write a review. They are a great way to introduce new readers to my books.

I love to hear from my readers, and you can connect with me through social media or my website.

All the best,

Alison Ragsdale

KEEP IN TOUCH WITH ALISON

www.alisonragsdale.com

facebook.com/authoralisonragsdale
x.com/AlisonRagsdale
instagram.com/alisonragsdalewrites

ACKNOWLEDGEMENTS

Thank you to my wonderful publisher, Bookouture. I am so fortunate to work with such a dedicated, talented, and supportive team. Special thanks to my stellar editor, Maisie, for her insight and expertise and for encouraging me to dig deeper, even when I think I can't.

Thanks also to Noelle, Jade, and Anne, and everyone who helped this story make its way into the world.

Thank you to the Royal National Lifeboat Institution and the Maritime and Coastguard Agency. Both organisations were invaluable in assisting with my research and in ensuring that I accurately represented the facts of a loss at sea, and the search and rescue procedures that would take place.

As always, a special thank you to my sisters, Lesley and Carly, my best friends, first readers and most reliable sounding boards.

Thank you also to all the friends, readers, reviewers, book bloggers and my Highlanders Club members and ARC crew who support me in my writing life. It means the world to me.

Finally, to my husband. Thank for being you – my staunchest supporter and best friend. I couldn't do this without you.

PUBLISHING TEAM

Turning a manuscript into a book requires the efforts of many people. The publishing team at Bookouture would like to acknowledge everyone who contributed to this publication.

Commercial
Lauren Morrissette
Hannah Richmond
Imogen Allport

Cover design
The Brewster Project

Data and analysis
Mark Alder
Mohamed Bussuri

Editorial
Maisie Lawrence
Ria Clare

Copyeditor
Jade Craddock

Proofreader
Anne O'Brien

Printed in Great Britain
by Amazon

44325620R00182